LEGACY OF THE SORCERESS

LISA BLACKWOOD

LEGACY OF THE SORCERESS

A Gargoyle and Sorceress Tale / Book 6

Lisa Blackwood

Legacy of the Sorceress

Gargoyle & Sorceress Book 6

COVER DESIGNED BY: Heather Hamilton-Senter

PROOFREAD BY: Tracy Vandervliet

Special Thanks to Stan H for his eagle eyes.

PRINT ISBN: 978-1-990608-52-0

EDITION: 10/27/2021

❀ Created with Vellum

BOOKS BY LISA BLACKWOOD

Gargoyle & Sorceress

Dawn of the Sorceress

Sorceress Awakening

Sorceress Rising

Sorceress Hunting

Sorceress at War

Sorceress Enraged

Legacy of the Sorceress

Sorcery & Firedrakes

Scion of the Sorceress

Sorceress Eternal

In Deception's Shadow Series (Epic Fantasy Romance)

Betrayal's Price

Herd Mistress

Maiden's Wolf

Death's Queen

The Prince's Gryphon (forthcoming)

Ishtar's Legacy Series (Epic Fantasy Romance)

Ishtar's Blade

The Blade's Beginning (short story)

Blade's Honor

Blade's Destiny

The Blade's Shadow

First Queen of the Gryphons

The King of the Anunnaki (forthcoming)

The Anunnaki's Blade (forthcoming)

Huntress vs Huntsman (Epic Fantasy Romance)

Master of the Hunt

Night Huntress

Dragon Archer

Soul Mage (forthcoming)

FREE BOOKS

GET TWO FREE STORIES FROM MY
BESTSELLING SERIES WHEN YOU SIGN UP FOR
MY NEWSLETTER.

I send regular monthly newsletters with details about new
releases,
special offers, freebies, and other bookish news.
If that's something you'd be interested in, just follow the
link below.

http://lisablackwood.com/join-the-newsletter-here/

ABOUT THE BOOK

Legacy of the Sorceress

A roll of the dice and Fate thrusts Corporal Anna Mackenzie into a new situation.

With her soul hanging in the balance, the young gargoyle, Shadowlight, makes a deal with the Lord of the Underworld to save Anna's life. The demigod saves her, then sends the pair to Haven, a city outside time, where they will heal.

The price?

Thirteen years. The length of time Anna will need to embrace the healing stone sleep of gargoyles. When she wakes, an adult gargoyle is waiting for her. He goes by the name Obsidian, but she'd once known him by another —Shadowlight.

Obsidian might be a stranger, but she'd promised Shadowlight she'd never leave him. Now his older self wants her to honor that promise and stay, training alongside him to become one of Lord Death's military leaders. To honor the memory of a gargoyle cub she'd once loved like a little brother, Anna agrees to join the Lord of the Underworld's cause.

Is she working for the good guys? Or has she traded in one Overlord for another?

Either way she's staying. Her promises don't come with an expiration date and the more she gets to know Obsidian, the more she sees Shadowlight in him. There's no way she's abandoning the kid a second time.

LEGACY OF THE SORCERESS

CHAPTER ONE

*R*eally, there are only three types of shit storms. First, there's the *'this is some bad shit, but I'll escape with only a few new scars.'* Second, there's the *'Oh, Mother of God, I'm screwed, but I'm damned well going to take down the other bastard before he kills all my buddies,'* and then as a grand finale there's the *'I'm fucked. You're fucked. Everybody is fucked. We're all going to die.'*

Anna decided her present situation was somewhere between the last two. She wasn't at all sure if the four-armed, four-legged monstrosity holding her broken body in two of his massive hands was trying to heal her or kill her.

To judge by the pain, she'd guess kill. But then again, the prolonged agony wasn't what she'd pegged as Lord Death's modus operandi. Wasn't Lord Death supposed to be the 'good' twin? Before all this started, didn't the Avatars consider him a friend?

Just then another wave of Death's acid-like power flowed across her skin and she screamed, her voice as broken as her battered body felt. Time was meaningless, the only certainty was that she'd been screaming for a frigging long time.

So much for a battle-hardened soldier.

The endless onslaught of Death's magic continued to rush across her skin and into her body. Deeper, always digging deeper. Was he trying to rip out her soul? God be merciful. Please let it end.

"Soon," a beautiful male voice whispered into her ravaged mind. *"It will be over soon. And I promise you, once this is done, you'll see that I am a friend."*

Friend? Dafuq you say! The Avatars needed better friends.

Anna blinked as sight slowly returned. Until then, she'd been blind to everything except the endless pain. A foot or two in front of her, a beloved and familiar, if a little blurry, image formed.

Shadowlight?

A muzzle dipped low and lapped at her face, washing the stinging sweat out of her eyes.

Yes. That was the kid. Did that mean this was almost over?

She blinked a few more times.

No. Not over. Lord Death was still holding her in his two lower hands while the upper two poised above her, pouring a torrent of power upon her. Shadowlight was sitting next to her, perched on Lord Death's thumb with his tail wrapped around the giant's wrist.

The sight made her feel something besides pain: tiny.

She felt as insignificant as a mosquito.

Her mind continued to clear. The pain grew less

intense. Still dazed, she shook her head and blinked up at Shadowlight. The power was flowing across his skin as well, but he seemed unharmed.

Anna licked her lips and forced her mouth to form words.

"You okay, kid?" The words came out more of a wheeze.

He bumped his muzzle against her cheek. "I'm fine. You're the one who nearly died."

"Nearly? You mean I'll actually survive this?" Whatever the fuck 'this' was.

Shadowlight glanced up at Lord Death. The giant nodded but continued to focus on his work. Which, apparently, was not peeling her like an orange to get to the juicy soul within.

Who would have guessed?

"Lord Death is working to undo the damage the blood witch's magic inflicted upon your soul," Shadowlight explained. "He says it's much more complicated when the soul is housed in flesh, but I begged him to save your life."

There was something more behind the words.

Oh, God. What had the kid bargained to save her life?

"Normally the Avatars lead my armies," Lord Death's voice wrapped around her, warm and strangely comforting. "However, the gargoyle half of that pair has been ignoring my summons. Now I wait to see if the female half will honor our old friendship."

I wouldn't hold your breath if I were you, she thought to herself.

The Lord of the Underworld chuckled, then broke into a deep, quaking laugh. It shouldn't have been a fear-inspiring event, and yet it was. The flash of deadly teeth, as long as she was fucking tall, caused her heart to pound. And that voice loud in merriment! Like thunder it boomed across the landscape and echoed back at them as she and Shadowlight rode out the god-created earthquake in this titan's hands.

She'd hate to witness his rage.

"I, too, doubt the Avatars will return to take up their old roles again. At least not in this lifetime. I saw a surprising new path open before them the moment the female half of the soul reunited with her proper body."

The power flowing into Anna ceased altogether. A sigh of relief escaped her before she could prevent it. Though, she doubted this reprieve would last long to judge by Lord Death's calculating expression.

Well, if she had to guess, that's how she'd interpret his slightly raised brow, somewhat narrowed eyes, and the slow flick of one ear.

But she'd based her guess on the fact his upper body shared similarities with a gargoyle. The rest of him, from what she could see from her current vantage point, looked more like a winged centaur or sphinx.

Lord Death tilted his head to study her with one eye. "If the Avatars will not lead my army, then I must find alternatives. And behold, the Divine Ones have delivered two powerful new beings into my keeping."

Yeah, that's where she thought his little speech was going. Had she and the kid traded one evil overlord for another?

"Not sure if it was your Divine Ones," Anna said, trying and failing to make her voice sound strong.

It was likely a foolish effort since she still twitched and

shook worse than an addict overdue for a hit, but, hell, she wanted to at least appear less helpless than she felt. To her great annoyance, she couldn't get her limbs to cooperate enough to sit.

"Of course it was." Lord Death seemed entirely unfazed by her doubt. "The Divine Ones put two children in my path. I will see that they grow in strength and wisdom until they are one day fit to lead my army."

"Children? For the record, I'm full grown." Baiting a titan probably wasn't the wisest of moves, but she needed to mount a defense.

Lord Death laughed like she'd said the most entertaining thing in the world.

Okay. Fine. She supposed to a being who was a bazillion years old, her twenty-four years was less than a blink in time. Still, she wouldn't just roll over, especially if Shadowlight had been forced to bargain to save her life. Time to find out the price of her continued existence.

"I owe you my life and all. Thanks for that, but do we get a say in any of this?"

"You always have a choice. Even when you were still my sister's prisoners, there was a choice."

"Yeah, about that. It was more of a serve or die scenario. This time I'm hoping for something a little more... flexible... with a happy ending."

"Flexible? Happy ending?" The giant grinned, flashing his teeth to full advantage again. "Some would say I deal out many joyful endings. I am the Lord of the Underworld. I bring death to the universe so there can be mercy, renewal, and rebirth."

"Not quite what I had in mind."

"I am aware." His toothy grin stretched wider for a moment before his expression smoothed into something more thoughtful. "Just because I wield a fearsome power, doesn't mean I am evil or share my sister's ambitions."

"Glad to hear it."

"I also don't believe in enslaving creatures to serve my needs. Nor do I force children into my armies. You and Shadowlight still have much learning and growing to do before you are ready to make the decision that will end with leading my army."

Anna glanced at Shadowlight and relief washed over her. At least the Lord of the Underworld wasn't planning to enslave the kid. This demigod seemed willing to give them a choice. Perhaps after she healed, he'd let her and Shadowlight go?

Now you're being naïve, Anna, she thought to herself.

"I don't enslave. I won't force either of you to lead my army." Lord Death's expression took on a hint of slyness. "But Shadowlight is a gargoyle, so too are you. That makes you my responsibility. I guide and protect all young gargoyles, only releasing them into the world once they are ready, after many years of training."

"I know I'm young compared to you—a child in your eyes, but I am an adult and have been looking out for myself for quite some time. And I have responsibilities to my people."

"Yes. I see that in you. The need to report back to them with what you've learned. A good soldier. And once you're fully healed and recovered, I will allow you to return to the humans if that's your wish." Another sly look. "However, Shadowlight is much more a child than you. He will stay with me until I deem him ready. Would you willingly leave him behind when you returned to your world and the Avatars?"

Why the four-armed bastard! He already knew her answer. He'd crawled in and out of her head enough times to know she wouldn't leave the kid.

"Never. If you don't release Shadowlight, you're stuck with me too." The words would have had more impact if she'd been able to cross her arms and frown at him. Hell, it would've had more impact if she could sit up when she made her pronouncement.

"Superb," Death's enchanting voice flowed over her, smooth, deep and rich, lulling her worries and soothing her soul-deep aches. "Sleep now, little hybrid. Find what renewal rest will grant you. Your long journey of healing is only beginning."

He bent his neck, his muzzle with its deadly fangs dipping far too close, and then he exhaled. His breath, warm and sweet, almost like flowers, blew over Anna. Her mind grew slow and her lids heavy.

She only had time for one swift regretful *'Fuck, I wasn't finished with this conversation'* before she knew nothing more.

CHAPTER TWO

ood. Anna dreamed of food, which, given what her dreams were usually like the last few weeks, was a departure she could embrace. The warm scent of bread—and something that smelled like oatmeal and some unidentifiable fruit reached her nose.

Her stomach growled.

Blinking open her eyes, she discovered it wasn't a dream at all.

Shadowlight sat on a cot across from her, scarfing down a bowl of something hot and steaming. She must have made a noise because he stopped eating and looked up.

"Anna! You're awake." He bounced off the bed and knocked into hers in his exuberance.

"I feel like rewarmed roadkill, so I suppose that means I'm alive." Her mind felt slow and foggy, sensations mute and muffled.

"Dray said you'd feel like that when you woke."

"Who the fuck is Dray?"

"The Lord of the Underworld goes by the name Draydrak. He says we can call him Dray."

Great. While she'd slept oblivious to everything around her, the kid and the demigod had continued to chat and were now on a first name basis. Just swell.

"It will continue to grow worse—the exhaustion." Shadowlight sounded unhappy as he imparted that bit of news.

"Why worse?"

"Dray said it's because you're still not healed."

"What? Wait. I thought that was the whole point of his burns-like-acid power." Though Anna didn't feel like she was dying, she couldn't say she felt healed either, now that she thought about it. Ever since Shadowlight had converted her with his blood, she'd always woken stronger after sleeping off an injury.

This time she didn't.

"Lord Death's power was destroying the blood witch's spell. It fought back. That's why it felt like a burning power to you. Dray later had to replace parts of your soul that had been... eaten away. But he's not a healer on the physical level. Your body needs to rest in stone. It's a natural part of healing now that you're pure gargoyle."

Part of her soul had been eaten away and needed to be repaired? Fuck, basic training sure as hell didn't cover this kind of shit. Yet Shadowlight's explanation needed some type of response, so she went with a pure vanilla one. "Sounds like a small price to pay for being alive. I'm lucky."

But if she was forced to take a stone nap, how vulnerable would it leave her and the kid?

"Yes, Dray said the blood witch nearly destroyed your soul. If we hadn't reached him when we did..." Shadowlight cleared his throat and glanced out the nearest window to hide his tears.

"Shh. It's okay. I survived." By some big-ass miracle. "So, I need to impersonate a stone statue for a while. I've been through worse."

"Yes," Shadowlight agreed in a small voice.

"Did... Dray... mention how long I might need to sleep?"

Shadowlight's tail wrapped around his own waist. "He said it would be years."

"Years..." *Fuck. We don't have years.* There's no way the Battle Goddess was giving her brother, or Earth, years to get ready.

"The cub is correct," said a new voice from several feet away.

She yelped in surprise as a big gargoyle materialized on the cot to her left. If she'd been able to move, she would have jumped up and faced this new and possibly perilous threat. But doing a face-plant wasn't likely to impress the newcomer. Besides, she didn't want to alarm Shadowlight or give him any bad ideas.

The older male—she assumed he was older since there couldn't be many gargoyles younger than Shadowlight running around—observed them calmly, even taking his unhurried time to arrange his tail so the tip came to rest against his muscular thigh.

Like Gregory, Darkness, and Shadowlight, this male didn't suffer from an overabundance of clothing. A loin-cloth and metal wrist and ankle bands were familiar. Though he also wore a matching metal collar that reminded her of a Celtic torc.

This male was big, both taller and stockier than either Gregory or Shadowlight's father. With another gargoyle to study, she noted a few other subtle variations in coloration and features. For one, his muzzle seemed a little blunter than Shadowlight's.

"I am Master Banrook, though my friends just call me Rook." He paused as he eyed first Anna and then Shadowlight. "You are welcome to call me Rook as we're likely to become close friends."

How did he make that sound like a threat?

Anna drew in a deep breath and studied his scent, but there were no betraying markers she could detect.

"What are you sensing from him, kid?"

"Honesty. Integrity. Determination."

Hmmm. So basic gargoyle nature. Could be worse.

"Draydrak has tasked me with overseeing your recovery and adjustment while you become familiar with our world and way of life." He flicked an ear at Shadowlight. "In other words, I will whip you both into proper gargoyles and do my damn best to undo whatever that manipulative Battle Goddess has hammered into your heads."

Anna cleared her throat. "I'd be very grateful for any aid in digging out whatever the Battle Goddess did to us both, but what if we don't want to become 'proper' gargoyles?"

Rook snorted. "Too late for that. Whatever else you are, you're both gargoyles, and that makes you Dray's responsibility. I'll be aiding him during your healing and later training. As you've already discovered, your full healing will take years."

Well, no one said those 'years' had to be here, in this Realm.

Anna glanced to her right. *"Kid, don't get too comfortable here. We need to escape back to Earth first chance we get."*

Shadowlight looked a little uncertain at her words. Yeah, she probably looked like crap, but surely the Avatars could heal whatever the blood witch had done to her and the kid.

"If you leave," the older male speared Anna with a look that made sweat break out along her back, "you will die. The Avatars cannot heal you fast enough while in the Mortal Realm. Your death will affect the cub in ways not even Lord Draydrak can fully see."

"You can read minds?" Anna tried and failed to keep the thread of hostility out of her voice. She'd mastered the ability to keep everyone, other than Draydrak, out of her head months ago. How was this big brute getting in?

"It's a gift. One granted by Lord Dray to aid me in the shaping and training of our younglings. But I don't do it maliciously." His tail tip thumped against his thigh once before stilling again. "We need to know your thought processes and your self-doubts so we can put them to rest."

Anna grunted but didn't challenge his words. He'd been open and honest about it at least. She didn't like having someone able to rummage through her head any time he wanted but admitted if she'd possessed the same gift, she'd have used it, considering where she and Shadowlight had spent the last few months.

"So..." Anna paused. A yawn snuck up out of nowhere and threatened to crack her jaws. She gave herself a little shake. "How's this going to work if Lord Dray wants us to lead his army and yet my healing might take years? There's no way the Battle Goddess is giving her brother years to prepare. Her armies might even now be marching."

"Actually, my spies report that the Avatars and a group of humans caused a rather large disturbance in her kingdom." Banrook gave her a wolfish grin. "They killed several of the Battle Goddess's captains and even grievously wounded the blood witch. For now, our enemies lick their wounds."

"Gryton?" Shadowlight asked suddenly.

Rook's ears flicked to the side, his expression darkening. "That one survived."

Huh. Big surprise. It would probably just be Gryton and the cockroaches after the apocalypse.

Though, there was a silver lining. Sounded like the Blood Witch Taryin had gotten a good smackdown. Fleetingly, she wondered what had happened to Vaspara, Sorac, and Bervicta. While she couldn't condone their choice of master, there were other people higher up Anna's shit list she'd like to see in the ground first.

"So," Banrook continued, "The Lady of Battles won't be sending her armies just yet. But when she does, she'll find a nasty surprise. Unfortunately, you don't have time to hear all the details now."

He gestured at her midsection and slowly drew the blanket down.

Underneath she was wearing an old-fashioned baggy shirt and a pair of matching drawstring pants. It struck her as odd that gargoyles would have human-type clothing, but that was a question for later.

When she tugged up the shirt's undyed fabric, her gaze

homed in on what looked like raw meat, old scar tissue and a hardy dose of burned flesh. It extended across the expanse of her abdomen. It didn't hurt. At all.

Even with top of the line pain meds, she should have been feeling something.

She'd seen some ugly-ass wounds before and knew the injury should be fatal.

That she still breathed was only at the whim of a demigod.

"The outside is ugly enough, but the true damage is internal. Souls are anchored to the body in seven places—" Banrook tapped the crown of her head, between her eyebrows, a flick across her throat, and an impersonal stroke between her breasts. Next, he gestured at the twisted mass of tissue covering her navel area, then circled a talon above her womb before moving lower to indicate the base of her spine.

"Your soul was nearly shredded from your body. Dray unraveled the blood witch's spell before it could finish its work, but your body will still need the long sleep to fully repair the damage."

Shadowlight hesitantly touched the ravaged skin. "She should already be stone."

"Yes. Dray thought you'd like to say goodbye first and to give us time to put your Kyrsu's mind at ease. I will show you both where you will be staying. A safe home, far beyond the Battle Goddess's reach."

Goodbye? It was that exact moment she understood she'd be abandoning the kid for a good long time. She couldn't help it. There was no getting around this wound.

It did not pain her but that was because her body was

shutting down. She sensed it, her instincts warning her of the danger, the need to find a safe place to rest.

This gargoyle, or another like him, would become Shadowlight's guardian until Gregory and Lillian came to take him back to Earth. There was no telling how long that would be since the Avatars didn't seem to be on conversational terms with Lord Death.

Oh, she knew it was better than where they'd just escaped—so much better. But strangers would still care for Shadowlight. Without her.

God. She only hoped Gregory and Lillian would come soon.

"Do I have your permission to carry you to another location?" Master Banrook asked. "It's too far for you to walk in your condition,"

She would have preferred to walk, but her limbs were growing heavy. "Yes."

"Let's get this over with," she whispered to the kid.

Banrook nodded and then carefully scooped her up like she weighed nothing. When he started away, it occurred to her they were in a medical ward.

Outside, the hallway was constructed of the same dark grey stone with faint green veins running through it. Carpets and wall hangings softened the otherwise hard edges. Every ten feet, wall sconces held lit torches. But the light cast by them was too ethereal—an unnatural soft shimmering blue—to be anything but magic in origin.

Strangely she couldn't sense or taste the foreign power. Eh. She was bad off if she couldn't feel the magic fueling the blue-white flames.

"Can you still hear me?" Anna asked Shadowlight across their shared mind link.

"Yes. But you're faint."

His ears wilted as his expression morphed into sorrow and grief. A sheen of tears shimmered in his big, dark eyes.

Ah, hell. This would be far harder on the kid than her.

That realization made her feel even worse.

"Is there nothing I can do to remain awake while I heal?" She asked the older gargoyle. "Shadowlight has lost so much."

Banrook shook his head. "No. Some ailments only stone can heal. But rest assured, we will protect and love our young brother in your absence."

Anna stared up at the ceiling and fought back a surprising wash of tears. If she slept for years, Shadowlight would grow up without her. Would she even recognize him when she woke?

"My Kyrsu, you will," Shadowlight said with a tearful huff. "I am your Rasoren. We are family and will always know each other."

That might be true, but it wouldn't be the same as watching him grow. The kid, her little brother, would be gone when she awoke.

As she wallowed in her emotional pain, Banrook came to a circular stairwell that led down into darkness. As they descended deeper, she noted a few details through her fading senses. The air wasn't damp or stale. It was fresh and held the briny essence of the ocean, as strong as when they'd been above ground.

A slight breeze even ruffled the older gargoyle's mane.

"There is great power here." Shadowlight's voice held a

hint of awe, and he eased closer to Anna and Banrook until he could nuzzle her hair.

"Do you sense danger?"

"No."

Despite his words, nervousness reasserted itself.

For his part, Banrook continued as if unaware of their silent exchange, though he'd already revealed his secret ability to listen in.

They walked in silence after that. A creeping lethargy soon spread through her limbs and a new, strange instinct to struggle out of Banrook's arms was rearing up inside her. She needed to go find a place to rest.

Sensing her distress, Banrook crooned softly. "Fear not. You still have enough time to see what I wish and to speak your goodbyes to the child."

Anna nodded weakly, having to trust in his words since Fate had taken away all other options.

"Ah, see?" he said only minutes later. "Here we are."

Banrook descended the last few steps and then they were once again on level ground.

She wasn't sure what she was supposed to see. They'd emerged into a chamber thick with shadows.

It was disappointing after all the buildup.

"Patience, young one." Using his muzzle, Banrook gestured ahead of him. Three other gargoyles stood twenty feet from the stairs. "I'd like you to meet Master Verroc, and Adepts Soryn and Shorban. Together we will be Shadowlight's primary instructors and mentors. Yours as well, once you're healed and ready to start your training."

If she'd been more alert, she might have been better able to assess the three new gargoyles, but as it was, she was having trouble remembering their names. Master Verr and Tor and Shore-something-or-other. It was all she could do to keep her eyes open.

"Kid, you still there?"

"Yes, Anna."

"What do you feel coming from these three?"

"The one called Verroc seems suspicious of us, but he's loyal to Lord Death and will follow his commands. The one called Soryn feels undecided. And Shorban—he and Soryn are brothers to judge by their scent—he is openly curious about us. Well, about you anyway to judge by how he's studying you."

"Huh, maybe he's just wondering if Banrook will be carrying a stone statue in the next thirty seconds."

"Anna," Banrook called her name and gave her a little shake. "Stay with us for a few moments more. We're almost there." He nodded to the other three gargoyles, jolting her with the motion.

It was enough to rouse her into witnessing one of the gargoyles, Verroc maybe, reach out and run his talons along a stalagmite rising from the cavern floor. One of the brothers did the same to a second stalagmite situated six feet from the first one.

A moment later a ripple of power flowed through the cavern, shivering and shaking the air currents. More magic crackled upwards, circling each stalagmite, snapping and dancing in a fiercely beautiful spectacle.

When the blue radiance covered both pillars from root to tip, the power from the separate mineral structures arched toward each other. When they touched, a loud ringing filled the air.

Banrook raised his tail to shade her eyes and seconds

later a blinding light flashed out from the two stalagmites. Even with a tail shielding her eyes from the worst of the radiance, it still took a few seconds for the spots to vanish from her vision.

Once her vision cleared, she continued to blink a few more times, just in case her eyes were playing tricks on her. But nope. Where before there was nothing but space between the pillars, a door to another place now stood.

The stalagmites had transformed into a large stone frame for a double set of iron-bound doors made of some pale wood. When one of the gargoyles—they'd all moved, so she didn't know who was who—pushed on the right door, it swung open on silent hinges.

Beyond was daylight and the scent of green, growing things. She'd seen stranger things in the last few months, but this made her laugh until she was light-headed.

"Fantasyland has magic portal doors. Go figure."

"She's going into shock again," Banrook said as he hurried through the doorway.

Once they crossed the threshold, they reappeared in a room that looked exactly like the one they'd just left, but Shadowlight's cautious sniffing as he sought new dangers told her they were somewhere else.

Banrook continued to stride forward, then swiftly ran up the stairs that were identical to the ones in the other place. Before long, Anna found herself back on the surface of the island. Or an island. This one was far more lushly covered in trees and greenery than the one they'd just left.

Beside her Shadowlight exhaled a startled huff, seeing or sensing something more than she could.

Why was that important?

Her eyes drifted closed.

"Anna, they are all hamadryads."

She cracked open one eyelid to scan the trees. Hamadryads? There must be a shit-ton of dryads hidden around here somewhere. But how was that going to help win a war with the Battle Goddess? Dryads were skilled at hiding and healing but were no warriors.

"The dryad nation answered Lord Draydrak's secret summons. They have been mating my species to increase our numbers for many years," Banrook explained. "It has been working rather well. We now have an army a hundred times greater than the Battle Goddess will expect."

"The Lady of Battles will have spies," Anna heard Shadowlight say. "She must know of this place."

Banrook snorted. "Our enemy does not know of our plans, and she won't learn of it until far too late. We are in a time before the Divine Ones used their Avatars to give birth to Lord Draydrak and his misguided twin. Here we are far in the past, but also outside the normal flow of time."

Banrook sounded very proud, and Anna could only take him at his word. Because this new knowledge was almost too much for her tired, foggy mind to assimilate.

"There are so many gargoyles here," Shadowlight whispered in awe. "More than my father's memories show. Many, many more."

"Yes," Banrook explained. "Stalks the Darkness, like all the other gargoyle soldiers born in the future, are unaware of this place. It must be this way to protect our secret, for the border guards always face the possibility of capture. We cannot risk the Lady of Battles learning our master's ultimate plan for her. Only the Council of Elders and a few guards with the sacred duty of protecting the time portal are privy to this secret and travel freely between times to carry out our duties."

"Yet you showed us," Shadowlight said, suspicion coloring his voice. "Now we can't go back without risking this secret."

That's my kid, Anna thought a little proudly. *Trust no one.*

"Yes," Banrook agreed. "This place will keep you safe from the blood witch's influence and well away from Death's sister. Here Anna can heal while you mature naturally and learn to be a proper gargoyle. Once Anna has healed, we will see to her training."

Banrook shifted Anna in his arms until she was standing. Well, not really standing. She'd have fallen in a crumpled heap if he wasn't holding her upright by a firm grip under her arms.

Shadowlight stepped forward, wrapping her in his arms. "I'll miss you."

His voice broke, and his shoulders shook. If Anna could have moved her arms, she would have wrapped him in a fierce embrace. Instead, she was as limp as a doll in his arms.

Only thoughts and emotions remained.

"I love you, cub. Remember that. Always."

Shadowlight cried harder.

"Oh, kid. I'm a tough bitch. When I return to you, I'll be stronger than ever, and we'll give the baddies a smackdown of epic proportions."

"Promise?"

"Yes. Have I ever broken one to you?"

"No." A warm tongue swept across her cheek, but the sensation felt dull and distant.

"This isn't goodbye. It's a see you later. And I will return. Promise."

"I'll be waiting."

"She's shifting to stone," a deeper voice said. "Hurry. Place her on the ground."

Distantly, she felt herself being shifted into a fetal position. Soft grass tickled her nose and cheek.

"There. She won't fall on her face the first time she wakes."

"Can I stay with her?" Shadowlight's voice grew fainter.

"As much as your training allows."

They continued to speak, but Anna only heard a few words, and then even those few snatches of conversation drifted away, and she knew nothing more.

CHAPTER THREE

Obsidian paced beside Truth as they traversed the bridge network suspended between the ancient hamadryad trees. Flying would have been faster, but Obsidian ached too much from training to enjoy even a short evening flight.

Besides, walking gave them time to talk on the way home. Obsidian eyed the other gargoyle out of the corner of his eye. "I can't believe you won't give me any pointers I can use when it's time for me to take the Adept Trial."

Truth snorted and flicked an ear in Obsidian's direction. "And have Master Banrook chew my tail off and beat me to death with it? Nope. Even if I shared, it wouldn't help. My mentors claim they tailor each test to the individual undergoing it. So, if it's all the same to you, I'd prefer not to get my new rank stripped away for sharing secrets with an uninitiated."

Obsidian huffed though it was more for show than any real annoyance at his friend. He'd expected the answer, anyway. It wasn't like he'd thought the straight-laced gargoyle would speak even if the mentors allowed it. Even for a gargoyle, Truth had an overly developed sense of honor.

"Will you celebrate with a drink?" Truth asked. "Lark and Meadow will be there."

Truth was delusional if he thought dropping the names of two dryads—no matter how pretty and appealing they might be—would sway him into coming.

Mentally snorting, he admitted he didn't have time for a relationship even if he wanted one, which was likely for the best since a heaping pile of other complications stood between him and the possibility of a serious courtship. Sighing, he turned back to his conversation with Truth.

"I doubt you'd find a stone statue good company." Sleeping in his stone form had become a regular occurrence.

"Again? Which mentor did you have today? Shorban or Soryn?"

"Both. At my request."

"Goddess, I swear you like getting your ass kicked."

"Who said it was my ass getting kicked?" Obsidian grinned. He had done rather well today. The exhaustion was a good type. Though he also had to admit even if he wasn't that tired, he'd still have returned to his quarters.

"Fine," Truth said, a sullen little note in his tone. "Sleep. You will need it because there will not be much of that going on these next three days. Spring Rites are upon us if you hadn't noticed, you great reclusive ogre. There's no way you will escape the dryads' eye again this year. They already have plans for a great feast."

Obsidian snorted. "That's not the only thing they have planned."

"Exactly. I fancy none, so you better have my back. Unless—" Truth's eyes narrowed suddenly. "Have you and one of the dryads already come to a consensus?"

Rather than answer his friend, Obsidian quickened his pace.

Several dryads had approached him. He'd turned them all down.

It was no secret that the fastest way to seduce a gargoyle was through his stomach. If he could have avoided the feast, he would, finding certain dryads overly aggressive in their hunt for future mates.

Ahead the path branched, the left bridge leading to the group of platforms that housed Truth's home and a few other gargoyles in the same level of training. The bridge's right fork led to a more secluded area away from other lodgings.

At the fork, they paused, saying their goodbyes and Obsidian even agreed to meet the other gargoyle in the morning to hunt food for the dryads to cook. Usually, both species shared in the duty of hunting and cooking, but during the Spring Rites, the dryads pampered their gargoyle counterparts, and no gargoyle would complain about that. In the fall, the gargoyles returned the favor during the harvest festival.

With a final goodbye, they went their separate ways— Obsidian taking the right fork of the bridge to the more secluded area where he'd made his home. Growing up, he'd never entirely felt like he belonged, his size and heritage setting him apart from the other gargoyles.

Yes, he'd made friends, and he valued those friendships —but the feeling of not wholly belonging never fully went away.

Alone now, Obsidian dropped to all fours and trotted toward his destination, the usual eagerness temporarily dispelling some of his weariness.

Grinning to himself, he turned down another branch of the bridge system that spread throughout the vast hamadryad forest. Overhead he could catch a few glimpses of stars between the dense foliage. Other nights, he would have taken a pleasure flight before bed. But not tonight. His nest called to him.

Rounding a large trunk of an ancient hamadryad, Obsidian came to a halt as the breeze carried the scents and sounds of others to him. It was unusual to find others out here this time of night. Hmm.

"Come on! We're out of time. Obsidian is likely already finishing up with the brothers." The words came from a somewhat young sounding voice.

A moment later Obsidian placed the speaker. It was Novice Oath, a gargoyle several years behind him in training. They'd struck up a friendship all the same. But what was the youth doing here this time of night? He should be in his own bed by now.

"Well. If you were worried about getting caught, why did you come?"

Ah. That voice belonged to Lark, a dryad in Warpath's training group.

"Why did you?" Oath countered.

Had Lark come to his place to ask him to join her at the fires and then found the younger gargoyle outside?

Obsidian sighed mentally at the thought. But that made little sense either since he was now picking up Nightshade and Meadow's scent. That was surprising.

Lark snorted. "I don't think we have much to worry about. Soryn is a tough old bastard. If he gets tired, Shorban will take over. They'll keep Obsidian busy well past second moonrise."

Usually, Lark's words would be correct, but his mentors released him early in a rare showing of sympathy. Now, Obsidian was back early and had interrupted some mischief.

"If he catches us, he'll put us on extra cleaning details," Nightshade whined. He was likely only here because Lark was present. Nightshade's infatuation with the older dryad was almost comical.

"He's not an adept yet," Lark said.

Sounding more concerned by the minute, Nightshade whispered, "But Truth is."

"I'd volunteer to take extra shifts for a chance to see the human." Oath again, awe ringing clear in his voice.

"But she's spelled into stone. There's not going to be much to see," Meadow complained.

"Doesn't matter," Lark countered. He could practically hear Lark's jaw clench with determination. "I agree with Oath. The risk is worth the reward. We'll be the first beside the council to see Obsidian's Kyrsu. Don't you want to see the female who will one day command us?"

Ah! Obsidian grinned with a new understanding. The human locked safely away in his dwelling had finally become too great a temptation for his peers. Their curiosity had led them to this rash action.

His grin grew broader. He'd been just like them only a few short years ago.

"We should go." Fear of discovery tinted Meadow's words. Her scent as well. It wasn't the only emotion on display. Mortification lay thick in the air. She must find the entire situation embarrassing, and yet, here she remained.

"He'll be coming back soon, and even if we're gone, he'll be able to scent that we were here." Meadow again, sounding more stressed.

"So little faith," Lark interjected. "My magic casting has advanced far enough to weave a spell that will erase our scents."

"He'll know someone was here if we tamper with the entryway spells. This is a stupid idea." Meadow's tone was more exasperated than embarrassed now. "I'm leaving. It's not like you'll be able to get past his protective spells, anyway."

Obsidian called on his shadow magic to hide. As his mentors could attest, he'd grown proficient with magic. The mischief makers wouldn't see or smell his presence until he wanted them to.

With power shrouding his form, he stalked forward, determined to cause a little mischief of his own. Ahead, he could see the small group of miscreants.

Oath stood closest to the entrance of the dwelling, his muzzle nearly pressing against the spell covering the door. "It's too complicated for you. This smells like Master Banrook had a hand in its making."

"You're right," Lark said. "If I had to breach one of Rook's spells on my own, I'd be here for another twelve moon cycles, but I was here with Truth early this morning when Obsidian was resetting it. I saw the composition of the trigger spell."

Why, that determined little dryad. The nerve! He'd get Truth to assign her to weeding the fields on the mainland.

Meadow halted and turned on her heels, her expression torn between doing what was right and satisfying a curiosity that had hounded many of the island's residents. "You can open that?"

"Yes."

After a long hesitation, Meadow returned to the other three.

"Fine, just a quick peek, and then we get out of here."

Obsidian waited until Lark had taken down the spell. The four were bunching close to the door, preparing to enter, when he ghosted up behind them.

Lark and Meadow, he tapped on their shoulders. Nightshade he thumped with the edge of his wing. As for Oath, his tail was too tempting a target, and he stomped on it with all his weight.

The dryads yelled. Nightshade huffed and choked like he'd swallowed his tongue and Oath yowled like a wounded cat.

"Very impressive," Obsidian said with a dose of satisfaction as he released his shadow magic and appeared behind them. "Would you like me to hold open the door for you?"

"Obsidian!"

"Sorry!"

"We're sorry!"

"Didn't think you'd be back yet!"

Sheepish looks accompanied the chorus of apologies.

"Next time you wish to enter, you should simply ask."

Oath bounced up and down, still holding his tail, but his ears swung forward with eagerness. "Would you have let us see her if we'd just asked?"

"No," Obsidian said with a big grin. Then seeing Oath's crestfallen look, he softened the blow. "It's not my right."

Oath's face fell. "Why did you say to ask then?"

"So you would think about the privacy of others." He pushed past them and opened the polished dark wood door. Then turning to face them, he grinned again. "Good night. I assume I'll see you all tomorrow during the preparations for the festival."

With that, he closed the door in their startled faces.

A flick of his wrist reset the wards protecting his small domain. A faint blue glow emanated from the polished wood door and the surrounding walls.

Floating balls of magic provided the only other heat and light. Not that he needed much of either to be comfortable, but he kept them burning in case Corporal Anna Mackenzie awoke from her healing stone sleep when he was away.

After giving the room with its carved walls and vine-shrouded windows a once over, he set aside his weapons and armor and shed his ward-spelled wrist and armbands. And then he paced to the center of the homey room where a concave nest cradled Anna's stone form.

She looked as she always did, her expression unchanged. Only the slight warmth rising from the stone and the slow beat of her heart suggested she was a living creature. None of those things hinted when she would finally wake and take up her destiny. Though, surely, it must be soon.

Feeling the familiar sadness, he dropped to all fours and crawled into the nest, arranging blankets and pillows how he liked before curling around her.

Even though she couldn't converse with him in return, he'd always told her how his day had gone, sharing his greatest joys and most profound defeats. When he slept and dreamed, his mind would touch hers and share much of what he'd learned that day.

His mentors encouraged it, saying when she finally woke it would speed her training along. But even if there were no tactical benefits to sharing his day with Anna, he'd still do it, the closeness giving him much-needed comfort.

Snuggling nearer, he settled a wing over them both. His one hand pressed against her chest, where, if he waited long enough, he would feel the slow thump of her heart.

That too had always comforted him.

"I miss you," he whispered along their mental link. *"Return to me soon."*

Closing his eyes, he waited. Only after he felt three of the familiar slow thumps of her heart did he surrender to his own stone sleep.

CHAPTER FOUR

A rich, dark scent, one reminiscent of patchouli forest incense and a hint of her favorite café mocha, teased her senses. Because no pleasant dream was complete without coffee and chocolate.

Hmmm. Some dreams were better than others.

Her mind roused further. Well, perhaps it was a rather odd combination. She hadn't smelled the patchouli incense since she'd last been home, what seemed like ages ago now. She took another breath, inhaling deeply.

Ah. No. That wasn't exactly what she smelled, but it was familiar all the same, and it reminded her of home. It really was a delightful scent. She would have been happy to drink in the fragrance for days and days if another part of her consciousness hadn't been piecing together more disturbing details.

She stiffened as she came fully awake.

What the fuck!

She was lying in a fetal position with a big, male body spooning her.

Fuck! Fuck! Fuck!

Why couldn't she remember what had happened or how she'd gotten here? She jerked in surprise as old memories surfaced from where she'd buried them to die. No! She wouldn't think of that time. She was stronger than the memories. They held no power over her now.

But the memories didn't care about her mental denials and continued to rise to the surface.

Fuck them and fuck the jackass who'd just roofied me!

She embraced the rage—it was far better than paralyzing fear.

I'll rip his balls off and stuff them down his throat!

Anna tried to bolt upright only to be brought up short by a weight across her waist. An arm—yep that was an arm —slung around her torso like he owned her.

His hand was cupping her right boob. She reached up to break his thumb, and the feel of large talons gave her pause.

What kind of sicko was she tangled up with now?

Never mind. Neutralize the threat first and worry about what the actual fuck was going on later. Her brothers had taught her that one.

She jackknifed her body, then came back down, slamming the back of her skull into his face. Lifting her pelvis for better leverage, she raised her right leg and kicked back with all her strength. Her heel made a direct hit to his balls.

Without pause, she grabbed his hand and twisted the

thumb of the offending hand back hard. The move would have broken a typical guy's thumb, but the big brute behind her merely grunted out an age-old sound of male pain at the hit to his jewels. His thumb seemed not to register at all.

"I will kill you!" She punctuated the sentence with another savage twist and kick.

"Anna!" He howled as broad wings folded back, showing her a glimpse of her surroundings.

More memories returned—newer ones—crashing into her mind like waves racing to shore. Blinking down at herself, she acknowledged she was fully dressed. So was he. Well, as much as gargoyles ever were. No one had roofied her.

Still, her spotty memories didn't explain what she was doing in a strange gargoyle's bed. A moment later, the male in question released his hold on her, likely so he could protect his nuts from further damage. Anna wasted no time in rolling away from him and to her feet.

The room spun, and she feared she'd collapse face-first into the pillows and blankets. Worse, the fabric was threatening to tangle up her feet and trip her. But after a few stumbling steps, she righted herself and crawled out of the strange nest.

The male was still hunched over in pain, so she glanced around the room, searching for other dangers. Power glowed, bright lines of magic forming a protective framework over the carved wood of the walls behind. She scanned for an exit, but nothing jumped out at her.

Great.

She didn't spare the room further study, swinging her gaze back to her opponent.

The gargoyle was straightening up. And, fuck, was he ever a big, brawny beast. Shoulders, wider than even Gregory possessed, flexed and rippled with strength as he stretched, limbering up stiff muscles. Thighs like proverbial tree trunks and biceps that might actually be bigger around than her waist only added to the 'I will break you in two' look he had going.

She desperately hoped he was big, slow, and dumb—a living stereotype. Otherwise fighting her way free would really suck.

She supposed she should try reason first. Though, really, what excuse could he come up with after she'd woken up in this dude's bed getting groped?

"Hey, big fella, mind explaining what's going on here?" While she talked to distract him, she inched her way closer to a rack of weapons she'd spotted on one wall. There was an assortment of quarterstaffs, spears, bows, swords, and knives.

A sword would be the most useful. She'd done a little training with a quarterstaff while under the tender care of the Battle Goddess's captains but didn't want to trust her life to those skills just yet. And a knife probably wouldn't even make him flinch.

She was within four feet of the weapons rack when the big fellow released a deep, unhappy sounding huff.

"Don't you know me?"

Know him? Huh? No. "Never seen you before. And it's not like I've met a lot of gargoyles. Would've remembered one as big as you."

"Is your nose still stone?" He paced closer. "It's me. How can you not know me?"

His scent wafted stronger the closer he got, and perhaps he was partially correct. Fully awake now, her sense of smell sharpened, telling her something impossible.

No.

Hell. No.

It couldn't be, not unless Shadowlight and Lillian had an older brother or... years and years and years had spun by while she'd slept and healed in her stone sleep. Like the elder gargoyle had said.

But it felt like she'd only just fallen asleep.

Surely it hadn't been...

She studied the big gargoyle standing across from her. Ears drooped, wingtips dragging on the floor, tail curled around his midriff, he looked the picture of absolute dejection.

"Shadowlight?"

His one ear flicked forward before flattening against his mane, but he inched forward in the slow, methodical way the kid sometimes would when he wanted a treat he knew he shouldn't have but was stubbornly determined to have it anyway, consequences be damned.

Even though she was half expecting the crushing bear hug, his speed and strength surprised a gasp from her. Then his arms and wings were folding her in a fierce embrace, and the magic of their link flared to life as if it, too, were just waking from a long sleep. But there was no denying the evidence of their mental and magical link.

"Shadowlight!" she shouted his name and hugged him back.

He was shaking with emotion. She probably was too.

"I missed you," he said, his voice deep, thickening with

raw emotion, or maybe it was normally a baritone now. He snuffled in her hair, nuzzling the side of her neck.

"I'm sorry I left you alone." And she was. But now she had questions. "How long?"

"Years. You slept for years like Banrook said you would. I didn't want to believe it would be that long. I always thought you'd wake sooner than this. I never stopped hoping." There was a world of loneliness in his words, and she'd examine them later, but, for now, she had more significant concerns.

"How many years exactly?" Anna leaned back to look up into his face, trying to see something of the Shadowlight she'd known. It was there, she realized with a sigh of relief. There was still something of Shadowlight's familiar soul reflecting back at her when she looked into his eyes. But, gods, how he'd grown!

"Almost thirteen years."

"Thirteen?" God. That long. But she supposed she should be thankful since it could have been far longer. No wonder she hadn't recognized him at first. He'd be, what? Twenty-one now?

Well, at least he was still younger than her. While he might not permit her to call him a kid anymore, he was still her little brother. Nothing would change that.

"Far too long," he agreed.

Shadowlight leaned down and gave her face a big swipe with his tongue. Then, his voice deepening with accusations, he said, "You thought I was big, slow and stupid. You didn't even recognize me!"

"Er. Sorry?" Anna rubbed at the back of her neck, only then realizing her hair wasn't in its customary rows. Damn it. Some do-gooder had taken them out. Or maybe that had happened when Lord Death had blasted away much of the blood witch's taint with his chilling power.

She glanced down at her clothes in more detail this time. A pair of plain drawstring pants and lace-up shirt covered her from neck to ankle. It was the same outfit she'd been wearing when she'd first woken up in the healer's quarters after Lord Death had finished working on her.

To her, it felt like no time had passed. But looking upon Shadowlight, she knew so much had changed.

"I...Oh, Shadowlight, I don't even know where to begin or what questions to ask."

He bumped his muzzle in her hair and dragged in a few deep breaths before speaking. "Well, I go by the name Obsidian now. Journeyman Obsidian. Or Rasoren if we're being formal."

"They changed your name?"

If they'd forced a new name upon him what other things had been forced upon him as well?

"Be at peace. It's part of the gargoyle legion's hierarchy. Novices keep the names their dryad mothers gave them until they reach Journeyman status. Once at that level—when a gargoyle is what you would call a young adult—we take on a new name of our choosing. I chose the name Obsidian Shadow."

"Huh." Well, at least they hadn't forced a name upon him. Though she was curious why he'd picked that name, she had other more immediate concerns.

"What's it like here?" She tried to use their mental link, wanting to feel the emotion behind his words, to see if he

was hiding something, but she came up against a smooth impenetrable barrier.

Obsidian grinned at her startled look. "I've been training hard for over a decade, and my command of magic is almost greater than my mentors'. Since gargoyles naturally use mind magic more than other races, one of the first things my mentors taught me was how to erect a mental wall when privacy is required. It's far more advanced than what we learned in the Battle Goddess's domain."

"Oh." He didn't want her in his head. She supposed she didn't blame him. They were almost strangers to each other now. It drove home how unprepared she was for this new life. He knew so much more than her.

He'd no longer need to look to her for guidance. That knowledge left a hollow ache in her heart. She'd look at those tangled feelings in more detail later.

Unaware of her turmoil, Shadowlight... er... it was Obsidian now wasn't it? He merely wrapped an arm around her shoulder and guided her over to a bench to sit.

"Come, sit. You'll be weak. Your body's resources depleted after so long in the stone sleep. Let me get you a drink." He went over to his weapons rack, took down a canteen and returned to her side swiftly. "Here, drink this. It's a tea fortified with minerals and herbs to replenish a weary body. Its taste leaves much to be desired, but it will hold you over until I can hunt up something more solid for you to eat."

Anna took the offered canteen, hesitated a second as she scanned Obsidian's expression—there was no deceit evident—and then drank deeply of the liquid. It was room temperature and had a mildly bitter, metallic sort of flavor to it. Kind of like chewing on a vitamin pill, Anna decided.

Not the tastiest drink, but now that moisture had hit her mouth, she realized how parched she was and swiftly took several more swallows. After she drank half the contents of the canteen, she sat it on her lap and looked up at Shadowlight again.

"It's Obsidian," he said in gentle reminder.

"You can read my thoughts, but I can't read yours. That's hardly fair."

"I'm much stronger than I was last time you were awake. Our link is now imbalanced. I don't trust that my mind won't overwhelm yours. Best we wait until your body is strong before we embark upon the first of your new magic lessons."

"Fair enough." For now, she agreed. But later she planned to get inside his head and gather intel about this place and her new, mature Rasoren. Maybe then she could reclaim some of the old Shadowlight.

Anna wasn't a complete emotional cripple. She'd known she'd loved the kid more than her own life. He was family. He was oh so easy to love. He'd been the first to breach the barriers she'd built around her heart after the 'incident' three years ago and to her surprise, she'd been fine with that chink in her armor.

He'd been safe, void of threat or peril. Because of that, she'd been able to love him in a platonic way that didn't risk stirring memories better left buried.

But looking at him now, she feared that love was lost—impossible to reclaim because he was no longer a safe, uncomplicated child. He'd grown into an adult. It was like Shadowlight had died.

Sorrow welled up. New pain to add to all the old. With a great deal of difficulty, she shoved all the emotion back deep inside. She wouldn't think or feel. She'd just adapt and survive like she always did.

"I'm still him. Still Shadowlight. Never a threat to you." He knelt before her. "A name change doesn't erase all that I was. Now I am just more. You'll come to see that before long. In the meantime, I'm happy to answer questions you might have while you eat. Afterward, if you still don't trust me or are unsatisfied with the answers, we can attempt the link."

Right. Mind reader.

"I promise I will answer all your questions, but first you need food. Come with me."

Food was always an excellent way to break the ice with a gargoyle and get him talking. Besides, he was correct. She was starving. But she needed to do a couple of things first.

Anna patted her hair and glanced down at her baggy clothing. "Don't suppose you have a proper change of clothing and a magic wand hanging around to tame this?" She pointed at her hair.

She spoke only half in jest.

If she were to venture forth where she might meet other gargoyles, she'd at least like to be presentable. Underwear was always a good start. Followed by real clothing and a tamed bedhead.

Obsidian's brow scrunched in thought. "Your hair will take too long to braid again, but you can borrow one of my mane tiebacks." He went over to a row of shelves along one wall and produced a strip of leather.

Anna took it and then finger combed her hair into a tamer version of its earlier self and tied it all back at the base of her neck.

Next, Obsidian rummaged in a lower drawer until he pulled out a few items. She recognized the beaded loin cloth preferred by gargoyles and accompanying it was what looked a little like a matching beaded sports bra.

"I knew you'd eventually wake and need these. Plus, it will be safer to wear something that will shape-shift with you until your gargoyle nature is entirely under your control. While you might be weak and hungry now, once you've sated your hunger and replenished needed stores, your gargoyle nature will reassert itself swiftly.

In other words, wear clothing that shapeshifts with the wearer to avoid wardrobe malfunctions.

"You can change and attend to other needs through there." He summoned a small bit of shadow magic and then gestured to a door that suddenly appeared in the wall and opened into another room. Camouflaged doors would take getting used to. Though, the carved wood of the walls and hidden door had a pretty artistry she admired.

Glancing inside the room, a rudimentary bathroom met her gaze. After testing a few handles, she discovered both hot and cold water. Basic plumbing. Things couldn't be all bad.

CHAPTER FIVE

When Anna exited the bathroom a short time later, she found Obsidian rummaging through his shelves again, randomly shoving items into a satchel. She drew close and peered into the sack.

"Water, rations, and more of the rejuvenating tonic to hold you over while I build a fire and go hunting."

"I won't perish, but I can gather wood and build a fire while you do the hunting."

"It's my duty to look after my Kyrsu while she is still recovering."

"Do I look like an invalid?"

He glanced sharply at her, his expression turning thoughtful. "I didn't say you were. But, Anna, how many times did you see to my protection and needs while I was a child? I'd like a chance to return the favor."

Eh?

Damn. He had a point. Besides, it would give her a chance to think.

She took the offered bag with a shrug. Never hurt to have supplies.

With that Obsidian triggered the door's spell and led her outside. She got the first look at her new surroundings, which didn't tell her much since it was the dark of a moonless night, but her eyes still picked out the outlines of leaves and branches. From the size of the branches, they were a good way off the ground.

"The third moon has just set. It will be dawn in an hour. You'll be able to see it better then if your gargoyle nature doesn't reassert itself before and give you back your night vision."

Anna nodded, adding that detail to the little she knew. This place, whatever it was, had three moons like the Magic Realm. Though, if she remembered Banrook's words correctly when he'd carried her here, this land was outside time. In a past that had never been.

"Your memory is correct. Though this place has a name: Haven."

"Haven, eh? It's an island, right? Even nose dead me can smell the brine. So that means you live in tree houses, on an island, in the middle of an ocean? You sure Lord Death hasn't left his temple in eons? 'Cause this sounds like the setting of Swiss Family Robinson."

"I'm unfamiliar with that family."

"Fictional book. Old classic. Should have found time to read it to you when you were a kid. You'd probably have liked it." The reminder that the Shadowlight she knew was gone caused another spike of pain.

To distract herself, Anna walked to the railing. It

circled the sides of the dwelling not attached to the tree's trunk. Leaning over, she asked, "How high up are we?"

"About two-thirds of the way to the top."

Which told her absolutely nothing since she didn't know the height of the tree or how far away the ground was, obscured by the sweeping branches of the gigantic tree.

"It's not a tree. It's a hamadryad. They continue to flourish and grow as long as the dryad lives," Obsidian explained. "And these hamadryads are larger than most, fed by gargoyle blood to keep them strong."

"Huh." Studying her surroundings, she picked out other such structures in nearby trees. Between them stretched bridges and ladders.

"We should go. It will be dawn before we know it and others will come looking for me the hour after sunrise."

Obsidian gestured for her to take the walkway leading right. She did, walking ahead of him and following his softly uttered instructions when they came to interconnecting bridges. At last, they came to a large platform she'd taken for a dead end until she spotted the ladder.

"I'll fly you the rest of the way." He squeezed past her and dropped to all fours, dipping a wing for her to mount.

"I don't think I'm ready to fly yet." She kept the nervous note out of her voice. "I'll take the ladder and meet you at the bottom."

"We're high up. Flying down will be faster." But he folded his wings back tight to his side and reared to stand on two feet. "But if you think you'll fall off, then I'll carry you."

The one-way mind-reading thing was getting old.

Obsidian chuckled. "If I'm honest, I doubt I'd stop it even if I could. It's been so long since I felt your conscious mind, I can't close myself off from you completely. It will stop once you recover enough to rebuild your mental shields."

The link flared briefly, proving it wasn't as one way as she'd thought. It let her glimpse a tiny peek into his mind. Just a fraction of a second but it was enough. In that moment of absolute clarity, she knew as difficult as she was finding this new situation, it had been much harder for him. "The link—or at least its absence—it was difficult to endure, wasn't it?"

"Yes." His expression was placid, but he couldn't fully control the agitated flicking of his tail.

"I'm so sorry I wasn't able to be there for you." She rested a hand on his shoulder, and he turned his head to nuzzle her fingers.

"You're here now. That is a blessing I shall thank the Divine Ones for daily."

The link that bound them had claimed a heavy price. She saw that now. Her absence had left him feeling like a part of his soul was missing, just beyond his reach. As a child, his mentors had thought it grief, but as he grew older, both he and his teachers came to understand it was more.

And now that she was awake at last, he desperately wanted to regain her trust, he craved it, needed to restore what time had stolen from them.

But he was patiently waiting for her to make her own decision. Anna glanced at the ladder. She could be stubborn and embrace her unease, or she could begin the process that might one day restore the absolute bond of trust they'd once shared.

Ah, hell, she'd never been a fan of rope ladders, anyway.

"I'll take the ride, but don't get used to it. I'll be doing my own flying as soon as I'm able." Anna stepped into his space and craned her neck. "A little help, please? You're enormous."

Relief washed down their link a second before Obsidian scooped her up in his arms and he laughed joyously. Anna scrambled for a grip around his neck as the big idiot launched himself over the edge and was suddenly twisting, flipping and gliding through the branches at breakneck speed.

Gonna die. Gonna die. Gonna die.

"Never!" Obsidian's voice rang loud in her head.

They dropped faster and faster; the branches getting bigger the lower they flew, and then suddenly they were out of the dense canopy. Obsidian tightened his arms around her body and then spread his wings wide, soaring thirty feet above the ground. Now the only obstacles in his path were the wide trunks of the hamadryads which he navigated with ease.

"A little warning next time would be nice." But she wasn't angry at him. They both knew it. In fact, his joy was filling her, shoving aside her uncertainties and dark memories. And she didn't miss how he hugged her just a little closer.

"Whiner," he mouthed into her hair.

"Jerk." Anna grinned up at him while she adjusted the satchel she still had gripped in one hand. "You're lucky I didn't drop the supply bag."

"You're too well trained for that."

"Training, my ass. Sheer terror had my fingers locked in a death grip."

Obsidian continued to pick up speed during his reckless flight through the trees. In this one moment, she had Shadowlight back. She didn't know how long it would last, but for now she was thankful all the same.

"You didn't scream."

"Jaws were locked."

He grinned. "Better lock them again then."

A moment later he went vertical, missing a low-hanging branch by inches and then rolled on his side to squeeze between two closely spaced tree trunks. Using one leg to push off from the nearest trunk, he changed directions.

"You call that a warning?" She was just talking shit now though. Like old times.

"That was an *advanced* warning."

"Still a jerk." She grinned and gave his neck a squeeze.

Again, joy sparked down their link, the emotion too powerful for him to block. She'd done the right thing by accepting the flight.

Eventually, they arrived at their destination—a cliff with trees running right up to its jagged edge. As far as Anna could tell, these were just regular old trees.

"Yes, we use this area for harvesting wood for the cooking fires." Obsidian circled lower, giving her a good look at the area before coming in for a landing. "We're less likely to get discovered out here, especially since it isn't yet dawn."

He gently placed her on her feet and then stepped back, searching the ground for a natural depression.

Without a word, he swiftly used his talons to clear the area of debris and enlarge the hollow.

Straightening, he stretched and sniffed. "I smell little in the way of prey here. I'll build a fire and then go hunt in the shallows for fish."

"I'll gather some loose rocks for a fire ring while you gather the wood."

Obsidian huffed in disdain and then waved his one hand at the ground. At first, nothing happened, and then the shadows shivered and rocks came loose from the ground, rolling toward the hollowed-out area.

Anna watched with bemusement. "Show-off."

In under a minute, the stones had formed a fire ring.

"I will be back shortly. We'll talk more then."

She nodded her agreement, and then he vanished into the forest way faster than someone of his size should be able to move.

CHAPTER SIX

Four leaf-wrapped bundles of fish were cooking on flat stones shoved half in the fire. Anna, too impatient to wait, peeled back the charred leaves of a fifth packet to get at the meat inside. Fish used to be one of her least liked foods, but her new gargoyle nature hadn't yet met a meat she didn't like.

"Eat these first." Obsidian held out some berries he'd found nearby. She popped a few in her mouth, then got hit with a rush of musty tartness and a hint of hot spice. Grimacing at him around a mouthful of the nasty crap, she gave him the finger.

"You did that on purpose!" she accused once her mouth was mostly empty.

"They are high in vitamins and minerals. Eat them."

Anna made a face but swiftly popped another handful into her mouth and chewed them as she continued to unwrap the fish. "Tastes like the devil's ass. Better be worth it."

Obsidian shrugged in apology. "They are much better dried and eaten in trail rations."

"Well, they couldn't get any worse, could they?"

After finishing the berries, she swished her mouth with water and then started in on the fish, burning her fingers but too hungry to care. She polished off the first bundle of fish and Obsidian immediately handed her another.

Nodding, she took it gratefully. After the sharp edge of hunger was sated, she looked over at Obsidian where he was polishing off his own fish.

It was so peculiar to know this was Shadowlight, and yet he looked like a stranger.

"It is strange for me, too," he admitted with a sigh. "I think I always just thought we'd pick up where we'd left off when you woke. But I'm not the gargoyle you remember. While I don't feel like I've changed that much, I understand that you need to come to terms with everything."

His words only highlighted the extent of the changes.

Shadowlight would have just brushed aside her concerns, told her she was foolish, and given her a big, sloppy gargoyle kiss. She'd have half-heartedly swatted him but then agreed, and they'd have found a solution to the present situation.

"There's a simple solution to this 'problem' if you're open."

Anna arched a brow at him.

"We talk. Ask me anything. I'll share everything with you. It might take days or even months, but I promise, we can be what we were before."

"I'd like that." Her heart swelled painfully, and she

glanced down at the fire so he wouldn't see the glimmer of foolish tears.

"Then ask me anything."

She scrambled as her mind blanked for a moment. Then went with the first question that popped into her head. "Have you created other gargoyles?"

"No." He gave an accompanying flick of his tail. "My mentors say it is unnatural and they wish to study your development before deciding whether it is something we should use to further grow the gargoyle legion."

Anna hastily swallowed a mouthful of fish. "I thought they'd give a resounding 'hell no' to any power linked to the Battle Goddess."

"Normally, yes. But they've studied me for many years now and know I am not her puppet."

Looking at him, his size, his control of magic, the impenetrable shield around his mind, Anna wasn't so sure she wasn't looking at the culmination of the Battle Goddess's plans.

He gazed at her, a hint of hurt creeping into his expression. "I thought we'd been through enough to know I'd never serve her."

"Sorry. I didn't mean it like that—I meant physically. You've grown into what she'd intended. The potential she'd strived to create to use as her vengeance." Anna resisted the urge to give the big brute a hug. "But your soul—that is a thing entirely of the Light. Thirteen years. A hundred years. A thousand. Nothing will ever change your core goodness."

And now that she was getting over her earlier shock,

she could see bits of the gargoyle cub she'd known in the adult who sat across the fire from her.

He huffed softly and returned to his food.

Time for a new topic. "Do you like it here? Do they treat you well?"

"Yes, this is my home now. I have friends, instructors, favorite mentors, even a few rivals in training. It is as Gregory said. We can trust Lord Draydrak. As fierce as his power is, he is nothing like his sister."

All his answers felt natural and unscripted, not brainwashed. A weight lifted off her chest. Shadowlight might have changed into this stranger... this Obsidian, but he wasn't unhappy. He'd just grown up on her.

Her throat grew tight again, and an ache that was becoming a familiar throb in her chest returned. She'd never again be able to read Shadowlight a story before bed or help him steal his favorite cookies from Gran's kitchen.

Considering what could have happened, this was the best outcome, even if she silently grieved the loss of Shadowlight.

Across the fire, Obsidian stood suddenly and then came around and knelt next to her. A moment later he was pulling her into his arms, his wings wrapping around her. "Shadowlight isn't gone. I'm still here. Look into my mind and you will see it's true"

There was no hesitation, just a familiar power and the warm brush of a mind she'd missed. But unlike when he was a child, the link was much stronger; the emotions bleeding across it as strong as if she was experiencing them herself.

Distantly, she heard him grunt in surprise at the unexpected strength of their link. She didn't have time to worry though, for in the next moment, she was Obsidian.

The gargoyle she'd once known as Shadowlight had trained for years, sunup 'til sundown, preparing for the time when he would lead an army of gargoyles against the Lady of Battles.

It was his own determination that drove him—not his mentors'. Though they shaped and guided his energy, that will to become the weapon that would strike a devastating blow to the Lady of Battles was all his. It was Shadowlight himself who'd first taken the steps down that path because he wanted to be a warrior worthy of his partner, his Kyrsu.

Together they would be powerful enough to destroy anyone or anything foolish enough to challenge them. Never again would he experience the helplessness he'd felt when Anna was struck down by the blood witch.

They were a team. Two halves of a whole. Together they would be near invincible.

Obsidian issued a little hissing growl, and suddenly Anna felt their link fade. The big gargoyle folded his wings and stood, taking a few steps back.

"My apologies." His voice came out gruff. "I knew our link would be stronger, but I expected nothing quite so..."

"Overwhelming," Anna supplied for him.

"Yes." He gave himself a little shake as if still struggling free of the binding magic linking them. "I was you for a few moments."

"Yeah. And I was you. Guess that answers some of my questions."

"That is... good." His tone was a little doubtful and

cautious as if he were trying to determine what all she'd seen in his head. "I thought I'd be able to control it even though you were untrained, but perhaps we should await direction from our mentors before trying again."

"Probably a good idea. However," Anna pointed to the place where he'd been sitting before, "I still have questions."

Against her will, her mind spun back to earlier, when she'd first awakened. She'd intentionally tried not to think about it because he'd known every other private thought that crossed her mind, so there was no way he'd miss this one.

Across the fire, Obsidian stiffened and shoved an overly large piece of fish in his mouth.

Huh. Got that one too, did you?

He was taking an inordinately long time to chew his meal. Well then. Two could play that game.

She bit off a chunk of her own fish, chewing slowly. Obsidian echoed her.

Another half a minute passed in silence. Ah, hell with it. When had she turned into such a chicken, anyway?

"Earlier, when I first woke up, what was that about?"

His ears flicked forward in question, but his expression was as placid as a lake on a breezeless day.

Play the mute all you want. It will not stop me from dragging an answer from you.

She waited a moment more. Nothing.

Fine.

"The 'hand on boob' and let's not forget the 'spooning me like a champion' thing."

She was damn sure if blushes could show on his jet-black gargoyle hide, he'd have been beet red.

"Ah, that... there was nothing untoward. Though a human might mistake it for something else."

"Don't try that 'she's a human, she won't understand' card on me."

He cleared his throat nervously, then gave the fire a couple of good pokes, but he eventually ran out of distractions and glanced up at her.

"For years, after a long day of lessons, I would come and curl up next to you. Hearing and feeling your slow heartbeat always reassured me, made me feel less homesick in those earlier days. My mentors said I should keep it up because I was sharing power with you, feeding your body energy it needed to aid in its healing."

He stared into the fire for long moments before continuing. "It also had the added benefit of allowing me to share some of what I learned with you. Though you may not be able to use what I gave you yet—it takes a very disciplined mind to control dreams and access what I shared. But in time you'll master that ability."

The bit about the sharing of knowledge was interesting. Once training starts, that could come in handy.

As for the rest?

Well, maybe she'd been barking up the wrong tree. But still. The gargoyle sitting next to her was an adult male. And life experience had taught her the only men she could trust were blood relatives. All others had ulterior motives, even Obsidian, even if he hadn't yet realized it.

"I don't... not like what you fear. I sleep in my stone

form every night to rejuvenate from the rigors of my strenuous training." His response sounded a little defensive. "As I did last night. I'd only just returned to my flesh and blood form moments before you did."

He was telling the truth. Her gargoyle nature stirred awake enough to let her know that.

With guilt, Anna remembered how she'd reacted and his snarl of pain. "Hey. Yeah. Sorry for any misunderstanding."

"If I'd known you would wake... I'd have..." He used the excuse of rescuing the last bundle of fish from the fire to stall. After unwrapping it, he offered half to her and then shoved the rest in his mouth.

"You'd have what? Not been fondling my boob?" She added helpfully after his words failed him.

Obsidian coughed and sputtered like he'd swallowed his tongue. Anna came around to his side of the fire and thumped him a few times in the middle of the back. After he'd cleared his airways, he laughed, a sound that was full and rich and surprisingly pleasant.

"Exactly so," he agreed at last. "Anna Mackenzie, please forgive me for that. I assure you, I didn't have ulterior motives besides wishing to share my strength, magic, and knowledge with you."

"I see that now." And she did.

After that, much of the earlier tension vanished, and they continued to eat in a companionable way. Occasionally, she'd ask a question, and he'd answer. Other times, he'd offer some exciting bit of his history she hadn't thought to ask.

But eventually, he looked up at the sky, sighed and stretched, then said they should return to his dwelling to get ready for the day. He couldn't put off taking her before the elders any longer.

CHAPTER SEVEN

While Anna was using his bathing chamber to wash up before going to meet with the elders, he mulled over his options. Unfortunately, he saw no way to scratch together more alone time to give her a chance to adjust to the new him. As soon as others knew she was awake, they would monopolize her time, distracting her.

It was one reason he'd taken her to the cliff instead of just going to the communal fires where there was usually food. He'd even debated taking her for a flight to one of the other islands that dotted the ocean in this region. But if he didn't show up for the festival preparations, it would draw suspicion.

But, curse the dark, she was his Kyrsu, and he wanted to cement that bond before venturing forth. Selfish of him, but true.

He was still digging for more options when a pounding rattled the door.

"I know you're in there," Truth called through the wood. "I don't want to be late for the assignments. You know I want to get picked for the hunt. Get your lazy backside out of that nest!"

Obsidian huffed at Truth's timing. Now there would be no way to keep Anna's waking a secret for a few hours more. "I'll be there in a moment. I slept in."

"Liar! You never sleep in." A fat pause followed a deep huffing breath. "God and Goddess! Do you actually have a woman in there with you?"

There was more loud sniffing and huffing laughter from outside. At which point Obsidian realized there were others out there with Truth. Just his luck.

"I came to apologize," Oath piped up. "But we'll come back later."

"No, we won't," Hunts in the Storm injected with a hearty laugh. "I've waited too long for the mighty Obsidian to fall. Now maybe a dryad will look in my direction."

"Storm!" Truth growled out a warning.

Damnation! Truth's younger brother was back from the mainland early? Storm was renowned for his tracking skills, but also for hunting down the truth. He never left any leaf unturned in that quest.

There was a snort from behind Obsidian.

"Friends of yours?" Anna asked.

"Not for much longer," he grumbled.

"Hah! You *do* have a woman in there!" Deeper sniffing sounded.

Anna made her way to the hidden door. She jabbed a thumb at the shielding magic. With a nod, he pressed his palm against a geometric section of spell work and released a tiny surge of power. After the slightest of pauses, the magic covering the door shivered and drew away to the sides of the frame.

Swiftly feeling along the door, Anna soon found the recessed latch hidden among the carvings decorating the entrance. With a click, the latch released, and she pulled open the door.

"Hello." She grinned at the rabble outside his door. Truth was there with Oath, Nightshade, Storm, Lark, and Meadow.

To a one, their expressions all reflected shocked surprise.

"I'm Corporal Anna Mackenzie, but I suppose my military rank is worth as much as spit here, so you can just call me Anna."

The two dryads were more composed, bowing their heads and uttering hesitant welcomes. The four gargoyles were still speechless, but Obsidian didn't miss how they leaned forward ever so slightly and drew in deeper breaths.

He resisted the urge to slap each of them alongside the head. Instead he marched past them, forcing them to move aside for Anna, or get run down by him.

"My Kyrsu is newly awakened and in need of clothing, boots, belts, and weapons. Why don't you five," he eyed Oath, Nightshade, Storm, Lark, and Meadow one at a time, "See if you can round up some of those items while we speak with the Council of Elders. While you're at it, why don't one of you inform the healers? They'll wish to examine Anna no doubt. And, Oath, you're quick, run ahead and inform the council we are coming."

The others, especially Oath, looked crestfallen until

Anna spoke up. "Aren't you going to introduce them before you go chasing them off?"

Obsidian huffed his displeasure. *"You've just tossed open gates that were better left closed and barred. But have it your way."*

He made quick introductions and then chased them away before they could bombard Anna with a thousand questions. After the others were gone, Truth came to pace at Obsidian's shoulder while Anna walked a little way ahead. The other gargoyle bumped his shoulder.

"Sly bastard," Truth said, using human words he'd learned from Obsidian while he'd dwelled on Earth. *"Is she why you didn't want to come celebrate with me last night? Not that I can blame you. After catching her scent, I'd be tempted to lock myself away with her too. I had no idea humans smelled so good."*

Obsidian cuffed Truth. *"Watch your tone when you speak of my Kyrsu. Besides, she didn't wake until just before dawn."*

"Aren't you touchy today?"

"Do you want a second cuff?"

Anna cleared her throat. "I might not hear the words, but I know you're doing that silent communication thing again."

Obsidian winced. "Forgive me. It won't happen again."

Then he side-eyed Truth.

The other gargoyle only gave him a toothy grin in return. The look promised more trouble from that front later.

"Treehouses. I still can't believe you live in tree houses." Anna leaned over one of the bridge railings to study her surroundings again. "They're even more spectacular by daylight."

"Yes, I suppose," Obsidian said distractedly as he shouldered past Truth to stand beside Anna.

"Getting stuff up this high must suck balls."

Obsidian grinned, only now coming to understand how much Anna had shaped his personality.

It did 'suck balls' as he could attest from having to haul up items. "I'll give you the full tour once we've seen the elders."

"Looking forward to it."

CHAPTER EIGHT

*A*nna kept her banter light and social while she studied every little detail for unseen danger and routes of escape, just in case things went sideways.

And things always went sideways, eventually.

"No one will harm you." Obsidian's thoughts flowed through her mind. It felt so much like Shadowlight her throat tightened again in that foolish way. Yet, it was different, too. There was a strength and discipline his younger self had lacked.

"None would dare. Not after Lord Draydrak went to so much work to save you and has made his wishes known. And even if someone is foolish enough to question Death's judgment, they will face me first. No one hurts what is dear to me."

A low growl accompanied his last sentence. The sound echoed through the air and Truth made a nervous questioning huff.

Obsidian's unearthly growl was nothing like Shadowlight's. Might as well compare a wiener dog to a wolfhound.

And while she was sure his words were meant to inspire, they didn't.

In fact, her internal 'shit's going to hit the fan' early warning system was screaming an alert. Shadowlight's adoration had been an innocent infatuation, and she'd viewed it as sweet and harmless. Something he'd outgrow.

But he hadn't, had he? If anything, this new Obsidian had somehow shaped that innocent adoration into something far more possessive. Bloody fuck.

"Now who's talking mind to mind and excluding the third wheel from the conversation?" Truth asked with a wink directed at Anna.

"Third wheel?" Anna muttered and then cast a questioning glance at Obsidian.

He shrugged. "I picked up many things when I was on Earth. Apparently, others soon picked up on my odd turns of speech. And as my mentors sometimes say—it spread like a wind-driven fire through dry grass."

"Well, something got lost in translation."

Truth leaned forward. "How so?"

"It's complicated." Anna wasn't about to waste time on explaining dates and third wheels when she had a more valuable way of using the time, like learning everything she could about Haven and its citizens.

But just then the section of the bridge they were traveling ended in a square platform.

"There are stairs and ladders for the dryads' use," Obsidian indicated the rope ladder, and then pointed across the way to a larger tree where wooden stairs circled the massive trunk. "The younger trees support smaller structures, but the ancient hamadryads can carry a much greater load. If you're still not up to climbing the ladder, I can fly or carry you."

Truth's snort was a sound rich in unspoken innuendo.

Obsidian half turned to give his friend a small lip curl and a flash of fangs.

"Thanks, but I'll climb. I'm feeling stronger now, and I'm sure I could use the exercise." And there was no way she was letting him carry her around like a child or— she glanced at Obsidian's massive size—like a child's favorite stuffed toy.

Booming laughter rang through the trees, telling Anna he'd been in her head for that one, too. After aiming a grin at Obsidian, she started down the ladder.

Truth just sort of hurtled himself over the side of the bridge and jumped from tree branch to tree branch, using his wings to slow his speed and his tail like a rudder. The gargoyle swiftly outpaced Anna. Glancing up, she sought Obsidian, but he wasn't above her.

"Here."

Anna turned toward the soft call to find him perched on a branch less than two feet away. Hell, she hadn't even heard him move. Man, he was stealthy for a big dude. His big bulk hadn't even shifted the branch enough to make the leaves shake.

"You will teach me how you do that." Her statement came out a demand, not a question.

"Just as soon as you can shape-shift."

"Damn straight."

Obsidian's gentle smile grew into a grin. "I have missed you very much, Anna Mackenzie."

"I'm glad to be back, too.'

Anna reached the ground without incident, but it took longer than she thought. The tree was tall, the bridge system about two-thirds of the way up, which left a lot of ground to cover.

While she didn't fear heights, it was nice to have her feet firmly on the ground again. The sickly swaying motion of a rope ladder was never her favorite sensation. Not that she'd admit to fear or weakness.

When Obsidian led the way, she followed. Truth brought up the rear.

They'd only made it a few hundred meters when Obsidian muttered a curse and came to a halt. Anna skirted around his wings and spotted a group ahead.

This group was a mix of three gargoyles and four dryads. One gargoyle towered over the other members of the group. She'd bet if he stood next to Obsidian, he'd only be an inch or two shorter.

What the heck was the Lord of the Underworld feeding his gargoyles? Growth hormones? Stem cells? GMO foods? Magic potions?

Though, this new fellow wasn't as heavily muscled as her two companions.

"Friends?" Anna asked sarcastically, knowing from Obsidian's stiff posture that this group was anything but friendly.

Obsidian huffed again, sounding less happy than before. "Do you remember earlier when I said I was happy here? That I had mentors, friends, acquaintances, even a few rivals? Well, here comes a rival."

"Figured as much." Anna moved to lean against a tree

trunk, cocking her leg while she waited for the newcomers to reach them.

"I see the abomination has finally awoken," the biggest of the newcomers said.

Whoa, Mr. Sunshine. Nice to meet you too.

Obsidian rumbled low in warning, but Anna reacted faster.

"The abomination has a name." She pushed off from the tree and circled to the left, forcing the dryad standing in her path to move or get run down.

The dryad studied Anna's approach with hostility but moved out of the way. Anna gave the dryad a searching look but decided the Fae wasn't a real threat. Her attention swung back to the big, belligerent fellow.

"Name's Anna. Though I'm more curious why you hate me so much when you don't even know me."

"I know *what* you are—a human with magic, an unnatural abomination created by our enemy—that's more than enough reason."

Obsidian snarled.

Turning, Anna arched an eyebrow when she saw Truth holding Obsidian back—barely.

"Who's the prick?" She jerked a thumb at the bigot.

"Reaver." The word came out harsh and ugly. Matched the name perfectly. "If you give her so much as a bruise, I'll break both your wings."

Anna grimaced. She'd learned enough. A minor scuffle didn't scare her, but for fuck's sake, the ones standing before her were the good guys, supposedly.

"Look, Reaver, I have better things to do than stand here and take part in some pissing contest. You don't like me. I think you're a prick. And even the Battle Goddess's lowest minions had better manners than you, so fuck off until you can at least match their conduct." Anna continued to walk around him, sizing him up.

"You would compare me to one of the enemies?" Rage rolled off his words.

"You bet. You wanna know what else? I get why you don't trust me. I wouldn't either, coming from there, but the least you could do is treat me with enough respect to give me a chance to prove my worth before judging me and deciding I'm an enemy."

Reaver's expression shifted into something even less pleasant.

"Eh? That's how it will be?"

"I'm taking you before the elders," Reaver lunged forward.

Anna allowed him to capture her wrist. She kept her body relaxed, and when Obsidian charged forward as she knew he would, she used the distraction to twist free of Reaver's hold.

Now, close to his side, she grabbed the outer edge of his right wing, then darting around behind him, she jerked the wing along with her. Gargoyle wings were strong and flexible, but even they could only be forced so far without breaking.

Obsidian, having guessed her strategy had taken hold of Reaver's forearm, preventing him from spinning and freeing his wing.

Anna forced the wing more, but even then Reaver only hissed in pain.

"Now, Reaver, what do you think will happen first? Will

the bone shatter? Or will the entire wing dislocate?" Anna bounced the wing gently in warning. "If you continue to be a jerk, we'll all get to discover the answer."

Reaver snarled, but after a moment his rage-filled eyes focused on her. "I yield."

"Hmmm." Anna glanced at Obsidian. "Wonder why I don't believe him?"

"Because it's a lie." Obsidian's lips curled back, exposing his impressive fangs. "He only plans to surrender for now. He's prepared to continue this later."

Sighing, Anna patted Reaver's muzzle with her free hand. He didn't bite her fingers. Smart boy. "Surrender for now, then. We can work through the root of your animosity later."

The male snarled again. Anna glanced where Obsidian's claws were digging into Reaver's forearm hard enough to draw blood.

"I'd listen to her, if I were you, Reaver," Truth said, entering the conversation for the first time.

"Someone must bring her before the elders." Reaver's reply was sullen and anger still shimmered in his deep tones as he stared death at Obsidian.

"Dumb fuck," Anna smacked him alongside his muzzle to get his attention. "Where do you think Obsidian was taking me before you jumped us?"

Muttering under her breath, she released his wing and stepped back. Obsidian used the opportunity to get right in his face. "Anna is my Kyrsu. Pick a fight with her, and you pick a fight with us both."

Finished with his dressing down, Obsidian shoved the other male away hard enough to make him stumble. Then without a word or backward glance, Obsidian started forward. Anna followed, then paused when she was even with Reaver.

"Next time you pick a fight, I won't be so nice. And in case you think I'm an easy kill, you might want to find out what I did to a blood witch."

Reaver wasn't cowed though and spat 'unnatural' at her in passing.

"Yes," Obsidian agreed, suddenly back at her shoulder, his blade-tipped tail pressing against Reaver's throat hard enough to draw blood. "We are unnatural. We are also a very formidable team. If you choose not to respect that, then I won't be held responsible for your death."

The fierce, proud tone when he said the word 'team' reminded Anna of Shadowlight's ferocious loyalty.

As if sensing her emotions—and he likely was—he bumped his muzzle against her cheek and then turned and marched off again. Though this time his tail had curled behind her back to ensure she followed.

Once they were well out of earshot, Truth bent double laughing. "Goddess, seeing Reaver get trounced by the tiny human—" More chuckling disrupted his sentence. "Best thing I've seen in half a year."

"Watch it, or Anna will come for you next." Obsidian's gruff tone was at odds with the glint of humor in his eyes.

Truth chuckled louder but glanced at her and issued a hasty apology for calling her tiny. "I'm sorry. Truly. It's just that Obsidian normally lets the verbal barbs slide off without so much as a flinch or flick of an ear."

"Eh? Well, if people are dicks, they better be ready for the consequences. I'm not as nice as Obsidian."

Obsidian's tail twitched, tightening a fraction around her waist before relaxing again. "I may ignore insults aimed at me, but no one challenges my Kyrsu without consequences."

Anna glanced up at him "That goes both ways. If someone is stupid enough to pick a fight with my little brother, then they deal with me too. It's the Mackenzie way."

"Little brother?" Truth rolled the words around as if he found a secret delight in them.

Anna shrugged. "I may have just slept thirteen years away, but Obsidian is still only twenty-one to my twenty-four. He's still younger than me. So 'little brother' is still officially correct."

Her glower dared anyone to claim differently at their peril.

Truth nodded and grinned, a great flash of white teeth. Then he leaned closer and sniffed at Anna. She doubted she'd ever get used to the utter bloody rudeness of gargoyles. They were touchy-feely and had absolutely no concept of personal space, or that it was impolite to sniff at a person.

"Truth," Obsidian warned, his earlier humor absent from his deep timber. "Know 'little brother' will bust the horns off any male who goes sniffing around Anna uninvited."

Truth choked on more laughter but took a couple of steps back in a show of obedience. Eventually Obsidian had his fill of glowering at his friend and turned his attention back to her.

"As much as Reaver annoys, don't challenge him unless I'm near. He is dangerous."

"I have a hard time keeping my mouth shut when I'm confronted by pricks. But I'll try to behave."

"Thank you. Reaver tests the patience of even Banrook, and he's the easiest going of the mentors. Reaver's personality is likely why he hasn't yet been called to take his Adepts Trial."

"And that burns his tail," Truth interjected from behind. "He's three times as old as me—I'm almost thirty-nine. In fact, you never had a chance of Reaver liking you. You're Obsidian's Kyrsu, guilty by association. This great lout," he patted Obsidian's shoulder, "has outstripped all of us. It's likely that he'll make Adept before his twenty-second name day. Reaver is one hundred and eighteen and still a journeyman."

Anna only half listened to Truth's words, still stuck on Reaver's age. She'd thought him Obsidian's peer, but he was old enough to be their great-great grandfather.

Beside her Obsidian snorted.

"What?" Truth's brows folded down.

"Anna mentioned Reaver's old enough to be our grandfather if he'd been human. I was just thinking that a dryad would actually have to take an interest in him first."

The other male's eyes widened in surprise and then turned thoughtful. "Honestly? A grandfather? Humans breed so swiftly?"

"Shorter lives," Anna clarified for him. "If we live to a hundred, it's considered extremely old."

"Ah." Truth seemed intrigued but continued with his earlier explanation why Reaver hated Obsidian so much.

"So, when you and Obsidian—mere novices—nearly defeated a blood witch..."

Was that a mix of awe and fear in Truth's voice?

"Well, we were lucky. The witch and the other captains underestimated us. We wouldn't be as lucky a second time."

"No. I suppose not."

Anna was about to turn the discussion in another direction when the trees along the manicured path thinned. She could also now hear the low rumble of many conversations over the breeze rustling the thick canopy of leaves. Only, it wasn't entirely the breeze stirring the leaves.

Above them, the canopy shook with an unknown number of gargoyles making their way toward what she assumed was a clearing in the dense forest. Her senses still weren't sharp enough to pinpoint the exact number of gargoyles overhead, but she'd guess at least ten. To either side, more pale cobblestone pathways snaked their way through the forest from other directions, all leading toward a central point.

"Come closer." Obsidian held out a wing. "I'll hide you using shadow magic. That way the others won't see you and swamp us with questions until after we've met with the Council of Elders and my other mentors."

After meeting with Reaver, she could only agree with his logic. She stepped in closer until his wing curved around her, blocking out the forest and much of the noise.

"Just curious. But what will others see when they look at you?"

"They'll see me carrying a saddle and using my wing for

balance to prevent it from bumping against my side with each step."

"A saddle?"

"Gargoyles wear saddles when we need to carry the dryads to the mainland or for a hunt."

That was logical.

Behind them, Truth snorted with renewed humor. "Normal gargoyles carrying a saddle isn't a strange sight. Obsidian carrying one? That's something no one has seen. Even though your 'little brother' is sought after by many a dryad, he's never allowed himself to be saddled or carry a rider. His appearance with a saddle will spawn much speculation about who has finally netted him."

"Let them speculate. They'll know the reason for the deception soon enough."

On that note, Obsidian ushered Anna along the path until it ended in a clearing. Trees lined the vast space on the north, west, and east sides, leaving the south open to the sky where a cliff dropped into the ocean.

She'd had loved to see if she could spot the mainland Truth had mentioned, but sightseeing would have to wait. There were a few hundred gargoyles between her and the ocean, and somewhere in the mass Obsidian's mentors would be waiting to see her.

CHAPTER NINE

*E*yeing the meadow, Anna watched as several dryads and gargoyles dragged wood into piles she hoped were for giant bonfires and not pyres for sacrifices. There were sixteen piles so far, in various degrees of completion, but to gauge by the space, there was room for another ten.

Around the outside edge of the meadow, many smaller cooking fires already burned with pots and spits suspended over them.

With amusement, Anna couldn't help but think it looked like a super-sized version of the Mackenzie family reunion.

"Here comes Oath."

Obsidian was facing east, and sure enough, the youngster was running through the crowds toward them.

"That was fast," Truth mumbled. "Wonder if he took time to say anything beyond 'Anna' and 'awake' before charging back here at full speed?"

Obsidian grunted. "Not likely."

Oath skidded to a halt, searching for Anna, but his gaze failed to find her. Next, he tried to get a good sniff but was blocked by Obsidian's wing. Undeterred, the youngster sidled up next to the bigger gargoyle.

"Nice try. Were you able to find the Masters?"

"I found Maradryn first. She's in her usual spot." Oath glanced over his shoulder at the eastern tree line. "Nightshade, Lark, Meadow, and Storm are all making their way to the other Elders currently in Haven. Maradryn said to have them meet at her cooking fire."

"That is likely wise," Obsidian agreed.

Together they headed toward the eastern tree-line. Skirting the worst of the crowds, Obsidian homed in on a campfire where a dryad was tossing pieces of cut-up vegetables and meat into a cauldron suspended over a large bed of embers. When they reached the cookfire, Obsidian released his shadow magic but kept his one wing mantled around Anna to hide her from the rest of the gathering behind them.

The dryad didn't halt her work, merely nodding at Obsidian and then finished slicing a few more tubers and tossing them in after the rest. She moved with the natural grace all dryads possessed, but that wasn't what seized Anna's attention.

This dryad's eyes missed nothing. And while her body might appear relaxed, she contained a shimmering intensity all predators, or highly skilled warriors, possessed.

Upon closer examination, the other woman was taller than Anna, wider across the shoulders, and had more muscular arms. She was a positive Amazon. Close cropped dark hair and a lack of adornments suggested this woman wasted very little time on vanities.

Anna liked her already.

When at last they reached the campfire, the Amazon looked up and smiled at Obsidian, transforming her somewhat strong features into something softer.

"My heart, I'm glad you came to me. I'd be hurt if you'd gone to Rook first."

"I know you and Banrook keep some kind of point system as if to discover which of you I adore more. It's pointless. I love you both equally." Obsidian leaned down, giving the woman an affectionate nuzzle.

In return, she reached up into his mane and gave him a good head scratch. Obsidian purred happily. Eventually, he turned back to Anna.

"I'd like you to meet Master Maradryn. She was one of the first island residents to take me in and mother me. She is also one of our greatest dryad healers."

The Amazon was a healer? She looked like she'd be more skilled at breaking people open than stitching them back up again.

And master, not mistress? They must not differentiate between the genders. Could this society be a study in true gender equality?

Interesting. But perhaps not so surprising. Both species were a single gender. Anna supposed that meant dryads and gargoyles might lack the usual gender bias.

She scanned the woman, her magic stirring to aid her study. Looking for she knew not what, but if she was to guess, it was to discover if this woman was worthy of Obsidian's evident devotion.

Anna stepped out from Obsidian's wing and then held out a hand.

The dryad's expression was inscrutable as she stared at Anna's offered hand. She didn't take it. Instead, her gaze followed the hand up the arm and on to her face. Maradryn's gaze searched Anna's, studying her in the same way she'd studied the dryad earlier, seeking to find something that would prove Anna was worthy of Obsidian's devotion.

"Anna Mackenzie at your service." Anna gave the other woman a nod of respect. "Previously known as Shadowlight's big sister, protector, and doer of whatever nasty things that needed doing. Don't quite know what I am now, but willing to help out in the war against the Battle Goddess in any way I can."

The other woman's dour expression melted away into delight and she laughed. "Anna Mackenzie, your role will not change. You will become Obsidian's Kyrsu, as Lord Death decrees, and continue to protect your gargoyle partner ferociously and do great violence to his enemies. Which is a great and noble thing, but before we go into all that, I wish to thank you for protecting my much-beloved Obsidian when he couldn't yet fully protect himself."

Anna bowed her head. "I will strive to make everyone proud."

"Good. Continue to keep a sharp eye out. While there's no darkness here, not like there was deep within the Battle Goddess's domain, there are still a few who do not trust Obsidian's power or how swiftly he has advanced. They would have preferred he developed slower to more fully examine his nature. You understand what I'm saying?"

"Yes." Anna did, completely.

"Good, because those resentments will only flare up brighter when our strong young gargoyle here takes his Adept Trial. So, Anna Mackenzie, snarl and bite, prowl and hunt. Take down anyone who is foolish enough to raise a hand against your Rasoren."

The older woman fell silent for a moment as she gave the fire a stir. When she looked up again, it was to smile good-naturedly. "But for now, eat and grow strong once more. You will need it."

CHAPTER TEN

Obsidian glanced at the woman he viewed as a mother and then back at Anna. He probably should be more insulted than amused that the two women thought he needed protection. Hadn't he been looking out for himself for many years now?

In truth, he looked forward to paying Anna back for her protection and guidance when he'd been a child. He'd start by helping her navigate these new waters.

Surprisingly, her concern also made him happy. It meant she was relating to him like she'd used to when he was Shadowlight, her beloved little brother and teammate.

Maradryn gestured for them to sit and eat, which he was always happy to do.

Anna didn't turn down the offer of food either. Maradryn happily kept up a one-sided conversation as they ate, filling Anna in on some of what she'd missed while asleep. Like a proud mama, the woman took particular pleasure in telling stories about his prowess as a hunter and warrior.

She even mentioned how many of the dryads had been so impressed they sought him out over older gargoyles. The praise and commentary made heat suffuse his cheeks, but he didn't rise to her baiting. Especially since she had her own agenda about whose affection he should return.

The Council of Elders had, upon occasion, seen fit to interfere with his life, but mostly, they butted out of his personal relationships. Though, clearly, Maradryn would like to have more influence.

"Well, you're no fun," she said with a grin.

"Try not to be." His tone mimicked one he'd heard Anna use many times.

Maradryn rolled her eyes and then gazed at Anna. "I should likely refrain from questioning you until the rest of the Elders arrive. However, I have a few subjects I'd like to broach before the rest of the council sidetracks you with yet more questions."

Obsidian drew breath to interrupt and was waved to silence before he'd even uttered a word.

"Yes, yes. You've told us everything you knew. However, you were a child. Anna will have a different outlook on events. Perhaps she even caught nuances that went over your head."

Anna nodded slowly in agreement though she didn't look like she welcomed an additional line of questioning before the official debriefing.

When the two women sat down across the fire and discussed past events, his thoughts turned inward.

When he was younger, it hadn't once occurred to him that Anna might not want to be a gargoyle, that she might seek to return to her purely human existence if that had been an option. He had been so starved for love, and Anna was the only one with the time or inclination to lavish it upon him, he'd taken her love as a sign of acceptance of her fate.

But as he grew older, he realized that it wasn't acceptance so much as it was her innate nature to look ahead, survive, escape, endure—all without whining about what fate had thrust upon her.

That didn't mean Anna was happy with her situation.

Now he only hoped she didn't grow to hate him for what he'd done to save her life all those years ago. And that she'd be willing to be his Kyrsu and fight by his side until they defeated all their enemies. He didn't know what he'd do if she asked to return to her life on Earth without him.

Anna glanced sidelong at him and patted the ground, her steady presence reaching out to him as Maradryn continued to ask questions. Not needing a second invitation, he sat and then scooted closer, using one wing to hide her from view of anyone passing by.

"Relax, I'm not going anywhere without you. We're a team. I made you that promise, and it doesn't have an expiration date. Lifelong, my friend. Get used to it." Humor accompanied her thoughts.

The tension between his shoulder blades eased. Grinning as foolish exuberance gripped his soul, he leaned down and gave Anna a gargoyle kiss.

"Gross," she muttered and wiped the back of her hand

across her cheek. *"But it's true. I'll always have your back, and I won't even mouth off to the elders like I did with that Reaver jackass. Promise."*

A snort from the other side of the fire drew his attention back to Maradryn.

"You do the nonverbal communication better than Rook and me. And we've known each other close to nine hundred years." She looked at Anna. "You really are his Kyrsu. That's the only time I've seen such a natural, unified front. Did you know you move together, mirroring each other? By the light, your resting breath and pulse are the same. You're completely attuned to each other, and you don't even realize it. No wonder Lord Draydrak is so keen to groom you both to be his war leaders. On the field of battle, you'll think as one mind but possess two bodies. You'll be lethal."

Maradryn continued to scrutinize them until Obsidian had the urge to squirm under her gaze.

At last, she changed the subject. "Oath tells me you've already had to drive off that thick-headed Reaver."

He growled, his earlier good feelings vanishing. "Yes, Reaver came upon us on our way here. Predictably, he insulted Anna."

"That boy will never make Adept if he doesn't learn humility, compassion, tolerance, and patience."

'I'd settle for basic intelligence,' Obsidian thought.

"I fear one or all of those objectives may be beyond him." Maradryn's expression darkened. "If he continues to give Anna trouble, I will speak with the other Masters. We'll act to discipline him."

"Thank you." Obsidian bowed his head in respect. "However, Anna cut him down with a few verbal spars and soon had him in retreat."

The memory of Anna winning the skirmish with words alone still made him ridiculously proud.

Meadow returned and politely bowed to Maradryn and then informed the group that the other council members were on their way.

"Stay," Maradryn told the other dryad. "Obsidian's friends are always welcome at my fire."

Meadow murmured her thanks before settling to Obsidian's left. He nodded to her. When he glanced back Anna's direction, it was to find Oath lying on the ground, his head resting on his forearms and his tail coiled around him as he looked upon Anna with absolute adoration.

"You won a fight against Reaver using words alone?"

"Wasn't that hard. He's not that bright."

The worshipful look in Oath's eyes almost made Obsidian laugh. She may not even realize she'd gained her first admirer among the citizens of Haven.

Others would soon see all the qualities that made him so proud of Anna. She would win them over—the ones worthy of the effort. The rest, like Reaver, Obsidian would break to his will or simply break them.

Maradryn soon turned the topic to Earth, and Anna explained about such things as politics, military, and various technologies with broad, sweeping hand gestures.

Partway through the conversation Meadow rummaged in a woven basket she'd brought with her.

From inside, she removed six of the clay-fired urns used

for storing wine and other fermented drink. The tops were sealed with wax stamped with her family's mark. It was one of her family's specialties and was always in demand at the festivals. "Banrook said I should bring some of these in case the council gets thirsty. There is enough for everyone."

Meadow offered Anna the first goblet, showing Obsidian's Kyrsu the respect she was due.

Anna smiled her thanks and took a careful sip. After a moment, her eyes lit up. "The good stuff. Don't be surprised if I come begging for more at some later date."

Maradryn leaned forward, holding out her goblet to fill. Truth, bored with waiting, stole an urn for himself and Oath while Meadow filled Obsidian's cup.

"Will you and Truth still be coming to my family's fire tomorrow after the hunt? That is, if you're not too busy now. Anna is welcome." Meadow's ordinarily outgoing and cheerful demeanor was absent, replaced by a more subdued and shy countenance. He thought he knew why, and it sparked a bit of unease in his belly.

"I..." He didn't want to give her false hope, but she was also his friend and he didn't want to hurt her feelings. "Of course I'll come. I'm sure Anna would like to meet your family."

"Later, for the dancing..." Meadow let her sentence die as she glanced over uncertainly at Anna, where she was still sitting sheltered under his opposite wing talking with Maradryn.

Oh. So that's the reason Meadow was suddenly awkward. She didn't know what kind of relationship he and

Anna would now share. Or how Anna's awakening would influence Obsidian's newer friendships.

Anna was...

She was his... friend.

But more than that, she was his—

Hmmm....

Why was he having trouble classifying their relationship?

Because, whispered a tiny voice in his head, she's more than just a friend. She's your trusted confidant, big sister, teammate, and many times she was the only safe option to love.

Yet, even though all those terms were accurate, when he'd been younger, he'd also thought once he'd matured enough, Anna would just become his partner in all things... eventually taking on the role of mate.

It was a silly childhood wish.

But none of those terms did her justice. Anna was so much more.

She was his Kyrsu. She completed and complemented his soul. They were two spirits joined by magic and shared experiences. No romance existed to muddy those glorious facts.

But what if their relationship developed and shifted toward something less platonic?

The thought made him flush self-consciously. No. He was being foolish. Anna was just... Anna. A force of nature he needed in his life.

It was better—safer certainly—that she continued to think of him in a brotherly fashion.

His mentors had always warned him not to project his

wishes upon his Kyrsu or risk stealing her will and stripping away any kind of choice from her.

Hadn't Banrook been drilling discipline into him all these years for just this day?

He would do all in his power to keep Anna safe from what his dark gift yearned to do to her.

A hand patted his knee and Anna was suddenly leaning forward to peer around him and meet Meadow's eyes.

"Shadowlight used to like music. I can't imagine Obsidian has changed so much." Anna's shit-eating grin was firmly in place. "If he tries to chicken out, I'll make sure he still puts in an appearance."

Meadow likely didn't know the meaning of 'chicken out,' but the answering smile that lit up her face transformed it from merely pretty into something warm and beautiful. Yet Meadow, lovely though she was, stirred nothing within him. Not knowing what else to do, he raised his goblet for a big drink.

When he looked up again, Anna was still grinning at him.

But a throat being cleared drew his attention back toward Master Maradryn. "Don't worry. You'll have lots of time to socialize later, but for now, the council has business that needs tending."

Meadow and Truth came to their feet swifter than if one of their mentors barked an order. The bigger gargoyle prodded Oath in the ribs when he didn't move fast enough.

Anna pushed on Obsidian's wing until he lowered it enough she could look over the top and watch the approaching Council of Elders. After noting their position, she leaned in close to his ear. "Meadow, she's sweet. It's obvious she likes you. If you two aren't already a thing, you should be."

He huffed in surprise at the pleasant sensation of Anna's warm breath against his ear and where his mind flashed to in that moment.

No, Meadow didn't stir him, but his Kyrsu just had.

$\mathcal{A}$nna didn't have a freaking clue what had possessed her to add her two cents about Meadow. It wasn't like she was any good at matchmaking, but there was something about Meadow—a wholesomeness tempered with an inner strength that just made Anna think the young dryad would be a good match for Obsidian.

Admit it, Mackenzie, Anna thought to herself. *If he's romantically involved with one of the dryads, then he becomes 'safe' and you like the sound of that a lot better than a bachelor Obsidian who might set his sights on his Kyrsu.*

Time to put that whole can of worms out of her mind. She didn't need further complications until she knew the inner workings of Haven. It had taken her weeks of careful observation to learn enough about the Battle Goddess's domain to benefit. If she'd been a crier, she might have teared up at the knowledge she was now starting from scratch.

At least Obsidian had a thirteen-year head start. She planned to mine him for intel later. For now, she had a Council of Elders to win over.

The newly arrived council members—there were only three, two gargoyles and one dryad—joined them around Maradryn's fire.

Banrook she remembered from before. Forgetting someone as big as him was hard. Obsidian was now the larger of the two, but Banrook was one of those types who sucked up all the oxygen in a room just by the magnitude of his personality.

"Anna, you may remember Master Verroc from when you crossed the time portal." Obsidian pointed to the less muscular gargoyle.

Anna nodded respectfully to the elder.

She'd started picking out other little details that differentiated one gargoyle from another at a glance. Some, like Verroc, wore distinctive jewelry. At least she hoped the silver ear-stud with its pale blue stone was distinctive and there weren't a hundred others just like it to confuse her.

"Don't let Verroc's smaller stature fool you." Obsidian sent along their link. *"He can and will hand you your own ass in the practice ring."*

"Speaking from personal experience?"

"Yes."

"And this is Master Sumdara," Obsidian said aloud like they hadn't just been having a private conversation. "She's one of our greatest dryad trackers."

Sumdara lacked Maradryn's Amazonian height, but she still possessed a warrior's body, well-muscled and marred by more than a few scars.

Anna acknowledged this new dryad with the same respect she'd allotted the gargoyles.

Verroc cleared his throat. "Now it's time to speak of things better not heard by others just yet."

With that gruff utterance, he raised a hand above his head and summoned shadow magic. The darkness between the nearest trunks shivered and shook before pulling away from under the trees which had first cast the shade.

With another soft utterance, Verroc ordered the magic to form a dome over them all, sealing them behind a shimmering silver-grey substance that blocked out sound from the outside.

"There. Now we'll have privacy. No one except this council knows the full extent of your power. They know you're a human with magic, one altered by the Battle Goddess, but your gargoyle nature is still a secret. We'd like to keep it that way, at least until you've settled in and get to know Haven's residents."

"I thank you for that, but how haven't they figured it out? That I was sleeping in stone seems like common knowledge."

"Yes. But all think it was Lord Dray's magic which accomplished the deed. We never corrected that erroneous notion."

Dray. It was so strange that a being with such frightening powers and a title like 'Lord of the Underworld' was merely called Dray by his friends.

But Anna wasn't given long to dwell on that thought for the Elders soon launched into what was apparently an interrogation. She answered them truthfully, holding nothing back—they'd sense any lie even if she'd wanted to keep something secret.

During a lull in the questioning, Anna reflected on that ability. An interrogator able to smell a lie, possess eyes sharp enough to catch the tiniest of tells, and even read surface thoughts?

Yep, back on Earth, that would be any intelligence agency's wet dream. When all of this was over, maybe she could orchestrate a peaceful joint operation between gargoyles and a few of the acronym agencies. It never hurt to think about future career choices.

Obsidian touched her mind. *"You'll already have a career, a gargoyle war-leader."*

"Never hurts to diversify."

But the council soon agreed on a line of questioning focused on her abilities. At first, she'd thought they looked for weaknesses to use against her. Then they talked about training. Ah. This interrogation wasn't for devious purposes. It was for school.

Her time in the Battle Goddess's kingdom had been more like a magical basic training package. This new training sounded a lot more academic.

Eventually, they finished grilling her and turned to discussing Obsidian's training and how he was progressing.

"Well," Banrook said as he gathered his feet under him, "I suppose we should release Obsidian and Anna, so they can enjoy the festival. Your training will resume the afternoon after the Spring Rites, but first, Lord Draydrak will want to see you both. Report to the temple that morning before your lessons."

"We will be there." Obsidian rose and then bowed his head at each of the Elders. Anna mimicked him.

"Besides," Banrook added, "if we hold you up too much longer, some of our brothers and sisters might expire of curiosity. That Lord Draydrak has made it known he desires a human to share command of his army has generated rather a lot of speculation."

"To put it mildly," Master Verroc added in his dour tones.

Banrook gestured toward the surrounding shadow magic shield. A second later the dome misted away. "Go. Use the time before the hunt to introduce Anna to the others."

"Would you prefer to sit the hunt out? The Elders will understand if you don't feel up to it yet." Obsidian asked after they'd left the council members.

She glanced over his shoulder to find those in the crowd nearest to their location staring with rapt attention. "Nope. I'm good. A hunt sounds perfect."

Because, surely, not everyone at the gathering would come? The hunt would offer an escape from the scrutiny for a short time.

"Very well." Obsidian sounded distracted, and when she looked up, it was to see him staring back at the crowd of gargoyles and dryads gathered a short distance away. They were talking amongst themselves now but still stared openly. "I think we'll still be required to 'show you off' to the legion first before we can escape on a hunt."

"Oh, come on. I'm a human, not a rare and mystical unicorn. Hell, humans and dryads don't even look that different."

"True. But they are also curious about where you're from—Earth. To them, Earth is far more mystical than a unicorn. And they know Lord Dray has seen something in you that makes you worthy to lead. They want to see if they can spot it too."

"Great. If I'm going to be under a microscope, might as well get it out of the way."

Obsidian agreed with a deep chuckle. "In that case, I think we should find a place to dig in and make them come to us."

"Works for me." Maybe some of them would be too busy to take time from their duties to gawk at the Earthling.

CHAPTER TWELVE

As it turned out, no one at the gathering was too busy to meet Obsidian's human Kyrsu. Anna had even grudgingly admitted it wasn't as bad as she'd expected. But flying free was going to be much more enjoyable. The breeze blowing off the ocean flipped her thick ponytail from side to side. They weren't even in the air yet and the wind was already working hard to loosen her hair. First chance she got she needed to put it back in rows.

"Here, take these." He handed her a bow and a quiver full of arrows. That done, he dropped to all fours and bumped his muzzle under her hand in eagerness.

"Jeez, grow some patience," Anna laughed. "I'm hurrying."

Lifting his wing out of her way, he waited with a humorous glint in his eye again.

"Now who's uncertain?"

"You're impatient and delusional." She swung a leg over his back and settled into place. While she waited for the rest of the dryads to mount up, she checked her quiver and harness.

Anna leaned forward to brace her hands on his shoulders and noted her nose was almost buried in his thick mane.

"Next time, we're doing your hair in cornrows. By the end of this hunt, I will be *so* done with getting flogged in the face."

"Stop whining!" Then he was flexing his powerful hindquarters and launching them off the cliff into empty space. "Enjoy the freedom of the day!"

Laughing, Anna spread her arms wide and embraced the sheer sense of freedom and belonging in this one perfect moment. Then the thunder of wings filled the sky as the hunting party took flight behind him.

It was at that exact moment she knew she would be all right; Shadowlight wasn't really gone at all. He'd just changed his name and grown up a little. This life, strange as it might seem to her old self, was hers now. Now it was up to her to claim it.

Slowly, Anna's wildly beating heart calmed, but she couldn't wholly vanquish the childlike wonder of flying gargoyle-back above the bright blue waves.

The sun shone hot, but the wind was pleasantly cool. Below them, a pod of dolphins cut through the waves.

"The Magic Realm has dolphins?"

Obsidian had been looking ahead toward the mainland in the distance, but he tilted his head, scanning the ocean and swiftly spotted the pod.

He banked to the left, dropping lower suddenly. Anna's stomach lodged itself in her throat for a moment.

"Some warning next time."

"Is my Kyrsu whining? Is that what I hear?"

"Just wait. You haven't experienced whining yet."

"Look closer," he said suddenly.

She did. There was a metallic greenish-silver streak dipping and darting between the dolphins. "Fuck me! A mermaid!"

Just then the mermaid leaped high above the waves, splashing one of the low-flying gargoyles. The leanly built male dipped closer to the water as his dryad rider cursed both her mount and the mermaid.

"That's Breaker. He and the sirens are good friends and often hunt the shallows together."

Anna's eyebrow lodged itself nearly in her hairline. "Gargoyles are good swimmers?"

She'd never had the chance to try but figured the wings would be a problem.

"Most aren't as good in the water as Breaker. The running joke is that he's spent so much time with the sirens, they've been secretly adapting him to a life in water. He moves like one of those..." He hesitated, obviously not remembering a word. "One of those flightless, ocean-dwelling birds back on Earth."

"Penguins," she supplied.

"Yes. He uses his wings underwater like one."

"Have you tried that?"

He grunted in answer. "Yes. Once. Think I nearly swallowed half the ocean."

"I'll give that a hard pass."

Obsidian veered back higher into the sky and a moment later a second siren broke the surface in a graceful arc before disappearing back into the blue depths, her tail flick insufficient to spray them twenty feet above the waves.

If Anna had been paying attention earlier, she would have recognized other magic wielders. It was a sharp reminder she needed to remain alert and not get seduced by the warm sun, cool breeze, and blue waves. Danger was never more than a few steps away.

"Those sirens are our allies," Obsidian informed her. "You need not fear them. They serve Lord Dray and patrol the waters around the island even as we patrol the sky."

Anna furrowed her brows. "Sirens. Read about them before. When my team was attacked by the Riven, there was a siren involved in that mess. Never saw her in person. Too busy dying at that time, but I read the file afterward. She'd originally come to enslave Gregory and Lillian and wipe out a good chunk of humanity. Those are the same creatures swimming down there?"

"Yes. They take their duties seriously. The one in the report was trying to protect her ocean realm."

"There are better ways than mass genocide."

Obsidian just shrugged.

Seriously. A shrug?

Anna arched an eyebrow at the back of his head. "You sure the ones down there are friendly?"

"I did not say that." He tilted his head to catch her eye. "I only said the sirens below serve Lord Dray and help protect our lands. If someone was to trespass and their intentions were not pure..."

"Mmm... Fish food. Got it. Don't go swimming in the ocean."

"You are safe from them."

Anna wasn't feeling particularly convinced. Humans didn't seem to be a favorite race in the Magic Realm. 'What'd we ever do to them?'

"You seem to forget we have that siren back on Earth to thank for our meeting," Obsidian pointed out. "If she hadn't helped us to destroy the Riven in the Mortal Realm, there would have been many more to clean up, delaying me from finding you until it was too late. If not for that siren, you might have been the first Riven I killed on my own. That thought upsets me."

"I..." The thought of never meeting Shadowlight, being saved by the fiercest gargoyle cub ever born, made her soul take a chill. "I never thought of it like that. You're right. Even though I don't condone that siren's methods, or what she was trying to do, I owe her my life."

"And I likely owe her mine as well." Strong emotion bled across the link. "I don't know if I would have survived all that has happened without you there at my side."

"I never intend to leave you again." Anna patted his shoulder. "The past is behind us. It's enough we survived it and our friendship was born. Now it's time to look to the future. And our immediate future has a hunt in it."

"Yes," he agreed, his tone still abnormally subdued.

A distraction was in order. "I'm about to take part in a hunt, but I don't even know what the prey will be."

"We call them cliff jumpers. They're a large cloven-hoofed beast that's woolly like an Earth sheep but moves with the agility of a goat. Though, it's much larger than both. Good eating."

"Sounds charming."

"They're so ugly, they're almost cute," Obsidian added. "We save them for feast days, so we don't have to work so hard on our days off."

"Like keeping a stocked pond."

Obsidian shrugged again and nearly unseated her this time.

"Stop that!"

His ears pinned back with embarrassment. "I'm sorry. I didn't think."

"Don't worry about it. Just don't do it again."

Anna scanned ahead, studying the topography of the mainland growing larger by the wing beat. If she hadn't been squinting, she might have missed the so-called cliff jumpers. Their coats were camouflaged to look like the cliff wall.

"What the heck needs camouflage perched precariously on the side of a cliff like that? What predator is dumb enough to risk killing itself for a mouthful of meat, no matter how tasty?"

"One with wings." Obsidian laughed and then beat his wings harder.

The other gargoyles surged after them. When she spotted the other dryad's drawing arrows from their quivers, Anna swiftly followed suit.

At least her time in the Battle Goddess's domain had made her proficient with the bow. And the woolly, ugly goat-sheep-muskox beasts were as broad as a barn door.

Don't miss, she told herself. *No screwing up the first day.*

Anna picked out her target as Obsidian streaked closer. When she judged they were in range, she released the arrow.

"Obsidian. Above you! Look out!" More than one voice cried the warning, but Anna was too busy tracking the danger. A vast black shadow arrowed from above. Time slowed in that strange way it did in the seconds before an accident. She could see everything.

Reaver was diving from higher up, his speed tremendous and his angle intersecting Obsidian's path. Her gargoyle partner reared back, going vertical in the air to avoid a collision with the other gargoyle.

The fool missed them by inches, but as he slid past, his powerful tail smashed Obsidian in the chest, throwing him backward. They spun through the air in a wild arc. Their link flared to life instinctively.

Then she was falling, dropping away as he righted himself in the air. Below, the razor-sharp rocks at the bottom of the cliff waited eagerly to shred her flesh and shatter her bones. Magic burned inside, her gargoyle nature rushing to the surface.

CHAPTER THIRTEEN

Moments before the shift took her, Obsidian was there, his tail wrapped viselike around her torso. Wings snapped out to stretch wide, halting their descent so suddenly all the air was smashed out of her lungs. His tail was a punishing and lifesaving pressure around her middle.

Death averted, she swallowed back her rising gargoyle nature.

In a small part of her mind not devoted to that task, she cataloged her injuries. She'd be aching and sore later. Likely a broad assortment of bruises would circle her chest and waist where his tail was even now holding so tight she couldn't breathe. But she was alive.

Obsidian continued to beat his wings, rising higher. She'd successfully mastered her gargoyle nature by now. Good thing too. She was on the verge of blacking out. With an ever-narrowing field of vision, she watched as he came in for a landing midway up the cliff's face where there was a ledge wide enough to hold them both.

"Anna!" The word was bellowed in her ears. It was only then she realized he'd been yelling her name for some time, but she'd been too busy swallowing back her gargoyle nature and assessing her injuries.

"Anna!"

Hmmm? That was a very panicked sounding Obsidian. Then he loosened his hold enough that she could breathe.

"Anna, please talk to me. Did I break anything? Crush your ribs?"

Poor fellow was so upset he forgot to use their link. "I'm okay. Sore. Nothing broken. Tomorrow morning's gonna suck."

"I'll take you to a healer."

He touched down on the ledge, and the jolt renewed the pain in her ribs. Yep. Gonna feel like crap warmed over with a side order of roadkill. The muscular tail unwound from around her waist. His hands took its place.

He poked and prodded. She hissed and cursed. Eventually, they both stopped.

After a moment's hesitation, the big gargoyle reached out and oh so carefully gathered her in his arms. Even with all his loving gentleness, her abused ribs complained at the new pressure.

Obsidian shook with adrenaline and reaction and their link flared with a secondary pain. He'd been hurt snatching her back from death, but it was dwarfed by his emotional distress.

Her ribs would keep; her partner needed reassurance.

She mumbled nonsense at him like she had done when

he was a child and hugged him back. When that didn't seem enough, she patted his back and projected her love. Anything to comfort him.

"I'll hunt Reaver down and murder him for what he tried to do."

"As tempting as that sounds, neither of us is up for that kind of hunt. Let's hunt up some healers instead." Anna continued to hold him even though her ribs were starting in with a new relentless throb.

"Some of your ribs are cracked." He nuzzled her hair, breath still coming in great gasps. "I'll use shadow magic to wrap your ribs until the healers can mend the fractures."

"You're hurt too. I can sense it, a burning ache all down your spine. Did you dislocate your tail?"

"Doesn't work that way. It's part of my spine." He shifted his wings and tail, testing them. "Might have a couple small fractures. I'm still flight-worthy."

That's good, Anna thought. *Should probably let him go now.*

"It's nice." Obsidian's tone was gentler, the rage melting away further. "I'd forgotten how nice this was."

"I'll give you a proper bear hug later, once the ribs heal up." Anna winced and stepped away. "I know you're not a child anymore, but you'll always be huggable Shadowlight to me. Get used to it."

Obsidian laughed, a deep, genuine sound of relief. "You're sure you're okay?"

"Yeah. You? I know that tail grab maneuver did something to your back. There are better ways to get a lumbar adjustment."

"I'll be fine."

Anna moved farther from Obsidian as another gargoyle

landed on the already crowded ledge.

It was Truth and his rider, Brooke. The dryad didn't dismount—there wasn't room.

"Obsidian, are you and Anna all right?" Truth paced closer and sniffed them over.

"I'll be better when I have Reaver cornered." A growl punctuated the end of his sentence.

Brooke leaned over Truth's shoulders. "Are you sure you're able to fly?"

"Yes."

The dryad wasn't put off by his gruff tone. "Truth can carry Anna and me if you need to reduce your load for the return trip."

"No." New menace rolled from Obsidian. "Anna flies with me."

"Easy," Truth said. "We will not separate you. But you don't have to worry about dealing with Reaver. Everyone saw what that fool did. He's already being escorted back to Haven where the elders will be made aware of what he did. He was flying above you the entire time and says he didn't realize until after that Anna wasn't secured in a saddle. He was telling the truth."

Gargoyles could scent lies as quickly as identifying their favorite food by smell. If the others didn't sense a lie, then Reaver wasn't a murderous asshole. He was just an asshole. That didn't mean she would not rip him a new one the first chance she got.

Truth was directing his words at Obsidian along a private link, but Anna still heard. Her mental connection with her gargoyle partner was much stronger now that she'd come so close to shifting.

"You're certain you can make it to the island?" Truth asked. *"There's no shame in asking the healers to come to you."*

"I can make it." Obsidian's voice still held an underlying low, menacing growl. *"But have the healers waiting when we get back. I want Anna checked over. She has a few cracked or broken ribs."*

Truth's ears tilted, scrutinizing Obsidian. *"You're being stupid you know. You should just let me carry double."*

Obsidian's answering growl didn't require words.

"As you wish." Truth backed away and then launched himself off the ledge and into the air.

Obsidian turned back to her. "Let me bind your ribs in bands of shadow magic for now, until the healers can see to them properly."

She wasn't about to argue with that and stood docile while he spun out a shadowy substance that looked something like cloth but was cooler to the touch than the surrounding air. Slowly she raised her arms out away from her body and allowed him to wrap her chest from just under her armpits down to her belly button.

Then he ordered the shadow wrap to tighten a little at a time.

"It's not a freaking corset. That's tight enough."

"It's supposed to be tight." But Obsidian loosened the spell a tiny bit.

"By the way, thanks again for that." Then Anna arched her brow at Obsidian. "You sure it's wise to ignore Truth's suggestion?"

"I will be fine."

"Well, I will totally say 'I told you so' if I have to shift and carry your heavy ass the rest of the way to the island."

"Part of my training focuses on pushing beyond physical limits. I've suffered worse training accidents than this and continued the session."

"Fine. Be a bonehead. We'll go see the healers together later."

Obsidian merely huffed and then dropped to all fours, presenting her with his tail and well-muscled backside. She suppressed the urge to slap his stubborn ass.

The ledge wasn't wide enough for her to circle around and stand beside him to mount, so she'd have to attempt one of those running gymnastic maneuvers where the rider vaults onto the horse's back. Or like they did in track and field.

Fuck. This would hurt.

He glanced over his shoulder, reading the hesitation. "I'll carry you."

"Do I look like a damsel in distress?" She took three long strides, planted her hands on his rump, and sprang up and over to land heavily on his back.

They both grunted under the impact.

"Told you this would suck," she wheezed out.

Then she carefully leaned forward, bracing one arm against her ribs and the other between his wing joins. A bloody motorcycle ride over three kilometers of potholes would likely be more comfortable than this short flight, but she didn't have a choice unless she fancied getting carried back like some fainting damsel in Obsidian's arms.

When Anna thumped his back, he leaped off the ledge and into the sky. His wings caught the air and forced it to submit to his will, and soon he was climbing higher as he headed toward his island home.

Obsidian held onto his rage by the tips of his talons. If Reaver had been within sight and if Anna wasn't clinging to his back, he would have engaged in aerial combat with the other male without so much as a second thought.

Reaver might plead stupidity versus hatred for Obsidian's Kyrsu. It might even be true. But that didn't mean he wasn't going to go after Reaver and break his wings and whatever other body part he could sink his talons into.

"Cool it, Obsidian. You're not shielding half as well as you think. I feel what you feel."

Anna's thoughts washed through his mind like a refreshing rain.

"Come on, you great brute." Affection and exasperation were equally clear in her tone. "You're hurt. I can feel as each wingbeat jolts through your body like a hundred little sparks of pain running from the base of your neck all the way down to the tip of your tail. By the time we make it back to the island, you'll be in no shape to deal with Reaver anyway."

He wanted to growl loud denials at her words, but they were all *too* true.

Though, it was also true that he'd trained to overcome pain and was fit enough to discipline Reaver once he reached the island.

"I know what you're thinking! Pretty damn sure your mentors won't appreciate it if you decide to do their job for them."

Again, his Kyrsu was correct. His mentors would punish him if he sought revenge against his rival. He grinned suddenly. A little punishment never bothered him.

"Oh, for fuck's sake. I. Can. Still. Hear. You." Anna thumped him on the shoulder. "You're ten times more stubborn now than you were as a kid."

"That's likely true," he admitted, humor rising above the rage.

Though even humor couldn't neutralize his rage completely. It still simmered below the surface. With good reason. Anna's return was like a vital part of him had been restored. He dreaded her vanishing out of his life again. Reaver's careless act had come far too close to stealing Anna away.

She sighed. "Fine. Do what you're gonna do. I've got your back... I've always got your back. Even when it's likely to get us banished or sent to the brig."

Obsidian couldn't help a grin. They were still a team. That hadn't changed in the thirteen years Anna had been asleep.

He was still dwelling on that when he touched down a tad gracelessly at the edge of the cliff.

Other gargoyles from the hunt were already cleaning their kills. He stomped past them with barely a glance, intent on the circle of curious bystanders around the elders.

"Hey, I'm still here in case you forgot." Anna's words were punctuated with a few more thumps upon his shoulder. "I'd like to get down and walk."

"Of course." It was best that Anna wasn't on his back for what he planned to do next.

When Obsidian finally halted to allow her to dismount, she knew it likely wasn't her words that had swayed him. It probably had to do with the growing pain she felt in his body.

"Let's go see that healer you mentioned earlier."

"We will," he agreed as she slid to the ground.

Good. Reasonable was good. She could work with reasonable.

"Hey, how long do you think it will be before the—"

Between one second and the next, Obsidian was gone, racing across the distance to the circle gathered around the elders.

Well fuck.

So much for the peaceful 'let's let the mentors handle it' method.

Giving chase, Anna winced as her bruised ribs bitched about the jarring pace. Sending a glower at the sight of

Obsidian's muscled rump disappearing through the crowd, she cursed as he swiftly outpaced her.

"Fuck!"

She darted around the bystanders in her way and soon spotted Obsidian again. She hadn't covered even half the distance when Obsidian leaped, going up and over a crowd surrounding the mentors. He moved like he had rockets strapped to his ass. To go by his appearance, no one would suspect he was injured.

A moment later sounds of snarling, growling and shouting rang through the air. Bystanders along the west side of the gathering suddenly flew backward as Reaver rolled across the ground, his limbs flopping in a way that made her think he was already unconscious.

But a moment later, when he came to a stop, he drew his limbs under him and half rolled onto his side. Stunned. Not unconscious. At least not yet. But he would be, or worse, by the time Obsidian was done with him.

When she touched the mental link connecting them, it was to find Obsidian consumed by an unnatural need to protect. She'd encountered this a time or two before—had, in fact, experienced it herself the first time she'd shifted to full gargoyle form to protect Shadowlight.

Yep. He'd totally lost his shit.

Gritting her teeth, she forced herself to run faster.

By the time she reached him, the mentors had recovered from their momentary surprise and were advancing on Reaver and Obsidian, shadow magic swirling around them.

"Obsidian ease up. The elders are summoning some badass looking magic."

Her Rasoren paused his pounding of the other male to

narrow his eyes at the approaching elders. Anna eyed the male on the ground. His muzzle had a pronounced bend that hadn't been there before. Broken likely. Blood oozed from his mouth, nose, even the corners of his eyes. If Reaver had been anything other than a gargoyle, he'd already be dead.

Tearing her gaze from the male, she turned back to the elders and held up her hands as she put herself between them and her Rasoren.

"Easy," she shouted to be heard over Obsidian's loud snarls as he faced the approaching elders. "Let me calm Obsidian, or there will be a bloodbath. This isn't his fault. I can calm him."

She desperately hoped that wasn't a lie.

When the elders turned their attention entirely on her, her body hair stood on end.

Yeah. Don't mess with the elders.

Banrook held out a hand, signaling the other elders to halt and give Anna a chance. "Work swiftly, Anna Mackenzie. I've never felt such mindless rage in a gargoyle before."

"Come on, Obsidian," she said as she reached out to touch him on one shoulder. "Time to get your shit back together."

When her hand touched his skin, their gift flared wide, immersing her in his thoughts and emotions. The wellspring of bitter feelings and chilling power stole her breath.

"That's enough." Her words were an order, launched spear-like into the rolling turbulence that was his mind. *"We need to pacify the elders. They are far more dangerous to us than that useless male."*

Obsidian's gaze narrowed into slits as he studied the

elders and their magic, looking for weaknesses she realized. Damn it!

"Obsidian. I need you to look at me, to see me, to hear me. Can you hear me? Can you understand?"

He looked at her, his mind becoming less chaotic, but still he didn't speak.

"See those mentors? Yes, them. They are going to force you to submit. You can fight, but it's going to be long, ugly and messy. I'll stand and fight at your side. I'll always fight. We're a team. But I'd much rather not fight them in battle. It isn't needed. This isn't about survival. It's about revenge. You're better than this. We're both better than this. Peace."

His muzzle lowered to sniff her hair. Then he was blinking and swallowing back all the rage. She witnessed his internal fight and her heart bled for him. Then taking his bloody hands in hers, she squeezed them and sent her deep understanding and camaraderie down their link.

"That's it. Come back to me. The Battle Goddess doesn't get to control us now."

"Anna?" His voice sounded like he was waking from a dream or nightmare.

"Yeah. That's it. Come back to me."

He allowed her to lead him farther from Reaver. She halted once they were a good ten feet away. Then in a sudden move, he dropped to his knees and pressed his face against her stomach, his horns a hard pressure to either side of her ribcage.

The position drew her attention back to her own aching body, but she would not shove Obsidian away for any reason.

"When I caught his scent, something rose up inside me. I

couldn't stop it. If you let me go, I will kill him. I don't want that. Please, don't let me go." Obsidian's words were an anguished mental sob only she could hear.

"Shh. If someone's going to kill that idiot, it will be me. But since I'm not going to kill him, no one will."

Crooning soft nonsense, she wrapped her arms around his head and gently ran her fingers through his mane.

They stayed like that—him on his knees, her stroking her hand down his mane while he clung to her. The meadow was eerily silent. Only the sound of mellow flame, logs shifting, and the drip and hiss of juices cooking out of the meat disturbed the uncanny silence.

She looked up. Everyone gathered in the clearing was staring at her and Obsidian.

Oh, she thought, *you see us for what we truly are. Monsters among you.*

She didn't know how Shadowlight had managed to win them over when he'd first arrived, but somehow, he'd managed to hide the depth of what the Battle Goddess had done to him from the gargoyles of this place.

Anna's eyes met those of Banrook. Well, perhaps Obsidian hadn't duped all the gargoyles, but he'd fooled some.

"I am not the Battle Goddess's tool," Obsidian whispered into her mind. *"I've overcome this darkness."*

"Shh. I know."

"I was cured—thought I was. But it's only been asleep, waiting for its match."

Waiting for me, Anna realized, *waiting for that which completes it. The darkness inside me.*

She shuddered with growing horror. While she'd slept,

Shadowlight had been able to overcome the darkness within him, her absence somehow starving it into submission.

"The full extent of the Battle Goddess's changes didn't come into effect until I turned fourteen. Gargoyles normally emerge from their mother's hamadryads during their tenth summer. At which point, we're physically mature and ready to begin our training."

Anna had been briefed on gargoyle and dryad reproduction. None of this was new. Which meant if he brought it up, then there was more to the story she didn't yet know.

"When my tenth year came and went without anything bad happening, my mentors and I took it as a good sign."

Linked with him, Anna could see the story unfolding in her mind. *"But you didn't stop growing."*

"No. I soon surpassed even the largest gargoyles in height and weight until I was fourteen. That's when my physical growth stopped, but my magical strength continued. Something else came with it. A new darkness—a violence. It would rise and consume my mind when I perceived a threat to you. It was that same berserker rage you would descend into when I was threatened."

Yep. The reactions were sounding far too much the same. Though she wondered what threats he was referring to.

"What happened to make you think I was in danger during the time I was asleep?" Because she'd love to know if she had other enemies gunning for her. Say among the Council of Elders.

"Several of the healers studied you while you slept. They learned a great deal about how our powers work. Years ago, some of them brought a plan before the council. They wished to wake you for short intervals to further their studies. Maradryn was one

of the few who disagreed." Obsidian's hand loosened from its death grip and relaxed enough to rub the small of her back as if he was giving comfort to her.

"*Go on,*" she nudged gently.

"*My power, that darkness which dwells within me, decided that the healers' planned course was an unnecessary threat to you; that you would be better served to sleep and heal naturally. The other Masters agreed with the healers.*" Obsidian paused at length. Then at last, with a deep, weary sigh, he continued. "*When they attempted to wake you the first time, I attacked. I couldn't stop myself, didn't want to stop myself. I was protecting my Kyrsu, and it felt glorious.*"

Anna gave him another pat, not knowing what else to do. "*I presume by your earlier wording that you eventually mastered your darkness with the help of your mentors?*"

"*Yes. At least we thought we had.*"

"*But you're not the only one with that darkness sleeping inside. I have it too.*"

Obsidian slowly pulled away without meeting her eyes. "*I'm sorry for that.*"

"*We've been over this before. I don't regret for a moment having you in my life. Sure, maybe I do the whole berserker thing from time to time when I sense a threat to you.*" Anna shrugged and then cupped the side of his face. "*That's a small price to pay for being alive and having you as the best little brother ever.*"

"*I should have allowed the healers to study you. Perhaps if they'd been able to study an immature version of what I possess, they'd have been able to dig it out of you before you woke.*"

"*Well, they can study me now.*" Anna's expression turned serious. "*I think your reaction is linked to my reawakening, that*

*my untrained and undisciplined mind somehow allowed your...
beast to escape."*

"Anna that's not—"

*"Hear me out. You already conquered and learned to control
your rage, but mine is young, wild and uncontrolled. If I can learn
to master it as you have yours, then it stands to reason we should be
able to live free of the berserker rages."*

Master Banrook halted next to them. Anna glanced
down at her hands and then back at the elder.

"Master Banrook, I'm in desperate need of a mentor
strong enough to help me conquer the darkness inside
before it can influence Obsidian greater than it already
does."

"Anna Mackenzie," Banrook tilted his head in a
respectful nod of acknowledgment. "I will mentor you, and
we will not allow the darkness to have you."

The tension between Anna's shoulders eased. "Thank
you, but before any kind of training, Obsidian and I really
need to see the healers."

Banrook merely nodded his silent agreement.

CHAPTER FIFTEEN

Even though Anna tried to take the blame, he still felt a soul-deep shame at how swiftly he'd fallen prey to the darkness.

Anna might be untrained and still prey to its whims, but he should be able to recognize its rising and prevent events like what just happened. If Anna hadn't maintained her senses and calmed him, he would have killed Reaver before the mentors stopped him. Their magic was formidable, but so was he and if they'd attacked, he would have retaliated in his mindless rage.

"Stop beating yourself up over something that was beyond your control, kid."

"I'm no child. A child isn't capable of putting his fist through Reaver's face."

Anna just shook her head and gave him her 'males-know-nothing' look.

"You'll always be my little brother, get used to it. Now

I'm going to call you kid because it annoys you." Her accompanying emotions soon turned darker and more serious, though. She then placed both hands on his shoulders and urged him up. "If you thought I didn't want to put my fist through his face, then you'd be very mistaken."

"But you didn't act upon your desire."

"No." Anna paused, her expression turning uneasy. "But I think I somehow made you act on it instead."

Her words held a hint of possibility. But his training was much more advanced than hers, his mind capable of building a wall not many of his mentors could breach. He should have been able to control himself and prevent the darkness from gaining hold.

He still hadn't come to terms with what he'd done when Banrook came over to him and put a wing around his shoulder.

"Come, young ones. Master Maradryn and the other healers will see to you three while the rest of us decide upon a suitable punishment for this..." The mentor looked toward the moaning Reaver. "Unfortunate incident."

Obsidian watched as three healers came forward. Two approached Anna, but his Kyrsu merely shook her head.

"Help him first." She pointed at Reaver. "Poor bastard can't even roll over to stand."

It was true. The damage inflicted upon the other male was beyond physical damage. When he'd attacked, he'd shredded Reaver's protective shields with ease and then went after the source of his power, where the wellspring of magic flowed from deep in a gargoyle's spirit.

If Anna hadn't called him off, he would have magically

gutted the other male in a matter of moments. It wasn't something that his gargoyle mentors had taught. No, this was something dark from back in the days when a blood witch had begun his teachings.

The elders hadn't come to realize the full extent of Reaver's injuries yet. He wasn't sure if Anna had realized what he'd done, but if they stayed, she'd come to understand what he'd done and where he'd learned that twisted bit of magic.

His shame swelled stronger.

So, when Banrook suggested they go to the healer's quarters, Obsidian was only too happy to obey.

"We'll speak more after you're healed." Banrook folded his arms across his chest. His glower speaking of his displeasure.

Obsidian nodded, the very picture of a docile subordinate, he hoped.

His mental link with Anna flared. *"We're about to get a good old-fashioned dressing down, aren't we?"*

"Yes. That puts my mind at ease. If they were going to toss me in some prison hole, there wouldn't be any niceties first."

"You guys actually have prison holes? Sounds more like a Tin Man type of punishment."

"No. We don't." His attention narrowed in on the term Tin Man. He hadn't heard Commander Gryton called that in years. For reasons he didn't fully understand, that old spark of jealousy flamed back to life at the mention of their captor-turned-ally-at-the-end.

Then he had a disturbing thought. Did Anna use it as half insult, half term of endearment?

It shouldn't matter to him.

Gryton was far away in the future.

He wouldn't use the link to investigate Anna's feelings.

But it was a great temptation.

CHAPTER SIXTEEN

The healers' quarters were irregularly shaped stone buildings forming a larger complex that twisted its way between the trunks of the towering hamadryads. Navigation would be a nightmare, but it made sense that healers' quarters would be on the ground since moving injured persons up and down through the branches would have been a monumental task.

Anna didn't get a chance to look around much, though. Almost as soon as they entered the first stone archway with its iron-bound wooden doors, the healers converged on them, fussing over them both, asking question after question, poking and prodding her and Obsidian the entire time.

Eventually, all but two of the healers went about their business—or Anna assumed—went to help with Reaver's injuries. The remaining two introduced themselves as Novice Mist and Adept Prairie Dancer. They led Anna and

Obsidian deeper into the complex, into one of the rooms branching off the main artery.

A short time later Obsidian was laid out on a bench with a healer on either side of him. It was as Anna expected. Obsidian's injuries were more significant than her cracked ribs. The two healers muttered among themselves for some minutes. Then one left.

"What's wrong?" Anna used their mental link. It was becoming as second nature as breathing. *"Her expression was concerned."*

"Annoyed more like."

Obsidian didn't bother to raise his head or open his eyes, his posture that of a dog lazing in the sun.

"Why? Because you were too stubborn and got into a fight with Reaver instead of coming to see a healer?" Anna let a good dose of I-told-you-so enter her thoughts.

"Actually, no. The healers think Reaver got what he deserved. They are having trouble getting past my natural resistance to magic, even healing magic." He paused and hissed as the remaining healer found a tender spot between the small of his back and the base of his tail.

Grunting, he opened his eyes and watched Anna. *"All gargoyles possess a natural resistance to foreign magic, even that of the dryads, but the trait is stronger in me. Likely will be in you as well. It makes healing me somewhat problematic. Novice Healer Mist has gone to find Maradryn to help."*

While Obsidian was explaining the particulars, Mist returned, Maradryn sweeping into the room on her heels. The elder glanced around, shook her head at the gargoyle and then instructed Prairie Dancer and Mist as they began working on Obsidian.

Anna learned that Prairie Dancer was Oath's cousin.

Since Obsidian trusted all the healers, Anna picked an out of the way spot along the wall and carefully leaned back. There was a second padded bench situated directly in front of him, but she didn't want to get underfoot. Sighing, she let her guard down, her mind going blank for the first time since waking. It had been an emotionally draining day, and her ribs were a now constant throb.

"Why isn't a healer seeing to Anna?" Obsidian raised his head, turning to look at her with both eyes. With an unhappy grunt, he levered himself a bit higher off the bench.

"Stay down," Maradryn ordered before Anna could say the same. "Prairie Dancer will see to your Kyrsu momentarily. We just need a bit of extra power to breach your defenses."

He grunted unhappily but stayed put. Though his tail flicked in agitation.

The three healers summoned a warm, soothing power that reminded Anna of lazy summer days and green, growing things. Oddly, the magic was a shimmering silver. As tree Fae, Anna had somehow expected their power to be green.

Unaware of Anna's frivolous thoughts, the three healers worked with a quiet efficiency. They were using what looked like a cross between physiotherapy, massage, and magic to realign and repair the damage to Obsidian's spine and connective tissue.

"This stubborn idiot would have turned to stone on you if he hadn't gotten here when he did." Maradryn smacked at his flicking tail. "He never outgrew that stubborn streak."

"I'm no more stubborn than the average gargoyle."

The healers rolled their eyes and continued their work, but their healing magic must have been doing the trick because they soon reduced Obsidian to a wing-quivering, groaning, and sometimes purring pile of gargoyle.

Glancing away, she sought somewhere else to look and settled on staring out one of the narrow windows at the north end of the room. She watched the patterns on a hamadryad trunk where a rare ray of sunshine penetrated the dense canopy overhead and created a small patch of dappled shadows on the rough bark.

The link between them was still active even though she wasn't trying to access it, a full array of emotions and sensations flowed, ghost-like through her mind. They were working their way toward his tail when things got weird. Discomfort hummed through their mind link. At first, she thought it was pain.

Oh, boy. That wasn't caused by his injuries...

Anna pretended interest in the scenery and walked to the next window, putting that much more distance between them to give Obsidian the illusion of privacy.

"Anna, where are you going?" Maradryn called from her position at Obsidian's head. "Prairie Dancer and Mist are almost done here and one of them will attend to your injuries shortly."

"Oh, yeah, sure. I'll be right over."

"Is there something amiss?" Maradryn asked, a knowing look in her eyes.

"Nope." Just sharing a doctor's office with a horny gargoyle. Nothing wrong at all.

A wave of something hot flowed along their link, then cut off abruptly as Obsidian erected a shield. Anna winced and grabbed her head.

"Is something wrong?" Prairie Dancer asked, not realizing what Anna and Maradryn had already surmised.

"It's nothing," Obsidian said.

Anna returned to staring off into space. She didn't pry, because she didn't want to accidentally break his mental shields and get an eyeful of his thoughts. He obviously had a thing for either Prairie Dancer or Mist. Hell, he was a young male. Maybe he liked them both.

Maradryn glanced up at the other healers. "Mist, why don't you go see how Reaver's healing is coming. Prairie Dancer, you can see to Anna's injuries now. I'll finish up here."

Anna could have kissed the woman. Observant and discreet—the best kind of ally.

At least that's what she thought until Prairie Dancer walked over to the other bench and patted the blanket covered surface. "Take a seat here."

Anna groaned mentally, and then glared at the dryad's back as the woman turned to go retrieve some forgotten supplies. If she suggested they move to another room, it would only serve to highlight that she was embarrassed.

She'd die first.

Sealing her lips, she settled on the bench and faced forward. At least she couldn't see Obsidian unless she turned her head. Small blessings.

Prairie Dancer soon returned. "Can you raise your shirt for me?"

Anna obeyed. The movement made all the hurts flare with renewed throbbing. She hissed.

Beside her Obsidian made a sound of sympathy. "It was the only way I could catch you in time."

"I know." She glanced sideways to meet his eyes briefly before returning to studying the damages.

Well, she thought, *that's a little uglier than I'd expected.*

Her brown skin was several shades darker around her torso. An inky purple coloration started at her last rib and extended all the way to her waist. Damn. That was some bruising. Internal bleeding?

She probed gently at her abdomen, but it didn't feel hard, and no sharp pains greeted the touch.

Anna glanced back up and found Prairie Dancer staring at her shadow magic sports bra where the lower half was exposed by her raised shirt.

What? Did a boob pop out or something? She glanced down to check. Nope. The girls were where they were supposed to be.

"You're wearing..." Prairie Dancer's mouth fell open. "But those are only worn..."

The dryad's gaze cut away to study Obsidian. "Only gargoyles need clothing that will shapeshift with them."

Disbelief laced her voice, but then her healer's instincts must have kicked in because her gaze narrowed again as she scanned Anna's injuries.

"Those bruises already look more than two days old. Only gargoyles heal that fast..."

Maradryn halted her work on Obsidian and came and

placed a hand on Prairie Dancer's shoulder. "I didn't think. I should have expected this after everything Obsidian told the council." She looked away from Anna to stare down at the younger dryad. "You will heal Anna's injuries, and once you are finished, you will tell no one what you've seen here. Do you understand?"

"Yes, Master Maradryn," Prairie Dancer breathed softly.

"Good. I'll assign you to be Anna's primary healer. If she is injured in training, you will be the one to heal her. The council wishes this to remain a secret until Anna has earned the Legion's trust. You understand?"

"Yes, Elder. You have my word of honor." The dryad healer sounded more than a touch in awe of what she'd discovered.

"Good. Then heal poor Anna." With that, she returned to working on Obsidian.

It wasn't until Obsidian settled his head back on his folded arms that Anna realized he'd been ready to pounce if the dryad had responded in any way that might endanger their secret.

"Jeez, you need to chill bro."

Obsidian rumbled something low and unintelligible into his folded arms.

Unaware of the undercurrent passing between Anna and her gargoyle partner, Prairie Dancer made sounds of sympathy as she began to heal the worst of Anna's broken bones. A few light touches, a warm power that was just this side of too hot, some deeper probing, and then the dryad was leaning back to admire her work.

"There. Almost done." Silver magic dancing between

her fingers, the healer administered another round of the hot, healing spells. "You should already have full mobility back, though the bruises will take another day to fade completely."

Her injuries didn't take near as long as healing Obsidian's, which told Anna just how much damage the stubborn gargoyle had sustained without asking for help.

"Never should've let you carry me back," she sent along their link. *"It only did a number on your already strained ligaments."*

"Wasn't going to trust anyone else to carry you." His voice came out a deep, rumbling purr.

"Is there anything else you'd like me to do?" Prairie Dancer asked the elder.

"No, that will be all." The elder never took her eyes off her work.

Prairie Dancer nodded and then backed away.

The room grew silent, and Anna found herself watching Maradryn work. There was something mesmerizing about watching her hands knead flesh, tissue, and bone back into proper alignment. Anna even found the silvery magic the healer summoned fascinating to watch as it whirled and dipped and swayed to some unseen breeze. Would she and Obsidian ever be able to manipulate that kind of magic? It would be handy, certainly.

Hell, maybe he already had the ability.

There were so many things she didn't know about him. But one thing was for sure, he was bound to have learned many things in the thirteen years he'd been here.

"Once you complete your novice tests, I'll be able to help you learn at a swifter rate than I did," Obsidian whispered sleepily

into her mind, lowering his mental shields for the first time since he slammed them up hard enough to make her teeth rattle.

"I'm sorry I hurt you. I'll be more careful in the future."

"It's all right. Don't worry about it."

Because really, Anna thought to herself, *please keep the shield up next time you get horny. I totally don't want to see that.*

Obsidian chuckled, telling her he'd caught her internal thought. But he didn't seem insulted. Anna relaxed. *"This strange stream of consciousness we're sharing is going to be a touch awkward at times."*

"We'll be too busy training to worry," Obsidian countered.

"Or too busy dodging trouble more like."

"Might have noticed that, yes." Lifting his head from his arms, he grinned at her. *"That's how I ended up needing a healer."*

"At least Reaver looked worse off than you. That's something. Think they assigned an entire team of healers to him."

"I totally owned his ass, didn't I?"

"You sound drunk. Cocky and drunk." Anna felt herself grinning at him again.

"The drunk feeling—it's one of the side effects of healing magic."

"What about horny? That one of its side effects too?" Frick! Where did that come from?

"You sound a little drunk, yourself." His thoughts had a drawl to them. *"Feeling a little warm and tingly?"*

"Nope."

"Really? I've had females flirt with me before. I know the signs."

Damn, this conversation had gone sideways in a hurry.

"Am not. Now get out of my head. I'm tired."

Obsidian nodded and lowered his head back down on his forearms.

She thought he was finished until he started again.

"The two dryads didn't stir my blood."

Gawd. *"Just stop. We can take up the conversation in the morning when we're not drunk from healing."*

"I just want you to know that it was the battle rage and blood-lust. It just morphed into other...things. It's nothing you need to be concerned about."

"Not concerned." Her own gargoyle nature whispered that her statement wasn't entirely accurate.

Argh! Her life had been less complicated before the magic.

Maradryn snorted. "Goddess! You two. I can hear every word of your conversation. And, Anna, he's telling the truth when he said he wasn't reacting to us dryads."

"Yep. Got that sorted."

Maradryn actually rolled her eyes. "I'm finished healing Obsidian, but I want you both to stay the night here in the healers' quarters. I'll check on you in the morning. Besides, if you venture outside in your present condition, one of you will likely reveal too much about your special bond to others."

Anna nodded in agreement. Besides, the last thing she wanted was to attempt rope ladders with a magic-drunk gargoyle in tow.

Obsidian grunted happily and soon fell asleep.

"There are blankets in the cupboards along the west wall. Feel free to use them." Maradryn went to a basin and washed her hands. "Sleep, you'll find yourself growing tired.

It's part of the healing magic. I'll return at first light to check you over."

Anna nodded.

The elder patted Anna's shoulder. "Later, after the festival is over, I'd like some time to study your gargoyle nature. I must admit to being fascinated. While you were locked away in stone, I even once asked the council to allow Shadowlight to convert another, so we could study the change."

Lifting her gaze, Anna met Maradryn's. Her earlier tiredness vanishing in a cloud of alertness. "Even after only one short meeting, I can't imagine that was popular with your fellow councilors."

"It wasn't. But that doesn't mean it's not important to learn as much as possible about what the Battle Goddess created."

"True."

"Then you'll allow me to study you and your new nature as time allows?"

"Sure." It wasn't like she could say no after promising Obsidian that she'd try to blend in. And this woman was like a mother to him. Anna wouldn't make her an enemy if she could help it.

With a nod, the older woman turned and retreated, leaving Anna in the room with a sleeping gargoyle.

Laying back on the bench, she stared up at the ceiling. A silly urge nagged at her until she finally gave in.

"Goodnight, Shadowlight. Love you."

A happy, sleepy grunt of acknowledgment came from the other bench.

Grinning, Anna closed her eyes.

CHAPTER SEVENTEEN

(The Present)

Servants and guards alike scurried to move aside for Captain Vaspara as she hurried down the corridor, her boot heels loud against the polished black floors. If she'd had a choice, her long-legged strides would be carrying her away from the Battle Goddess's altar room, not toward it.

But she didn't have a choice and now wasn't the time to be late, let alone absent.

After the debacle with Shadowlight and Anna escaping, Gryton turning traitor, and the Avatars arriving to wreak havoc, the Lady of Battles was in a foul mood. Vaspara considered each hour that she was still breathing a win.

Especially with Captain Taryin still among the living. More's the pity, that the Avatars hadn't had time to eradicate the blood witch. Even though she and Taryin served the Battle Goddess, Vaspara didn't trust the witch. Some magic was just too dark and chaotic to be controlled without consuming the user.

In a deep, dark part of her mind where impractical thoughts went to die, she wished Gryton had confided in her and Sorac. Together they might have found a way to use Anna and Shadowlight's escape to kill the blood witch and blame it on the hybrid and cub.

But Fate never sent her down the easy path.

Perhaps it was time to plan an escape. Even the Mortal Realm was starting to look appealing.

The corridor ahead intersected another, and she heard footsteps. Her magic confirmed it was Sorac a moment before he fell into stride next to her. They acknowledged each other with a nod.

Of all the denizens in the Battle Goddess's keep, the male next to her was the closest thing she had as a trusted confidant. They were both survivors and didn't trust anyone besides each other. Romance had no part in their relationship, nor did she consider him a food source. Though he'd once offered, somewhat reluctantly, to let her feed after she'd been hurt out on patrol.

She'd declined. Always a wise choice. Sex with a fire-drake-fertility god hybrid might ruin her taste for other men. And a half-breed succubus who couldn't feed wouldn't long survive. Besides, she wouldn't risk a child. Sorac had once joked he could get even the most barren of wombs to bring forth life.

"Who do you think is getting sacrificed to the blood witch today?" Sorac asked into the silence.

It wasn't asked in jest. The Battle Goddess had been impressed that the witch had survived a one on one attack with the Sorceress. There was speculation among the surviving captains that their goddess was now grooming Taryin to replace Gryton as Commander.

"Don't care as long as it's not one of our soldiers or us. Worked too damn hard to train them."

"We should subtly remind our goddess of that fact."

Vaspara snorted. "For what good it will do."

They continued in silence, and all too soon reached the altar room. When she and Sorac entered, they found they weren't the first or the last to arrive. Korsha and her younger sister, Ernya, had returned early from two of the border patrol units. The elegant half-sidhe, half-demoness women didn't have one silver-blonde hair out of place.

They were in stark contrast to the survivors of the unexpected attack by the Avatars. Vaspara's own skin was blemished by magical fire and bruises. She was lucky not to have sustained worse considering how unprepared they'd been.

At least the Battle Goddess was not yet here. A good sign.

As they waited, another of the surviving captains arrived. Bervicta limped over to stand with her and Sorac. The harpy was in worse shape than Vaspara or Sorac. The feathers of one wing were burned away, and a third of her olive-toned skin was now charred black and oozed clear liquid.

She was a tough old bird, though, and the injuries didn't diminish her fighting skills or cunning intelligence. In time, she'd heal, if something didn't happen to her first. For her part, Vaspara would do what she could to protect the other female.

"Looks like you finally got yourself a harem." Bervicta's sarcastic comment was aimed at Sorac.

The firedrake had already commented on how he was the sole surviving male captain still in service to the Lady of Battles.

"Not how I wished to achieve such a thing, but I did notice my fellow males did not fare so well. Let's not point that out to Taryin. I don't need the witch setting her sights on me. She tends to devour lovers who fail to please her."

Bervicta snorted. "Don't fear, Pretty One, Vaspara and I will protect you."

Vaspara laughed her agreement at the harpy's words. After all, she and Sorac needed all the allies they could get if they wished to displace the witch as the Battle Goddess's new favorite.

Not that she, Sorac, or Bervicta wanted to assume Gryton's role, but better it was one of them than the witch. And with six of the twelve captains killed with Anna and Shadowlight's escape and later the Avatars' attack, the pool of candidates was slim.

Vaspara would even happily serve under one of the half-sidhe sisters. They were honorable and far deadlier in a fight than their graceful appearance would suggest. One didn't become a captain by being weak after all.

Soon the soft rattle of chains drew Vaspara's mind back to the task at hand. Within moments the Lady of Battles walked into her altar room, chains dragging along behind her. She moved like she no longer felt them. Which, Vaspara wondered, if that meant the Avatar's ancient spell was growing weaker and the duality curse would one day fade.

That had been Vaspara's greatest wish when she'd been newly welcomed into the army, but over the years, her outlook had changed a bit. Oh, she was no bleeding heart, but she still knew that once the Lady of Battles was free, she'd be swift to resume her fight directly with Lord Death.

Last time, they'd nearly ripped the three realms apart.

Sorac brushed the side of his boot against hers in silent warning and Vaspara shut down the errant thoughts. The firedrake could sniff out strong emotions. If he sensed her turmoil, others might as well. If the Battle Goddess discerned her real thoughts, Vaspara would be dead faster than she could exhale.

Soon the swish of fabric joined the rattle of chains, and then the Lady of Battles walked part way down the stairs. The giantess towered over them all, her rage tangible, almost a shimmering in the air around her.

It made even the ordinarily confident Vaspara feel tiny and inconsequential. The sensation certainly didn't diminish as the Battle Goddess studied each of her captains in turn.

Then with a snort of disdain, their Lady brushed aside her skirts and sat upon the landing mid-way up the stairs. "You can relax. I won't be killing any of my captains this day. I can't afford to lose any more of you."

Sorac cleared his throat and bowed deeply. "We are ready to serve you, Great Queen."

The goddess laughed. "I should hope so. If we fail to

win the coming battle, the Avatars will see each and every one of you dead."

Unfortunately, their goddess was correct on that part, Vaspara thought.

"Each of you will select the most cunning and most skilled soldiers under your command and will begin grooming them to fill the new holes in your ranks. They have a moon cycle to prepare, and then they will meet on the practice fields. The survivors will be elevated to the role of captain."

Sorac coughed softly, catching the Battle Goddess's attention.

"Speak. You clearly have something you want to say."

"Don't take this as a sign of weakness on my part, for I know my choices will all be standing at the end of the matches, but as our ranks have been unexpectedly thinned, and if we're picking from the strongest and most intelligent, wouldn't it be better to avoid deathmatches? We might need the losers to step up later. Make them our new seconds."

"Cocky as always." But the Lady of Battles didn't seem angered by Sorac's candor. "It shall be as you say. No death matches then."

After that, the tension in the room eased, and the meeting turned to routine reporting, patrol assignments, and other various tasks and duties that now needed to be performed by new personnel.

Eventually, the meeting wound down, and the Battle Goddess was turning to leave when new footsteps—an uneven shuffling gait—reached Vaspara's ears.

Shortly, the blood witch limped in and bowed toward

the Battle Goddess. The bow wasn't her usual elegant movement, and if Vaspara wasn't mistaken, that was a piece of skin that just flaked off and floated to the polished stone floor.

The witch was hooded, but the light was good enough that she could see the new arrival's reflection on the floor. Burned, charred, and oozing skin was mixed with the bright pink of scar tissue. Her dark magic was healing her, but it would be many days before she was fully restored.

She was weakened in her present state, but far from defeated.

Vaspara waited for whatever news had brought the witch from her nest of spells so soon.

When the blood witch rose from her bow, she met their Lady's gaze. "My magic has returned enough that I was just able to discern something of strategic importance. Anna and Shadowlight aren't dead. Lord Draydrak has cleansed Anna of my blood spell. If we act quickly, we may still be able to recover them."

"That's not possible." The Battle Goddess leaned forward. "I felt them vanish, their lifeforces snuffed out."

"Oh, yes, they did vanish, but they are not dead. If Draydrak were going to kill the human hybrid, he wouldn't have worked so hard to untangle her from my spell work. He would have just killed her and then cleansed the soul afterward."

Vaspara could see that the Lady of Battles was mulling over what the witch had said.

"Go on."

"He's either secreted them away somewhere for questioning, or he's looked into their souls and thinks he can use them against us. But they live. If they were dead, my blood magic would have trailed them into the Spirit Realm."

"Then we must find a way to steal them from my brother or kill them. They are too powerful a tool to leave in his hands."

"Agreed. But first, we must find them. A task for which I am perfectly suited—once I'm fully recovered."

The Lady of Battles nodded once. "You can have as many non-combatants as you need to fuel your spells. But do not disappoint me, Witch. I've had my fill of failures."

"I shall not." The blood witch bowed again.

Vaspara and Sorac shared a look.

But then the meeting was over, the Battle Goddess retreated deeper into her temple, and the captains walked off, already focusing on finding the strongest and most skilled of their soldiers. Vaspara's own mind was already headed down those paths as she and Sorac left the hall.

Once they were well away and no one was in earshot, Vaspara leaned closer to Sorac. "We need to find a way to hide our servants from that creature before she eats them."

Sorac nodded agreement.

"I've been assigned to fly the outer borders tomorrow starting at dawn." He paused and speared her with a look. "I'll be leaving earlier, at second moon rise. If you want your servant family to survive, send them to meet with mine an hour before that. I can carry them all to the wildlands. If they can steal enough supplies, they'll have a chance at survival. Better than they would have here."

Vaspara wasn't accustomed to saying thank you, but

one bubbled up and out her mouth before she could rethink it.

Sorac looked down at her and grinned. "You can repay me once I return. I'll need someone to clean my chambers."

Vaspara flashed her fangs at him. "I don't clean, cook or mend clothing, but I'll come and stay with you and help protect you from the witch. She'll be none too pleased to learn she's short a few snacks."

"A deal. But with luck, she'll be too busy hunting for Anna and Shadowlight to pick a fight with us."

CHAPTER EIGHTEEN

As it was, Anna and Obsidian didn't wake until close to noon, Master Maradryn had left them to rest since they apparently needed it. After a few pokes and prods with her healing magic, she declared them fit to go.

After they left the healers' quarters, Anna's mind sharpened and went over the evening before. Every freaking embarrassing little detail.

At least when she'd woken this morning, her gargoyle nature was stronger, and she was able to build a proper mental shield. It wouldn't be enough to keep a determined Obsidian, or a mentor, out of her head, but it restored a little bit of privacy.

They were almost out of the larger healers' complex when Obsidian cleared his throat.

"Anna, about last night..."

"Don't worry. We were both under the influence of the healing magic. What happens in the healers' quarters, stays in the healers' quarters. Deal?"

Obsidian looked pensive for a moment then snorted. "Probably wise."

"So where to next?"

"My dwelling to clean up and get a change of clothing. Then food," Obsidian added plaintively. "I'm going to eat the Cliff Jumper you shot yesterday. If you're fast, I might save you some."

"Food sounds great. A shower sounds better." Anna paused, remembering that while Obsidian's tree house bathroom had running water, a basin and a flushable toilet of sorts, she hadn't seen a shower or bathtub.

Made sense since there was probably a limit to how much rainwater they could collect and store in the small tanks atop their dwelling.

"That reminds me, where do you all shower or bathe?"

"Since it isn't feasible for a gargoyle to squeeze into a human type shower, we have heated communal bathing pools that we use to soak away aches and pains from a long day of training. We can go there if you prefer."

She was so very tempted to say yes. Except the communal part was a bit of a deal breaker, at least for now. She'd tackle that issue later. For now, a good washing would do. Otherwise, if she had to wait, her stomach was going to chew its way out of her abdomen.

"Your place is good."

They exited the medical complex and found Obsidian's friends waiting.

"You were there for ages." Truth was the first to accost them. "Were you really hurt that much? The healers wouldn't let us visit you."

"The healers had to use a large dose of healing magic to

get past my defenses to repair the damage." Obsidian flicked his tail. The small tell speaking of his embarrassment at having to admit weakness.

He cleared his throat. "Master Maradryn was...generous. I had to sleep off the aftereffects."

"He means he was the equivalent of piss drunk," Anna added with a grin.

"I wish I'd seen that." There was no hiding the humorous note in Truth's tone.

Anna crossed the threshold into Obsidian's place, only then realizing the others hadn't followed. She ducked her head back out.

"What? Are you vampires and have to be invited in?" Her jest was lost on them, though, and Anna just waved them inside.

Meadow, she noticed, was hanging back, clearly more uncertain than ever about Anna and Obsidian's relationship.

You and me both, Anna thought a touch worriedly.

Anna would face down the blood witch, fight the Lady of Battles in hand to hand combat, have tea with fucking Tin Man if need be, but the thought of Obsidian expecting a romantic relationship terrified her, and predictably stirred up the old memories and night terrors.

There were two ways she could handle this. Cut him off at the knees and crush any romantic notions he might be harboring and likely do substantial emotional harm, or she could direct his attention to a more suitable female and let nature take its course.

Anna's gaze landed on Meadow again. Unless she was mistaken about the dryad's feelings, the early groundwork was already laid out, all she had to do was nudge Obsidian into Meadow's waiting arms. But first, she'd have to mend some fences. Otherwise, the dryad wouldn't know Anna's Rasoren was available.

Hmm, Anna thought to herself. *Best way to do that is to convince Meadow that Obsidian and I are like two siblings.*

This was more than just about Meadow, though.

Obsidian needed to continue growing and developing emotionally. It looked like he'd been doing just fine until she awoke. Now, he needed to get back to that level of emotional separation from her and the unnatural bond the Battle Goddess had forced upon them, or he'd never be independent.

Obsidian deserved a normal life.

And finding and falling in love with a nice girl—or dryad—was part of that.

Obsidian's happiness was important to her. She just couldn't be the cornerstone that he built his love life around. Besides, even if she hadn't been...damaged, the darkly possessive bond that linked them together nullified any chance of them having a relationship where they were both equals. He'd always have the ability to command her. Not that he would, but it would hang over any relationship.

"Anna, did you wish to go first?" Obsidian was gesturing at the second smaller room that functioned as a bathroom.

She shook her head. Obsidian nodded in acknowledgment and then entered the room himself.

Anna turned her attention back to the dryad. "So... this feast. What's the occasion, anyway? It's a big deal obviously."

Oath leaped on her question before Meadow could answer. "It celebrates spring and new life."

Anna mentally tripped over that detail. It was spring? It took her brain a moment to realign itself and remember she'd been asleep for thirteen years.

How bad could a spring festival be?

"Oath is young, so he's more interested in the food and music," Meadow clarified. "But this is also a dryad sacred rite, marking the beginning of when many of my sisters will enter their yearly fertility cycles."

Alrighty then. It was going to be that kind of shindig. Great time to wake up from your stone nap, Mackenzie.

"Not everyone will take part, only the ones who have hamadryads ready to carry a child and those dryads just entering their first fertility cycle and are yet unmated."

Meadow paused for a moment, thinking.

"The dryads of Haven are likely different than the ones you might be familiar with. We remain mated to our gargoyle partners for life, unlike normal dryads who lead solitary lives and pick a new mate for each fertility season. We're also physically and magically stronger, thanks to our gargoyle heritage."

"You make Haven dryads sound like a different species."

"I suppose we are. The earliest dryad sisters to arrive on this island were normal dryads. But after a few generations of selective matings with the gargoyles, we are now very close to becoming a different race."

"You really are the Amazons of the fairy folk."

Meadow's one brow arched in question and Anna explained what an Amazon was.

"Yes, we are a fiercer breed than our cousin dryads. Each subsequent generation grows stronger, and we have a higher ratio of full blood gargoyle sons. If a normal dryad mated with a gargoyle, she might have three or four daughters to one son. We're down to two daughters to one son."

The soft creak of hinges drew Anna's eyes to the bathroom door.

Her breath hitched, then froze in her lungs.

Breathe, you twit!

She managed to draw in a deep gulp which attracted the male's eyes.

Worse, she was sure her mouth was hanging open. But in her defense, one of the hottest dudes she'd ever laid eyes on was standing on the threshold. And she just gawked like a bystander at a house fire.

It was Obsidian. Her magic told her as much. It shouldn't have come as such a surprise. Shadowlight had once taken on human form—a gawky adolescent who had just happened to look like a younger version of one of her brothers.

However, this fellow didn't look much like a Mackenzie.

No, he had more of the young god vibe going for him, and his hair—he totally rocked the hell out of them dreads. She'd always suspected his thick, lustrous black mane would work beautifully done up in dreads.

Guess she had her answer.

Gold bands at the end of each dread clinked together

as he walked closer. Matching armbands circled his biceps, and he also had a wide collar made of hammered gold discs engraved with patterns that reminded her of Celtic knotwork. The rest of his chest was bare, which didn't surprise her as gargoyles weren't known to be big on clothing.

He'd traded in the traditional beaded loincloth for a paneled knee-length garment with a wide belt—also engraved gold—reminiscent of what ancient Roman gladiators wore.

Continuing farther down, her gaze reached his feet, encased in sensible leather sandals. It was the first time she ever recalled him wearing foot coverings.

Returning to his only familiar features, her gaze studied his eyes with their dark irises and vertical pupils; though, they were now human shaped instead of the larger, slanted orbs of a gargoyle.

Come to think of it, his eyes weren't the only familiar thing. He'd coordinated their skin tones like he'd grabbed a bunch of paint chips and meticulously matched them to her until he found the perfect one and then replicated the hell out of it. If they walked side by side, they'd look like matching horses on parade.

Briefly, she wondered if it was consciously or unconsciously done.

Either way, she wasn't sure if she should be flattered or freaked.

"Thump...and another female falls under Obsidian's spell." Truth's tone was humorous, no envy to be found.

Anna snorted and side-eyed the other male. "Pretty boys don't do it for me. Obsidian's safe. I was just taking in all the changes. He used to look like a younger version of one of my brothers."

Truth leaned forward, the picture of mischief. "And he doesn't now? Hmmm. Wonder why that is?"

Obsidian reached out and cuffed Truth. "All of you out so Anna can get changed."

She was going to point out that she could do that in the bathroom just fine, but Obsidian cut her off.

"Meadow, did you or Lark have any luck finding something for Anna to wear?"

"Yes actually." Meadow shrugged a pack off her back and proceeded to pull out several garments. "I could stay and help."

"Sure," Anna said before Obsidian could utter a response. "We can chat while you show me what's what. I'd love to hear stories about Shadowlight growing up."

Obsidian arched an eyebrow. "You could simply ask to look into my head if that's what you were really after. But it's not. I'm on to you. You won't learn anything juicy from my friends."

Anna returned his grin. Poor deluded male. Women always dug up the dirt and shared.

CHAPTER NINETEEN

*D*ecked out in her new outfit—composed of a short skirt, leggings, and midriff-baring top done in shades of forest green and sunset gold—Anna exited the dwelling with Meadow and rejoined the rest of the group. Obsidian was standing just outside like he'd been assigned guard duty.

"Anna, you look lovely." His voice, almost a low rumbling purr, made her stomach churn with nerves, and not the good kind.

It didn't help that his gaze had paused for a moment at her chest, where the top's fabric stretched a little too tightly, and then again at her hips where the shirt accented their flare. Dryads were generally a slimmer build than humans.

Sweat broke out along her palms, and she hunted for something sarcastic to say. Her gaze landed on his dreads.

"How in the hell did you find time to do them while Meadow and I were talking? We didn't gab that long."

"I used shadow magic to manipulate the strands."

"Fuck. You've been holding out on me."

He reached up and rubbed along his scalp, looking somewhat embarrassed. *"I tore out a chunk from my mane during the first attempt."*

"Eh? Really? Think I'll stick with the old-fashioned method."

Obsidian was still looking self-conscious as he turned and led the group away from his dwelling. Slowly Anna relaxed and then scolded herself for being a fool.

She hadn't been this off balance since just after the attack.

For fuck's sake. This was Obsidian. It didn't matter that he'd shifted and now looked like the world's sexiest guy. He'd harm her no more than Shadowlight would. And even if he was harboring ideas about nurturing a romantic relationship with her, she knew she could trust him to back the fuck off when she told him hell no.

He wasn't the monster that had haunted her dreams in the months after the assault.

Giving herself a mental shake and a reprimand for losing her shit over something as foolish as Obsidian's innocent compliment, Anna turned her attention back to her earlier conversation with Meadow.

She and the dryad had shared a bit of small talk, while the other woman had helped her pick an outfit but, unfortunately, Obsidian's earlier comment had proven correct. She was unable to get the dryad to open up about his childhood.

Now, as the group swiftly made their way across the bridges and rope ladders, wasn't the time to continue her previous chat with Meadow. It would have to wait until they were once again on the ground.

Luckily, they were soon on the ground. Anna soon saw other gargoyles shifted to appear human—or actually, dryad, she supposed.

Obsidian led them down a familiar path toward the larger gathering place. Sounds of a growing crowd could be heard just ahead. Music filled the surrounding forest. It was pretty and non-assuming. Exotic sounding woodwind and string instruments if she was to guess.

While they walked, Meadow continued her explanation of the Spring Rite from where she'd left off when Obsidian's appearance in his humanoid form had distracted them.

"Later, after the dinner, drink will begin to flow, and a horn will call the revelers to dance. The dryads begin the dance and seduce the gargoyles into taking part, but really most already know who's going to join the dance, since we ask days in advance."

"Sounds like just good old dating." Anna found herself grinning at the thought of gargoyles dating. It hadn't occurred to her before.

"Just because a dryad invites a gargoyle to the dance and he accepts doesn't mean it will end..."

Coughing sounded behind them, and Meadow glowered over her shoulder at Oath, who was making the universal 'girls are gross' look.

Anna grinned at Oath in silent agreement.

Meadow wouldn't be put off, though. "The singing and dancing spreads throughout the forest and often goes until dawn."

Yep. Have the picture, thanks.

"The new pairs will discover if they are compatible." She looked over her shoulder, saw that Oath and Nightshade had dropped back, and continued her tale. "There is both a physical and emotional component to the bond between a dryad and her gargoyle. Some bonds form quickly, others more slowly. The elders encourage such relations but require that we don't risk a child until we've completed our training at least to the level of Adept."

Anna glanced behind at the two younger males. "What about the youths? What do they do while the adults are adulting?"

Anna really hoped the answer was retire to their own place and sleep until dawn. That's how she'd prefer to end her night.

Meadow looked truly startled. "Why, they are already dancing and having fun. A gargoyle signals his interest in courtship by sitting until a dryad approaches him. He'll then only stand if he's interested in that dryad."

Great. So much for just sitting in a quiet corner and waiting it all out. Talk about an introvert's worst nightmare.

"What if I get tired and want to rest for a bit?"

"Rest?" Meadow laughed. "We're warriors. Think of this as an endurance test. The mentors will be watching."

Nightmare. Total fucking nightmare. Commander Gryton and the captains were starting to look good.

Finally taking pity on her, Meadow patted Anna's arm. "Don't worry. You won't be judged if you find this first full taste of our society too intimidating. Just follow Obsidian's lead. You're his Kyrsu. It's his responsibility to see to your welfare and introduction into our society."

She barely heard the dryad's last three sentences. Her mind was still on the implied cowardice. The hell with that!

She'd battled demonic Riven, demigods, a blood witch, and an assortment of other riffraff. A freaking country dance did not intimidate Corporal Anna Mackenzie!

"Obsidian has never remained seated. I think he will this time, though, since he shifted into his wingless form. That's another, more obvious sign, that a male has an interest in one particular female, and he wishes to impress her with his shapeshifting abilities."

Anna choked on spit. After sputtering and wheezing loud enough to draw everyone's attention, she managed a bored, "That so?"

"Yes. But in the past, there's been a lot of speculation, so who can really guess the mind of your Rasoren. Some think he just hasn't finished maturing. Others reason he doesn't like women. And then there are those who think he's holding out for his human Kyrsu." The dryad rushed on before Anna could refute that rumor. "Not that it's anyone's business. Those are just some of the general speculations. I thought you should know."

Damn. She'd have preferred to remain ignorant. Now she had something else to add to the list of things she'd need to hash out with Obsidian one day soon.

"You're very tranquil and hard to read," Meadow said suddenly, surprising Anna. "Most would have some kind of visible reaction."

"Tranquil?" Anna cracked a smile. "Not a word anyone who has known me for more than a couple of days would use. I've been on my best behavior so as not to embarrass my Rasoren. I'm stubborn, sarcastic, ambitious, judg-mental and have been known to fly into a rage easily. Not very pretty to see, I'm afraid."

Meadow laughed. "I see so much of Obsidian in you. Or maybe that's you in Obsidian."

You don't know the half of it, girl.

Just as they came to the end of the stone pathway where it opened into the vast clearing, Obsidian joined them. "Thank you, Meadow, for keeping Anna company while I spoke with Truth about tonight. Will you be joining us?"

"Unfortunately, no. I must help my mother with the wine, but I look forward to talking with your Kyrsu again soon."

Anna watched as the dryad vanished into the crowd, then she turned her attention to Obsidian. "I don't need a babysitter. If you want to go have fun with your friends without me, go."

"I'll not leave you after what Reaver did yesterday."

Sighing at his predictable answer, she glanced around until she spotted Oath and waved him over. "Oath, you and the rest of your underaged friends will all help to keep me entertained tonight, right?"

Oath nodded his head so fast it almost vibrated.

"See," she whispered along her mental link to Obsidian. *"I'll be protected, and you can go court whatever girl has caught your fancy."*

It sure as hell better not be me, Anna thought to herself.

"Oh, Anna. There is no girl."

"Really? You like guys?"

Obsidian snorted. *"It's far more complicated than that, but I'll tell you later. Not here."*

He wouldn't even tell her over their mental link? Dammit. It had to be bad.

"Okay, later it is."

Obsidian agreed and led her out into the gathering, his friends arrayed around them, once again acting as an honor guard and keeping the curious onlookers at bay for a little while longer.

As they made their way farther into the gathering, Anna spotted more of the humanoid looking males.

Anna's attention soon turned from the gargoyles in their hybrid forms to something even more interesting— tables laden with food. They sat in ten long rows at the center of the clearing, situated in a rough horseshoe shape. A wide variety of fruits, breads, meats, and vegetables covered the surfaces. It all smelled heavenly. Anna's mouth began to water.

Oath, Lark, and Nightshade peeled off to check out the food choices on the side tables, leaving only Truth walking at Obsidian's shoulder.

It wasn't until she was closer that she realized all the tables were made from magic.

"Wow. That must've taken someone some energy to shape all those from shadow magic."

"You can sense shadow magic?" Truth asked with sharp disbelief. "But you're human. That's not possible."

Fuck. She'd just stepped in the proverbial crap.

"Anna is unique. You must know that she was changed by the Battle Goddess even as I was." Obsidian speared

Truth with an intense stare. "Anna has many abilities the elders don't yet want revealed. Do I make myself clear?"

The sharp command in his tone nearly had Anna standing at attention. This was the voice of a Rasoren—prime war leader of the gargoyle Legion.

"Is she gargoyle stock?" Truth asked in a low voice. "Has our enemy found a way to breed gargoyles and humans?"

"No." The one word rang out.

It wasn't a lie. She didn't have gargoyle parents, after all. Truth must have sensed a hint of deception for his eyes narrowed, and his nostrils flared to take in Obsidian's scent.

"No more questions until after we've met with the Council of Elders."

"Well, if that's settled, I'm starved." Anna hooked an arm through each of theirs and guided them toward the food. "Let's go eat."

CHAPTER TWENTY

The evening went without further mishap. Obsidian's mood improved once he had a heaping plate of food in front of him. It might have helped that there were hundreds of different delicacies to be had. Soon his friends returned from wherever they'd gone and took seats at the table Obsidian had claimed as his own.

Music and song continued for the entire meal.

"How much longer will this be going on?" Anna asked.

"Do you wish to retire before the dance starts?"

"Is that an option? If so, then hell yes. Sign me up for some downtime."

"Not really, unless you aren't fully recovered. The mentors would understand if you were tired still from yesterday's events."

"Nah, I'm good."

Obsidian studied her in silence and for once she couldn't guess at his thoughts, but soon the meal concluded, and the music changed, a deep, throbbing drumbeat joining in.

Anna noted that all the dryads were now getting up and dragging their gargoyle counterparts up as well.

The music increased in volume. The crowd began clapping, stomping and swaying to the music. Anna attempted invisibility without actually calling on her shadow magic. But it didn't work, and Oath and Nightshade darted up on either side and grabbed Anna's hands and pulled her away from Obsidian before he could stop them.

Behind her, she could hear Obsidian and Truth laughing as they were dragged into the dance by others.

People spun by Anna at a dizzying speed. She soon found herself being handed off to strangers, but all were friendly and happy. Soon, even she began to relax and enjoy the dancing, which was a fast-paced mix between Celtic circle dancing and something of the stylized moves found at a powwow.

After an hour of dancing, more young dryads and gargoyles appeared, carrying large pitchers and ladles. When one young dryad child—she couldn't be more than fourteen—offered Anna a drink, she was happy to accept.

The first sip surprised her. It wasn't water or alcohol. It was a cold and sweet nectar-like drink, blessed with the gift of quenching thirst and delivering much-needed sweetness to fuel them for another few rounds of the circle dances.

The three moons of this planet rose higher in the sky, casting the revelers in a surreal silvery glow. Thick mist rose from the warm ground, adding to the magical feel.

After another hour, the dancers took a rest, returning

to the tables where they sipped drinks and laughed and nibbled at food.

It was during one such rest period that Obsidian's foster mother, Master Maradryn, joined them at their table. She eyed them in silence for a moment before just spitting out her concern.

"I've come to caution Obsidian against entering into a relationship with a dryad this day if that is his plan." She eyed his wingless form.

"I know the rules." Obsidian sounded sullen.

"But Anna must be curious and if I know you at all, you haven't told her." Maradryn tilted her head as if challenging him to deny her words. "A normal Rasoren and Kyrsu can be father and son, brothers, long-standing friends, or if unrelated, the pair might even be lovers. But they also need to get along off the battlefield as well. If they are unmated when they first form the bond, they both must pick mates together, and those mates need to tolerate each other at the very minimum."

Anna's poker face cracked in two and she was left gawking at them with her mouth gaped open. "That's one hell of a tall order."

"Yes. And that's with a normal bond. What you and he share goes beyond that. Your power seems to naturally share everything. Strength. Knowledge. Pain. Likely pleasure too."

"Oh, my God. I want off this ride." Anna muttered under her breath, then cleared her throat. "I'm not sure how things are around here, but I'm not down with any kind of three-way poly relationship. I don't swing that way. And in case you have forgotten, Obsidian is like a brother.

There's going to be a whole lot of nope during this conversation."

Speaking about little brother, he was awfully tight-lipped. She turned to him to find him deep in thought and looking unhappy.

At last he sighed and joined the conversation.

"Why are you even bringing this up, Maradryn? The council still doesn't want me to court anyone, because of my...condition. Has that changed? No? Then why does any of this matter? We all know the spring rite can't be anything more than a fanciful diversion for me. It means nothing."

"Then why did you take on your wingless form?"

"I don't know!"

The last came out so scathing even Anna winced.

Maradryn just huffed. It was almost a laugh. "I'm not a gargoyle, but I know a lie when I hear one that obvious."

"I don't...I know I can't..."

"Surely you must have realized we didn't mean for you to never take a mate. All we wanted is for you to wait until everyone knows and is comfortable about what Anna is. Then once you find that one woman you wish to spend your life with, bring her to the council, and we will explain the full ramifications."

Okay. There was way, way more going on than Anna knew.

Maradryn touched Obsidian on the shoulder. "Though I think you've already set your heart on one particular female to be your lifemate, haven't you my dear?"

"What is going on? No cryptic talk. I want clear, uncomplicated answers."

Maradryn chuckled. "Then you are sure to be disappointed. I don't think there is anything uncomplicated about either of you."

The music swelled louder, the drums drowning out Maradryn's words until she leaned closer and whispered in Anna's ear.

"He'll tell you everything later. I'll just say it's unfortunate you look upon him as a younger brother. It would solve many issues if you didn't."

What the hell? She loved him like a brother. End of story. She wasn't being obtuse, naïve or stubborn. It just was how she loved him.

The only way she *could* love him.

CHAPTER TWENTY-ONE

*A*nna was unsettled. Obsidian knew it, felt her spike of uneasiness like a shivery essence flowing along their link. It took a lot to upset his Kyrsu, but he'd sensed her unease many times since she'd woke from her healing sleep. That he was the cause left a churning void in his soul.

Well, to be honest, he was now more than a little unsettled, too.

After last night in the healers' quarters, he'd awoken with the knowledge that he wanted Anna. Heck, he'd known even that first night, when he'd shifted from stone to flesh and found Anna awake and in his arms.

The need to let her know his interest was the reason he'd shifted to this hybrid form. Well, that and to let others know his intentions. He was interested in only one woman. The woman sitting across from him now.

A woman who was absolutely horrified at the thought of him as anything other than her brother. His less than subtle decision to shift to this form was now circling back to bite him.

There was no avoiding the final dance now that he'd announced his interest in courting a female. When no dryad succeeded in seducing him off a bench later tonight, everyone would know Anna was the object of his desire, which had been his plan. But he hadn't counted on Anna's near horror at the thought of them becoming a couple.

Some trauma had occurred in her past that made it hard for her to trust males. He knew that, but he hadn't thought it extended to him, or at least he thought he'd regained her trust in the last two days. But it wasn't enough time. In her moment of horrified disbelief, he'd seen into her unguarded thoughts, a glimpse of what she kept hidden.

Now Anna stood there waiting for him to say something. If he didn't want to make things worse between them, he needed to be truthful but also soothe her fears.

With a sense of desperation, he returned to the subject Maradryn had opened. At least he wouldn't have to lie about that.

"After the dancing is over," he whispered along their link. *"I will fill you in on everything my mentors and I have discovered about our bond. But it is a long conversation, best carried out when we are alone and have no distractions to interrupt us."*

"Sounds serious," Anna said. *"That all you're going to give me?"*

"I..." He scrambled for something else to say. Then at last an idea occurred to him. *"The nature of how I can convert other species to gargoyles has changed a bit as I matured. The council wishes for me to remain celibate until they fully determine*

any dangers I might represent to the dryads. They have not yet finished their study."

Her eyebrow arched nearly to her hairline. *"Yeah. Okay. I see why this is a conversation for later."*

A new throb echoed through the air, saving him from searching for further safe conversation.

The new drumbeat rose and fell like the surging of some great beast's pulse. Around him, several of his brethren were extracting themselves from the crowd and making their way over to the benches where the unmated were expected to go and present themselves.

A few curious onlookers were casting furtive glances in his direction. They were expecting him to join the others moving toward the benches.

"Oh, for fuck's sake. You look like a deer staring down a truck's high beams."

That sounded more like the Anna from his youth.

"This new look," she indicated his hybrid form in a sweeping gesture, "Going by what Meadow and Maradryn said, it's to say you're seeking courtship, isn't it?"

He swallowed around a lump in his throat and nodded.

Anna compressed her lips and switched to their link. *"Is there a dryad you're hoping will come dance for you?"*

"There is none."

Her expression shifted subtly, like she was approaching a dangerous beast. *"Is this for me?"*

He glanced off into the darkness for many moments and then issued a soft 'yes' that was barely above a whisper.

"You going to lose face with the legion when you're left still sitting at the end of the night?"

"There is no shame in not being chosen."

Anna rolled her eyes at him and muttered under her breath. *"That's not the answer to the question I asked."*

"It was my foolish decision. As my mentors would say, I will have reaped what I deserve."

"But you are also Rasoren, future war leader of the legion. Are they going to judge you differently?"

Obsidian looked around, eyes searching the crowds. He remained deep in thought for several minutes. At last with shoulders slumped, he admitted the truth he'd been too stubborn to see. *"I should have thought this out better."*

"Like thought to ask your Kyrsu her opinion first?"

"Yes that." He glanced down at his hands and started to chuckle bitterly. *"Why should they put their trust in a leader who doesn't even take the time to learn his second in command's thoughts?"*

"Okay. You can stop beating yourself up now. This is how this is going down. We're going to go sit over on one of those benches, you're going to magic us up a checkerboard using some of your shadow voodoo you've learned while I slept, then we're going to play a few rounds, ignoring everything and everyone around us."

"I can do that. But..."

Anna just cut him off.

"Onlookers gonna speculate. Let them. They can stew on what we might be to each other until they die of old age and they still won't have a clue how deep our bond runs. But I know what we are. We're a team. I've always got your back."

She glanced heavenward as if praying for divine deliverance. "Even if it's during a freaking dryad fertility rite."

"There is..."

"You're welcome. Just don't take this the wrong way. I have no intentions of getting hitched to my little bro."

The other revelers decided just then that he was taking too long and gently pushed him in the direction of the benches with a great deal of laughter and even a few innuendoes.

"If this turns into a fucking bachelor party, you owe me big time," Anna hissed under her breath as she followed close on his heels.

While he and Anna were guided toward the benches where the other single gargoyles sat, the youngest, including Oath and his peers, were herded off toward the tree line and onto the stone pathways that led deeper into the forest.

"By the way, if I see any stripteases or lap dances, I'm calling my shadow magic and vanishing in front of everyone, the Council of Elders be damned."

"Don't worry. If that kind of thing goes on, it's saved for more secluded locations."

"I'm warning you...if I see jiggly titty, I'm outta here."

Anna's crass words caused a grin, and he relaxed. Perhaps he hadn't made so great an error in announcing his willingness to court his Kyrsu. Sure, she had—to borrow one of her phrases—shot him down, but that was because of something that had happened in her past. She was fierce and resilient. In time, if he was patient and didn't screw things up, she might come to love him romantically.

Until then, he'd be a loyal training partner and friend.

With hope a warmth in his belly, he led a grumpy Anna to the nearest empty bench.

"They came, they danced, they went away again. Is it over?" Anna was clenching her jaws to stop a yawn, but he sensed her weariness. It had been a long two days.

"I have fulfilled my role as tradition requires. We can go now if you'd like."

"Hell yes. I've eaten enough tonight to descend into a food coma until noon tomorrow."

Obsidian was still smiling gently at Anna's words when Truth came up to them.

"Banrook cornered me after the dance. He wants to talk to you sooner than the council meeting tomorrow."

Obsidian mentally cursed. He'd expected the other council members to notice his shifted form and knew they would want a word with him, but he'd hoped they'd wait until the meeting in the morning.

"They want to speak to me, too?" Anna was suddenly bright-eyed and suspicious again.

"Banrook didn't name you, so no." Truth shrugged. "I'll walk you back to Obsidian's place while he speaks with his mentor. It will likely put your Rasoren's mind at ease knowing you have protection against any more of Reaver's surprises."

"I won't waste your time. You must have better things to do than babysit me. I can find my own way back."

"It's no chore."

Was Truth interested in Anna?

Obsidian narrowed his eyes as something dark and possessive reared its head. He knew well what it was, and he did his best to ignore it. "Anna, it *would* put my mind at ease if you would accept his offer this time."

Anna merely shrugged and then bobbed her head in

Truth's direction. "Lead on. Obsidian can catch up once he's seen to whatever his mentor wants."

Truth's grin stretched wider, the flash of white teeth glowing in the darkness. He held out a hand.

"Do I look like a lady to you?" Anna snorted, and her long-legged strides soon outpaced the startled gargoyle.

"Anna hates coddling." As usual, a note of pride entered his voice when he spoke of her.

"Apparently." Then Truth looked back at Obsidian. "I see why you're enamored. But that very ferocity will be what makes her so hard to win."

"I wouldn't have it any other way."

"I still don't envy you the hunt, my friend."

Then under the light of the three moons, they went their separate ways. Truth to chase down Anna, and Obsidian to hunt up his mentor.

CHAPTER TWENTY-TWO

Anna matched Truth's pace and cast random looks in his direction, wondering how long it would take the gargoyle to spit out what was bothering him. They were halfway back to Obsidian's place, and Truth still hadn't said anything. At last, she took pity on him.

"You might as well just say what's on your mind."

"To what are you referring?"

Mister Uptight I have you figured out. "Let's get to the meat of the subject. You like Meadow. Meadow likes Obsidian. You're wondering if Obsidian approached me with his suit and if I'm now going to encourage him? Sound about right?"

Truth broke stride for a step, but he recovered in the next moment. "It's that painfully obvious?"

"Not really. I'm just good a reading people." *Like way, way, way better than I was before I took a stone nap.*

"Very accurately." Pain entered his voice. "In the last year Obsidian *seemed* to be warming up to Meadow's gentle courtship, but I was uncertain if Meadow's feelings were reciprocated or if he was just being kind to her."

"And since you, Obsidian and Meadow are all friends, you didn't want to cause friction," Anna guessed.

"Goddess, yes. Meadow and Obsidian are my closest friends. I don't want anything to jeopardize that, but I..."

"But the heart isn't logical," she finished for him.

He nodded, a helpless sigh of distress escaping him.

"Love sucks," Anna said as she continued to walk along the bridge in the direction of Obsidian's dwelling.

"You've managed to discover in two days something I haven't even told Obsidian. And we share a great deal."

When she looked sideways to meet his gaze, it was to find his eyes narrowed in thought. "Your perception is uncanny."

Sighing, she figured Truth could be trusted. "It's something to do with my bond with Obsidian and what the Battle Goddess's plans set in motion. With time and training, I think I'll be able to read and command gargoyles like a Rasoren."

"You're not just his second, are you? How deep is your bond with him?"

"Powerful. It's always been powerful. I was told it would only grow stronger as he matured. I think the Battle Goddess modeled us after the Avatars. One mind. One being. Two bodies. A deadly and loyal fighting unit that would answer only to her." Anna shuddered.

After a few deep breaths, she continued. "I'm incredibly glad Shadowlight and I escaped that fate. Yet we can't change what we are. Instead, we bury our darker natures, but some things, like the ability to read each other's thoughts and the emotions of other gargoyles, slip beyond our control. But we don't have to be controlled by our power or become the mated pair the Battle Goddess intended. I sure as hell don't plan on being forced into that role."

Truth's dark eyes grew wide in surprise and understanding. "But you love him anyway. He's literally your other half like the Avatars." His sentence died off in a whisper.

"Yes!" The one word escaped her control, but it also lifted a weight off her chest. "We weren't given a choice, but we don't have to become what the Battle Goddess wants. I can shape how I love him. I can love him as a brother. He can be free to love elsewhere."

Truth was silent for a while, but he wasn't willing to give up. "Are you so sure you can control it? That Obsidian can?"

No, I'm not, Anna whispered in the private darkness of her mind. "While I can't fill the role he wants, I *will* fight tooth and nail to give Obsidian the happiness he deserves. If that is with Meadow, or another dryad, I will do what I can to smooth the path for them."

Truth's ears perked forward, his expression entirely too happy for a fellow who knew the woman of his dreams loved another man.

"After tonight's events Meadow will know you hold his heart, and I'll have my chance with her."

What the actual fuck? Was she speaking a different language?

"Hold up one minute. Your logic has one big flaw. I don't love him in a romantic sense."

Truth laughed. "Say that again in a year, ten, a hundred years from now. See if it's still the truth. I'm quite certain it will be a lie that you won't even bother to utter."

Damned opinionated gargoyle.

"I'm going to hold you to this," he muttered happily. "That's a promise, Corporal Anna Mackenzie."

She flailed for something to say, but her mind refused to turn over, like a truck sitting in the cold for too long. Growling at him in frustration, she fought her gargoyle nature as it flared, scenting a challenge.

Truth tilted his head at her growl and gave her a toothy grin. "See? You're already so firmly a part of him you even sound like a gargoyle."

You don't know the half of it, Anna thought to herself. And then added aloud, "Fine. What are the stakes of this bet?"

"Stakes?"

"Yes. In a normal wager, the winner gets something from the loser. What are the stakes if I prove you wrong?"

Truth shrugged. "The winner gets to hold the victory over the loser for however long they like?"

"Bragging rights?"

His grin grew bolder. "Yes. I like that term. Though, I think the true reward will be that both parties will have what their hearts desire."

"Speak for yourself." But Anna took his hand and gave it a strong pump. "I accept your wager, Truth in Shadows. Now you should know that I've never lost once I put my mind to something. Consider this fair warning."

"Very well, future Kyrsu of the Legion, but you should know that no one wins all the time. And I feel the certainty in this. You will lose, you should prepare yourself."

"What makes you so cocky?"

"Because you already love him, you just don't know it yet."

Anna was working up another logical denial when they arrived at Obsidian's place and she had to focus on opening the door shield instead. She'd seen him trigger the release spell once before. The magic was a familiar pattern now. With a wave of her hand, a touch of magic, and a good deal of will power, the ward spell rolled back, exposing the door's latch.

"I'll see you at the training session tomorrow. Good night, Anna Mackenzie. Think about what I've said. The sooner you concede the wager, the less I'll embarrass you later."

She gave him the finger.

Truth only laughed, before turning and jumping off the bridge.

The cowardly fucker.

CHAPTER TWENTY-THREE

Obsidian returned to his quarters in what would have been an unseemly rush if anyone had noted his passage, but no one was in this section of the bridge system, and more importantly, he didn't care if anyone saw him running back to Anna.

He'd been sensing something he couldn't fully identify rolling off her since shortly after she started her walk back with Truth. Her shields were in place, and much stronger than they'd been even a day ago so he couldn't hear what she and Truth were discussing without blasting through her mental barriers, which would be a gross break in etiquette, not to mention surely pissing Anna off.

Keeping a close rein on his own emotions, he rushed back, hoping to learn what was going on between her and Truth. Though he was undoubtedly the topic of conversation. That made him more than a little uneasy.

As he raced down the last section of the bridge, his

dwelling's door opened, and Anna stepped out, forcing him to skid to a halt or run her down.

"Where's the fire?" Her old shit-eating grin was firmly in place.

Obsidian grunted, hesitating while he thought up a good excuse to explain his haste that wasn't a lie.

"I felt your magic flare. Was there a threat?"

"No," Anna rolled her eyes and then turned and entered his home. "Truth and I were just talking shit and made a wager."

"What kind of wager?" Obsidian flared his nostrils, dragging in a deep breath of her scent. There were no stress markers to indicate she was annoyed, afraid, or bothered.

"The kind that's between him and me."

"Was it about events tonight? Surely you can tell me that much."

Anna sighed. "Yes, if you must know. But it's completely innocent."

She wasn't lying. He'd have scented that.

"How did your meeting with Banrook go?"

That wasn't something he really wanted to talk about with her. Besides, if she could use the 'it's personal' defense, so could he.

"It's nothing to concern yourself over. Just a conversation with my mentor."

"Touché."

Obsidian didn't know the meaning of the word and her mind was shielding against him, so he just nodded in acknowledgment.

Their conversation apparently over, for now, Anna glanced around the main living area of his dwelling.

"Since no one's had time to find me lodgings or set me up in a storage room someplace, where did you want me to sleep?" Anna eyed the nest doubtfully.

His eyes tracked in the same direction.

"Yeah. I'll just grab a couple of blankets and pillows and sleep along the wall." Anna walked toward the nest to retrieve said items.

Something shifted inside him, and he barked out a sound of humor. "Who are you and where have you put my Kyrsu? She wouldn't be afraid to share a nest with me."

"I'm not afraid of you. I'm just not sleeping with you. You probably snore."

He snorted again. "I don't."

"How would you know?"

He shrugged, though he was still confident he didn't snore. "If I snore, it would be just as loud over by the wall."

"No, it wouldn't."

Now she was just being silly or dragging her feet for another reason.

"I know you don't love me romantically, but this new behavior now begs a different question. Are you actually afraid of me?"

"No, of course not. I've known you since you were a child."

"Afraid of me as an adult male, then?"

"Nope."

"Is it this body, then?" His voice dropped until it was a vibration in his chest. "Do you find my new body desirable and that frightens you?"

He didn't know what demon possessed his mouth and made him say those things, but he discovered he wanted to learn that answer. Curiosity was a dangerous and seductive emotion.

"Still nope. And as much as I freely admit to liking your scent, it doesn't stir anything more than a little appreciation."

"We both need rest." Though, was that mild disappointment he felt at her words? Yes, it was. His pride hurt more than a little. He'd worked hard designing and mastering his new form so that he could one day court Anna. "There is no reason for us not to share a sleeping area until I can make one for you."

Anna shrugged, saying 'fine' in that most neutral way.

"Excellent. And if you're not too exhausted to stay awake for a few minutes, I'll fill you in on what Maradryn was talking about earlier."

"As long as it isn't a long story."

"I'll keep it short."

"Still, let's get ready for bed first, that way if I fall asleep, you can continue in the morning."

Obsidian stood before the washbasin as he shed his hybrid body for his true form, wanting his more familiar shape to ease any fears Anna might still have. At least that was his hope.

When he exited the smaller chamber, Anna was already sitting in the middle of the nest with her hands buried in her fluffy head of hair.

"The hell with this. I'm going to fall asleep before I get the first one in. You remember how to do rows? Want to help?"

Obsidian nodded. Sometimes, when he'd been a child, Anna would read to him while he did her hair. Or he'd read to her while she did his. He'd missed those times ferociously when he'd first come to Haven. "Can you do mine up in a couple braids first?"

"Sure thing."

Grinning with happiness, he padded over to sit in front of her. She used a bit of the mane oil he'd given her earlier and finger combed that through before starting to section it into lengths. Enthralled by the steady pressure of her fingers, he fought not to purr.

"By the way, what did Maradryn want you to tell me?"

Anna's voice dragged him back to the present. Suddenly he wished he could wait until morning, because he feared after he told her the full extent of what the healers had learned, it would destroy the fragile thing growing between them. But Anna deserved to know. It affected her as well.

"When I was younger, only my blood was powerful enough to convert another into a gargoyle."

Anna's fingers stilled against his scalp. "It's not just your blood anymore, is it?"

"No. Any bodily fluid can now begin the process. Even my saliva. Though, the agent in my blood is much more potent than what's found in my saliva." Obsidian coughed and folded his hands across his lap.

"Go on."

"My seed is almost as potent as my blood. The healers

say it's designed to convert and impregnate a female at the same time."

He heard Anna's teeth click together as she closed her mouth. After another ten seconds, she drew a deep breath. "Holy hell. That's some badass STD."

"STD?" He didn't know the term from his time on Earth.

"Sexually transmitted disease."

He wrapped his head around the term. "Yes, that describes it accurately."

"Gargoylism is now an STD. Talk about the need for safe sex." Anna paused then whistled. "So, you've never been laid?"

He shook his head.

"The Council of Elders wants me to wait until they know the full extent of my abilities. Some believe I won't come into my full power until your magic finishes maturing." He halted and looked at her over his shoulder. "Even if the elders didn't require it, I'd still have been cautious. I don't ever want to steal anyone's choice again.

"Well, that's...er...complicated for you." She paused again and then dropped her hands to rest on his shoulders. She gave him a squeeze.

With his back to her, he couldn't read her expression, but he could read her scent, and her mind opened to him a small crack.

She was softening toward him, sympathizing with what he'd had to go through growing up while learning how different he was from other gargoyles.

"Obsidian, I did choose. You seem to forget that fact. Even though you were a child, you gave me the choice of being healed by your power or ending my life to save my soul from the Riven."

"But you didn't know the power would tie you to me as close as it has. It might as well be enslavement."

Anna didn't deny his words, but she gave him another squeeze before returning to work on his mane. "I don't regret it."

He drew in a steady breath. "And now that I'm Obsidian instead of your beloved Shadowlight?"

She smacked him on the side of the head. "I still don't regret it, you big idiot. You'll always be my beloved Shadowlight."

Obsidian sighed, a catch in his throat making it impossible to speak for a few moments. When he could, he continued. "The healers did confirm that the darkness inside me was only designed to create one Kyrsu to be my second."

Anna chuckled. "Always knew I was one of a kind."

After finishing his mane, she stood and then came around to sit in front of him.

"One moment." He stood and went to the shelves running along one wall and sorted through them until he found the bowl containing gold beads and clips that he wished to work into her hair. Then after one more glance at her head, he went back and grabbed a small hand mirror.

"You can tell me if I'm doing them wrong," he said as he handed it to her. "It's been years, and I wasn't very good at it back then."

"At this point, I'd settle for pigtails if I don't have to do it myself." Anna yawned and rolled her shoulders.

Pigtails? He huffed with disdain. His Kyrsu would get

something better than a hairstyle that was inspired by a pig's tail.

He settled down behind her and arranged his supplies close at hand while he began to systematically map out the shape of her skull and decided what pattern would best accentuate her features.

"It must be like a virus." Anna started up the conversation again. "I don't know why I didn't think of that before. I just assumed magic was this amorphous substance that could be shaped into any tool, but what you describe sounds much more like a virus. Somehow the Battle Goddess figured out how to take a virus and mutated it with magic until it was capable of doing what she needed it to do."

"I'm only vaguely familiar with your Earth science and medicine, but that seems logical."

Anna just shook her head. "She created the ultimate biological weapon, one that would convert her enemies into her own enslaved army."

"Indeed."

"How contagious are you?" Anna paused. "Obviously, I don't have to worry since I've already been converted. But what about other people? How dangerous are you to them?"

"How contagious are we, you mean," he continued, finally working up to tell her what she hadn't yet come to realize herself.

"We?" She turned her head to look at him over her shoulder. "Of course I'm a carrier."

"Yes."

"God. We're biohazardous."

She had to explain the word, but once he understood, he agreed with her assessment. They were dangerous.

"How bad is it? Not airborne, obviously, or the healers wouldn't have let us intermingle with the other island residents." Anna's fingers drummed against her thigh.

"A direct fluid exposure is needed," he said as he started on a second braid.

"Then the virus can't live outside a host for long?"

"The healers do not believe so."

"Good. Otherwise, we'd risk infecting others by a simple touch."

Obsidian nodded. "The one small blessing is that it takes several exchanges over the course of a few days before the virus has changed the new host body enough to survive in it long-term."

"So even if you accidentally exposed someone to your blood during a session in the training ring, they wouldn't be converted immediately."

"No. That only happens after several willful exchanges,"

"That's a relief."

"Yes."

"You've put a lot of thought into this."

"Yes."

They were silent for a time after that, the only sound the slide of his fingers against her hair.

By the time he was nearly finished braiding her hair, the moons were lower in the sky, and Anna's head was tipping forward.

"I'm almost finished."

She mumbled a sleepy acknowledgment.

After he tied off the last braid, he tucked her against

his chest and lowered them into his nest. She never woke, merely shifting until she was more comfortable.

He briefly thought about leaving his nest to her and sleeping over by the wall as she'd planned to do. While he was no longer a frightened child locked away in a dungeon cell, he had missed the comforting warmth of curling next to his Kyrsu.

Holding Anna in his arms was a balm for his loneliness. Only she'd ever been able to soothe away his worries.

So, with no guilt, he curled around her and was soon asleep.

CHAPTER TWENTY-FOUR

*B*ands of pressure wrapped her chest and thighs. As she swam out of sleep, she wondered when and how she'd managed to get injured again. She blinked open her eyes to discover she wasn't wounded. Nope. She was presently being smothered to death by a seven-limbed octopus.

The octopus was actually her big brute of a Rasoren. Presently he'd mistaken her for his teddy bear.

Obsidian slept oblivious that she was awake. If the situation had been different—say she was marooned in the Arctic—being folded in his arms, wings, and coiled tail might be appealing. But since they weren't, they needed to set some ground rules.

As she stared up at the wooden rafters of the peaked ceiling, she catalogued the sensation of waking up in his arms. He had damn fine pecs, rock hard abs, and an absolutely lovely scent clinging to his warm skin. She hadn't noticed it this strongly before.

She breathed in a deeper lungful. Mmm. Nice.

Obsidian might just be her new favorite scent. It took her a minute to realize she'd turned her head to rub her cheek against his skin.

A touch of reason slowly returned.

What the hell was wrong with her?

"Your gargoyle body is entering sexual maturity." A sleepy purr accompanied his words. Moments later Obsidian ran his muzzle along her arm, his tongue darting out to lick her skin in places. "I can taste the pheromones in your sweat. Your first fertility cycle."

"What are you talking about? I had my first period when I was eleven."

"Hmmm." He took another sniff as if to make sure and another little purr escaped him before he continued his previous train of thought. "But when I converted you, I was only eight, so my blood and magic only changed you into a preadolescent gargoyle. It likely took the magic raised during last night's dance to trigger your change. The healing magic might have helped things along as well."

He continued to sniff along her skin in a way she knew her rational mind wouldn't like. The problem was, she wasn't feeling too rational, and she wasn't nearly as both-ered by his words or actions as she likely should be.

"I had not thought of this complication. I suppose I'd always just assumed you were sexually mature." He continued to nuzzle the skin of her shoulder and back of her neck.

She'd likely find this awkward later.

"Maybe you should let me up now?"

"Very well." Obsidian's rumbled agreement held a hint

of disappointment, but he released his hold on her as his wings folded back.

She rolled to her knees. Now that she was away from his scent, she felt more alert. She studied him suspiciously. He ignored her. Too busy stretching, rolling, and arching his back like a cat in a patch of catnip. Jeez, he was even purring for fuck's sake.

The entire session was far too weirdly sensual for her peace of mind. She cast a glance down south of his belt. He was a big fellow. It would be noticeable if he were sporting morning wood. Whatever was going on in his mind, it didn't seem to include a raging desire for her. At least that was a relief.

"Morning wood?" Obsidian laughed. "I think that's just a human condition. At least, I've never suffered it."

That might be true, but something was going on, and Anna didn't like it. "Stop reading my mind."

"I'm not. You initiated the link. Your magic is running back along our link, teasing my senses. It's an invitation, I think."

"The hell it is!" But when she reached for their link, her magic was already flowing along it like he'd said, and there was no reason it should be doing that since he wasn't hurt.

She slammed up her mental shields and stopped the flow of magic. Feeling an unusual heat in her cheeks, she tried to ignore the fiery blush as she focused on him.

"Sorry about that. Wouldn't have done it knowingly."

"I know." Obsidian shrugged a little. "I'd be lying if I said I wasn't flattered. Though I know this part of our bond makes you uneasy, so I'll try to prevent it from happening in the future. You caught me unawares this time."

"Don't apologize. Wasn't your fault." It was her stubborn and apparently *frisky* gargoyle nature that was the issue here. She needed to find a way to shut that shit down.

"We should likely go to the healers. They might have something that will help. As it is now, the first male to catch your scent will begin to speculate if you're really human at all."

"Healers? Why didn't you start the conversation with that? We could already have been half-way there."

He rolled his eyes at her. "There's no hurry. It's not life or death."

She gave him her best death glare.

"Fine. I'm coming."

Obsidian muttered something under his breath that didn't sound too complimentary.

Maradryn walked across the length of her workroom to one of the shelves running along the west wall. After shifting a few jars aside, she found the one she wanted. "Anna, Obsidian is correct. Your gargoyle nature has matured overnight. There was no sign of it yesterday morning or even last night when we chatted. You're most certainly entering your first fertility cycle. But considering a string of gargoyles didn't follow you here, I think it's safe to assume the pheromone is only designed to entice your Rasoren."

Fan-fucking-tastic.

If she'd had the ability, she'd have melted between the seams in the stone floor and vanished into the dirt.

But as the healer said, she was lucky it didn't affect all gargoyles.

Anna stared at her sandals and grit her teeth. "Please tell me you have something to make my body stop producing this shit."

"No, but I have something that should help Obsidian." She unscrewed the lid of the jar she held, gave the contents a little sniff, scrunched up her nose and then reached in and scooped a bit of the pale green paste onto her fingers. "This cream is made from a tree possessing a substance in its bark and sap that contains a mildly caustic compound. The cream completely burns out a gargoyle's ability to smell for a good half a day. That should give him a reprieve until you learn to neutralize your pheromones using a shadow magic shield."

Maradryn paused and looked up at Obsidian. "And you shouldn't have any trouble focusing on your training session today."

Obsidian didn't move his feet, but his upper body leaned away from the approaching healer. "I'm sure I'll be able to manage just fine. The cream isn't necessary."

"Ha! Says you until you get distracted and come to me for healing after you get a sword thrust through your gut." Maradryn deftly snagged his lower jaw and pulled him down to her level. Then fast as a snake striking, three of the fingers covered in the cream, smeared a strip under his nostrils.

He reared back and whined, his eyes already streaming.

Shit. He'd actually whined.

When the healer held out the jar, its lid now safely tapped back in place, he took a few more steps back and grunted in denial.

Anna held out her hand. "I'll keep that somewhere safe in case we need it again."

"Be careful. That is at full strength. As you can see, he only needed a little bit to do the job."

"Yep. Got that from the whine." But she wouldn't ask Obsidian to use something she wouldn't try herself. Anna popped the cork and dipped in one finger and then cautiously held it up to her nose.

It was almost a pleasant scent until it detonated like a bomb going off in her face.

A pungent scent invaded her nose, mouth, and eyes. A frosty eucalyptus-like burn swiftly amped up into a 'mouthwash on steroids' sensation. From there it increased in unpleasantness until it was like she'd borrowed the devil's own brand of aftershave, mixed in a little vapor rub, then added a dash of napalm for good measure.

Sputtering and gasping, her eyes and nose streaming, she managed to wheeze out a weak, "Fuck me!"

Maradryn arched a brow.

"Fuck! Shit burns. What's this crap normally used for? Torture sessions?"

"Training sessions. Though usually a more dilute form. One of the tasks for the Adept Trial requires the student to learn to hunt and track using senses other than their nose. Not all enemies can be tracked by scent. This replicates that handicap."

Thank God the burning sensation soon mellowed into a kind of numbness.

"Guess if someone sees me with this in my stuff, I can say it's for training."

"Fear not. No one would guess that evil crap has any beneficial use," Obsidian growled from behind her.

She turned to find him sharp-eyed and clear-headed. No more purring. She breathed a sigh of relief.

"Nice to see you're back with us."

Obsidian huffed. "That stuff would revive the dead. I'm fine now."

Anna bumped shoulders with him. "Sorry that it was necessary. I didn't know about my gargoyle nature's newest trick. I'm almost afraid to learn what else the Battle Goddess has engineered into us."

He bumped her shoulder gently in return. "Whatever surprises arise, we'll get through them together."

"Partners," she agreed with a grin.

"Let's go find something to eat before we're due at the council chambers."

CHAPTER TWENTY-FIVE

Anna walked up the last few steps and emerged into the as-of-yet empty council chambers. Which, she realized as she walked farther in, wasn't a chamber at all. Located three-quarters of the way up the most massive tree on the island, the structure was a broad platform circling the enormous hamadryad's trunk.

There were no walls, just a waist-high carved railing that ringed the platform and provided a breathtaking view of the surrounding tree canopy, the velvet green mountain peaks to the west, and the vast ocean all around. In the distance, she could see the mainland.

Overhead, a beautiful filigree lattice covered in flowering vines provided cover from the sun. Her gargoyle nature was quick to detect a shimmering dome just a few inches above the vines. Upon closer examination, her magic discovered its primary function was protection against the elements, but a few adjustments to the knotted spell work would transform it into a defensive shield against any outside attacks.

"It's never been needed to serve that function. A few tropical storms are the worst it has had to repel." Obsidian's mind touched hers briefly and then retreated, as if unsure of his welcome.

Earlier, during breakfast, she'd discovered her mental barrier kept slipping. Hell, that was an understatement. Her gargoyle nature kept sabotaging her efforts. That wasn't Obsidian's fault, though. And in this instance, it was beneficial to have their minds linked.

"Keep the little insights coming, especially anything you have on the Masters."

They'd come early enough that none of the council had arrived yet. Which was both good and bad. Good, because it gave her time to compose herself. Bad, because it gave her time to worry about Obsidian's punishment.

Banrook had promised the council would assign punishment to both Obsidian and Reaver today.

"Do not worry. I welcome any punishment. Beating Reaver unconscious for what he caused..." A growl cut off his sentence, and he had to clear his throat to continue. "Whatever comes, I will accept my punishment with grace, and we can then begin our training."

Anna wasn't so sure if her gargoyle nature would be willing to sit back and chill while someone was harming her Rasoren. It didn't help that they didn't yet know his punishment.

As they walked farther along the platform, she spotted the floor to ceiling shelves filled with scrolls and whatnot. Obsidian led her around the long curve of the hamadryad's trunk, revealing what was on the opposite side of the platform from the stairs.

A sizeable crescent-shaped table made of a cherry-colored wood and polished until it gleamed in the light dominated the space. Behind the table sat six padded benches, upholstered in a dark green, velvet-like fabric. The seats were also subtly curved to mimic the curve of the hamadryad's trunk behind them.

Her eyes were drawn up to a hulking symbol with gold inlay that was carved and poured directly into the hamadryad's bark. It was done in a style similar to ornate filigree crossed with Celtic knot-work; though it was its own unique style she was coming to recognize as the art of either the dryads or the gargoyles who lived here.

"It's a blending of both." Obsidian supplied.

She thought she was seeing an emblem of a winged tree. But after a moment's study she spotted the two stylized gargoyles standing guard on either side. Below the tree, four swords with their hilts crossed, added a more war-like element to the artistic beauty of the insignia.

"It's the symbol of Haven and the new gargoyle legion."

He might have said more, but just then his ears twitched and swung toward the stairs. Anna turned in that direction as well. A full minute later she heard the approach of others.

"I'm surprised they didn't fly."

"They likely did fly part way, like we did, but the buffeting of wings as they breach the shield tends to clear the table of scrolls and reports placed there by their aides."

Anna's eyes tracked back to the long, crescent-shaped table.

As each of the masters arrived, Obsidian bowed, Anna following suit. She recognized each of them from the last couple days. Banrook entered first, coming to Obsidian and cuffing him affectionately on the shoulder before taking his seat at the table. Maradryn nodded a greeting. There was some secret amusement in her eye that made Anna think the other masters likely now knew of her gargoyle nature's newest surprise.

Next came the dour-faced Verroc.

Sumdara, the dryad tracker she hadn't seen since their first introduction, brought up the rear.

That left two empty seats. The masters were shuffling through the various reports on the table, so Anna used the lull. *"Who else are we waiting for?"*

"Likely no one. Thayn is the oldest of the gargoyles and leader of the council, but his duties usually require him in the future, and he only makes the trip back a few times a season. The other seat belongs to Rook's daughter, Brinrook. She and her mate reside in the future, still recovering after they sacrificed most of their magical power to strengthen their son and make him battle worthy to fight even though he'd been born early like me."

"Who's their son?"

"Gregory."

"Wow. Wait? Rook is Gregory's grandad? When were you going to get around to telling me that bit of news?"

"As things came up?"

Anna rolled her eyes at him but didn't show any other outward signs of displeasure. Not when the council looked to be almost ready to begin.

But just as Master Verroc opened his mouth to speak, a mighty beating of wings heralded the arrival of another.

Papers and scrolls flew off the table and swirled around in the air for a time and then with a few more powerful down-beats the gargoyle landed, sending a flurry of parchment and quills skittering off the edge of the platform to flutter away on the ocean breeze.

"Thayn!" Verroc growl. "How many times—"

The newcomer snorted. "Greetings to you too Verroc."

Verroc scowled but didn't say anything else.

Then the gargoyle Verroc had addressed as Thayn turned to Anna and grinned in welcome.

"Hello, young one. I'm glad you've finally awakened. Now, perhaps, we can take Obsidian's training to the next level."

The male then grabbed her shoulders and pulled her into the biggest bear hug she'd ever received in her entire life. Her ribs complained at the sudden pressure and she wondered if he was trying to pop her head off. But then he released her a second later.

When she could breathe again, he patted her shoulders and then leaned closer to whisper in a conspiratorial tone. "I'm too old to bother with stairs. When you get to be my age, you'll understand. Besides, Verroc is far too stuffy. I do what I can to help him unbend."

With that he turned and marched over to the table, taking one of the last two seats.

The mischievous tones and the spark of secret humor in his eyes reminded her of someone. It took a moment, but then she realized she'd just met the male version of Gran.

"By the way, he just stole something from you," Obsidian warned.

"What are you talking about?"

"You'll be missing something that you had on your person a moment ago. It's his favorite trick."

"I'd know if he took something." But then her eyes locked on the little jar of cream Thayn was spinning like a top on the polished surface of the council table. Once it started to slow, he snatched it back up and pried off the cork stopper and gave the contents a sniff.

He wheezed. "Goddess, that should count as punishment fulfilled all on its own."

Why that old...

"However, reports have reached our Lord about what transpired the first day Anna awoke. Dray has suggested a worthy punishment." Thayn grinned. "It's really quite delightful."

After she heard the details of Obsidian's 'punishment' Anna grew very concerned. But not for what the masters would do to him, but because of what he would do to them.

She grabbed his hand to hold him back, but he just marched forward, dragging her along with him until his thighs bumped the table.

"You cannot be serious!" A fist slamming against the wood punctuated his words. "I'll take any punishment you wish, but don't make Reaver and Anna training partners!"

Anna wasn't exactly thrilled about the idea, but it was kind of ingenious—in a twisted, cynical way. And made for a perfect punishment for Reaver.

Reaver's ascension from journeyman to adept depended on Anna passing her novice test. She'd gathered from Obsidian's thoughts that he'd been looking forward to helping her with those skills. Not that he'd expected it to be hard for her. They'd learned the basics of battle magic during their stay in the Lady of Battles kingdom.

She should be able to complete the tasks quickly, perhaps within a day or less if the elders would allow her to streamline it that much.

But Obsidian wouldn't be the one to test her skills after walking her through each task. No, for whatever reason, Lord Death thought it a better punishment for Reaver.

"Come on, Obsidian. I've got this. I'll pass the test and Reaver will be out of our life."

His one ear flicked back to acknowledge her words, but he continued his debate with the Elders.

"Any journeyman or adept level student can initiate a novice. Anyone is better than Reaver. He'll be seeking revenge and will think Anna is the easier target." His gaze traveled to each of the Elders sitting across the table, but none of them so much as blinked at his words. "I'm sure Truth would agree to mentor her. Or Swift Hunter if Truth is too busy with new novices."

She placed her hand on Obsidian's arm. "Reaver, as much as he doesn't care for outsiders, is a gargoyle. I've faced the Battle Goddess's captains. He is only one gargoyle. I'll be fine."

"Gargoyles are capable of holding their own against the Battle Goddess's minions," Verroc said, no emotion showing on his face or the tilt of his ears. Even his tail remained still.

"I will not tolerate Reaver as Anna's teacher!" The words were more of a growl, the threat clear, but the wildly chaotic emotions bleeding down the link just reinforced that the berserker darkness was rising to the surface.

"For fuck's sake, keep your shit together. Shit! Together!"

"I'm fine."

"No, you're not. Bring it down a few notches, or I'll do it for you!"

Obsidian flicked an ear in her direction. Suddenly, his tail was snaking around her waist, dragging her closer, and then he tucked her against his side as if he was planning to snatch her and run.

"Don't do it! Piss mamma bear off at your peril."

Thayn leaned forward, doubling up over the table as chuckles burst forth. Banrook's lips quivered, and his chest started to shake a moment before he, too, howled in laughter. Sumdara and Maradryn wore big grins. Only Verroc managed to maintain a straight face, though it looked a little like he was sucking lemons.

Oh crap! The Elders had picked up on her conversation with Obsidian.

Well fuck. This day was just getting better and better. Maybe she could ask Obsidian to show her how to turn back to stone. Sleeping for another decade was looking good.

"Oh, Obsidian," Banrook said with tears running down his cheeks. "Worry not for Anna Mackenzie's safety. She's fully capable of handling Reaver. A whipping from her sharp tongue will defeat that prideful male."

Obsidian huffed loudly but didn't add words to the

sound. His disdain at the thought of Anna having to work with Reaver needed no accompanying words.

Thayn got control over his chuckles and looked her in the eye. "Anna, you will do fine. And, Obsidian," his gaze tracked away from Anna to land on her gargoyle partner next. "You will do as you're told in this. Anna will take her Novice test as required. However, I will make one small allowance. Reaver will still be her opponent, but you may be her instructor."

"Thank you," Anna said swiftly. Obsidian was far too slow in answering, so she reached under his wing and pinched his ass hard enough to make him jump.

"I agree," he blurted out.

"And if Reaver attempts to harm your Kyrsu again after we've strictly forbidden it, you, or she, may do to him as you please with no repercussions from the council, by Lord Dray's edict."

Obsidian perked up a little at Thayn's last words.

"Or," Thayn tossed the small jar of cream back to Anna, "she could just use this on him full strength if he attempts anything."

Anna caught the jar and slid it back in her pocket. Thayn had said it as a joke, but there were possibilities in the idea.

CHAPTER TWENTY-SIX

The training field wasn't, in fact, a field. It was a multi-tiered complex crawling up the side of the island's third highest peak. A series of terraces provided flat ground for the actual training rings, but many stairs and pathways also led up the side of the mountain and would provide a challenging route if someone wanted the trainees to run a tour.

Obsidian's earlier rage had dissipated as he walked her up to the fifth level of the terraces. On the way, she'd spied other outdoor obstacles. There were also many smaller domed structures made from stone, which he'd said were used for learning the more dangerous spell work.

They reached their destination to find many of the other novices and mentors present.

"There are not normally so many here this early, especially after the feast day. They've come to watch my Kyrsu fight for the first time." There was pride in his tone, and Anna didn't want to disappoint him.

"How do you want me to handle this? Give it my all—short of actually shifting forms—or pull my punches and let Reaver score some points?" She'd already determined that she could take Reaver in a fight. Her gargoyle nature had assessed his abilities that first day and her training at the hands of the Battle Goddess's minions ensured she could use his weaknesses against him.

Obsidian flashed his teeth at her. *"Kick his ass. I want everyone to know my Kyrsu can protect herself. But don't go so far as to reveal your true form."*

"Got it." She paused as she looked at the growing number of onlookers. *"You going to tell me what to expect, or not?"*

"It's a series of tests designed to show how much you already know so the Council of Elders can adjust their training plans and possibly switch up who will mentor you. Though I imagine they'll keep us under the same mentors to improve our integrations as a single fighting unit as our bond is designed to emulate."

"Doesn't sound so bad so far."

"Unfortunately, Reaver will likely attempt to do his worst even with the council's warning. But I think that's what Lord Dray and the council seek. They want to test your limits."

"And what if my limits are far beyond what they're expecting?" She asked only half in jest.

"Harm Reaver as much as you like. The healers can patch him up later. Just don't kill him. Gargoyles never kill gargoyles."

Anna snorted and then continued the conversation aloud. "Could have fooled me by the way you were going at him after the hunt."

"That's different." Obsidian shrugged and then continued to explain the test. "There are five tasks. The first three, combat with knives, sword, and staff, are all to first blood."

"Got it."

"He would normally outmatch you with his size and speed, but your nature and magic will allow you to draw first blood quickly."

"Ah, so no drawing it out and making him look really bad? You're no fun."

"I don't care about how bad you bruise his pride. I'm selfish. I don't want you in the ring with him any longer than necessary."

Anna just nodded, not wanting to push Obsidian with the bond shortening their respective fuses when it came to each other and potential danger.

Obsidian was apparently still feeling edgy and protective. Best not to make it worse.

"Under normal circumstances, his years of training with both sword and staff would give him the advantage. However, each night, while you slept in stone, I shared what I learned that day with you." Obsidian paused to allow a group to move farther down the pathway. "It won't be the same as muscle memory, but it will be an advantage. Use it."

"Anything else of importance I should know?"

"The quarterstaff is Reaver's strong suit." Obsidian bumped his muzzle against her cheek and planted a kiss. "Don't be ashamed if he beats you, you'll be able to make up points in the ground course. With that test, there are several obstacles where a lack of wings will be an advantage. To win, you simply have to complete all the obstacles and arrive back at the starting point before Reaver catches you."

"So, I have to complete them all and he doesn't?"

"The course imitates a spy attempting to return back across enemy lines into friendly territory. Or in Reaver's case, following and stopping the spy before she can deliver her valuable intel to her commanders." Obsidian's mind touched hers. *"You're allowed to use any of your gargoyle skills in the ground obstacle. He won't know you command shadow magic, and we won't inform him either."*

"So shadow magic is fine as long as no one sees."

"Exactly," he said, returning to speaking aloud.

"You said there were five initial tasks. What's the fifth one?"

"Archery. But it's incorporated into the ground obstacle test. There will be a bow and arrows at one of the obstacles, and you'll need to hit the target before continuing.

Anna rolled her shoulders. She'd gone bow hunting with her father and brothers as a teen. Later, during her time in the Battle Goddess's domain, Vaspara and Sorac had resurrected that skill and put several layers of polish on it.

"Only the quarterstaff is likely to give me trouble."

Obsidian snorted. "None of it will be easy by normal standards, but you'll still make me proud."

"No pressure."

"Come. It's time."

CHAPTER TWENTY-SEVEN

Anna and Reaver stared at each other balefully as they waited for the signal to start the ground course. As Obsidian had predicted, she'd won the sword fight, but Reaver was victorious with the quarterstaff. Though she'd made the bastard work for the win.

For this task, Obsidian was forced to wait at the starting line, but each of the course's obstacles would have a mentor or older student stationed there to judge her skill at each task.

She was presently waiting for all the observers to get into position.

At last, the call of a horn rang out, and the two gargoyles standing with crossed spears at the starting line lifted them up and away.

Wasting no time, Anna darted through the opening. She'd only been given a short head start. Just enough to make it to where the map she'd studied said the course branched into five different directions. She could take any one and complete the obstacles in any order. She just had to stay ahead of Reaver.

If she completed the tasks and made it out of the ground course first, she was the winner. If not, then he'd win. And she'd already lost to him as much she planned to today.

Anna darted down the far-left pathway. After a short sprint, she came to a rope bridge over a mud pit. Slowing, she studied it for traps but found none and swiftly made her way across and hauled ass to where the map had shown the next obstacle waited. This one turned out to be a climbing obstacle. The wall must be close to twenty-five feet tall. Ropes hung down the sides, suggesting even a gargoyle was supposed to climb not fly.

She scanned the area and swiftly homed in on the observer. It was Sumdara. She nodded to the elder.

Scanning the area with her magic and not sensing a trap, Anna ran at the obstacle, launched herself a few feet into the air and then grabbed the rope and began to climb. The wall took a little longer than the other two, but she was soon up and over and lowering herself down the other side.

She was just rising from the ground when she heard someone approaching at a run from behind. It could only be one person.

Diving off the path, she called shadow magic to hide. She'd acted just in time. The gargoyle burst onto the track twenty feet behind and sprinted toward the wall. He was running on all fours. His leap landed him three-quarters of the way up the wall. He swiftly climbed the rest, and his tail vanished over the top a moment later.

Show off.

She waited for another minute to be sure he was out of earshot before she continued to run. Two legs were a bitch'n disadvantage compared to four, but she wasn't about to lose to the arrogant prick again. Ten feet ahead, the pathway branched again. Not wanting to accidentally catch up to him, she took the opposite fork as him.

Reaching deep, she called her gargoyle nature, needing the speed and agility, but stopped short of shifting.

With her magic strengthening her, she darted down the path to the next obstacle. A rockfall. She leaped over rock to rock and only acknowledged Master Banrook with a barked 'Greetings Elder' as she passed him. His peal of laughter followed her.

She completed five more obstacles. Some required going through water or swinging over it. Well, others involved climbing through narrow tunnels—which would have been far more difficult in gargoyle form. She even had to belly crawl through mud which sent a spike of home-sickness through her. If she ever made it back to Earth, her debriefing was going to take days.

But then she came to the next obstacle—a narrow timber spanning a ten-foot ditch and she turned her atten-tion back to this newest rendition of military training.

At each of the more difficult obstacles, there was either a dryad or gargoyle present to watch her attempt and judge her performance. Only a handful were people she'd met, but many of them were likely adepts or masters to judge by the power she felt radiating off them. Though there were a few younger students mixed in. She briefly wondered if they had been assigned their positions as some kind of reward.

A couple were likely even novices since their eyes widened at the ease with which she completed some of the tasks.

"Your display is winning over more than a few of my brothers and sisters," Obsidian whispered into her mind.

She'd sensed him watching along their link more than once, but this was the first time he spoke.

"I'm pretty sure you're not supposed to be in my head while I do this test."

"I'm not giving you pointers." He sounded offended.

She grinned to herself, then added, *"Get out of my head. I don't need the distraction. There's no way I'm letting Reaver win again."*

"Better get a move on then," came his laughing reply.

Yeah, someone was having way too much fun watching her compete against Reaver. When Anna reached the next obstacle, she immediately noticed something wrong.

Three archery targets were set up at the end of a long tree-lined lane. Ten feet in front of her, a longbow rested against a post. Three feet in front of that a glowing line of power had been burned into the ground, clearly the designated position to shoot from.

There was only one problem: no arrows.

She scanned the area twice more with no luck.

"He took them with him after he completed the task." A gargoyle stood in the trees, just off to the side of the post. A little growl had accompanied his words, but his anger hadn't been focused on her. "That male has no honor."

"Could've told you that within two minutes of meeting him."

The powerfully built gargoyle laughed at that. He wasn't as big and bulky as Obsidian, Reaver or Banrook, but he should have been a match for Reaver. "You could have stopped him if you wanted."

"*Actually, he can't.*" Obsidian's voice was burrowing deeper into her mind along with his emotions. Their link flared wider and she got a peek at his thoughts. He very much wanted to get his hands around Reaver's neck again.

He wasn't the only one.

"As observers, we are only allowed to watch and record how each participant does. We're not allowed to interfere in the test, not even to stop one such as Reaver from cheating. I would gladly have fought him myself if it was permitted."

"What's your rank and name?"

"Journeyman Frostburn."

Frostburn. Already she wanted to call him Frostbite. She was going to mess his name up more than a few times.

"Thank you, Frostburn, for the gift of your name and your honesty."

After all, the observers weren't required to talk either.

"Anna Mackenzie, Reaver thinks to make you confront him at one of the other archery obstacles. You don't have to if you know how to make arrows. He left the bow behind."

She stared at him in silence.

He gestured wide. "The forest can provide the raw material you need."

While that might be true and if she needed to hunt up some dinner, she might try her hand at making arrows, but she wasn't stopping long enough to make some field arrows and give Reaver this win.

"Obsidian?"

"Now you want to talk?"

"You following what's afoot?"

"Yes. Thayn said I can do what I want if Reaver messes with you again."

"Not what the elder had in mind."

"He's still mine to challenge."

"Won't be needed after I beat his ass in this test. Can Journeyman Frostburn be trusted with a little show of shadow magic?"

"Yes, he's honorable, and once an elder speaks with him, he'll keep his lips sealed. What are you planning?"

"This." Anna walked to the post and picked up the bow. Then she walked until her toes were almost brushing the glowing line of power burned into the ground.

While Frostburn looked on in confusion that turned to astonishment as she drew the bow, she summoned shadow magic and formed it into three perfectly elegant arrows. Then in one smooth motion, she nocked the arrows and let them fly.

Each flew true and buried itself in its intended target. While the gleaming ebony staffs continued to vibrate softly, she propped the bow against the post.

She then turned back to Frostburn and smiled at his stunned expression. "Don't share what you saw here today. A mentor is sure to come to speak with you."

Frostburn surprised her by dropping into a deep bow.

"As the Kyrsu commands." His voice softened a bit. "Well played, Anna Mackenzie. May you win fairly."

"I plan to." Anna nodded goodbye to the gargoyle and darted off. The archery target was the last required obstacle.

"You did very well," Obsidian sent over the link. *"Reaver is farther from the end than you. If you hurry, you'll be able to reach the finish first."*

"Good, I can't wait to see his face when he exits to see me already outside."

"Now who's enjoying this?"

"Never said I wasn't," she countered.

"Hurry back to me. We can watch his expression together."

Anna nodded even though he wouldn't see it, and then sprinted back to the beginning of the course.

As promised, Obsidian was already there with no Reaver in sight.

Beside him, Thayn stood with a horn clasped in his hands. He blew on it then, alerting everyone still in the depths of the field course that there was a winner.

A few minutes later, gargoyles started to emerge. Eventually, Reaver arrived. He spotted her and growled.

"How did you manage to complete all the obstacles?"

"Very carefully. I even had to stop and make three arrows for the final one."

His nostrils flared. "You completed all the tasks?"

"Yes."

He jerked like she'd slapped him. "That's not possible. I'm far from the slowest gargoyle, and there is no way a human could complete that course faster than a gargoyle."

"I'm just fast by any standard."

His expression was comical. His face was scowling, but his ears were in a forward questioning pose. Poor boy was trying to solve a puzzle when he didn't have all the pieces.

"You cheated. Not knowingly. I'd sense that, but you must have unknowingly missed some of the obstacles. Once all the observers are here, I will question them and see which one you missed."

"Go ahead. It won't change the outcome." Anna shrugged and then turned to Obsidian. "Let's go find some training knives for the next test. I might as well get some practice in while Reaver satisfies his suspicions."

Grunting agreement, Obsidian swung an arm around her shoulder and guided her past a fuming Reaver.

Once they were away from the others, she relaxed. Only then discovering how nervous she'd been. It wasn't the training; it was keeping her true nature a secret.

"What I am is going to come out, and that will make it look like we both were trying to hide what the Battle Goddess did to me. Reaver is suspicious, but he isn't actually stupid. Just a jackass."

Obsidian shrugged. "You're worrying too much over something that simply is. Yes, your nature will be revealed one day. Perhaps before the elders intended that to happen. But the residents of Haven already know we were changed by our time in the Battle Goddess's kingdom."

"Yeah but..."

"They will adjust. No doubt some will initially respond like Reaver, but they will come around once they realize what the Battle Goddess did to you did not reach your heart, mind, or soul."

Their talk had carried them to one of the training rings, and a sand-covered field greeted her sight.

"Fine, but better let me get some practice in before Reaver gets here. His mood isn't going to improve once he questions the observers and realizes I did complete all the required tasks."

CHAPTER TWENTY-EIGHT

After selecting from a bunch of weapons already laid out, Anna tested the eight small throwing knives and the two long daggers. They were well-made, their balance good in her hand.

Obsidian snorted. "These are training quality, nothing more. Once you are assigned mentors, they'll commission a set of weapons and armor made for you. Ones superior to these."

"These will do for now."

By the time Reaver appeared, Anna was landing knives consistently in the targets.

She went to retrieve her blades. When she returned, Banrook was already standing and glowering at Reaver and Obsidian.

"There will be no more questioning Anna's loyalties. She is Kyrsu to Obsidian and chosen by Lord Draydrak to be co-leader for the legion. If you have a problem with that, you can take it up with Lord Death."

Reaver bowed his head and muttered an apology, but when Anna joined them, he glowered at her instead.

There was still bad blood there for sure.

Obsidian was suddenly there in her mind, his anger rising again.

"Hey. I've got this." Though, she was really getting tired of Reaver's lousy attitude. It was time to put him in his place.

"And I'll put new holes in his hide if he tries anything other than what he's supposed to do."

"You know how to give a girl the warm fuzzies."

Obsidian growled. *"Go kick his ass, he deserves it even more after what he did at the archery obstacle."*

Reaver grew impatient at what he perceived as a fearful hesitation and came at her. Anna held still until the last moment, then she sidestepped faster than he could react. Dipping low to avoid his wing, she allowed his momentum to carry him past her, then she flicked her wrist, her dagger opening a red line on his thigh.

"First blood," she called while he swung around to face her.

He'd braced one hand to his wound, but paid it no notice, studying her instead. His look was one of speculation, not the arrogance or anger she'd expected. After a moment, he released his hold on his leg and drew a second dagger.

Then he was upon her again, calmer this time. Determined.

She danced with him, studying him in turn, waiting for an opening. When she saw it, she darted in close to land a strike, but he blocked her.

"Humans of the Mortal Realm would not have a chance against a legion-trained gargoyle. You, Anna Mackenzie, are not human. You smell of gargoyle and unwholesome magic."

Anna swore in her head. Of course, close combat had forced him inside the shield she'd been using to filter out her betraying gargoyle scent.

"Enough," Obsidian bellowed to be heard over the crowd. "The match was to first blood. Anna landed the first blow. The bout is finished. Reaver, concede!"

Out of the corner of her eye, she spotted Master Banrook rise from the bench where he was sitting. "Enough. As pretty as her style is to witness, Obsidian is correct. We've seen enough to gauge her ability. Thank you for your assistance Reaver. You are no longer needed."

Her opponent hissed his displeasure, but obliged, bowing to the master.

Then he straightened and turned to leave without a backward glance at her.

Well, that was a more pleasant end than she'd expected. When Anna turned to bow for Master Banrook and the other mentors, her gargoyle nature warned of danger.

Instinctively, she summoned shadow magic. It raced to answer her call, forming a shield in the air mere seconds before Reaver spun, plucking a throwing knife from each wrist brace and sent them flying toward her.

More shadow magic darted up from the ground. Reaver's throwing knives struck the barrier and then bounced off to land in the sand. Her gargoyle nature missed nothing, not the subtle shift of his muscles, not the slight cloud of dust raised by their fight and not the menacing growl from Obsidian.

"See?" Reaver roared. "She is no human. She even smells like some bastardized crossbreed between a gargoyle and a human."

From somewhere behind her, Obsidian snarled again. Using the link, she determined Obsidian was being held back—barely—by Banrook, Verroc, and Thayn.

With her partner safely out of the way, Anna addressed Reaver. "You must like getting the shit kicked out of you. Eventually, my Rasoren will escape. When he does, I'm going to be very, very tempted to just sit back and watch him shred your magic. When he's done, even the healers won't be able to fix you."

The gathering had fallen eerily silent.

After thirty seconds, the silence was broken by snorting laughter.

Anna glanced swiftly to where the three masters were holding Obsidian.

Thayn had released his hold and was watching Anna with amusement.

"Dray was correct. You're a fierce one. A little blood-thirsty, but I like what I see so far." The eldest of the gargoyles marched up to her but turned his gaze upon Reaver, his humor vanishing. "You, on the other hand, are a very misguided cub. And if you persist, I will make you my own personal apprentice. You will not enjoy the experience."

The big male's entire body flinched, and his wings gave

an involuntary shudder. The eldest of the gargoyles must be one scary dude to garner such a response. She made a note not to get on his shit list.

Reaver recovered his composure somewhat, and by the way he was staring at her, he wasn't ready to give up. "But she doesn't even deny my words!"

Banrook stormed up to them, glowering at Reaver. "You have acted rashly. Shaming your other mentors. Again! Continue like this and you'll never achieve your full potential. As it is now, you'll be lucky to make island guard!"

"But she is hiding what she is! Her deceit is a threat to everyone."

"Enough out of you. You will listen." Thayn slapped the journeyman across the muzzle and then turned to address the rest of the gathering. "Anna has only followed the council's orders. After seeing how many distrusted Shadowlight when he first arrived—and he only an innocent child—we thought it best to allow Anna time to adjust to our ways and prove herself before her true nature was revealed."

"I can assure everyone, that while Anna and Shadowlight spent time in the Battle Goddess's kingdom, it wasn't willingly, and they managed to resist her dark power. These two young souls are not our enemy's work, they are the work of the Divine Ones."

Murmurs of surprise sounded throughout the gathering. Thayn just raised his voice above them. "The Avatars have made a choice—their allegiance is now divided. To compensate for that complication, the Divine Ones have chosen two new souls to take up their cause."

"I..." Reaver trailed off, sounding uncertain.

"Do you still doubt the wisdom of the Divine Ones, Lord Dray's choice, and the council's plans?"

"No, Master Thayn." Reaver bowed his head in defeat.

"Good. Now go wait in Rook's workroom. I'm sure he'll think up something suitable to cure you of your rashness." The oldest gargoyle dismissed the journeyman.

Reaver bowed and departed. Only after he was gone did Anna release her hold on the shadow magic shield.

Banrook signaled for Obsidian to come forward. He did and preceded to sniff her over for injuries. When he found none, he sat on his haunches and waited.

Thayn patted first Obsidian's shoulder and then Anna's. "I'm sorry that your secret was revealed in such a spectacular fashion, and while it's not what the council may have wished, now you don't have to work so hard to hide what you are."

"There is that," she agreed.

"We'll discuss your skills and determine which mentors to assign you, but from what we've all seen, I believe we'll start you with Obsidian's mentors first. But I'll leave that to Rook to oversee."

Anna's gaze darted toward Banrook, but he was too busy working on crowd control. "What are you all waiting for? Off with you! Go."

The crowd departed, slowly. And then only because Rook's words weren't a suggestion.

"I must admit I'm curious to witness your gargoyle form." Thayn was eyeing her up and down as if trying to imagine her with wings and horns. "Obsidian said you were spectacular in the air as well as being a fierce protector and warrior—a berserker even."

"Don't know what he's been claiming, but that side doesn't come out very often."

Thayn rubbed his jaw in thought. "We will have to see if we can lure that part of you out for the healers to study. While berserkers are extraordinary on the battlefield, they aren't quite so beneficial in everyday life. We'll test out a few training methods to see if we can find a way to harness all the destructive energy into something positive."

Thayn soon dismissed them but Master Maradryn arrived before they could make their escape. "Maybe now I'll have that chance to study your gargoyle form."

Anna bowed to acknowledge the older healer, but she wasn't enthusiastic at the idea.

"Of, course." *So much fun. Can't wait.*

"Not what I'd call fun," Obsidian replied as he bumped his muzzle against her shoulder.

"Do you need another application of the cream?"

"No!" He jerked back and eyed her suspiciously. "Come on, you're getting grumpy, which means you're hungry."

Anna just muttered under her breath as she let him lead her in the direction of food.

CHAPTER TWENTY-NINE

Food wasn't the only thing they found when they arrived at the community fires. Anna's ability to call shadow magic caused much excitement and many questions.

Seeing all the eagerness, Anna seized on the opportunity and suggested she shift to show the depth of her abilities. He'd agreed. Better they were honest and forthright about it now. Of course, as soon as she shifted to her gargoyle form, crowds of onlookers gathered, and it took the rest of the evening meal and well into the night to satisfy the worst of the curiosity.

But for better or worse it was done. He no longer had to lie to his friends or fellow students.

At last, after far too many questions, the crowds diminished allowing he and his Kyrsu to seek their rest.

They were halfway back to his dwelling when Anna suddenly halted and looked over her shoulder at him.

"I'm dead on my feet, but I want a bath—a real bath—

before bed. Where are these public baths you mentioned yesterday?"

"Not far if we travel on the wing." While he had been tired, the thought of flying with Anna gave him a renewed surge of energy.

"Let's go then. But have mercy. I'll be rusty. Don't want to go smacking into trees."

With a huffing laugh, he squeezed by Anna, then dropped to all fours and continued down the bridge at a jog. She followed so close behind, she playfully nipped at his swaying tail. It became a game of sorts. Him trying to anticipate when her next attack was going to come; her trying to land little nips without getting smacked in the muzzle.

When he reached the end of the bridge, he leaped up into the air, his wings opening wide to capture the wind. Three heartbeats later, Anna was flying beside him. Warmth and joy flowed along their link. She'd missed this too.

When the trees ahead grew too thick and forced them into single file, Anna curled the tip of one wing and glided until she was just ahead and slightly lower. He'd forgotten how graceful she was in the air.

Their wings moving as one, they sailed through the moonlit forest, silent as owls. From this vantage point, he studied the flow of her long mane. Her shift from human to gargoyle had freed her hair from the braids.

She'd likely grump about it later, but he didn't mind putting them back in. He looked forward to anything that brought them close and allowed him to touch her.

Gargoyles were naturally a tactile bunch, but some

component of their bond intensified that need. He suspected it was the same for Anna even if she wasn't ready to admit that yet. To satisfy their need, he'd make sure to keep things playful and platonic for now.

A subtle shift of muscles along her spine and hips warned him a moment before she banked, gliding around a tree in her path. He followed instinctively and then closed the gap between them, so they were in perfect alignment, their wings rising and falling together.

He skimmed just above her, so close he could feel her body heat against his skin. It would be so easy to reach out and grasp her hips, entwine his tail with hers and lick the delicate skin at the base of her neck. New heat spread throughout his body at the thought.

"Hey, what part of 'I'm rusty' don't you understand?" She dipped lower. "No acrobatics or I might fall out of the sky."

He grunted at her interruption but realized how close he'd come to doing something stupid that would likely only drive her away from him.

Platonic. Keep it platonic, he chanted to himself.

Belatedly, he realized her statement required some response from him. "You don't give yourself enough credit."

"And you give me too much." She glanced over her shoulder at him. "Where are these baths anyway?"

"The stone pathway just below us—follow it until it forks. Take the left branch, and you'll see the waterfall that feeds all the constructed streams and pools."

She nodded and followed the path until the baths could be seen ahead. Dropping lower, she came in for a landing.

He dropped down beside her.

"This way. The water is cooler at this side of the baths because it's farther from the main heating spell at the base of the waterfall, but it will be quieter. I figured you'd prefer a little privacy since you're still in your gargoyle form."

"Yeah. Sounds like a plan. Been ogled enough for one night."

Obsidian trotted toward the most private of the baths, hoping it would be empty this time of night. It had nothing to do with the fact he'd get to have her all to himself for a while. There was also a secondary reason for seeking out one of the more secluded private pools.

Flying wing-tip to wing-tip with Anna had stirred his blood a little too vigorously.

"You're awfully quiet, what's up?"

He snorted at her wording and turned it into a cough to cover up. Well, something was up, wasn't it? But she didn't need to know that. If he remained in his four-legged form with his wings drooping slightly, she wouldn't notice anything. He hoped.

"Just thinking about the future." *And hoping you'll accept me as your mate one day.*

A few of the pathways leading to the pools were marked with piles of brightly painted stones to show those pools were already in use. Even without the artful piles of rocks, the occasional soft voice, seductive laugh or deep moan would have told him which pools were in use.

"Oh, geez," Anna reared and shifted to walk on two feet, and then cast a glower in his direction. "If I see any live-action gargoyle smut, I'm so gone."

"As am I," he agreed with a chuckle. He could smell her

embarrassment and couldn't resist one little dig. "Unless I'm misremembering, it was your idea to come for a very late-night bath, wasn't it?"

"In your dreams."

"Now you're giving me ideas."

Her swaying tail froze in place, the end quivering ever so slightly. Then one ear flicked forward and the other back as if she didn't know how to respond. Goddess, she was adorable when she was caught off guard.

At last, her eyes narrowed upon him. "It's just a phrase."

"I know. But I couldn't resist."

"Jackass."

"You swear too much."

"Who died and made you Gran?" Her snarky tone was ruined by the corners of her lips curling up.

He stalked up to her and bumped his muzzle under her hand and was rewarded by the feel of her talons gently working his scalp.

"Seriously, though, I don't want a bath badly enough to accidentally interrupt someone's one on one time."

"See those painted stones?" He pointed with his muzzle as he trotted past. "When they are scattered, they are telling others that the pool is empty. A straight line means it's occupied, but others are welcome. Rocks stacked in a tower means the occupants wish to be left alone."

"Piled up rocks—bow chicka wow wow. Got it."

Obsidian laughed. He couldn't help himself. Soon the laughter included snorts. In turn, Anna started laughing at him.

"It wasn't that funny." She managed between chuckles.

"Yes, it was." He was still grinning as he shifted a circle of rocks into a line. That done, he gestured her to go ahead of him.

He watched Anna as she surveyed the area as they walked the rest of the short distance to the pool. Her gaze went to the small waterfall first, moving to the pool next, and then the overflow last, where the old water vanished into an irrigation channel that would deliver the water to the hamadryads.

"Magic Realm hot tub. Cool." She stuck one talon-tipped toe in the water. "Nice."

Turning back to him, she made a shooing motion.

He flexed his jaw. "I'm staying."

"Like hell."

She pinned her ears back and looked a little like she might bite. His blood surged a little more hotly at the thought. Which probably wasn't the reaction she was going for. He cleared his throat. "If it were safe, I'd give you as much privacy as you wanted. But after Reaver forced you to reveal your shadow magic, I can't guarantee that others won't feel the same as him. I'm staying."

Anna glanced away from him, studying the area with new eyes. He nodded when she looked back at him. "Yes. Someone wishing to sneak up on you would have the tactical advantage. The waterfalls will drown out any noise of approach, and the scent of soaps and flowering vines will help disguise and muddy any warning your nose might normally give you."

After a moment her gaze returned to his. "Sorry. I thought you had less pure reasons. You can join me."

She faced the pool and reached behind her back and

under her wings to untie her top. Casting it aside, she reached for the knots tying her loincloth in place. Obsidian fought to keep his breathing even as he watched her. He shouldn't be staring. But he was mesmerized by the subtle shift of muscle beneath her skin and the play of shadow and moonlight upon her supple body.

When she started forward, he hurried to shed his loin-cloth, wanting to get into the water as quickly as possible. As the ties released, he sighed in pleasure as the constricting fabric fell away. With luck, it was dark enough that the shadows below the surface of the pool would hide his problem.

As she moved across the pool, closer to the waterfall, he swiftly descended the stairs cut into the side. Once he was safely chest-deep in the water, he waded closer. "See that basket to your right sitting on the lip of the pool? That holds body soaps and gentler products for your mane."

Anna waded over to check out the items. He drew closer, intent on grabbing one of the small washing towels and some soap from one of the jars, but his thoughts scattered as her tail brushed along his thigh. It was an accidental touch, and she quickly pulled her tail away, but his entire body jerked at the contact.

Goddess, this was a bad idea.

"This one smells a little like jasmine, but prettier. Though, it's a little on the strong side." Anna half turned and waved the jar at him. "What do you think?"

'I think I'm going to embarrass myself profoundly if you brush up against me again.' Then out loud, he said, "It's nice. The scent will fade once you dry off."

His gaze followed the curve of her neck to her shoulders and then to where the water lapped against the upper swells of her breasts. Her skin was all creamy darkness, just a shade lighter than the shadowy water.

Realizing he'd been staring, he looked back to her eyes to find them on his face. He didn't know what that look in her eyes was, but it seemed a little haunted.

She gave herself a little shake and then slipped by him and waded back toward the waterfall with her supplies. He prayed she hadn't caught that last thought. He'd been keeping his shields locked tight since she mentioned wanting a bath. So surely not.

They washed in silence for a time.

She seemed to have relaxed around him again, so he did his best to ignore his body and carry on a conversation about training.

"How the heck do you guys manage to wash the parts of your wings you can't reach?" She twisted and turned, but no matter what she did she couldn't reach the section of wing closest to her body. "I used to shift back to my human form during baths. But you guys must have some secret voodoo. Time to share."

"No magic. We use our tails and a cloth, or if we're in the communal bathing area, we just ask our nearest neighbor to wash our wings."

"Nope to the second." She stood looking at the bit of cloth in her hand and then her tail emerged from the water. With a little experimenting, she got the rag balanced on her blade-tipped tail, then attempted to scrub her own back.

He managed not to laugh at her failed attempts.

Then after about the fifteenth try of the cloth slipping off her tail and vanishing under the water again, she smacked her hands against the surface.

"Fuck it! Get over here and scrub my damn wings!" She paused, her voice softening slightly on an awkward, "Please. I'll do yours first."

Grinning he went to her aid, all too eager to accept her offer and present his back. Then, even though it was just an impersonal washing, he had to fight back more of his purring as she rubbed the stout membrane between his wings and the area where the joints met. Then she started on his back. The entire time he fought to keep his tail still at the bottom of the pool.

Her touch was glorious and over far too soon.

Before disappointment swamped him, she was offering her back, her wings spread slightly. He touched her reverently. And if his knuckles grazed her skin in places instead of the rag? She didn't seem to mind.

He was lost in the moment, enjoying the pure pleasure of touching his Kyrsu in a way she permitted, when suddenly her tail swirled through the water and wrapped around his thigh. While he was still registering the not so subtle pressure and warmth, she reached behind her to touch his waist.

A surprised grunt escaped him.

"Easy," she whispered. "I can feel your hunger. If you let me, I can help take the edge off so you can sleep."

"I'm not sure—"

But she was stepping back into him, the base of her tail going between his legs, the firm globes of her backside pressing into his groin. Another grunt of surprise escaped him as his hips jerked forward instinctively.

She reached for his hands and wrapped them around her waist as she rocked her hips back against him again. His thoughts scattered as the aching length of him ground against the small of her back.

He tightened his hold on her middle as helpless purrs of pleasure escaped him.

She chuckled, the tone deeper and more seductive than before. "I think your purr is the sexiest thing I've ever heard."

Purr? He was purring. There was a reason that was bad, right?

Before he could remember why, Anna was turning in his arms, her breasts brushing against his chest as she leaned in and nuzzled him under the throat. Her tongue flicked out, caressing him there even as her hands were trailing a slow, seductive path down his chest.

Simultaneously, she nipped his shoulder and her fingers closed around him under the water. They were strong and sure, working up and down his length, making him rise nearly onto his toes as he chased the sensation.

"Goddess! Anna...I..."

"You like that."

It hadn't been phrased as a question, but if he'd been able to speak, he'd have told her it was better than anything he'd experienced in his life.

Something was nagging at his conscience, but it was hard to think when she was touching him. That was it, though, wasn't it? The fact she was touching him at all. Anna didn't desire him in this way.

No. Oh, great Mother Goddess, no.

Was this her gargoyle nature's fertility cycle overwhelming her? Or perhaps it was even worse than that. Was she reacting to some silent command his need had somehow issued? Had he stolen her will?

He couldn't know for sure which it was with her skilled fingers working to drive him into a frenzy. But he knew this wasn't his Anna. This was conditioning implanted in her by the darkness that slept in their blood.

He'd promised that he'd never steal her will.

"Stop." He let authority ring in his voice for once. "Not here."

She didn't step away, but she did stop.

"What's wrong?" The skin along her muzzle scrunched up as she sniffed at him, attempting to read his emotions and thoughts.

"I want to return to our nest."

Her tail was caressing him below the water but thank the Divine Ones she'd released him from her fingers' grasp.

"Are you shy?"

"Does it matter?" he asked suddenly as he stepped back. He continued until he was at the steps and then walked up them backward so as not to take his eyes off her. "Let us dress and fly back to my quarters. We can talk more there."

"Talk?" Her delicate snort told him she thought they'd continue current activities there.

He didn't enlighten her. First, he had to get her someplace safe and then he planned to turn them both to stone for the rest of the night if that's what it took to return them both to sanity.

As he fled the pool and got dressed, Anna followed him and pulled on her clothing. Though she reached out to caress a shoulder or wing every so often as if to reassure herself that he was still there, warm and willing.

"You are a magnificent male."

He sighed, his heart aching along with his body. If Anna had said those words, she would have quickly brought him to his knees, but now that he had the space to think, he knew he'd forced this upon his beloved Kyrsu. His desire had bled over into her, and their link had shaped it into a command, forcing her to want to please him.

It was wrong. He couldn't have Anna.

Not like this.

Never like this.

It would still be force, no matter how willing she might seem.

As they returned to his dwelling, Anna flew just behind him. The night air cleared her head and cooled her blood, and she almost wished she could pull the persona of the gargoyle back over her mind. It was better than having to face Obsidian after what she'd done.

All too soon they were landing outside his place. He'd dismantled the ward spell over the door in record time and was hurrying inside before she'd even landed. She hesitated outside, debating flying deep into the island interior for the night, so she wouldn't have to face Obsidian.

Had he run back there at the pool because he'd lost his nerve or was he eagerly running home, so they could continue? The first opened a well of guilt inside her. The second made fear churn in her gut.

Gods, this was such a mess.

But then he was back, standing in front of her with a white smear of cream on his upper lip and his eyes streaming. She recognized the potion by scent and didn't struggle as he reached to smear some under her nose.

While it burned away her sense of smell, she shifted back, secretly hoping Obsidian wouldn't find her human form as appealing.

"Anna, I'm so sorry."

"I'm sorry too. I don't know what came over me."

Obsidian glanced down at the little jar he still carried. "I know exactly what came over you. That's why I'm so sorry. I...my wish...my desire. Our link turned it into a command. Are you alright?"

"Yeah, I'm fine. But I don't think it would have had such an effect if I wasn't in heat. I'm pretty sure my gargoyle didn't need much encouragement."

A greater wave of guilt made her flush as she remembered how eager and willing she'd been. Even though he was only a couple of years younger than her, she was certain Obsidian was pretty damn innocent. And she just teased him until he'd nearly spilled in her hand. Only his noble nature and knowing her actions weren't really hers, prevented him from giving over to his own desires.

She certainly hadn't been able to slow herself down.

"Are you sure you're fine?" he asked softly. "I didn't traumatize you when I stole your will?"

"No, of course you didn't traumatize me. I should be asking you the same."

Obsidian laughed for the first time since they'd returned to his place. "You need not fear on that front. I enjoyed it very much. If it had been your choice and not our link or your gargoyle nature forcing you to do those things, I would have gladly stayed there in that pool until dawn."

He was so damn earnest and sweet. He loved her.

Anna felt herself flush with a sickly heat. It was a mix of guilt, embarrassment, and anger.

Her gargoyle nature wasn't afraid of intimacy. For the first time since the fucking attack, she'd been confident enough to overcome her fears and dark memories. She'd even become the aggressor, wanting to give Obsidian pleasure but also seeking it herself. For close to three years, she'd wanted to get back to who she'd been before her personal life imploded.

But that confidence wasn't real. What she felt—none of it was real. It was all just a compulsion.

While she was angry and guilty, she was also envious of her gargoyle's boldness and resilience. Now that she'd returned to her human form, she couldn't even find the fucking courage to tell Obsidian why she was too messed up to give him more of her heart. He still thought it was their bond she feared, that loss of freedom.

While that was concerning, it wasn't the root of her fear.

"Anna, I'm going to hug you now."

"What?" But then she felt the wetness tracking down her cheeks. What the hell? She didn't cry. She didn't. Not even directly after...

His approach was slow and non-threatening. It might

almost be comical if it wasn't for the haunted look in his eyes. "You desperately need a hug."

Standing there frozen, she allowed him to take her in his arms. After a moment, he crushed her to his chest, and Anna reached around his waist to give him a hard squeeze in return.

"I don't know what caused this pain," he was saying his voice muffled in her hair. "But it's eating you up inside. One day you must share this with someone and lance the festering wound. I hope it will be with me, but I understand if this is something you don't want to share with a male."

"Oh, God. You've been in my head. You've seen."

Bands of pressure were squeezing her chest. Her lungs burned. She was holding her breath and gasped a deep lungful of air. Still, it did nothing to combat the dread.

"No. You've kept the memories from me, but I can feel the pain. It's not hard to figure out what must be the cause. You'll speak of it one day when you're ready."

Anna wasn't sure she'd ever be ready.

CHAPTER THIRTY

The next morning could have been far more awkward if they had time to think and talk. But Anna was saved from that by a pre-dawn knock at Obsidian's door. Master Banrook informed them that Lord Draydrak wished to speak with the pair.

Which was why she now stood in a chamber in Death's temple several floors below ground. She had a vague recollection of this place from her time after she'd been injured and Banrook had carried her through these passages with a frightened Shadowlight trailing behind.

Now Obsidian stood beside her, confident and ready to face Death.

While Anna might not be feeling such surety when they were about to meet a demigod, she wasn't frightened either. Just cautious. This demigod had had ample opportunity to do her and Obsidian harm over the years. As far as she could tell, he hadn't.

He had, in fact, given Shadowlight a safe place to be a kid for a while before growing up.

So, she stood staring up at the 'viewing mirror' where it shimmered in the center of the chamber. The mirror was of a size with even the most pretentious of drive-in theater screens. Presently, it showed what one might mistake as a mirror image of the room they were standing in, except for the fact she and Obsidian weren't in the reflection.

Her gargoyle partner had confirmed they were looking into the future. Their own time to be precise. When she'd asked if this was like the time portal they'd crossed to get here, he'd shaken his head and brushed his knuckles against the spell. The simple touch had sent ripples through the image for half a minute before it calmed again.

They'd waited maybe five minutes when Anna heard the clopping sound of massive hooves on stone. She drew in a quick breath and waited. A vast shadow arrived a few strides before the Lord of the Underworld appeared, dwarfing the expansive room with its hundred and fifty-foot ceiling.

The four armed, four-legged god of death tilted his gargoyle-like head downward and then down some more until his eyes locked upon them.

"Greetings my Rasoren and Kyrsu." He circled once and then twice more before folding his legs under him and reclining. A second later his tail wrapped around his body in a cat-like manner.

Her brain still hadn't settled on what kind of animal he'd modeled his form after. The head was gargoyle-like certainly, as were the wings and tail, but his neck, shoulders, and body with its four sturdy legs had a more equine quality. But he didn't move like either of those species. The graceful and flowing movement, almost like he didn't have joints, was rather like one of the big cats.

"Corporal Anna Mackenzie, I am older than all those species." It was said in a humorous tone.

Thankfully.

She didn't need to start out this meeting by offending a demigod of death with a foolish thought.

"I have summoned you because now that Anna has awakened you both have a decision to make. It is no secret that I wish for you both to serve as leaders for my army. But I have no interest in slaves. You must choose this path willingly." Lord Draydrak paused. "Obsidian is now old enough and far enough in his training to make his decision, but, Anna, you have much to learn first. It is not a decision to be made lightly. You have a year as Haven counts time to decide. That will give you time to train and catch up to Obsidian's level. After that, if you wish to return to your place and time, I will release you."

Beside her Obsidian was practically twitching with the need to speak, but Lord Dray laughed at him. "Easy, my Rasoren. If Anna chooses to go and you wish to go with her, I will release you from my service as well."

Obsidian dropped into a deep bow. "Thank you, my Lord."

"Though as gargoyles, you will always hear my summons and be bound to come, but I shall always rerelease you. I cannot undo what you are."

Anna understood that all gargoyles were somehow bound to serve the demigod. So the last part wasn't entirely new. Though it was likely to cause trouble later down the road.

"I have a secondary reason to call you before me. Your mentors have reported the trouble with the Journeyman named Reaver. I shall speak with him. You need not worry about further trouble on that front. However, I have also felt a disturbance between you."

He shifted, two hands coming to rest on the ground directly between them.

"Nothing can come between your bond without creating a weakness. If a wound—even an emotional one—is left to fester, it will sicken you both, taint your spirits and your magic. That is the nature of your bond. But your greatest gift and strength is that your bond can also be used to create a unity that will be equal to the Avatars. The kind of strength even the darkest of evil cannot touch."

Shit. The demigod sensed the flaw in her armor. But it wouldn't remain just her flaw. It would become Obsidian's as well if she didn't find a way to fix herself. The dread she'd felt last night returned tenfold.

"Do you understand what I'm telling you? Your link will not be complete—will, in fact, be a liability—until you both learn to merge your hearts, minds, and souls completely."

Damn it. He was saying if she didn't get her shit together and her head screwed on straight, she could get Obsidian killed in battle.

"Do not judge yourself so harshly, Kyrsu." Draydrak's expression softened. "What you suffered did not lessen your strength, your spirit, or your will. And you are not the only one with fears holding you back. Obsidian has his own. Ones he's only now fully realizing. But together, you and he can heal those unseen wounds and find a peace you've never known."

Anna swallowed and stared at her feet for a moment. Then, spine stiffening and shoulders straightening, she looked up and met the demigod's eyes. She was done with being weak. "I will not disappoint you, Obsidian, or myself. I will become the Kyrsu my Rasoren will need in the coming war."

"You will," Lord Draydrak agreed.

Beside her, Obsidian shifted, his one wing coming to curl around her shoulders. *"You already are the Kyrsu I need, but together we will heal you, so these dark memories no longer haunt your days."*

CHAPTER THIRTY-ONE

(The Present)

Vaspara once again found herself marching in a direction she'd rather not be heading. This time Sorac, Bervicta, and the sidhe-demoness sisters were with her. They'd been ordered by their goddess to find out how the blood witch's spell was coming. She hadn't reported in over three days.

If they were lucky, the witch had miscalculated and been eaten by her own spell. But Vaspara was never so fortunate. Otherwise, she and Sorac would have been shipped out on patrol yesterday and would have missed the Battle Goddess's latest summons. But Korsha and Ernya were late getting back with their newest trainees because winter storms had closed off the passes. And even magic could only do so much.

The faint whiff of death that always clung to this section of corridors was growing stronger by the step. Another hundred steps and it was all she could smell. Fifty more steps and she could taste death on her lips.

"Goddess," Sorac choked, raising his hand to his face and slowing. "If that gets any worse, I'm just going to torch the entire section."

"I'd wait until the bodies have been removed before burning them, were I you. Otherwise, the entire keep will smell like a charnel house." Vaspara rounded the corner and halted so suddenly Sorac ran into her from behind.

"You sure you don't want me to just burn the entire keep?" Sorac asked as he peered over her shoulder. "We could rebuild. Probably quicker, too."

Bervicta craned her neck and then whistled. "That's just nasty."

Bodies were stacked seven high on both sides of the corridor as far as the eye could see.

Behind her one of the sidhe-demoness sisters made an offended sound. "Why haven't the servants cleaned this mess up yet?"

"The 'mess' is the servants," Sorac said in a low voice. "Since you just got back from a patrol, I assume you haven't been to your quarters yet. You'll notice something missing."

Vaspara was glad Sorac had been able to spirit her servants away on the same trip he'd delivered his to safety. Once it was safe, he'd go retrieve them. She'd later learned, Bervicta had stashed her own servants in preservation spells and sank them to the bottom of the lake beside the training field.

Bervicta was glancing back at the line of young trainees still following in their mistress's wake. The harpy's expression was dark as she looked back to Vaspara. "Should we suggest they clean up the dead, so the witch doesn't use the youngsters as a snack? I think Korsha and her sister are only now starting to realize the true depth of Taryin's darkness."

Vaspara turned. "You there!"

The foremost of the soldiers started at being addressed by one of the other captains.

"Yes, you. Stop looking toward your mistress for permission. Gather your men and clean this mess up. Take the bodies out to the edge of the practice yard and burn them to ash."

Korsha's eyes widened slightly in understanding, and she turned to her men to give them further instructions on how to find the nearest exit from the keep.

Then the five captains continued up the hall in single file until they reached the door to the witch's workroom. Here the smell of death was almost overpowered by the taint of blood magic. Almost, but not quite.

Vaspara called through the door twice. When she got no response, she really did start to wonder if the witch had fallen prey to one of her creations. A surge of hope welled in Vaspara's dark little heart as she pushed open the heavy door.

The first sight of the room snuffed out that hope.

Taryin lay slumped across her worktable. Alive. Though barely.

Above her, a dark, churning power hung in the air. Inside its swirling mass, ebony shadows danced with a rusty red mist. The speed and pattern of its shifting energy currents changed between heartbeats. Sometimes it was slow, almost graceful in its movements. Other times it was quick and jerky, reminding her of something in its death throes.

"I don't think I've been so unlucky as to witness anything half as evil as that...thing...until now." Sorac's voice was colored with awe and revulsion.

"Not unless you count the unconscious witch."

"Well. True. But we could do something about that."

Vaspara eyed the spell. "We could. If that thing will allow us to get close enough."

When she stepped closer to the spell, it spun with more excitement.

"Hold up," Sorac warned. "I think that thing can read our intentions."

"You might be right." Curse it. They might not get another opportunity like this to take out the witch. But Sorac was correct. The spell calmed when she set aside the idea of terminating the witch.

"Besides, we need the witch to control that thing."

"I'll distract the spell. You see if you can get Taryin and escape with her."

"I'm not leaving you in a room with that thing." Sorac's brows were drawn down into a line above his nose.

"I'm not suicidal. I am not staying. We'll leave together and then put some powerful wards around this chamber before we go report to the Battle Goddess." Vaspara eyed the slowly spinning evil once more. "Whatever the witch has sought to create, I think she was successful."

"Yes," Sorac agreed. "I feel sorry for Anna and that poor gargoyle cub of hers."

Vaspara was more concerned about their own asses but admitted she didn't like the idea of that thing hunting any of her trainees, even escaped ones.

"Come on. Let's do this and report back to our Lady."

CHAPTER THIRTY-TWO

Anna's first two weeks at Haven went smoothly after the minor hiccup with Reaver and the not-so-minor encounter with Obsidian in the baths. But at least her heat cycle only lasted three days. She was all too happy it was behind her now.

But in the days after that incident, it was easy to see Obsidian still blamed himself for what had happened. She didn't know how to erase that fear; she just hoped showing him that she trusted him completely would soothe over the worst of it.

Her plan seemed to be working. Slowly he began to relax around her again.

As for day to day life, their routine was quickly established. She went to the healers early each morning to allow them to study her and to be sure the previous day's work wasn't too much for her system after sleeping in healing stone for thirteen years.

Overall, they seemed pleased with her progress and

gave her a clean bill of health, which her instructors then took as permission to test her limits.

Her official gargoyle mentors were Master Verroc and Adept Shorban. Though Banrook, or Rook as he *strongly* preferred, attended all her sessions and took part in a good half. Her dryad instructors were usually Master Maradryn and Adept Takara. Both were calm, level-headed women.

Her new mentors regularly pitted her against other opponents as well. Of her training sessions, over two-thirds were combat based, leaving every third afternoon set aside for history lessons with various Journeymen.

All in all, it wasn't so very different from what her daily routine had been like in the Battle Goddess's kingdom. Well, except for the parts about not having to fear such things as the possibility of getting fed upon by an incubus, warding off an amorous Gryton, or finding a way to save innocent people from being sucked dry by a blood witch's spells.

Anna had soon come to another realization. Here she could form friendships and alliances and not have to worry about the possibility of crossing swords with them on the battlefield in some future time. Not having to kill friends was always a plus.

Typically, this time of day, she would be practicing, but today Obsidian was training for his Adept Trial.

She was looking forward to seeing him fight.

They'd been spending so much time on her, keeping her busy, she hadn't had time to see the full extent of what Obsidian could do.

Now she was getting her chance.

But when they reached the practice rings, Obsidian continued without slowing.

"I thought the elders were going to give you a workout?"

"They are, but not here. They have something more advanced in mind."

Advanced might be his word for it, but Anna could think of far more apt words for the steep course with its dozens of obstacles spilling down the side of the mountain. While the ground course she'd run during her novice test had been relatively simple, this one was every extreme sports junkie's wet dream.

The course was all stone pillars, rope bridges, broad jumps and tall walls that would give even the most diehard parkour nut pause.

"That's one hellish looking obstacle course." Anna scanned the terrain from the valley floor all the way up to the cloud-shrouded peaks.

"It's fun."

"Only a gargoyle would find that hot mess fun. You're all insane."

Obsidian snorted. "You'll be glad to know the mentors want you to follow me down as I hunt and 'kill' as many opponents as I can find."

"So...suicide hide and seek parkour. Yep, still sounds insane."

"Come. Fly up to the top. Then you can shadow me all the way down. Don't get separated. There's a fair amount of risk for the unwary. So, stay focused and silent. Even a misstep can alert the others to our location."

"You're insane."

He grinned suddenly and slapped his tail against her flank. "So are you for following me."

Then he leaped into the air, his wings beating mightily as he began the steep aerial climb up the mountain.

Instinctively, Anna spread her wings and followed.

Her gargoyle nature didn't flag those words as a lie.

Her initial assessment was correct. This course was a nightmare on a scale that she'd never experienced before.

Obsidian's breakneck speed only made it worse. At least she had wings if anything went drastically wrong.

"Flying, even just a short glide, will get you disqualified," Obsidian sent along their link. *"Now focus your mind and concentrate."*

Duly reprimanded, Anna returned her focus upon their immediate environment and Obsidian's well-muscled rump as he zig-zagged his way down the mountainside. He moved with a fluid grace that was positively impressive for one as big as him.

It took all her skills, instincts and endurance to keep up with him. And if it weren't for their bond that burned with potent magic, linking them subconsciously, so they moved as one, she never would have kept up with him.

She used to be the swifter of the two, but he was breathtaking.

As they hurled themselves across a rock fall, Obsidian twisted in the air, rolling onto his back to launch a spear of shadow magic at the gargoyle rising out of a crevice ten feet behind them.

Anna had only spotted the gargoyle after Obsidian had targeted him.

His aim was true. A shower of bright sparks rained down, marking her partner's seventeenth 'kill' so far.

"Keep up," he barked out.

Damn. They'd fallen out of sync and Obsidian was now twenty feet ahead of her. Determined to regain that almost addictive feeling of oneness, she put on a burst of speed to catch up even as she focused her mind on the thread of sensations flowing down their link to her.

When she was alongside him once again, he slapped her flank playfully with his tail. Then he surprised her again by bumping her muzzle affectionately with his. "You're doing well, but don't allow yourself to get distracted. I don't want to see you get hurt again."

"Now who's distracted?"

He rumbled and smacked her halfheartedly with his tail a second time "You make me so proud, though I'll admit that sometimes your beauty and strength distracts me."

But just then, two gargoyles appeared on the path ahead.

Together, she and Obsidian dispatched these next opponents. It was supposed to be training, but it was so much more than that.

This was right. This was how it supposed to be. Just the two of them against all comers. They moved as one. They breathed as one. They thought as one.

CHAPTER THIRTY-THREE

The next four weeks sped by in a blur. Anna thought she'd been doing well until this morning when Rook had come to them and said Lord Draydrak was concerned with one facet of their training and wished to speak with them.

But once Rook had delivered his message, she knew what it was about. She and Obsidian had never again achieved that same level of unity they'd shared racing down the side of a mountain together.

Now they stood before the viewing mirror once more.

As Anna waited for the death god to make himself comfortable on the other side, she replayed his words the last time they'd been here. That time he'd said she and Obsidian needed to overcome their fears and merge their hearts, bodies and souls if they wanted to survive the coming war.

It had been six weeks, and while Anna had advanced in her physical and magical training, she still wasn't ready to let Obsidian into her mind—to see the depths of her fears and the damage to her battered heart. She couldn't shake the notion that he would see her differently and know her tough exterior was a lie.

When Dray was comfortable, he studied Anna in silence.

And yeah. I suck. We both see it. No need to mention it out loud.

Dray grinned and shook his head at her. It was the first time she'd seen him smile. The flash of teeth was impossible to miss, and would have been frightening, but Anna was used to gargoyle grins by now.

And there was just something peaceful and...pleasant? Yes, pleasant, about spending time with this demigod. Looking back, she realized she'd first sensed it when she was dying. Though she'd been too scared for Shadowlight at the time to be calmed by it. Now she could detect it more easily. A kindness. A purity. Something that clung to the Lord of the Underworld and was able to travel between the viewing mirror and touch her here in the past.

She allowed it to calm her.

"Rest easy Anna. This meeting isn't about you. It's about your Rasoren."

Obsidian stiffened and bowed his head in shame.

What the hell was this all about?

Dray watched them calmly for a moment, then sighed. "Obsidian. I know what it is to fear love."

"I've tried to be the partner Anna needs. To be a Rasoren to make you proud, my Lord. But I have failed."

He didn't look up, his braids falling forward to partially

hide his face. But Anna didn't need to see his expression to feel his anguish.

"I love her too much. My desire distracts me, and if I continue like this, my resolve will weaken until I lose control." He drew in a ragged breath. "When that happens Anna won't have a choice. She'll love me because the link will force her too. I don't want our link to twist my love into something evil. That would destroy a part of my soul."

Obsidian's feeling might sound a touch dramatic, but knowing what the link had already tried, his fears weren't unfounded. Still, she'd never really been afraid of Obsidian, and strangely, she still wasn't, even after his confession.

They'd been in a lot of tight spots. They'd get through this one too. Anna just wasn't sure how yet.

"Speaking one's fears is always the start to overcoming them." Lord Dray's soft, soothing tones washed over Anna, and she saw Obsidian's wings relax ever so slightly. "Another way is to face them head-on."

Obsidian looked up at last.

"Yes, my Rasoren. There is a way to free yourself from this fear that threatens to cripple you. Throw down all your mental barriers and truly embrace your link. When a normal Rasoren and Kyrsu are first establishing their bond, they must become one mind for a short time. Considering the nature of your bond, that step is likely even more crucial. Allow Anna to experience your love and fear. I think you'll find she is strong enough to push back and stand her ground."

"I...I don't trust myself."

"That is easy enough to solve." Draydrak spread his arms wide. "You may have the pick of the masters or any of the other mentors to watch over you. If it is as you fear, and you cannot yet control the link, they will be able to stop you before things develop too far."

"I..." Obsidian cleared his throat and then stiffened his spine, drawing up to his full height. "I will do as you ask, but only if Anna is in agreement."

"I am." If this was what it took for Obsidian to regain his confidence, then she'd even risk him seeing what she desperately didn't want him to see.

"Very well. Make your selection this day. There is no point putting this off."

Anna thought Dray was finished with them, but his expression turned thoughtful. "Perhaps if I share my greatest fear, it will help to lessen yours?"

Anna somehow doubted that, but merely nodded her head. Beside her, Obsidian was doing his best to restore some of his composure.

Needing to do something for him, and not caring if Lord Dray thought it a weakness, Anna came to stand next to her partner and wrapped a wing around his larger form.

He shuddered and leaned into her.

"Shhh...I'm here. We'll find a solution to this newest complication."

"Oh, goddess, if we don't, I'll...I'll. We just can't let that happen."

"We won't. Lord Dray will help us."

The demigod, shifted his legs, seeking a more comfortable position. "The Avatars once shared with me an ancient prophecy. It tells of how the first female gargoyles will mark the coming of Death's Mate. Lillian is the first female gargoyle. You are the second."

Anna nodded. *Because, really, what else did you do when a demigod was telling stories?*

"While I can see the possible futures of all living creatures, that gift does not extend to my own future or my twin's. But now there is another being whose future I cannot see." He paused as if deep in thought, then gave himself a little shake and continued. "The Avatars' youngest child—her future I cannot see. That suggests it will be entwined with mine."

Anna knew about Lillian and Gregory's unborn child. But Lord Death's wording was strange. Youngest child. Not only child.

"Do the Avatars have more than one child?" Anna blurted out.

Lord Dray's one ear flicked forward, then he grinned again. "You caught that, did you? That is a story for another time."

Yeah. It probably was.

The Lord of the Underworld held all four of his hands clasped loosely against his abdomen. "I fear Lillian and Gregory's girl child is the mate the Divine Ones promised me."

"You don't sound too enthusiastic about that."

"Why should I be?" He shrugged. "I have been alone all of my existence. I am at peace with what I am. And after seeing what the Avatars have suffered for love, and what it did to my twin, do you blame me for wishing to avoid that?"

"No, I suppose not." Anna didn't know what he wanted to hear, but she did think she understood why he was sharing. He was telling them that they weren't alone in fearing love and what it could do to them.

Nice gesture, but Anna didn't think what was wrong with her, and now Obsidian, could be healed with a story.

"But not all love is painful. For many, it is a glorious thing."

Yeah. But it wasn't for everyone.

"At least you don't have to worry about the Avatars' child for a few years yet. She hasn't even been born yet."

Dray just flashed his teeth at her. "The outlook of a mortal. For me, the wait for her birth and then growth will be but a blink in time."

Anna compressed her lips, realizing something else. "You've said it yourself. You don't know your future. Or the girl's. With war looming, nothing is guaranteed."

"That is the truth." Dray agreed softly. "The future isn't set. There are always many, many possible futures. And in many of them, I see you and Obsidian overcoming your fears and sharing a love that rivals the Avatars."

And in others he must have seen us fail, destroyed by a love twisted into something of darkness, Anna thought, *or else he wouldn't have needed to warn us of the danger.*

CHAPTER THIRTY-FOUR

Anna and Obsidian sat across from each other in the center of the sand ring. She tried to ignore all the places where sand was infiltrating as she listened to Rook's deep voice.

"The first step to deepening your link is to lower your mental shields and let each other fully into your minds." He paused, giving them a moment to begin. When nothing happened, he continued in a soothing voice—the first she'd ever heard him use.

Who would have thought Rook had a gentler side?

"Obsidian, you worry that your mind will take command of Anna's, that what might be a benefit in battle, could also cause trouble in your day-to-day life." Rook patted the younger gargoyle on the shoulder. "But you forget, Anna is equally as strong in both mind and soul. She simply must remember that and know when to fight and when to give. This is just another part of your training."

"That doesn't sound so terrible, as far as a magical link goes, does it?"

Obsidian snorted. *"Talk to me again when my emotions bleed over, and you find yourself suddenly and inexplicably seeing through my eyes and feeling what I feel."*

"Both of you, stop muttering in each other's heads and concentrate!"

Damn it. Sometimes she forgot Rook had the gift to see inside his student's minds.

She concentrated on her breathing, the deep sound of her pulse, the warmth of the sand. Of Obsidian's steady breath, his scent, the thrum of his strong heart.

"Now discard everything I taught you about building shields." Rook's voice came from different directions as he paced a circle around them. "That's it. No barriers. Reach for each other without fear."

Anna sighed out a long breath and then visualized surrendering the last shield blocking Obsidian from her mind.

The shield lowered.

She waited.

Nothing happened.

Her eyes popped open to stare at her partner. His head was bowed, eyes closed, but his mind was still locked up tight. But even then, he couldn't block their link entirely and a hint of fear, like a bitter fruit, flowed down it to her.

"It's okay to be scared," she whispered into his thoughts.

Obsidian still didn't respond.

Rook huffed. "Obsidian, you haven't been afraid of any part of your training. Why is this so different? You can trust Anna to protect herself. Have faith in her."

The tilt of Obsidian's ears and the firm press of his lips over his fangs looked a touch more belligerent than he had a moment before.

"We're a team." Anna reminded him softly. *"Have you forgotten that? We can survive anything if we work together. This is just the newest obstacle. We'll work through this, but you must come halfway. You can trust me."*

"I do trust you." At last he released his hold on the mental shields holding her, and the rest of the world, at bay.

Her power reacted faster than her brain, reaching for him. His strength, his essence, reached back. The two energies met in one swift rush. Then they were one mind for an endless moment. Distantly, they felt Anna's body sway closer to their male half as magical power built in a wave between them.

Then there was a shift in the balance and Obsidian's mind expanded to become her world. He was everywhere, he surrounded her mind, and she was home.

He loved her. The emotion was such a beautiful, incandescent radiance, she couldn't help but be in awe of it. His spirit drew her in and what he felt sharpened. Yes, his body hungered like any healthy young male's, but there was nothing of darkness about that. He did not want to force her. He just wanted her to return his feelings, to welcome him.

Regret that she couldn't be what he needed, because some other thoughtless prick had just taken what he wanted, lit a spark of anger in her soul.

But that was from the time before. It couldn't touch

what they shared now. Nothing could. That was the beautiful and seductive promise of the link.

His fears weren't unfounded. What he feared the most *was* possible if they didn't guard against it. She saw how easy their bond made it should he wish to seduce her. But she also saw that weakness ran in both directions. Should she ever wish to exert her will upon him, she could.

Like any relationship, for their bond to be healthy, they needed their minds and hearts in balance.

"Tell you what, I'll be strong when you are weak, and you'll be strong when I am weak. How's that for a start? Does that suit you?"

"Yes, my beautiful, fierce one."

Their minds slowly pulled away from each other and Anna sensed movement around her.

Slowly, she recognized voices. A warm body circled protectively around her. Her nose buried in his mane. Her arms and wings surrounded him. Protecting. Sheltering.

It was only then that she realized he was sobbing wordlessly into her neck.

"I didn't... I didn't enslave you."

"Of course you didn't." Anna stroked a hand along his back, under his wings. Hoping her touch conveyed her love, even if it wasn't the type of love he craved.

"But I wanted to. I wasn't sure if I could stop once I started."

"I'm sorry you had to go through that. But it's done... And I think it worked. Our bond feels like it did that day we raced down the mountainside." She looked to Rook for confirmation.

"Your link burns brighter than before. Lord Dray's plan

worked. You both should be ready for the next level of your training.”

Obsidian was slow to uncurl, and when he did, Rook patted his shoulder.

“How do you feel?” Anna asked.

“I am well.” He met her gaze, then glanced away into the distance. She wasn’t at all sure he was okay, though.

He was still shaking with reaction.

Something warm unfurled within her at his show of vulnerability. She’d never seen him like this. Even as a child, he’d rarely cried. Soon, he would pull his mental armor back in place and hide that part from her.

Before he could, Anna stood and wrapped her arms around him again, opening her mind and offering him shelter, comforting him as only his Kyrsu could. “We’ve got this.”

Obsidian shuddered against her. She could almost feel it as he drank up her love in deep, grateful gulps. Eventually, his wings stopped their quivering, and he reluctantly pulled away. Then, with a look of absolute tenderness on his face, he reached out and stroked a knuckle down her cheek.

“I do not deserve you.”

Anna’s heart gave a betraying little lurch at his words. She’d only wanted to provide him with comfort, and if she was truthful, take some in return. Though she feared she was foolishly trying to give him something else in return— her shriveled little heart.

But it was more than half dead. It was no fit gift to give. Anna needed to lighten the mood.

“No. You certainly didn’t deserve to get saddled with

me and my baggage. Wonder what god you pissed off in your last life?"

Obsidian snorted with humor. "I'll have to thank him."

"Come. You're exhausted. I think the mentors are going to give us the rest of the day off. Why don't we go round up something good to eat and indulge ourselves?"

Obsidian nodded in agreement and Anna was glad that the strange intimacy from the strengthening bond seemed to be fading a bit. She wasn't ready to deal with that level of intimacy all the time.

It was lucky, she supposed, that he'd been so focused on his own fears that he hadn't noticed her new, and very, unsisterly feelings toward him.

Later, she would examine them, catalog them, and then bury them somewhere deep inside the darkest corner of her soul where they'd wither and die. Only then could she guarantee this relationship wouldn't get fucked up like all her others.

She couldn't screw this up. She wasn't sure if she could survive without him. If he learned she wasn't as strong or fierce as he thought, he might turn from her. That would do more than destroy her bruised and battered heart. It would destroy her soul.

God. She sounded pathetic just thinking about it.

But the familiar self-loathing soon shifted to numbness. And with a little convincing, she was able to assume her tough as nails, badass bitch armor.

No one would know of the weakness deep inside.

CHAPTER THIRTY-FIVE

(The Present)

It took three days for Taryin to regain consciousness. Vaspara would have been fine if the blood witch had never recovered from creating her spell. But she had, and once again the captains had been called before the Battle Goddess.

Sorac stood at Vaspara's right shoulder; Bervicta at her left. Korsha and Ernya stood on the harpy's other side. All of them studied the blood witch while they awaited the arrival of their goddess.

They didn't have long to wait. The Lady of Battles arrived in a swirl of skirts and the rattle of chains.

"My witch, I am glad to see you're awake. The other captains reported that you were successful with your spell, though, they couldn't tell me its purpose."

"My Goddess, I think you will be pleased with my spell." Taryin bowed gracefully, fully recovered. Apparently, she'd healed from what the Mother's Sorceress had unleashed as well as from whatever toll her own dark magic's cost had exacted.

When she straightened from her bow, the witch drew herself to her full height. "My spell is one for spying. It's a magic even a gargoyle will not sense."

That was an ambitious statement. Gargoyles didn't miss much. They certainly would scent blood magic. Taryin must have enslaved some magic-rich creature or traded with an upper-level demon to complete her spell.

The witch smiled at Vaspara as if she knew the succubus' thoughts. Though it was more likely Taryin was just reading her expressions. Still, she tightened her mental barriers another notch.

"I summoned a djinn."

"You what?!" The Battle Goddess shouted, nearly deafening her captains.

"A djinn, my Goddess, is the only creature with magic that is similar enough to a gargoyle's to hide my blood magic from their sharp noses. But fear not, I captured this djinn and trapped him in a vessel made in the Mortal Realm. He cannot escape swiftly. And once you are freed from the duality curse, you can carry him to one of the planets in the Mortal Realm, and safely release him there or simply leave him to free himself. In the meantime, I can siphon some of his power from the storage vessel and use that to fuel more spells."

Beside Vaspara, the harpy made a strangled sound. She didn't blame Bervicta. A djinn. As far as she knew, there were less than ten left in all existence. Once there had been many more, but their numbers had dwindled over time as they were used in long ago wars, djinn pitted against djinn, forced to kill each other for the benefit of their temporary masters.

Temporary because a djinn always found a way to escape his or her prison eventually. And when they did, they always leveled their master's kingdom. Or the whole damn planet.

Some speculated it was not revenge, but just that opening a portal to the Spirit Realm and having an uncontrolled amount of power from that plain mix with that of the Magic Realm always resulted in an explosive event.

But the Avatars could travel between the realms and call spirit magic without blowing big holes in the universe. Didn't that suggest a djinn could do so as well? If they wished.

Likely they were just vengeful.

That was part of the reason no one was foolish enough to attempt to summon a djinn any longer. The other reason was that as each djinn died, their power was transferred to their brothers and sisters, making each remaining djinn stronger.

But that was a long-ago time even before the Battle Goddess had been chained to her temple.

Now, the few remaining djinns dwelled in the Spirit Realm, safely out of reach. Or so Vaspara had believed. Somehow the witch had risked the old magic and summoned one of them forth.

"Tell me more about your spell." Their goddess's chilling voice said she was still displeased that the blood witch had gone ahead with such a dangerous plan without consulting her.

"The spell I created must first be carried into the gargoyles' territory." Taryin paused as if thinking. "I'd suggest a trusted lieutenant, one skilled enough to hold his own against a gargoyle and capable of landing a grievous wound on his opponent."

The Battle Goddess made a humming sound and signaled the witch to continue.

"The moment the lieutenant dies, his death will trigger and feed the spell, so it is strong enough to invade the gargoyle who landed the death blow. The gargoyle will lose consciousness and turn to stone while the spell melds with his spirit. When he wakes, he'll just think it was a normal wound requiring their healing stone sleep."

"That sounds promising," the Lady of Battles admitted. "Go on."

"Once he wakes, he will become our spy and won't even realize it. The spell is also sentient. When it finds a hint of Anna or Shadowlight, it will begin influencing the host until it finds them, then it will transmit their exact location to me." Taryin paused, her expression calm as she waited to see if the Battle Goddess would find this spell worthy of the risk of summoning a djinn.

At last, the Lady of Battles shook back her hair and straightened. "Your contribution is enough that I shall not kill you for your unsanctioned actions. This time. If you ever again make such a decision without speaking to me first, you will not find me so forgiving."

"I would expect nothing less, my Lady." Taryin paused and bowed again. When she straightened, she met the demigoddess's eyes. "Once the spell reports their location, did you want an assassination or a rescue mission? The spell will be able to carry out an assassination. A rescue will take far more resources."

"We shall wait to see what your spell finds first, then I will decide."

"Very well my Lady."

"And give me the djinn," the Battle Goddess commanded. "I shall keep him in my temple where he's less likely to find a mind he can influence."

"Of course, my Goddess." The blood witch reached into her robe and withdrew a beautiful, jewel-encrusted drinking vessel. Its top was corked and sealed with wax and layer upon layer of spells.

Taryin carefully placed it in the Lady's outstretched hand.

Taking the vessel, the Battle Goddess folded her fingers over it and then brought it up to her breastplate where she carefully tucked it between her cleavage.

The vessel hadn't been any longer than Vaspara's arm.

Strange that something so small could hold a power great enough to level worlds.

CHAPTER THIRTY-SIX

Obsidian stomped beside Anna as they made their way along one of the bridges on their way to the main cliffside gathering.

"Why don't you just growl, snarl or beat the shit out of some poor training target? It might make you feel better." Anna said in a light tone.

"I'm fine! The healers are just coddling me. The wing joint is almost completely healed."

"Sure, it is. That's why we're walking then?"

He and another gargoyle had collided during one of their aerial combat sessions. This exercise had reminded her of a medieval melee in the sky. The other gargoyle—a novice—had been at fault. Knowing they were going to crash, Obsidian had turned in the air, taking the brunt of the impact when they'd hit the ground. It had been a chivalrous gesture to protect the youngling from getting crushed under his heavier mass.

"You're lucky you didn't break your wing joints. The healers are correct. You need another day to heal."

He huffed and muttered under his breath.

"Relax, Truth said the mentors agreed to partner us, so you can rest assured I'll be in good hands."

"I could take you out in a couple of days after I'm healed."

Anna snorted. "What, and have the dryads be all pissed that we didn't bring in enough of the octopus things?"

Another reason she wanted to go fishing was because the healers had plied him with copious amounts of magic to repair his wings and back, and now he was feeling amorous again. He couldn't help that side effect, but she didn't need to be around making it worse for him.

It wouldn't be an issue if she had her own place, but she was still rooming with Obsidian, since Rook had said they needed to be together at night, so their sleeping minds could use the link to process all they'd learned that day.

"Anna." He reached out and forced her to halt and face him. "Be safe. Don't take risks or allow yourself to get distracted. The ocean currents at the base of the cliff are dangerous."

"Yes, Mom!"

~

Obsidian could only watch as Anna, in the company of Truth and the rest of the hunting party, took off, launching themselves from the cliff with wild abandon.

If he hadn't been injured, it would have been him flying

wingtip to wingtip with his Kyrsu and then teaching her how to swim in the rough coastal waters.

During the Solstice Festival the gargoyles hunted for the dryads, bringing them their favorite delicacies. As such, he would typically be out hunting, but since he'd been injured, he'd expected to get grounded. He'd naively been looking forward to spending the afternoon with Anna, but she'd gone behind his back and talked with Truth, who'd gone to the mentors.

Why did it feel like the two people he loved most were working against him today?

Truth? Huh. He was probably trying to be helpful. But Anna? He wasn't blind.

Obsidian knew it was because he'd been subtly trying to court Anna ever since they'd linked minds and he'd discovered that they were both strong enough to love each other without enslaving each other.

The healers' magic would likely embolden him later, and his Kyrsu knew that and was in full panic mode. Outwardly, she was all business, almost aloof. Inwardly, she was running because she didn't want him to get close enough to learn whatever secret she was trying to keep buried. Though he doubted she even understood that yet herself.

Anna's acceptance and belief in him had allowed him to overcome his fears. Now it was his turn to fix what was broken in her.

Unfortunately, the damned healing magic had got his blood up. If he could trust their link not to flare and share something distracting with Anna, he'd have been tempted to return to his dwelling and deal with the issue.

But he couldn't do anything that might distract Anna while she was hunting.

Perhaps a long soak in the baths would help take his mind off his Kyrsu for a time.

Sometime later, in the seclusion of one of the smaller private bathing pools, Obsidian stripped and descended into the water, allowing the current to tug him in the direction of one of the carved sitting alcoves.

The water was too warm to help cool his blood. Narrowing his eyes, he called on his shadow magic and soon that chilling power helped to cool the water. Leaning back, he closed his eyes and sighed.

The bath might have been more enjoyable if Anna had been here with him, but it was still nice. And he was weary. His eyelids grew heavy as he drifted closer to sleep.

CHAPTER THIRTY-SEVEN

There had been any number of what the fuck moments in the last few months. But if Anna ever wrote up that long overdue report, fishing for alien octopus with a gargoyle and mermaid—fine, they called themselves sirens—was likely to raise a few eyebrows.

"For the record," Anna shouted to be heard over the thunder of the waves as they skimmed above the white peaks. "This kinda sucks."

Truth laughed. "It does, doesn't it?"

They had already made over two dozen such dives, and Anna was growing weary. It was hard work. The gargoyles flew along the cliffs, within a few feet of the water while the sirens located where on the cliff wall the octopus-like creature was holed up.

A siren could only sense where the creatures lived, she couldn't get close enough to the razor-sharp rocks to pluck the octopus off the cliff base. That's where the gargoyles came in.

Once a siren located their target prey, a gargoyle would dive in just seconds before a wave hit and use their talons to cling to the cliff face as the water began to recede. While they clung to the wall, they'd snatched up as many of the octopuses as they could and then climbed higher before flying to safety ahead of the next massive, bone-jarring wave.

Anna's first attempt hadn't been successful. She wasn't so foolish to do that again. She would likely sport the bruises tomorrow after being slammed against the cliff. Luck had been with her, though, since those first waves had been small.

If it had been a more significant wave, like the ones rolling in now, she might have gotten pulled out to sea by the riptide.

Gargoyles were surprisingly strong swimmers, able to use their wings something like a penguin. It had been fun at first, but now that the currents were getting stronger, it was just plain old work.

Thankfully they were almost done, Truth claiming the group had gathered enough to satisfy both dryads and sirens.

"We just need to do three more dives each." Truth said, echoing her thoughts. He sounded as weary as she felt.

"Thank God. If the elders and mentors wanted to fast-track the novices and journeymen's stamina training, just assign them this on a daily basis."

Truth snorted again. "The dryads would grow fat and the octopuses would swiftly become over-hunted."

Below them, a head and shoulders broke the surface as one of the sirens called out two more locations.

"I think they are more demanding than our mentors. Or a dryad mate, for that matter," Truth said after the siren had ducked back under. "It's lucky we're not cross-fertile with them. We'd be enslaved for sure."

Truth's humorous quip was pleasantly diverting, but Anna had another dive to time perfectly.

Studying the waves as they rolled toward the cliff, Anna picked out the biggest one—the one she'd ride to the cliff.

One...two...now. She tucked her wings and dove, arrowing into the wave. Her momentum carried her forward as she skimmed just below the surface, her wings stretched wide to stabilize her, and her tail acting as a rudder. The wave moved her toward the cliff.

Seconds before impact with the rocky cliff, she reared upright, her upper body coming out of the water a moment before the wave hit the cliff.

The weight of the wave against her back was brutal, but her gargoyle body was designed to absorb punishment.

Reaching blindly in the white surf, her talons found hand and foot holds just in time. A moment later, the wave receded, dropping away from the rocky cliff base.

Anna spotted one of the octopus-like creatures, a size-able ten-armed beast almost as big as her upper body.

She was reaching to grab it when her link to Obsidian flared wildly and then opened a strong connection between them. She was still clinging to a cliff wall, angry surf crashing some distance below, but she was also, impossibly, back on the island in one of the private pools, seeing and feeling what Obsidian felt.

Oh, my God!

He had a woman under him, his body draped over her,

dwarfing her smaller form in the cage of his arms. His jaws were locked around the back of her neck as his hips jerked against her.

"I've been busting my ass all day, and you're getting your rocks off? Get out of my head!"

"Anna?"

His reply came startled and strained. He was likely as surprised as her by the unexpected link.

She didn't care. *"Get out of my head before you kill me you jackass."*

The vision of the bathing pool faded.

Anna heard Truth shouting at her a second before another massive wave slammed her into the cliff with rib-cracking force. A few short seconds of the ocean's roar in her ears and then the white water was receding, taking her with it. She scrambled for handholds, anything she could use to prevent herself from being dragged deeper, but her talons only brushed against the slick surface a couple of times before the churning water spun her in a circle and the riptide snatched her up.

Maybe twenty feet from the cliff, the current slammed her against another pile of rock, likely fallen from the cliff above some time ago, her mind noted in the odd way it did when time slowed, and death danced nearer.

She was dragged along for a few feet more, then she smashed into a sharp projection of rock. Red agony bloomed along her back and right wing. The current bumped her against rock again, jarring precious air from her lungs.

Clamping her muzzle and pinching her nostrils tightly closed, she fought the blinding pain and the ocean's currents. But with her one wing out of commission, she couldn't glide through the water even if she broke free of the riptide in the narrow channel she found herself in.

"Anna," Obsidian screamed into her mind, *"shift to stone. You can't drown in that form. I'll be there momentarily and will drag you through a portal to safety."*

In her mind, she could see what he planned to do.

The thought of Obsidian using magic to pull her to his side—to the very pool he and the unknown female had been screwing each other's brains out in—sparked rage deep in her soul.

The hot emotion gave her strength, fueling her weary muscles and when the current slammed her into the next piece of cliff, she used her powerful thigh muscles to push off. Swimming for all she was worth, she broke free of the current. With each mighty kick, she drove herself closer to the surface.

Her wing was still a sharp agony as bone grated on bone, but she used that to further fuel her rage and to fight for the surface.

There was no way she was going to let Obsidian come play hero, not after he'd been the reason for the distraction in the first place.

Above her, the sunlight reflected off the surface, bright and beautiful, but at the edge of her vision gray was creeping in. She fought on, forcing her weary limbs to kick and thrash. Her lungs burned, a spasm seized them, and she choked on water.

She wasn't going to make it.

She had to make it.

The damned ocean wasn't going to be the death of her.

She still had the blood witch to kill and a score to settle with the Battle Goddess.

"Anna! Don't make me command you!" Obsidian was still in her head. The bastard. And he was moments away from taking the choice away from her.

"Fuck you, Obsidian." Her vision narrowing further, she struggled closer to the surface.

Then a pale green, long-fingered hand wrapped around her wrist. The grip was surprisingly firm. Then with a near-violent tug, she was rocketing toward the surface.

The siren arched out of the water, breaching like a whale.

Anna popped up more like a buoy in rough seas, bouncing and bobbing as she coughed and retched on the air, her lungs burning anew as they relearned how to process air. A dark shadow appeared directly over her head and then Truth was grasping her shoulders with his hind feet. The talons dug in hard enough to draw blood, but she was too cold and exhausted to feel much in the way of pain.

She was too heavy, or maybe it was the raging seas which caught at her wings and created too much drag for him to haul her out of the water, but he managed to keep her head above the ocean waves and the siren returned, grasping Anna's hands and helping Truth drag her dead weight to shore.

"Anna," Obsidian shouted into her mind. *"I'm bringing healers."*

"I'd hate to inconvenience you. Maybe just send the healer."

Her words reverberated down the link, and she felt Obsidian jerk like she'd slapped him. Good. The stupid jackass deserved to feel a little guilt and remorse for almost killing his own damned Kyrsu while he was screwing the brains out of some female.

"There was no female."

"You don't need to lie. I saw. Now shut up and just get one of the damn healers here. My wing is killing me."

By the time Truth and the siren had her nearly to shore, Anna could already sense the gathering of shadow magic along the beach. There was something else mixed in with it. The chill of spirit magic. Sand blew in all directions as the power swirled and trailed up higher into the air.

Lances of silvery-blue magic sparkled between the dark shards of shadow. A disc-shaped portal opened a window between two locations.

Obsidian bolted through before it was fully formed. Seconds later, two healers raced after him.

The three newcomers ran into the surf and grabbed Anna from Truth and the siren.

"Give me a minute to thank them. They just saved my life."

"You can thank them later," Obsidian shouted as he hovered in front of her. "I've never been so frightened in my life."

"Yes, you have. So, get out of the way and let the healers do their thing."

Obsidian obeyed, for once. But he paced and snarled softly every time one of the healers poked too deeply and made her flinch.

"It's your fault, so stop growling at the poor healers."

"You think I don't know that?" His mind voice was full of anguish. *"I did not mean to fall asleep."*

"Fall asleep?"

"Yes." He blinked at her for a moment in understanding. *"It was a dream. You didn't know that?"*

"No."

"Ah." He paused, tilting his head and looking at her strangely. *"But didn't you recognize...?"*

She blinked up at him while the healers worked. Recognize what? It had all happened so fast. She tried to remember the vision. She hadn't seen the woman from the front, hadn't seen much at all. The strongest impressions were sensations of what he'd been doing, not who he'd been doing it with.

"I'd conjured you in my dreams."

A dream? Featuring her. Oh.

At that moment, Anna knew she'd been barking up the wrong tree.

"But it doesn't matter. It will never happen again." He pushed aside the healers, much to their annoyance, and wrapped her in his arms and wings.

There was something to be said for being held in big, strong arms after a harrowing experience.

It wasn't until he'd held her for a while that she realized the shivers racking her body weren't all hers. He was shuddering.

"Forgive me, Anna."

"Shh, it was an accident. There's nothing to forgive."

The healers poked and prodded at her more, ignoring the big gargoyle like he wasn't in their way. One healed muscles and joints while the other attended to scrapes and bruises and lacerations. The healers' warm magic was becoming familiar to her.

When they were finished, one of the healers gave her instructions. "If you return to human form for two days, when you shift back, your wing will be healed. But no flying for at least three days after that."

Anna nodded her understanding.

"Good. Shift now so we can aid you if need be."

But Obsidian shared power with her, and she was able to resume her human form without their aid.

The lack of wings felt strange. And her balance seemed off without a tail to act as a counterbalance. But she'd suffered worse.

The healers soon finished up and told her to sleep and then have a proper meal upon waking. With that, the healers packed up their supplies and headed back through the still-open portal.

As she watched, the gently spinning magic of the portal vanished like it had never been. With nothing else to do, she looked into Obsidian's eyes.

He was looking back at her with much the same shock and confusion she'd been feeling.

"Anna, we need to talk."

"I'm tired. Let's wait until tomorrow."

"No. We'll talk now. While I am sorry I distracted you enough for it to become a danger, there's more to it than that. When you thought I was with another female, it upset you a great deal."

"Please don't ask me to talk about it now." She bowed her head and then slowly sank to her knees.

"Anna?" Obsidian's voice softened, and then he knelt next to her and curled a wing around her shoulders. She felt safe and warm for the first time in hours.

"Do you love me?"

"I can't." Her voice quivered. She would have done anything to make it stop. "Even if I wanted to."

He breathed softly in her ear. "But you were hurt when you thought I was with another woman."

"No."

"My Kyrsu, that's a lie. I'm rather certain my fierce warrior woman is in love with me. But I must confess, I don't know why she hasn't just taken what I offer so freely."

"Because she can't." Anna glanced sidelong at him. "I'm too damaged. Unworthy."

"Why, by the Light, do you think you're unworthy?"

"Something happened years ago that made it so I can't love like that anymore."

Obsidian tilted his head, his dark eyes finding hers.

"If that was the case, and that part of you was indeed dead, then it wouldn't hurt to see me with another woman."

"I.." God. Why couldn't he just let it go?

"Because I love you."

"Oh god, Obsidian," Anna sobbed into her hands. "You are so easy to love. Even my dead, shriveled little heart foolishly wants to love you."

"Is that so terrible?"

"Yes, for you it is. I can't give you what you're seeking. I can't be your lover. Even my trust in you isn't enough to overcome and repair the damage done."

Her entire body shook, and she fought to keep herself from telling the rest.

"Anna, your pain can only mean that you do love me."

"But I can't love you, I can't. Not physically. It will destroy me. Shatter the last protections I have around my mind."

"That sounds far too dire, my Kyrsu. Share with me what happened to make you shun something as wonderful as love."

"No."

"Yes. Share your story with me, and I will take your pain. Please. I've only ever wanted you to be happy. You never were, but I didn't know how to fix that. Now I sense a way for you to find healing."

He held her and rocked her, and between that and the rhythmic sound of the waves, Anna found herself relaxing a small bit, and suddenly the story was flowing from her. The one she'd sworn she'd never tell another living soul.

But here it was falling from her lips.

"I've always picked the wrong guy. All through high school, I knew I wanted to follow in my father and brothers' footsteps and join the military. But I also wanted to have some fun before all that, so I tended to sneak out after curfew to hang out with the senior boys from my high school."

Anna sighed. "I would have gotten into a lot more trouble than I did if my best friend wasn't there to take me home after I'd partied a little too hard. Matt was always swooping in like a literal white knight."

Obsidian nuzzled her shoulder, and she stroked her fingers in his mane.

Calmer, she continued, "We grew up together. He's a lot like you, actually. Quiet, but noble. Fierce when he needed to be. At seventeen, I joined the military. Matt already knew he wanted to help people, but not in the same way. He wanted to study to become a nurse. Even though our career choices differed greatly and took up a lot of time, we grew closer."

"He sounds..." Obsidian paused. "Worthy enough to keep my Kyrsu company until I was born."

Anna smiled a touch. "Slowly, over several summer breaks and leaves, we became more than friends. I wasn't entirely surprised when he asked me to marry him. I said yes. We got engaged. If things had been different, I might have spent the rest of my life with him. We were young, only twenty-one, but my mother and father had been high school sweethearts, and they have a great marriage even though my father is away a lot. I figured Matt and I could do the same. Then everything changed one night when I went out to a bar with Resnick and the team to blow off some steam."

Anna looked out across the ocean and fell silent; she didn't want to go on. It would only make Obsidian pity her. And she damn well didn't want his pity

"I would never pity you. You're too strong. Besides, I've long suspected what caused your fear of relationships. Now you're going to continue so I'll know the name of the one I'll one day hunt down. Once I find him, I'll rip out his heart and bring it back to you."

Damn. He was serious.

Does that make me bloodthirsty for finding his offer sweet? Anna wondered.

She turned and rubbed her cheek against his shoulder. Telling him wasn't actually as hard as she thought it would be.

Taking a deep breath, she continued.

"I left my cell phone in the vehicle and went out to get it in case Matt texted me. He was sweet like that. Always keeping tabs, wanting to know how my day went. The good and the bad."

The ocean waves rolled in, hypnotic. Beside her, Obsidian was a substantial warm presence. His quietness was what allowed her to go on.

"I was on my way back to the bar when a guy came out of the bushes and tried to grab me. I could tell right away he was a civilian. I was in the process of handing him his own ass when I got hit on the head with something. A tire iron or a bit of pipe, maybe. Hadn't realized the jackass had a friend with him. Blacked out for a bit. Too long and not long enough if you know what I mean."

She swallowed around the lump in her throat and strived to remain detached. "Came to as the one jackass was just finishing. He put a sweaty hand over my mouth and nose before I could make a sound. When they were about to switch places, I rammed him in the face with my skull. Broke the fucker's face. Would have broken something else but Resnick had come looking and spotted my phone on the ground and knew something was wrong. The two guys ran off when Resnick came closer."

Obsidian growled more viciously than she'd ever heard. "I will kill them for you."

"That's not how justice works back home." But if she ever ran across those two again, they wouldn't survive to see the inside of a prison.

"We will take their balls, at the very least."

Anna gave him a brittle smile. "Tempting."

"If you won't let me kill them, will you let me hunt these males down and terrify them?"

"Won't do any good. Light was bad. Only saw the one guy's face in silhouette. Never got a good look at the other one."

"Their scent memory will be enough for me to shape a spell from shadow magic to find them."

"Humans don't have a sense of smell like a gargoyle. I was full human back then."

After a moment her brittle smile faltered. "As horrible as it was to live through, I would have put it behind me eventually. I knew the physical damage would heal, and even the humiliation of getting bested by a couple of untrained civilians would fade in time."

She drew patterns in the damp sand, her index finger creating lines to represent the waves. "Resnick handled a lot of stuff for me, and afterward, I was released on medical leave. All I wanted was to go home and forget. Maybe wrap myself up in my gentle fiancé's love. But when I came home, I discovered he was having an affair. Now that I look back, I can't believe I didn't see it."

Obsidian growled anew. "Another human I shall kill when I return to the Mortal Realm."

"You will not kill my ex-fiancé."

"Fine. What about the woman he cheated on you with?"

"There was no woman."

It took him a moment to change mental gears, but gargoyles and dryads seemed more open and accepting of same-sex pairings. "Your fiancé was a lover of men?"

She nodded.

"Matt begged me to stay and listen, claiming he loved me, always had and was just trying to make it work." She gave a bitter snort, then explained something Obsidian likely hadn't gleaned from his short time on Earth. "Matt's from a very traditional Italian family. Catholic."

Anna took the time to explain what that meant.

"He was too afraid to come out of the closet with his family, and his religion still called love between same-sex couples a perversion."

"I see." Obsidian still sounded like he wanted to eat someone. "This male, this Matt, he really did love you, just not how you'd thought."

"Yeah. Should have seen it though. He was never the instigator in bed, but he was the best friend and partner I could ever want in other areas. Attentive, sweet, humorous. Hell, he was even a great cook. And he didn't hide the fact he wanted kids. I guess he thought marriage to his best friend wasn't a terrible life choice considering his religious background and his family's expectations."

"So, you and he are still friends?"

"No. I was in shock and hurting. Not capable of rational thought at the time. I screamed at him and the other dude for like three minutes straight and then grabbed my shit and went to my parent's place."

She cleared her throat. "My family doesn't know about the rape. I swore Resnick to silence. I didn't want my father or brothers to look at me differently. My mom can't keep a secret to save her life. As far as they know, I just came home to surprise my fiancé and then found him with another man. That explained the rage and the tears I couldn't hide from my mom."

"I would take this hurt from your heart if I could." Obsidian nuzzled her again.

"I know." She pressed her cheek against his shoulder. "It's been three years. I've forgiven Matt, mostly. The other trauma only visits me in nightmares or when something triggers a memory, but I can bury that shit deep and function in daily life. I just can't get intimate with someone. I've tried a few times. All the dread just comes rushing back. I figured if I couldn't have love, I'd have my career. Screw anyone who thought they could tear me down."

She'd whitewashed the gory details and the worst of the emotional trauma. That was something Obsidian didn't need to know.

"I will never hurt you like that." His breath stirred her braids.

"I know. But I still can't..."

"Shh...I'm done pressuring you. My beloved Kyrsu, you can love me like a brother, and I will be content." He nuzzled her cheek again. "But I'll also be faithful."

Deep down, that's what she'd wanted, wasn't it? For him to be as asexual as she'd become. For him to be 'safe' for her to love. Yet now that she knew how deeply he loved her, she felt guilty for being so selfish.

He was silent for a time, then huffed out a sad sounding whine. "I've reawakened all these old memories, haven't I? Forgive me for that."

"You're not at fault. Life just has a way of sucking."

Obsidian gently rocked her in his arms. "I will become Shadowlight for you again."

"Shadowlight is gone. We can't go back to that uncomplicated relationship, but I'd love for Obsidian to become my rock."

Silently she mourned what they could have had if her life had been different.

"Of course. And in the future, I won't fall asleep under the influence of healing magic."

Anna snorted. "Well, maybe not while I'm out doing dangerous work. Getting caught up in your sexy-time dreams is a bit of a distraction."

He coughed, and she felt his embarrassment flow down their link. "I'm normally better at shielding my thoughts and emotions from you."

"You're not nearly as good as you think." A grin tugged at her lips, surprising her.

"I'm not?" He asked slowly.

"Well, that was the first vision I caught. Normally it's just emotions and a few heated thoughts when you're..." She made a jerking motion with one hand.

"Goddess." He cleared his throat nervously a second time. "I wasn't aware."

"I wasn't about to draw your attention to the issue during those times."

The big gargoyle looked like he wanted to disappear into the sand beneath his feet. She'd never seen Obsidian squirm before. Her grin bloomed full force.

"Don't worry. I never felt threatened by you during those times."

"I am glad."

It had actually been the opposite. Feeling Obsidian's desire, knowing what he was doing had been sexy. Not that she'd admit that to him.

Anna felt more lighthearted than she had in weeks.

But she was also exhausted, the healing magic lulling her toward sleep. "Do you mind if we stay here a while? I need a nap."

"I'll be here when you wake."

She curled into him and closed her eyes. Sleep was just reaching up to claim her when she heard his final whispered words.

"Sleep well, my love."

CHAPTER THIRTY-EIGHT

Obsidian took in Anna's peaceful expression and just enjoyed the rare moment when her guard was down. She'd finally trusted him enough to share her painful secret. Perhaps now healing would flow into her soul and wash away her darkest memories.

And maybe she'd even heal enough to love him. He'd be patient, offering whatever support she might accept and then one day perhaps she'd be able to love him like he did her. It would not come soon, he knew, but gargoyles were very long-lived. Patience was an innate trait they all shared.

"My young Rasoren," came the softly familiar voice of Lord Draydrak. *"Normally, I would praise the path you've chosen to help heal your Kyrsu. However, I have dire news."*

Magic arced up from the ground, twisting and spinning, stirring air and sand into a violent storm between Obsidian's position on the beach and where the ocean rolled in. He raised a shield of shadow magic around himself, preventing Anna from getting pelted with damp sand.

The magic storm lasted only moments, then it swiftly pulled in upon itself as a viewing mirror appeared. Lord Draydrak was already waiting on the other side. When the shimmering magic calmed, the demigod set his piercing gaze upon Obsidian.

"I promised Anna a year to decide whether she truly wished to aid you in leading my Legion, but my sister will not grant us that time. She's grown desperate enough to resurrect the old ways and summon a djinn from the Spirit Realm."

Obsidian sucked in a surprised breath. His studies had covered the history of the djinn, and he was aware of their destructive power. "Merciful Mother."

"Indeed. You might be well served to pray to my divine parents for guidance. I did the moment all the future paths shifted in subtle ways. What was clear just days ago has now been cast in doubt by the new futures born from the djinn's arrival."

"This is not good."

"No. Unfortunately, you can do nothing about the djinn in my sister's keeping at this time, but you will face him one day soon. And if you wish to survive a creature that even my sister and I would treat with extreme caution, then you and your Kyrsu must seal the bond between you and safeguard yourselves. This is the only way."

A chill swept through Obsidian's soul. He knew what the demigod was asking. "Anna isn't ready."

"We are all running out of time and must adapt our plans or see them fail."

"I do not disagree with you and would seal the bond

with Anna in a heartbeat if I only knew how. You said it would take time. And yet we no longer have that time."

Lord Death nodded. "Yes, the ideal way to seal your bond is slowly, over time as your two minds become more accustomed to working together. An unshakable unity would have grown out of that naturally. But it is not the only way to solidify your link. A bond forged by shared trauma can be just as strong and formed much quicker due to necessity."

Obsidian's blood rushed in his ears. Was the demigod really asking...

"Yes. I am asking that. Asking that you take Anna's worst memories and relive them yourself. You must become a cohesive unit. And that can't happen until Anna stops shielding her innermost mind from you. Only if you see and endure what she went through and then show her you will not turn away from her, will she be able to let you into her mind fully."

Dray might be correct, but there was one problem. "Anna will never agree to this."

"That is irrelevant. One thing my long existence has taught me is that sometimes we must do what we find distasteful for the greater good." Lord Death gestured to the world around them. "Sacrifice is a part of life. You must see her memories. Live them. Only then will she no longer have reason to guard her mind against you, to hide the pain and shame, because you will have experienced it and will know the fear. Then together, with the bond whole and strong, you will both start to heal.

But Lord Draydrak's plan left out one crucial detail.

"I won't do it. I'm not a monster. I won't betray Anna.

Our bond won't be formed on such a breach of trust. She's been raped once. I won't mind-rape my Kyrsu just to seal some link on the off chance we'll fight marginally better on the battlefield."

Lord Draydrak watched him silently. Though, he didn't appear upset.

Was this another test?

Had he passed?

Failed?

"No, Obsidian. You are no monster." Dray's voice sounded resigned. "But I am when the need arises."

The Lord of the Underworld clambered to his hooves, his hands going to the hilts of his four swords. They cleared their scabbards with reverberating tones. The lingering chime might have been beautiful if it had been anything other than Lord Death preparing to strike Obsidian down.

He was no match for Death, he knew it, but still, he raised his shields, layering more and more power into them.

Magic erupted along the lengths of Draydrak's blades. It raced from their deadly edges, crossed the space between them, and merged with the magic of the viewing mirror. The added power made the mirror's image distort and shiver, but the spell held together.

Moments later, the streams of magic darted from the mirror and collided with Obsidian's barriers.

But as he'd feared, his magic was no match for Death's strength.

Power rippled along the shield, tendrils reaching in to brush against Anna's skin. More energy flowed under his own and his back stiffened at the strange sensation of it burrowing deep. It found a vein and followed that deeper, the magic racing through his blood.

It eventually reached his heart but didn't command that muscle to stop.

Obsidian breathed, watching as Anna's chest continued to rise and fall with life.

Lord Dray didn't want them dead then.

Nor did he want them to move, either.

Even wiggling a talon was impossible.

Death's magic continued to flow through his bloodstream. His mind—he realized that was its destination.

Still staring down at Anna, he watched as magic continued to crawl across her body.

He could sense its path, mirroring what was flowing through his own body. Which was how he knew the exact moment it touched her mind because it affected his as well.

Anna's eyes flew open, and she gasped, but she wasn't awake, not truly.

She was trapped in her own mind as Death hunted for the memories he wanted. After a short time, which was still far too long, Anna's eyes closed, and she sighed, drifting back into a natural sleep.

But Death's magic wasn't finished yet.

It rose up out of her body, hovering above her skin a moment before racing along her body and forming tendrils that burrowed into his. Again, he felt the power speeding through his blood, to his heart, and then onward to his brain.

There it flicked and probed and whirled until the power began to slowly recede.

What? That was all? He'd expected Anna's stolen memories to overwhelm him immediately. But nothing happened.

He glanced down at Anna, drawing her sleeping body closer. That's when he realized he could move again.

"You have until the day after tomorrow before the spell sealing away her cloned memories fades and unleashes them to merge with your mind. When that happens, you won't be able to hide it from her, and she'll know what I've done."

Obsidian just sat there, panting as adrenaline, fear, and rage coursed through his body. He'd never felt so betrayed in his life.

"Make sure you are far away from others on that day. You'll be trapped in the memories until they play themselves out. Your magic will react to protect you from danger, but there will be no foe for it to strike."

Slowly, Dray's words sank in, though he still seethed inside.

"I understand." The words were harsh and bitten out.

"I know you are angry at me now, but it will fade as you come to understand that what I've set in motion is a good thing for your relationship with Anna." Dray laughed then. "And you might just live long enough to work out the last of your issues now that you have a chance against the djinn."

Lord Dray turned and started away, the viewing mirror's image fading. But he paused and glanced over his shoulder.

"There's another benefit for doing things my way. Now

your Kyrsu's anger will be firmly on me. She'll see you as a victim."

Obsidian's anger ebbed slightly. "You still should have told her about the djinn. She's a soldier. She would have accepted that this needed to be done now that the danger to Earth and the Magic Realm is that much greater than it was before."

"Yes, she would. And ever after she would blame herself for you having to endure her memories. This way she'll be too angry at me to blame herself or you."

Long after Lord Draydrak and the viewing mirror had vanished, Obsidian sat with his sleeping Kyrsu in his lap and stared out at the crashing waves. A storm was brewing on the horizon, dark clouds gathering to deliver damaging winds and rains to the mainland.

He couldn't help but think it was a metaphor for his own future as well.

CHAPTER THIRTY-NINE

(The Present)

Lieutenant Ridaner reflected on how his life was to end as he took one last look out over the ocean as he was led from the beach, deeper into Death's kingdom. He'd always imagined he'd die honorably in battle. Perhaps even falling to protect his beloved captain.

As Fate would have it, he wouldn't be sacrificing his life for Vaspara's. That was perhaps too much to ask. If he could not die protecting his superior, he could at least fulfill this, his last, mission.

The captains had all put out a call to the soldiers under their command, asking for volunteers. He did not know about the other captains, but Vaspara had laid out the brutal truth. This was a death mission. And while she didn't want to lose any of her soldiers, this mission's success was pivotal to all future victories.

He was not the greatest soldier under her command, but he was in the top thirty, which made him the perfect candidate. He wasn't the only volunteer either. Many others had asked for the honor.

Once a pool of candidates had been gathered from across all twelve companies, they were told the details of the mission that would take them into gargoyle territory. Nothing was left out, right down to the part where the volunteer's soul would fuel the blood witch's spell.

Again, the captains called for volunteers to reassert their willingness.

Far fewer had stepped forward that second time.

The Lady of Battles had then ordered the remaining volunteers to take their conviction with them to the practice fields, and there a winner would be decided.

Lieutenant Ridaner had won against all the challengers as he'd expected.

After all, long, long ago, Vaspara had once saved his soul from being devoured by a demon. He was indebted to her. And he always repaid a debt.

This one just had a very high cost.

Though he hadn't uttered a word as the blood witch called her terrible spell to inhabit his body, if Vaspara hadn't been standing, looking on, there might have been screaming.

But she was there, staying with him for the entirety of the ritual.

Afterward, he'd been weak, too weak to stand on his own, but Vaspara and Sorac had pulled him to his feet. The firedrake had then muttered in his ear about the foolishness of blind love and devotion.

There was wisdom in the firedrake's words, he decided.

His recovery had taken three days and then another nine to reach this location.

He could have carried out his mission by fighting the first gargoyle he'd come across and then transferring the hidden spell, but Vaspara had said it would be better if he could catch one of the Masters in the spell instead of a foot soldier.

The spell would have a greater chance of finding Anna and Shadowlight that way.

With that in mind, he'd allowed himself to be taken alive and escorted here to this island stronghold of the enemy. He was kept under guard the entire time, even after being put in the dungeon.

Several gargoyles came to interrogate him, but none of them were Masters.

That's when he'd begun suspecting they were off elsewhere. Studying the Battle Goddess's hybrids, perhaps?

A half a day passed.

He'd given up on the idea of infecting one of the Elders. The longer he waited, the greater the chance one of the gargoyles would sense the spell, even protected as it was with a djinn's magic.

Now he'd just settle for any gargoyle entering his cell alone.

Outside his cell door magic flared as the ward spells were deactivated.

Ridaner held his breath as he waited. He'd only heard three sets of footsteps approach.

New voices addressed the guards.

Then the door was shoved inward, and a hulking gargoyle entered, followed by two slightly smaller beasts. The biggest one glowered directly at him.

"Well, you don't look like much," the male said with a huff, but his eyes narrowed. "Which means you're actually either very dangerous or a deserter. My bet is on dangerous. Shall we start digging and see what traps we find?"

The darkly sentient spell inside Ridaner stirred awake, sensing danger to itself and its mission. It studied its surroundings with an attentive eye.

The gargoyles kept shadow magic shields tightly around them. Under normal circumstances they'd be nearly untouchable, their magic able to absorb or repel greater quantities of magic, depending on what they wished. He'd once seen a gargoyle absorb a magical attack and then launch it back at his opponent.

This time a djinn's magic would alter that outcome.

The gargoyles stepped nearer, calling on more of their shadow magic.

The sentient spell watched, waiting until they were closer.

From his position chained to a wall, Ridaner was only an observer. But between heartbeats the magic attacked, red and silver energy arced out of his body, ripping his chest open in sudden agonizing surprise as it rushed to escape.

Screaming in pain, his vision danced strangely. Then his legs gave out, and he half slumped to the floor, only held upright by the chains. A raw, tainted power drew all the heat from his body. Pain bled away with it.

He was left to watch with his fading vision as the power continued to lance outward, stabbing each of the gargoyles, even rushing out into the hall to attack the guards.

The magic pierced their shadowy defenses. Loud snarls followed.

With a mind that was growing fuzzy, he still saw the strategy in the spell's attack. It wished to appear random, like an attack designed to maim or kill as many as possible, not turn one gargoyle into a spy.

But the gargoyles were far from defeated.

A moment later they launched their own devastating attacks. A wave of force unlike anything he'd experienced in his life struck his dying body. The power invaded every cell, then a blink later burned them away to ash.

His body might be gone, yet his spirit remained, watching helplessly as the blood witch's spell shredded his soul for the energy it needed to inhabit another.

At first, he wasn't even sure which gargoyle the spell had chosen. Then he spotted the fading tether that linked his soul to the dark weaving. But that leash was weakening, fading away, having already taken what it needed from him.

Numb and hollowed out, he watched as the tether vanished, taking with it the only clue as to which gargoyle now was home to the witch's spell.

But he had fulfilled his mission.

Though, he no longer remembered what that was.

More gargoyles rushed into the dungeon, and not even their magic-enhanced sight could see what remained of his fading spirit.

He drifted for a time, watching as his form started to break apart.

Into the silence, a deep and soothing voice reached the shredded remains of his disembodied spirit. *"Poor battered soul. Come, and I shall heal you of whatever that infernal blood witch has done this day."*

"Who?" the spirit asked.

"I have been called by many names. You will know me as Draydrak, the Lord of the Underworld. Though, you may call me Dray."

Dray?

In life, he'd known Death would come for him one day—it was inescapable, even for a being who didn't age.

But this was nothing like how he'd thought it would go. Was it?

"Do you know why you're here?" the god of death asked.

"I...remember...little." That was true. And strange.

A soul was supposed to remember everything from their last life. And yet there were great voids in his memory.

"I suppose that's to be expected after what you've endured feeding that attack, but it's still unfortunate, since I haven't been able to see your future since the djinn's magic touched you." Lord Death sighed. *"Come. Once I restore you, perhaps then you can tell me what mischief my sister and her pet blood witch hoped to accomplish by sending you deep into my territory."*

All his life, Ridaner had fought on the opposite side from this demigod.

Now it seemed strange to be seeking his aid.

Yet he was tired, and Dray's power was like a welcome drink after days in a desert.

When the demigod called a second time, the wispy remains of a savaged soul followed him into the Light.

CHAPTER FORTY

The sun was already at its highest point in the sky when Anna woke the next day feeling more muzzy-headed than usual from the healers' magic. As her wits sharpened, she'd thought she'd feel awkward around Obsidian. But that was not the case. If anything, she felt lighter as if finally sharing her terrible secrets lessened the dread.

Oh, the memories were fresher than they'd been in months, but the emotional pain wasn't as severe. There was more anger than shame now. Perhaps one day she'd forgive herself for letting a couple of civilians get the better of her.

And Matt?

Looking back, she now knew Matt's hold on her heart paled in comparison to what she and Obsidian shared. And she and her gargoyle partner weren't even a couple.

At first, she'd been afraid Obsidian would act strangely around her, either pitying her or showing some new protectiveness, as if she was weaker now than she'd been just the day before.

But he didn't.

Instead, he greeted her with the usual gargoyle nuzzles. Then offered to fly her back to Haven since she was stuck in human form for another day while her gargoyle body healed. Or whatever the heck the magic did that allowed her to shift back and have a fully healed wing.

When they reached the island, Truth sought them out and told them that several of the Adept-level mentors had returned from the future and were now asking for Obsidian and Anna.

"I take a nap, and all hell breaks loose," Anna grumbled.

Obsidian shrugged. "It was a rather long nap. And Lord Draydrak actually spoke to me on the beach."

"He what?" Anna pivoted and jammed a finger at his chest. "Why didn't you wake me?"

"You needed the rest."

"Not that much, you overprotective idiot." But she softened her voice to take the sting out of her words. "Start talking."

He did, telling how Lord Dray had sensed a new, unwelcome development in the time streams. The Battle Goddess had summoned a djinn—and now everyone was in a tizzy.

Apparently, real-life genies were way more badass than in the legends.

Great.

Like they didn't have enough evil henchmen to deal with.

When they reached the council chamber, situated high in its towering hamadryad, all the Masters and several of the oldest Adepts were present and loudly discussing this newest development. Discussing? Hell, it looked more like a shouting match.

Rook was the calmest, standing with his brawny arms folded over his chest, looking on with an expression of boredom. Verroc was the second calmest, although he was a little more animated than usual.

Thayn, the eldest of the gargoyles, was here as well. He just looked plain delighted.

When he spotted them, he came over and joined them.

"Haven't seen this much excitement in years. A djinn. Wonder if I know him?" The ancient gargoyle just grinned at them.

Anna arched a brow and wondered why the old geezer found that amusing. It was on the tip of her tongue when Rook came up to them.

"I'm more concerned about the purpose of that attack," Rook muttered.

"What attack?" Obsidian asked what Anna was thinking.

Master Thayn explained how a scout had found one of the Battle Goddess's minions and brought him in for questioning.

"She was testing some new djinn-based battle magic. It was powerful and cut through even a Master's shielding magic." The elder rubbed at his chest where Anna could see a small, healing wound. "First scar someone has landed on me in ages. The magic came close to killing three of the guards."

"We must find out more about this battle magic and create better defenses." There was a determined glint in Rook's eye. "I say we address this issue at once."

Thayn snorted. "Normally, I'd agree. However, the power is far from perfected. The poor bastard she used to deliver the attack was torn open when he triggered the spell. Killing him was a mercy. If we can remove the djinn from the Battle Goddess's keeping, we'll have deprived her of her new weapon."

"Fine, if you won't let me send agents to learn more about this power, give me Obsidian. The others will be discussing these newest events for the next three days," Rook pointed his complaint firmly at Thayn. "While they're doing that, Obsidian can take his Adept Trial."

"You think our young Rasoren is ready?" Thayn rubbed his thumb under his jaw as he studied Obsidian.

"Yes."

Thayn grinned. "Then why are you three still here? Go down to the practice fields and make ready. The Legion might be needing its war leaders sooner rather than later. I'll inform the rest of the council, and we'll be along after we've finished discussing the djinn development."

Rook bowed to the elder. "We'll go at once."

"You'll do well." Thayn clapped Obsidian on the shoulder. "Wait. I've got a present for you."

The elder held out a belt with a dagger sheathed in an ornate scabbard. Obsidian took it with a laugh, thanking Thayn for his generosity. Anna didn't get a good look at it until they were walking down the stairs and Obsidian held it out to Rook.

The design was familiar, one she'd admired a time or

two herself. The old geezer had struck again. Rook just stared at what Obsidian held out, uncomprehending.

"Weren't you wearing that when we walked into the council chambers?" Anna asked sweetly.

Strangely Rook looked utterly surprised for a moment as if Thayn didn't pull that trick every time he visited, but then the Master just snatched up the belt and weapon and looked forward again.

They were halfway down the stairs circling the giant hamadryad when Rook commanded them to meet him at the arena. A moment later he took to the air.

Once he was well out of sight, and hopefully too far away for his mind-reading ability to work, Anna glanced at Obsidian. "That was odd. Wonder what's chewing his ass?"

"Thayn, I'd say."

But Obsidian's gaze watched the spot where they'd last seen Rook.

CHAPTER FORTY-ONE

Anna stood at Obsidian's side as he took in the number of people gathering in the corridor. By the noise, there were hundreds more outside.

"You nervous?" Anna asked from her location at his shoulder.

"No."

Anna snorted.

He gazed down at her and grinned. "Eh, that was a lie, wasn't it?"

"Just a little one. Tiny, like no bigger than this." She stood on her tiptoes and spread her arms as wide as they would go.

Her lighthearted humor had the effect on Obsidian she'd hoped, and he sighed, his shoulders relaxing as his mind calmed.

Together they walked out of the underground tunnel and onto the sands of the arena's floor.

Unlike regular practice rings, this one was vast. Impressively so, with it being a good three or four times the size of the next largest ring. And there were bench-like seats on three sides, carved into the very stone of the mountain. She doubted the amphitheater was natural. It was too symmetrical. More likely magic had cut it out of the side of the mountain.

As large as it was, it still wasn't large enough for the entire island's population, but that didn't stop them from trying, as a couple thousand gargoyles and dryads packed themselves into the space.

Above, a few gargoyles circled lazily on thermals as they waited for the first bout to begin.

"Seems like everyone wants to see you kick ass or get your ass kicked." She grinned up at him since she was still in human form and he towered over her.

"Adept Trials are more exciting because they pit the student against multiple partners," Obsidian explained. "They start with the student facing his peers. All of them. Then if he or she defeats them, they go on to face the mentors one at a time. If they defeat all their mentors—which can happen but is rare—then the student goes on to face off against all the newly titled Adepts from the past year."

"Yeah, because that sounds fair," Anna muttered.

"The student only has to defeat three of the Adepts, and they will be elevated to that level."

"That doesn't sound so bad."

"But if the student is very skilled, he or she must keep fighting Adept after Adept until they lose."

Anna eyed him up and down. "You hate losing a fight. We're going to be here all day, aren't we?"

Obsidian grinned. "Yes. I plan to win as many battles as I can."

"Master Obsidian. Is that the title you're really after?"

He snorted. "No. But I won't turn it down."

"So modest."

"The only way I'd get named a master today is if I fight Rook and win. No one ever wins against Rook during a Trial, or so I'm told."

"How do you get named a master? Kill a dragon or something?"

Obsidian rolled his eyes at her.

Well, how was she supposed to know? She hadn't covered that crap in her studies yet.

"It's like an Adept Trial in that the student must face all their peers and then face the Masters. The student has to beat at least one of the older masters."

"Only one?"

"A gargoyle becomes more powerful with age."

Their conversation was cut short by the arrival of Master Thayn. He bore a large silver bowl in his hands.

"What's that?" Anna asked along their mental link.

"That is why it's called a Trial."

Obsidian took the offered bowl and then drank from it, draining the dark, spicy smelling mixture.

"That wasn't something harmless like wine, was it?"

"No. It's a potion only known to Lord Dray and the council members. It cripples a gargoyle's shadow magic for a day." Obsidian licked at his lips as if it tingled or burned but handed the bowl back to Master Thayn without so much as a flinch.

His thoughts touched hers one final time. *"This Trial is*

designed to teach a gargoyle that he can't always count on his magic, that sometimes you must learn to take down opponents more powerful than yourself. Don't be alarmed if our link starts to fade or feels like it disappears. It will return soon enough."

"So, the old geezer is stealing your magic this time. Why does that not surprise me."

The elder turned and grinned at Anna a second before his thoughts touched hers. *"I'll have to think up some other surprise for you if this doesn't offer enough to be entertaining."*

Heat crept up Anna's face.

Right. Oldest gargoyle. Gargoyles get more powerful with age. Check.

After that Obsidian didn't say anything more. Anna wasn't sure if it was because he was mentally preparing to face his first opponents or if the drink worked that fast. Three more minutes crept by and the sensations that always flowed along their link, even when they were shielding their minds, suddenly stopped.

A heartbeat after that, their link blinked out of existence, leaving a hollow feeling in Anna's mind.

She had to shove away the panicky little feeling its absence caused.

It hadn't occurred to her how much their link was a part of them. She just took it for granted. Gods, what if only one of them survived the coming war? What would it do to the other? No. She wouldn't think like that.

They either both survived or they died together.

She found that thought strangely comforting and was soon able to focus upon Obsidian and his test.

It took most of the afternoon, but he defeated all comers, first the novices, and then his fellow journeymen.

He'd been magnificent to watch, making the defeats look easy, but up close she could see the toll.

The air near the arena's floor had been cooled by the summoning of shadow magic by his opponents. Steam now curled up from his body even as sweat dripped into the sand under his feet. That alone told her while he'd made it look easy, it wasn't.

Finally, Thayn called for a break.

Anna found herself rushing forward to check over her Rasoren for injuries before the healers had even made it to his side.

He laughed and touched a drop of sweat that was making its way along her hairline from temple to ear.

"You look like you've been battling your own demons, my Kyrsu." His voice was rich with humor, but she still heard the weariness in it.

Until that moment, she hadn't realized how much willpower it had taken to stand in the sidelines and watch her partner get beat on by opponent after opponent.

"It's not funny." Anna grabbed a bucket of water right out of one of the healer's hands and offered it to Obsidian. She needed to do something, to feel useful or her berserker gargoyle nature was going to come out and play.

"How much longer?" It was simmering just below the surface as it was. It wouldn't take much more to send her over the edge.

He shrugged. "Not that much longer. I've faced all the novices and over half my peers. I just have group combat and then to face and beat three of the adepts."

Obsidian held up the ladle for her to drink from before

he'd take anymore. "You're on edge. I can scent that even without the use of my magic. You need to calm."

Fuck calm.

She'd need something a whole lot stronger than water to feel mellow while Obsidian was battling half the gargoyle nation.

But soon more dryad healers arrived and began sponging him with cold water to help cool him down. Anna joined them.

After he was sufficiently cool, more arrived with a light meal and leftover treats from yesterday's feast. Drinks that were stronger than water by the smell were making the rounds out in the amphitheater's seating area.

"Wonder if there will be any of that alien octopus to try."

"I don't smell it. So, it was likely devoured yesterday." Obsidian whispered in her ear. "Tomorrow, I'll make sure to hunt some up for you to try."

"Focus on your test, not my stomach. I'll be fine. You might not."

"Fear not. No one has ever died."

"Comforting."

They shared a quick lunch. Obsidian didn't eat anything substantial, sticking to fruits high in water and sugar and a few of the dryad version of granola bars.

After the meal, Thayn called Obsidian back into the ring.

Then between one heartbeat and the next, the most skilled of the journeymen were rushing toward her partner, five to one. Anna fisted her hands and kept quiet. This was just part of a test, but that didn't mean she had to like it.

The fight was brutal, but even then, there was something breathtaking about how Obsidian moved. His sword a bright streak of silver, a flash of light and then with the ring of blade on blade, sparks rained down upon the sand.

He didn't move so much as glide from place to place.

Actually, he was good enough he didn't need to move, but he chose to dance.

And his deadly dance was stunning.

Between one strike and the next, his present opponent's sword was on the ground. But the match wasn't over, and before the slight cloud of dust had settled, two more opponents raised their blades to his.

When he beat his first five opponents, five more came to take their place.

Anna's fingertips began to burn, and her shoulder blades ached in that familiar way that spoke succinctly of her gargoyle's wish to come out and hurt something.

When Obsidian defeated the last group, Thayn called for another break.

"No wonder you take years to practice for this shit. It's so y'all don't drop dead midway through the test." Anna set down her bucket and squeezed out the rag on his overheated skin. Only after he seemed cooler did she offer him something to drink.

All too soon, Thayn was calling over the noisy crowd, ordering Obsidian to face the first Adept in the ring. Anna followed along behind. His first opponent was Adept Shorban. Others were already waiting at the edge of the ring for their turn.

She prepared herself for another long fight with her own gargoyle nature.

Shorban was followed by one of the warrior-dryads, a woman by the name of Adept Karlaryn. Then another gargoyle called Firethorn.

Midway through the present fight, threads of warning began fingering their way up Anna's spine. Her gargoyle nature roused stronger and studied Firethorn. No. He wasn't the cause.

The threat was emanating from closer to her position than Obsidian's.

Scanning the press of gargoyle bodies crowding close to the ring, she stalked in the direction her magic tugged her.

There. Where Rook and Thayn were watching from the side of the ring. Just behind them, Reaver stood at the ready, a spear in his hand.

If she shifted now, it would alert Reaver that she was stalking him.

Remaining human, she made her way toward him.

Just then Rook stepped away from the others, his blade coming free of its scabbard.

Swinging her eyes back to Reaver, she froze.

He was gone.

Pulse pounding, her eyes darted around the outside of the ring, scanning the crowd.

There!

Snarling, she shifted to her gargoyle form and bounded across the sand toward her prey.

Too late. Reaver wasn't alone. Three other gargoyles stood with him, and they launched their spears at staggered intervals, targeting Obsidian.

She tossed up a shadow magic shield between him and the airborne spears. Two of the spears struck her barrier.

The other two clipped the top and sent them spinning. One hit the sand, but by some unimaginable bit of ill luck, she heard a grunt of pain followed by Obsidian's snarl.

Anna growled in answer and adjusted her trajectory, racing through the crowd.

She'd kill the others once her Rasoren was safe.

CHAPTER FORTY-TWO

*S*ilence smothered the ring as the crowd fell silent in shock. Anna ignored them as she powered forward, sending bodies flying in her wake. At her mental call, more shadow magic rose up from the sands.

The temperature in the arena plummeted. Steam rolled off the sand and Anna's own breath condensed in the air. Any gargoyle in her way was shoved aside by her savage power.

There was no pain or fear or weariness. No limit to her power. There was only rage that these lesser beings had endeavored to harm her Rasoren. And now! Now they were daring to cage her.

Nothing could stop her when her partner was weaving between consciousness and oblivion. He was losing too much blood. She could smell it. And after drinking that potion, he couldn't call his magic to heal the wound or shift to stone.

It drove her into a frenzy of rage.

When she reached her Rasoren's side, he was surrounded by several other gargoyles.

She snarled a warning. Wisely, they darted away to what they thought was a safe distance. There was no safe distance for them to run if they meant Obsidian harm.

When she sniffed at him, she swiftly determined those others hadn't intended harm. They had cut the spear from his side and packed the wound to stop the bleeding until one of the healers could reach him.

"Anna," his voice came weak as shudders coursed down his body. He lay on his side, wings curled around him. "I need your magic. I can't summon my own."

His words a command she wanted to obey. Every fiber in her being vibrated with the need to obey, to belong, to be claimed by her Rasoren. They'd both been foolishly resisting the soul-deep bond for different reasons.

"My Anna, all will be fine," he whispered as his body began to feed on her power, draining strength and healing from her flesh.

Of course it was going to be all right now. She was here. They were together. She would kill all threats until he was well enough to move.

"No, Anna."

"Why not?" Her voice sounded scratchy to her own ears like she'd damaged it with her snarls and growls.

"Come, lie next to me, my lovely Kyrsu. We'll shift to stone and sleep side by side until we're both healed."

"You're still in danger." But denying him was so very hard.

"Am I?"

His words confused her until she examined the minds closest to them.

The others feared her.

As they should.

Hmmm. But she detected no hostility toward Obsidian.

That was strange. There'd been a definite threat before, but now it was gone.

It had to be a trap or a trick. That was the only reason.

"It was an accident."

"No. What I felt and what they did to you was no accident."

"It was part of the test," he assured her. "After it was over, I heard Rook yelling at Reaver and the others about their terrible aim. They were supposed to cause a flesh wound at most. I think Rook did it because he wanted to see this side of you."

His words made sense when compared with what she felt in the others' minds. But there had been some threat. She'd felt it. Sighing she gave herself a little shake, her fear and adrenaline slowly melted away.

She would listen to her Rasoren but only so far.

Concentrating, she summoned more magic and formed it into a powerful weaving. A moment later a protective dome surrounded them. Safe now, she curled up next to him and nosed at his wound.

Removing the packing placed there to slow the bleeding, she started to lap at the wound. Even as the healing compound in her saliva started on the surface, her magic worked its way into his body, finding the deepest point of the puncture wound.

The spear had bitten deep, perforating his liver. She summoned another wave of magic and sent it deep.

He hissed in pain.

But healing him was helping her to calm, so she continued.

"It serves you right for drinking something that would cripple your ability to summon your magic. Don't do that ever again, you great dolt!"

"Don't think I will."

"Good. It was very foolish."

"How are you feeling?" He asked, already sounding stronger from her healing.

What a strange question for him to ask her.

"I'm fine. You're the one who got his ass kicked up and down the arena floor and then used your liver to catch a spear."

"You're back with me?"

"Back from where? You delirious? Where the hell did you think I'd be when you're hurt?"

He gestured above them.

Anna spotted a shimmering dome of power. It smelled of her magic, and she had a foggy recollection of creating it. Outside was chaos, the sky black with gargoyle wings.

Then she noticed the bodies littering the arena floor.

"Oh, god. I went berserker, didn't I?" She knew she had because, while she could remember the events, they were blurry and dull, like she'd witnessed them through a dirty window.

"It's not your fault."

"The fuck it's not."

"No. The blame can be firmly placed on Rook's shoulders. This was his idea. He has wanted to witness your berserker nature for quite some time. Goddess only knows why he chose now to do it, in front of so many and with everything that's been going on."

"What the bloody hell did he think would happen?"

"Something like this I'd imagine? But on a smaller scale maybe. I don't know." Obsidian sounded exhausted.

She snuggled closer to him and glanced around once more.

"Do you need a healer?" she asked just to be certain, but it looked like her magic had sealed his wound, and his other injuries were gone. "I didn't even know I could heal like that."

"I didn't either, but it's good one of us does. We tend to get into a lot of trouble." He gave his side a cautious poke. "I don't think a healer can do any more for me than you already have."

"Good."

"Now all I need is my Kyrsu." He yawned and wrapped an arm around her waist.

She glanced around. First at the dome and then everyone on the outside. The dome's magic was impressive and damn near impenetrable. No one would be getting past it anytime soon. Not unless she allowed it and right at this moment, she wasn't feeling very magnanimous. They could just sit out there on their collective asses until she and Obsidian were healed and rested.

Besides, it looked like most of the bodies on the ground were picking themselves up or being helped up by others.

She'd likely feel guilty later, but now all she felt was numb. Emotionally empty.

Briefly, she wondered if the emotional numbness of a berserker was a little like being a psychopath. That the thought didn't inspire fear probably should have scared her.

But she couldn't even feel fear.

Yawning, she curled closer to Obsidian and then with a silent command and a wave of power, she ordered both their bodies to shift to their stone forms to recover.

CHAPTER FORTY-THREE

Obsidian yawned and stretched, feeling a little tender where the spear had thrust deep, but his injuries were healed, and the drug the elders had given him had been purged from his body.

All in all, he felt good, physically.

Mentally? That was another matter altogether.

But there was only so much Anna and the healers could do. Restoring his peace of mind wasn't one of them.

He'd woken from his stone sleep before Anna and found that Thayn, with the aid of Lord Draydrak, had been able to undo the spell his Kyrsu had hastily raised to protect them while they healed.

The elder had brought them to the healer's quarters, where he remained.

Obsidian's body was on the mend, but his mind was restless, thoughts and theories about why Rook had sabotaged the test churned endlessly.

If the elder had merely wanted to test Anna's tolerance

to threats directed at her Rasoren, the elder could have set something up during regular practice. It wasn't necessary to do it in front of everyone or was that the point?

Did Rook want the entire gargoyle legion to see what he and Anna were capable of before it was unleashed on the battlefield? That still seemed a poor excuse for such a spectacular risk. Others had been harmed. Rook was lucky there hadn't been any deaths. Anna in berserker mode wasn't known for mercy.

Perhaps she'd managed to retain enough of 'Anna' to reason that the legion gargoyles weren't a threat.

As for Rook, he could have done a series of smaller demonstrations throughout their training sessions. But the elder hadn't exercised caution. Now, in the blink of an eye, all Anna's hard work to gain the legion's trust had been undone. Could she ever regain their people's confidence, or would they judge her a threat?

A soft grunt drew his gaze down to Anna. His restless thoughts must have disturbed her sleep, for she'd still been stone up until a moment ago. The shimmer of magic even now danced along her skin, before being swallowed back.

Her eyes blinked open to stare at him.

Or at least she tried. Dawn's light angled in and struck her right in the eyes. Groaning, she rolled over onto her belly, shielding her face.

"Oh my god. What the fuck did I drink? Fuck, I don't care what it's called. Just don't let me drink it ever again."

"You're not drunk."

"Obviously. I'm all too sober now."

"It's a reaction from calling more magic than your body is trained to handle."

"Ugh. Remind me to go easy next time, will you?"

"I don't think you were in a receptive mood to listen to reason."

"Meh." She rested her face in her hands. "Stop talking. My head is going to explode."

"Stop whining and come here," he said with a grin.

When she didn't move, he sat cross-legged on the bench and then dragged her unresisting body closer to him until he could roll her over and position her head in his lap.

She groaned dramatically.

Calling a tiny bit of his shadow magic to the tips of his fingers, he gently worked them between the rows of her braids. He wasn't a natural healer like Anna or some of the dryads, but he'd learned this trick from Maradryn. The smallest trace of the tingling magic could sooth headaches.

"Oh, you're a god. Thank you." Anna's unguarded expression made him smile, but it wasn't likely to last. As soon as she remembered what she'd done, doubt and self-loathing would replace it.

Which was why he was in no hurry to have this rare peaceful moment end.

But eventually he'd rubbed away the worst of the pain, and her eyes opened and spotted the ceiling of the healers' quarters.

Her brows drew together in thought and then her earlier blissful expression became shuttered. She compressed her lips.

"I fucked up, didn't I?"

Following her progress along their link, he witnessed when she recalled all that had happened. Much of it would be blurry and hazy, but there was enough for her to piece together events.

"I flipped and hulked out on everyone when you were hurt, didn't I?"

He wasn't familiar with the term, but its meaning was clear enough in her mind. "Yes. Though, this wasn't your fault. You were just reacting to what you perceived as a danger to me."

Obsidian explained what he'd been theorizing about while she'd slept.

"So, you see, I think this was exactly what Rook wanted to happen—at least your going berserker part. Though I don't think he expected it to be quite so violent. At least I hope he didn't."

"Well, I for one am going to go ask him myself. Just as soon as I can stand up without the room spinning."

"Tomorrow will be soon enough for that," he said, and he gently brushed away some sand that was sticking to her temples.

If only his other worries were as easily brushed away.

CHAPTER FORTY-FOUR

The day after Obsidian's Adept Trial, Anna found herself high up on the slopes of the eastern peak picking berries with a group of novices and journeymen.

It was a mundane task, which was why the mentors had assigned it to her. Secretly, she was happy to do it because it got her away from most of the stares and whispers.

Reasonable, quiet, and unassuming had been her modus operandi since the morning she'd awoken in the healers' quarters with a splitting headache. Later she and Obsidian had confronted the elders.

Rook had admitted his plan had gone afoul. Thayn clarified by adding that when Anna had tossed up her first shield, it caused the spear—which was supposed to miss—to change its trajectory.

The spear was only supposed to have clipped him, causing a flesh wound.

They'd wanted something that would cause a threat

response in Anna, but nothing so dangerous to trigger a full berserker event.

Well, because Fate loved fucking with her, Rook and everyone else got to see the full package. Which was why she had been trying so hard to be quiet, unassuming, and mostly invisible today.

It didn't help that Obsidian had been sent off to a remote island for some traditional mumbo-jumbo where he was supposed to meditate on the duties that would now come with his new title of Adept.

While she was pleased that he'd completed the trial with flying colors and earned his title before everything had gone sideways, she preferred him near. Her gargoyle nature was still edgy. Since there were no reported dangers, it had to be the new fear and hostility some of the legion felt toward her after the berserker event.

She kept telling her gargoyle nature to sit down, shut up, and don't cause a stir. Obsidian didn't need his Kyrsu making any more of a ruckus.

Probably no one was buying her docile, good girl routine. Though, no one had organized a torch and pitchfork-carrying mob either, so she supposed she wasn't about to get lynched.

But that wasn't even her most significant concern.

The more she thought about it, the more she was sure Rook, that cagey bastard, had wanted her to go berserker for some reason other than to study her threat responses. But she didn't have proof. Sighing in frustration, she turned her attention back to her present task, for now.

Anna glowered unhappily at the berry bush she was presently picking bare of ripe fruit. Truth had laughed at her earlier when she popped a couple in her mouth and promptly spat them back out. He'd then informed her they were only used in cooking with honey to sweeten them. The jerk.

"By the way, how much longer do we have to do this?" Anna called to him where he was working on filling his basket farther up the slope.

He glanced in her direction, looking unhappier than picking a few hundred berries should merit.

Hmm...something was up.

"You." She glared at him. "What's that look about?"

Truth sighed and set down his woven basket. "We already have twice the berries we need. Obsidian wanted me to keep you busy today."

"Why?"

"I'm not sure. He wouldn't go into detail, only that he had a task to complete that required solitude."

"That's what he told me as well." Anna's fingers strummed her thigh. "I thought it was some traditional ritual after becoming an Adept."

"There is no tradition," Truth confirmed.

"Damn it! Why didn't I smell a lie?"

"He likely never told a lie, just didn't correct your false assumption."

"Fuck!" Anna abandoned her berry bushes and the baskets, half running up the slope toward a bare patch of rock where she had room to shift to gargoyle form.

She might be overreacting, but she couldn't ignore the fact the elders might be setting up a test of some sort to see if Obsidian was like her.

"Where are you going? Anna!" Truth called her name as he came running up behind her.

"I'm going after Obsidian. I don't know what the Masters have planned this time, but their last plan didn't go so well."

"What are you talking about?"

"I got my powers from Obsidian. I'm not the only berserker." She said in a rush. "As a child, Shadowlight had that trait, too. Milder, but I can only imagine the breath-taking scope of Obsidian's rage if they manage to trigger it, now, as an adult."

"That makes no sense. If it were the mentors, he would simply have told me that. Though I see why the elders might not want you there." Truth paused, and then said more softly. "It might not be the mentors."

"Who else?" But then Anna knew. Reaver and the other gargoyles who might have turned hostile toward her and her Rasoren.

Anna reached the flat stretch of rocky ground and shifted. Moments later her wings were unfurling as she launched herself off the steep slope and into the air. Truth continued to shout after her as she climbed higher into the air.

Rounding the mountain's peak, she spotted him beating his wings hard to catch up. She didn't wait for him and headed out to sea, using her link to Obsidian to pinpoint his location.

"Obsidian are you alright? Can you hear me?" No answering words or thoughts echoed back along their link.

He was about eighty miles out. Easy distance for their link, but he didn't respond, and she couldn't touch his mind. How was that possible? Even if he was stone, she could still feel his mind.

Fear sped her wings, and she swiftly out distanced Truth.

"I can't feel Obsidian. Can you?" she asked Truth along a private path.

"No. His mind is closed off to me." Concern tinted the gargoyle's thoughts. *"I don't like this."*

"I can't wait for you. Keep up as best you can."

"Go, go. I'm calling our friends. We'll meet you there as soon as possible."

"Thank you."

CHAPTER FORTY-FIVE

*B*elow, the ocean waves churned. They'd been growing larger the closer Anna got to Obsidian's distant little island. A high black wall of clouds billowed out across the sky from the same general area.

Unfortunately, she feared the storm wasn't natural, but fueled by uncontrolled magic. Obsidian's magic. The taste was heavy and familiar in the humid air. She didn't know what was being done to him, but her terror kept her wings beating at top speed even after fifty miles.

"Be at ease, young Kyrsu," Death's compelling voice was suddenly filling her head. *"While your Rasoren is experiencing something he finds greatly distressing, he is in no physical danger."*

His reassurance fell short of actually reassuring her. *"Why is he in distress?"*

"Because there is a djinn within the Magic Realm and you no longer have the time needed to seal your powerful bond slowly, over time, as I would have preferred. But there was a faster way

to see it molded into its potential. Obsidian is now undergoing the ordeal."

"*What is it? And was he willing?*"

Death sighed out a long, sad note in her mind. "*Your most traumatic memories. He's reliving them. When it's over, you'll have no reason to keep a shield up around your mind. Once it's done, he will understand as he never could have before, and you will be there to share in his pain and comfort him.*"

Her heart felt like it seized in her chest. Obsidian was never supposed to see those. Never. She shuddered and swooped lower. Realizing the danger, she beat her wings harder and arrowed back higher into the sky.

"*He was never supposed to see those. Why would he do this?*"

Why would he do this to me? I trusted him.

"*Your Rasoren can't do anything that he'd see as harming you. He's not physically capable. And he viewed what I asked him to do as a type of mind-rape. He's a noble soul. But we don't have time for noble. I forced him to take the memories.*"

So, Death had done this to Obsidian.

Her rising rage had a target at least.

"*Yes, I am the one who made a hard choice so neither of you would have to. Remember that before you decide to hate me forever.*" Draydrak's voice was filled with sadness. "*Go to your Rasoren. He needs you now. Remember what you felt after the trauma and how all you wanted was to be comforted by your beloved? Obsidian will shortly find himself in the same emotional hell, but unlike the first time, you will be there to comfort him. Out of this shared pain and self-forgiveness, your magic will forge an unparalleled soul bond. One strong enough to rival what the Avatars share, and they began as one soul.*"

Anna still seethed, but she would heed Draydrak's words. None of this was Obsidian's fault.

"I won't fail Obsidian."

"Good. Because your magical ability will increase tenfold and give you a fighting chance against a djinn of this one's strength."

"Go, Anna, rescue your Rasoren and forge a soul bond of a strength never seen before."

She did, winging her way closer with each heartbeat.

CHAPTER FORTY-SIX

Anna battled the storm as she circled the island in large loops, drawing closer with each revolution. Obsidian was down there somewhere. Her magic might not be able to separate him from the maelstrom created by his power, but her keen gargoyle sight served her well, scanning the land.

Ah, there.

He looked like nothing more than a tightly curled bit of darkness against the pale sand of the beach. But it was him.

Curling a wing, she changed direction and arrowed toward him.

The crosswinds and layers of wild magic buffeted her, tossing her around in the air. She overshot her planned landing site next to Obsidian and crashed into the surf at the edge of the beach instead.

Sand, wind, and rain pelted her in vicious waves. She

formed a translucent shield of magic to protect against the worst of it. Then dropping to all fours, she stalked across the beach, her talons digging in against the gale-force winds.

When she got closer to Obsidian's location, she saw why she'd overshot her target. He sat within a protective dome. The storm winds circled it like the eye of a hurricane.

Inside the air was calm, not even a little breeze to stir his mane.

She hoped this dome was the reason she couldn't touch his mind.

Though the way Obsidian was kneeling with his muzzle tucked against his chest, wings mantled around him, and rocking back and forth ever so slightly as magic continued to bleed off his skin didn't look good.

She shouted his name.

He didn't respond.

Or maybe it wasn't that he didn't respond. Perhaps he *couldn't*, his mind trapped inside the memories.

There was one ray of hope. His magic didn't consider her a threat, and she was able to touch the dome without harm. After a moment of gentle coercing, the magic of the dome-shield granted her entrance.

She went to him then and knelt without hesitation, placing a hand on his shoulders. His magic stirred in acknowledgment of her presence, licking and caressing along her skin in recognition, but it didn't attempt to drive her away or otherwise harm her.

Running her fingers along his spine, she moved them up under his thick mane until she could stroke the back of his neck. As a child, he'd always found that comforting. She hoped he still did.

While he couldn't respond, he might still be able to hear and feel.

"Oh, my brave Rasoren. I've failed to keep this horror from you. I'm sorrier than I can say but know I'm here with you. You're not alone." Her gargoyle nature stirred in response to his distress, her magic reaching out, seeking a way into his mind.

At first something within him resisted. Then the link flared strongly, sucking her deep into his thoughts, a passenger in his mind.

Freezing in surprised recognition, she looked around at the parking lot she found herself in. It was the dark of a November night, a familiar crispness in the air that promised winter's return. Light from the bar's neon sign reflected in the puddles.

Vicious ghosts from a dark point in her past were here as well, flowing around her, on the hunt.

Their voices, the tone of their laughter and excited grunts chillingly familiar. Their faces were clearer than they'd ever been before. The smell of fries, beer, and cigarette smoke strong.

But this time they were not hunting her.

She discovered a new horror as her link whispered that they were attacking her Rasoren. And in the nature of these past memories, he could not fight or change the outcome. He could only huddle on the alley's cold, wet pavement as he relived what had happened to her—a hapless passenger caught up in the memories.

Rage slowly built within her, replacing the horror and fear.

Seeing the vision-ghosts of her assailants no longer inspired dread. No. But it triggered something else—her berserker rage.

She welcomed it.

These lesser beings might once have harmed her, haunted her mind for months, but no more. They were weak. Easily torn to shreds with her talons.

The fools!

They thought to harm her Rasoren.

She struck out with her own magic, wrapping Obsidian's mind in layers of protection before she turned her attention to the vision-ghosts. Even as the rage urged her to act, her mind remained sharp. She continued with caution, very much aware this was no regular battlefield.

These were her memories transferred into her Rasoren's mind.

She wasn't really here. These weren't enemies she could just gut and claim victory over.

No. This would need a two-pronged attack.

First, she merged her mind with Obsidian's more firmly, feeding him her love and strength. Magic flaring, it expanded, surrounding him in a protective shield.

In the real-world, Obsidian moved closer, and Anna curled around him, drawing him into her warmth and vitality.

"We are not victims. Together we are far too strong for some wispy dark memories to do us harm." She came to kneel next to his shoulder and turned his face to look up at her. "Look upon the horror. Acknowledge what I once endured so there will be no more secrets between us. But then see me as I am now. Strong. Fierce. Whole. Know that I survived. I overcame that one dark night in my history. They did not tarnish my mind, my soul, or my sense of worth. I see that now. You showed me that."

"Anna?" He blinked up at her. Seeing her for the first time.

"Yes, that's it." Anna continued to caress his face.

"They were so strong. But I am stronger. How could I have not fought my way free?" He sounded lost and confused. In shock, most likely.

At that moment she hated the God of Death.

"In life, we sometimes meet opponents we cannot fight. But I will show you the way free of this nightmare."

"I understand."

"Good. Now follow your Kyrsu."

She went on the attack, her talons digging into the memories, shredding them as she summoned a second wave of magic. Beside her Obsidian came to his feet, shaking off whatever spell had held him immobile.

Together they destroyed all that remained of their tormentors.

When it was done, they started on the memory of the location, tearing it apart piece by piece.

Afterward, Anna and Obsidian reached for each other, burying their muzzles in the other's manes.

"Oh, my fierce, beautiful one," he whispered close to her ear, sadness thick in his voice. "I understand now."

"No, you don't, because you feel sadness. This moment is not about sadness." Her mind expanded more, sweeping him in, surrounding his consciousness until she was everything. And then she shared herself, her emotions, what they were to each other. What he meant to her.

In response, his mind and magic reached deep, mingling with hers until he was a part of her, their thoughts, emotions, memories, their very souls, joining to form a new wellspring of strength and power.

Now fully merged, their bond finally fulfilling its potential, their minds sought out every bit of fear, discomfort or scrap of loneliness and set about erasing it all with the warmth of their acceptance and love.

Their bond was a strong heartbeat in their minds. Immense strength flowed from it, feeding both their souls and their magic.

"I think this must be a little like what the Avatars feel," she said in soft wonder.

"Mmm," he agreed with a delighted mumble, almost a purr.

"I understand now what Death wanted us to experience. It wasn't the horror. It was this. Guess I won't hold it against him." Anna sighed and stretched. Though she was aware this present 'body' wasn't real. Her body was still sitting on a beach, inside a dome-shield with a hurricane raging outside.

Obsidian was still holding tight, but he lifted his head and looked around as if sensing the storm as well. "Ah. It's as Lord Dray said it would be."

"The storm?"

"He didn't say I'd call a hurricane to our shores, but he warned my power would slip my control."

"We need to deal with it before it destroys the island."

"Yes," he agreed.

They were both reluctant to let the other go, but at last, Obsidian released his hold on her waist, and she dropped her arms from around his shoulders. With those actions their minds disengaged.

Anna blinked to find herself alone in her own mind, sitting on a beach with Obsidian's body curled around her.

The dome still held, thank god.

While they'd been distracted, the storm had drifted to the east, heading toward the mainland.

"Damn. I'd say you leveled up." Anna added an accompanying whistle.

Obsidian raised his head, taking in the beast raging across the sky. "Are you up for this? You used a lot of magic to reach me. I can steer it off course and back out to sea by myself if needed."

Anna leaned forward, bumping him in the shoulder with her muzzle. "I'm good. Let's go put a leash on the monster."

"Come," he said as he took to the air, his larger wings sounding like thunder as he fought to get airborne in this wind.

Anna launched herself into the sky after him. When she caught up, she touched their link, *"You know how to control that thing?"*

"Of course." He rolled an eye in her direction. *"But do you?"*

"Not fair. You've got years more experience at wielding magic than me."

"What I know, you can access as well."

She wasn't about to trust her new knowledge during a

magic-induced hurricane. *"Let's work together. That hurricane is savage, and it isn't getting any prettier."*

Obsidian studied the storm. *"We will learn the limits of our new strength together."*

Then he opened his mind fully to her, and together they summoned more power. Though this time, they would be capturing the storm and reeling it in.

While he braided their power into an invisible tether, she created spells across the island to act as anchors.

The storm fought them, resenting being shifted off its course. But Obsidian was skilled, looping tether after tether around wind currents forming the storm until, at last, they'd managed to leash the monster.

Captured, they forced it to spin around its island anchor. It was still a huge monster, but it was under control.

Only their shields protected them from the buffeting winds, but they weren't done yet. Together, they directed more magic into the storm, spinning it out into a glimmering net, where it captured and drained away the storm's fury little by little.

After fifteen minutes, the winds dropped. The clouds soon began dissipating.

"Not half bad, partner." She lengthened the last word into a drawl and grinned at him. "We can add masters of meteorology to our resumes."

He gave her his best 'humans are odd' look. Then ruined it by nuzzling her nearest wing. She returned his warm affection in kind.

They wandered down the beach together, and then, neither of them in the mood to return to Haven yet, settled under one of the big leafed palm-like trees. There they sat and watched the still rough ocean in silence.

Their link remained open, thoughts flowing freely between them. They didn't need words. There was a profound understanding between them that required none.

She leaned into him, and he mantled a wing around her.

His invitation was more than physical, and she was soon looking into his mind as some of his youthful adventures with Truth and friends played out in his memories. She, in turn, showed him some of the long summer camping trips she took with her family as a kid.

"You miss them."

His words weren't a question.

"It feels like a lifetime since I saw any of my brothers or either of my parents." She shrugged. "Not that we ever see much of each outside of the Mackenzie family reunions. Too busy with careers and life. But we used to at least text or chat from time to time."

She paused as something else occurred to her. "I wonder what my family knows, if anything? My father is a brigadier general. He'd know all or at least some of what happened to me back on Earth, but the rest of my family probably wasn't granted clearance. I wonder if my father has given up hope and thinks we're dead."

Then his mind was answering even before his words. "While it has been thirteen years here in Haven, it will be like no time at all has elapsed in the present. For our families, it will only have been the few months that we were trapped in the Battle Goddess's kingdom."

"Right. I keep forgetting about the time travel part."

"I will do all in my power to see that you get to reunite with your human family."

"Deal. And I'll do everything in my power to make sure you get to see your sister again...and reunite with your father one day after he heals." She paused. "We can visit with your battle-ax of a mother as well, I suppose."

Obsidian snorted. "She'll be very pleased with you."

"I doubt that. She hates me."

"She admired you, actually."

"Really?" Doubt was probably etched on her face because he laughed at her.

"At first she didn't, but she soon saw how you protected me."

He fell silent and nuzzled her hair again. She thought he was finished talking, but he started up again, his tone soft and kind. His accompanying thoughts were as well.

"Years ago, back on Earth, do you remember the time Gryton invaded Gran's home by night and he tried to capture us? We were weaponless but fought him anyway. While I was keeping him busy, you got his dagger and used it against him."

Anna glanced sidelong at him and arched a brow, wondering what had triggered that memory. "Yep. The bastard just about charbroiled us."

"Just before that, while we were still fighting. I thought you the bravest and fiercest being I'd met. Your soul was lovely. I knew then that you were the one the Divine Ones had chosen for me."

"You were young. It was infatuation. A crush. But I am flattered." Usually, the dread would be kicking in at the mention of anything that smelled like a relationship conversation, but strangely she was okay with this.

"That's true. Though it grew into true love as I matured. What I feel now is a much more adult version of that same love."

A smile touched her lips, realizing something else.

"I loved Shadowlight like a little brother." She reached out to pat his cheek. "But you I now love as a partner. Just couldn't admit it right away. Waged a bloody, internal war to deny it, in fact. Looking back, I know it started that first night I woke here in Haven and you took me to the cliff side forest where we just talked. I was grieving the loss of Shadowlight, but even then, I knew this Obsidian fellow was a good sort and I could trust him."

"We agree we love each other?" His lips curled back in humor.

"Yes." It came out easily. That surprised her. "Still, I'm not certain..."

"If we're ready for romance?" He looked thoughtful, his mind on the other end of their newly strengthened link was calm. "I'm not either. I love you. You saw that in my mind, but our link is so new. And after everything that—"

"After everything that happened, we need time to process all of it and see how that affects us." She lay back on the sand and stared up at the stormy sky.

"Yes." He joined her, his wings spreading until one touched hers.

"You know, this island wouldn't be so bad with a cold beer and minus the storm clouds. We should come back here some time."

"We could bring lots of food with us. Make a day of it swimming and fishing." He sighed and stretched.

"You can do all the fishing you like. I'll be on the beach sunning myself."

"Hmm, that has merit too."

"Damn straight."

In that moment she knew her world was perfect.

CHAPTER FORTY-SEVEN

Three days after Obsidian had called a storm into being, Anna was back in the practice ring, facing off against Banrook. In other words, getting her ass kicked across the sands by the big brute. He'd grin occasionally and praise her.

Then he'd proceed to knock her on her ass.

After the ninth time, he just shook his head and called for a halt.

"Don't know why I bother," he said, sounding grumpier than usual. "Might as well take a break since your mind is not on the lesson."

It was true. Usually, Rook would have her full attention. Today it was divided between the ring and the council chambers. Rook had said it was more important that Anna continue her training since she still hadn't reached Obsidian's level of mastery.

That meant Obsidian was in the council chambers with the Masters discussing preparations to abandon Haven.

That a djinn had returned to the Magic Realm and might be able to sense the portal spell had created quite the stir. They also discussed what to do with the gargoyle legion.

If they just suddenly appeared in the present-day Magic Realm, the Battle Goddess would sense the shift in the magic flows. It would betray the gargoyles' numbers.

Because of that, Thayn had mentioned taking the gargoyle army to Earth instead. There they'd be able to hide their presence from the Battle Goddess.

"Yeah, that's going to go over real well back home," Anna said along their link.

Obsidian agreed, and then explained again about how the governance on Earth worked to the Council of Elders. He suggested a small contingent go first and negotiate to secure permission for the rest to come.

"I'm rubbing off on you. Don't think I've ever heard you use the word negotiate before."

Obsidian replied with a mental snort. *"You. Go back to your training before I start laughing to myself in front of the Masters."*

"Fine. But if you get tired of all the negotiation talks, give me a shout. We can trade. I'm sure Rook will happily kick your ass around the ring a few times."

"I'd love to switch," Obsidian said, truth ringing in his tone. *"But Rook wants your training accelerated as much as possible."*

"Gee, I must have missed that."

But just then Rook approached her bench with a drinking skin.

She touched Obsidian's mind once more. *"Have fun with the council. Talk more later."*

His mind brushed hers, acknowledgment and love flowing through that slight touch.

The bench dipped as Rook sat down. Anna found a drinking skin unceremoniously shoved in her face. Grinning, she uncorked it and took a swig.

Expecting water, she choked down the cold burn of something that was reminiscent of peppermint and alcohol. "Ugh. What is this crap?"

Rook just snorted and rolled an eye at her. "Drink it. Your pain will go away for a short time."

Eyeing the sand ring and then Rook as he stood up and went to retrieve a pair of quarterstaffs, Anna upended the skin and drank. If she was to guess, Rook planned on keeping her on the practice field until well past sunset.

A mind that wasn't Obsidian's touched hers and a familiar power swept over her being seconds before Lord Draydrak's voice was loud in her mind.

"Run! Run now!"

The God of Death's voice still echoed in her head.

"What?" But Anna was already on her feet.

"That is not Banrook."

His words still explained nothing, but Anna had come to trust this demigod's words. If he said that the gargoyle in front of her wasn't Rook, she believed him.

Even as she moved, she called on her protective magic. Or at least she tried. It was sluggish to respond. For five seconds she stared at her empty palms, where the magic had sputtered for half a second and then died.

Then she remembered the drink Obsidian had swallowed during his Adept Trial. The one that neutralized a gargoyle's magic. It had smelled minty.

Oh, fuck.

"There is no point in fighting," Rook who was not Rook said. "Your magic is gone for a short time. Long enough for me to return you to our goddess."

He was talking about the Lady of Battles. Anna didn't know what or who was standing in front of her, but he was an enemy.

Moreover, the Lord of the Underworld had just instructed her to run.

Leaping backward over the bench, she shifted in the air and then landed on all fours, darting away from the threat. She reached for Obsidian even as she ran, but like the time he'd drunk the potion, there was only a numbness where the tether tying them together should be.

Behind her Rook didn't give chase. She was realizing the implications just as she ran headlong into some kind of magic net. It contracted around her, squeezing tight. The numbness inside her continued to spread.

There was another power there too. She sensed it now. The coppery taint of old blood. Sickly sweet. Familiar. The work of a blood witch.

The power continued to cocoon her in ever tightening layers.

Rook standing over her was the last thing she saw before he tossed something over her head as well.

CHAPTER FORTY-EIGHT

Master Verroc was discussing the number of gargoyles to send to Earth for the first wave of negotiations, but Obsidian's mind was drifting. His new, stronger link with Anna was also addictive. It was work to focus on anything else.

He loved it, and yet it was a distraction in the current situation.

Still, he found himself reaching back along the link to briefly touch Anna's mind.

And ran into a barrier.

No...not a barrier.

He sucked in a surprised breath.

There was nothing to touch.

What? How?

Blood began to surge as he rose to his feet, no longer seeing the Elders gathered around the council table. He was drawing breath to warn them that something was wrong when Lord Draydrak's powerful mind touched his.

Wasting no time, the God of Death, shoved a vision at Obsidian, wordlessly telling him all that had happened.

"Go, my Rasoren. Rescue your Kyrsu. I will explain and rally the council." With those few words, the demigod was gone from his mind.

Obsidian didn't need any other prompting and bolted for the stairs. Once he was far enough away from the council chamber's protective shields, he took to the open sky, winging his way to the practice fields.

"She won't be there," Dray whispered, telling Obsidian the demigod was still with him. *"There is only one place this agent of my sister can run with his prize."*

"The time portal." Obsidian angled a wing edge and sliced a sharp turn in the air, winging his way as fast as he could in the new direction.

"Yes. It is his only hope of escape. His djinn magic allows him to hide, even from me to some extent, but he won't be able to hide from all my gargoyles. He'll try to make it to the portal with your Kyrsu. He knows if he can escape with her, you will follow."

"Always." Obsidian's fierce reply echoed through the air.

"I have been healing the soul of the soldier who carried this dark spell into our territory. The soul was severely damaged, and it took me time to heal him, and even longer for him to remember what his mission had been."

For once Dray's mellow voice failed to calm Obsidian, but he listened as the demigod provided valuable information on the creature who had stolen Anna.

"He was a carrier only. His death was used to fuel a spell created by the blood witch using magic from a djinn. It wasn't my sister who captured the djinn. It was the witch."

Obsidian didn't miss the mild relief that touched Death's voice, and he wondered at that.

"If my sister had lost the last of her sanity, she wouldn't have stopped with just one djinn. She would have summoned and captured them all. At least the blood witch has limits to her power."

"For now." But for how much longer, with a djinn to fuel her spells? But Obsidian couldn't dredge up the appropriate fear for that just now, not with Anna being held by one of their enemies. His only relief came in the knowledge that whatever controlled Rook wanted Anna alive. If not, his Kyrsu would already be dead.

When he reached the temple, he called his shadow magic. After sealing the bond with Anna, he'd surpassed even a Master's abilities. He might even be more powerful than Thayn now.

He hoped so, for this new enemy had taken one of the most powerful masters as its host, and only the power of a fully trained Rasoren or Kyrsu could hope to overpower one of the ancients.

Still, he continued with caution. There could be no berserker's rage or a blind rush to Anna's side. He had to be swift but cunning. If whatever was controlling Rook learned Obsidian was on the hunt, the creature might kill Anna if he couldn't escape.

I cannot lose my Kyrsu, he thought a little desperately.

Making his way deeper into the structure on silent feet, at last, he came to the chamber where the time portal resided. Rook was already there, standing before the two, as yet, dormant stalagmites.

Only the sight of magic already rising off Rook's body stopped Obsidian from attacking. Rook was feeding power into the portal. If Obsidian launched an attack now, that magic would join what was already in the spell work.

The time spell was both enduring and yet fragile. Too much power and it could collapse, trapping everyone here in this place.

Obsidian would wait until the spell was self-sufficient. As soon as Rook was far enough away, he'd launch his attack.

Rook continued to manipulate the trigger spell, unaware that he was being watched.

Twenty feet from the larger gargoyle, Anna lay on her side against a wall, wrapped in layers of the imposter Rook's shadow magic.

She was breathing.

She was still alive.

His gaze sought hers.

Oh. And she was pissed.

He hadn't seen her look that enraged since her time in the Battle Goddess's kingdom.

The breath he'd been holding released on a soft, unheard sigh.

Now all he had to do was stop Rook from dragging Anna through and keep him trapped here until Lord Death had rallied the council. They'd be here in a matter of minutes. The only reason they weren't was because only Anna could outpace him in the air.

He eyed the master's progress with the spell work and

then the distance between Anna and the portal. Rook must not have wanted to chance his spell might interfere with the portal's summoning. Obsidian's narrowed eyes tracked back to the enemy.

If Rook escaped through the portal, he couldn't be sure that the male wouldn't destroy it once through.

Though, Rook would only have taken Anna if he wanted her Rasoren, too. Which suggested the portal was safe until Obsidian crossed. At which point, the essence controlling Rook might decide to destroy the gateway.

While Obsidian mulled over his options, Rook continued to wake the dormant time spell.

Though he knew a select few of the masters traveled between the two times, Obsidian hadn't seen the inside of this room, or an active portal, since he'd first seen it as a child.

The stalagmite began to glow much the same as he remembered. This time he watched as Rook created the trigger spell. It was a complex and beautiful thing. One Obsidian was confident he could re-create now that he'd seen it.

As soon as the portal had stabilized, Rook slowly walked to where Anna lay on the floor.

Obsidian stalked forward, low to the ground, still shrouded by his shadow magic. He'd gotten better at hiding himself from his mentors during his recent training sessions, but he didn't trust that the elder wouldn't sense something.

Inching forward, Obsidian moved closer to the portal, until he was almost close enough for a successful charge. He needed to put himself between Rook and the portal so he could toss up protective spells around it the second he charged. It was the only way to protect both his Kyrsu and the gateway.

Rook leaned down and scooped up Anna. Instead of turning toward the portal, Rook faced Obsidian, a shard of shadow magic held against his Kyrsu's throat.

"You're very skilled. I wouldn't have noticed if the portal hadn't responded to the shift in power flow in the room," Rook said, addressing the room at large. "I don't have to see you to know you're here."

Obsidian froze, not speaking or moving. Only tensing his muscles to strike.

Rook sent other bits of shadowy magic dancing through the air.

Whichever angle of attack Obsidian took, the other male would be able to track his charge using the disturbed shadows as his guide. Gritting his teeth at Rook's cunning, he continued to sit and wait for the perfect time.

"If you attack, I'll kill your Kyrsu before you get to me. You know I can. She's quite magicless at the moment."

Obsidian's growl echoed around the room.

"Ah. You need a demonstration." One long, shimmering shard sliced a line along Anna's cheek.

She didn't make a noise. Obsidian didn't betray his location a second time either. Though it was a fight.

"Come now, Rasoren. We are supposed to be on the same side. You seem to have forgotten what you were created for." Rook sidestepped closer to the portal.

Obsidian triggered his own wall of magic, stopping the Master, who grimaced.

"The Lady of Battles will welcome you back. She'll be

delighted with your development. And the human is still new enough to her powers that the demigoddess shall be able to use her to control you. And this," Rook tipped his muzzle to gesture at his own body, "is just an added benefit. The Lady of Battles will be well pleased with my mistress's work."

"You won't escape alive." Obsidian used magic to project his voice from different locations throughout the room as he circled wider, heading in the direction of the room's northern wall, where he'd created his own shadow magic barrier to stop Rook escaping toward the gate.

If Obsidian was careful, he could hide from Rook's swirling tracking eddies. Most of them were situated in the central part of the room.

"Nice try." Rook slashed another line, down Anna's arm this time. The female gargoyle only growled louder.

He felt himself slipping closer to the berserker rage he shared with Anna. He couldn't let it win. Rook was too smart. That's what the other male wanted.

"You won't escape before the other masters arrive. I can feel them approaching. They're only a little way distant." He stalled for time. "Let's make a trade. Release Anna and I'll let you escape through the portal."

"And have you kill me later? No Rasoren. I'm not that foolish. However, if you allow me to approach the portal, I can get myself through and release Anna on the other side."

"Never."

Rook's shard grew into a proper dagger, and he drew it along the curve of her breast, just above where her gargoyle heart beat strong. "If I can't capture one or the other of you, I was instructed to kill you both."

The blade returned to Anna's throat.

"Don't think I will hesitate. I may be sentient, but I am a spell. I do not fear death because I am not alive."

All of that was likely true, but the complicated spell's primary objective was to gather information and carry it back, which gave Obsidian an idea. "A trade then. We'll approach the portal together. You give me Anna, and you can carry back all that you've learned here. The Master is a worthy prize. He knows more than Anna or me."

Rook tilted his head.

Got you now, Obsidian thought with a mental grin.

"A deal, Rasoren." Rook nodded his muzzle at Anna.

They both inched closer to the portal.

"You may attach anchors to the shadow magic I used to imprison her."

"Very well." He'd do that. But he'd also follow with Anna, and once she was safely away from Rook, he'd continue his original plan of attack. They'd just all go through the gateway together first. It was the best option of the ones available.

Rook and Obsidian mirrored each other's every move as they made their way closer to the time spell. When they were at last within touching distance of the glowing portal, Rook stiffened suddenly.

The hand holding the shadow magic dagger to Anna's throat was ripped away by a much greater force.

What was going on?

A moment later Rook lost control of his other limbs.

Anna's expression said she didn't know what was going

on either but darted toward Obsidian. He swiftly took her into his arms and triggered a spell of protection around them and the gate, sealing Rook on the outside.

Rook continued to arch his back, his wings stretched wide by some unseen force.

Another ten seconds dragged by as the master struggled.

Thayn strode through the portal. "Oh, no you don't! I know what you do when you die."

The most ancient of the masters struck Rook with a wave of power, shoving him across the floor. He gestured, his shadow magic dancing around him and more raced forward, dragging Rook halfway up the wall. There another powerful wave of focus slammed him against the stone. It would have vaporized a lesser being.

"Nasty bit of spell work that. But that should hold him." Thayn gave Rook a couple more shakes to be sure before pointing a talon at the center of the room. The unconscious gargoyle sailed back across the space to land in a heap before the portal.

"Thank you," Anna said.

"Well," Thayn said, circling the fallen male. "I was coming to warn of another danger entirely when our Lord touched my mind and told me what he'd learned from the enemy soldier and the purpose of the spell. I wasn't about to let it go slithering into either of you. Even I would be hard pressed to win a fight against our powerful young Rasoren."

Obsidian kept his attention on Thayn.

Can I trust him though? Both masters had been in the dungeon when the original spell triggered.

"Thayn is clean." Lord Draydrak confirmed. *"I've already searched his soul for signs of the spell. There are none. The others who were injured in the same attack are likewise unaffected. Only Rook was corrupted."*

Thayn grinned suddenly. "I'm not going to let the cocky brute live that down for a good long time."

Obsidian shredded the spells trapping Anna. When she was free, she came to her feet and looked down at Rook. "Who the hell is he?"

"A friend and an enemy," Thayn said with an accompanying ear flick. "Lord Dray will deal with Roo—."

The portal flared with power as a giant hand, talons extended, emerged. A second later it snatched up Rook. Then as swiftly as the massive hand had come, it was gone, the portal quiet once again.

Thayn blinked at the spot where Rook had been, his tail swaying and his ears cocked at the portal. "Dray does so hate when his sister plays with his gargoyles."

Ignoring the elder, Obsidian took Anna's chin in his hand and turned her face to his. Her eyes were still slightly widened in surprise. When he leaned closer, sniffing along her skin, he could smell the drug on her.

"Are you alright?" It was strange having to ask that after how strong their link had grown recently, but the potion Rook had tricked Anna into drinking would remain in her bloodstream until at least nightfall.

Her expression twisted into a bemused look. She must have come to the same conclusion as him. "I'm fine. He didn't harm me. Just my pride. He managed to capture me in thirty seconds flat."

"It's nothing to be ashamed of, especially not without

the use of your powers and against one as skilled as Banrook."

"Still. Pride stinging a little over here."

He drew her closer and wrapped her in his arms.

Slowly, some of his earlier fears dissipated but it would be a long time yet before he forgot how close a bit of shadow magic had come to slicing her throat. He'd been close enough that had the worst happened, he could have shared his magic with her, turning them both to stone to heal.

But that would have allowed Rook to escape, and that could have had far more dire consequences.

He never wanted to choose between Anna and the greater good.

He was just glad he had not needed to make such a decision this day.

If Fate were kind, he never would.

CHAPTER FORTY-NINE

When Obsidian and Anna faced Rook several hours later, his usual pride and assurance were absent. But Anna supposed that was expected after Lord Draydrak had carved away the djinn-fueled blood witch's spell that had been feeding on him.

After the Lord of the Underworld had finished with that task, he called them all together to inform his council of everything he'd learned.

In the real temple, in the real time.

They'd crossed over when Draydrak said it was no longer safe to stay. The legion was preparing to evacuate. But first, they had another problem to face and defeat.

The Lady of Battles hadn't left the task of retrieving Anna and Obsidian solely to the spy spell.

She'd sent an army.

That was the other threat Draydrak had discovered and sent Thayn back in time to warn Haven.

"We must stop them before they can come close

enough to sense the time portal and destabilize it," Rook said into the silence.

Thayn nodded sharply. "We will set an ambush for them."

On the far side of the room, the Lord of the Underworld paced with restless energy, his horse-like lower body moved with fluid grace.

The viewing mirror hadn't done him justice. He looked even bigger and scarier in real life.

"Rook, you will take the most skilled of the students and destroy this threat," Death interjected into the conversation. "All other available gargoyles will stay to guard the island in case the first line of defense fails. The first line of defense will not fail. Do I make myself clear?"

"Perfectly, my Lord," Master Banrook said with a salute in his tone.

Lord Draydrak turned next to ponder Anna. "It is time my Rasoren and Kyrsu test their skills in a real battle."

"As my Lord wishes." Obsidian echoed Anna's own words.

They thought as one, now it was time to discover just how well they fought as one.

CHAPTER FIFTY

Anna crouched low, almost hugging the ground. With her shadow magic a cloaking pressure around her, she was more concerned with disturbing the underbrush or some bird than having an advanced scout see through her disguise.

Ten feet to her right, Obsidian was waiting with his back pressed against a tree with shaggy bark. To others, he'd appear as part of the tree.

So far, they hadn't been discovered. The Battle Goddess's scouts continued into the ambush. The first scout made her way past Anna's position without so much as a flicker of unease.

The female's nearest companion, a lightly armored male, glided through the forest a couple hundred feet to the woman's right.

Another scout on the female's opposite side was walking very close to where Thayn waited, but the elder remained undiscovered.

Anna's gaze tracked farther back, deeper into the forest where she could even now hear other enemy soldiers approaching.

Ah. There. Three more scouts. According to the legion's scouting party, these six were the total number of advance scouts.

When the rearmost scout was even with Obsidian, Anna picked out her target. A large male in light armor less than twenty feet from her position.

"Now," Rook broadcasted out across the shared link.

Anna lunged, covering the distance in two long strides and then, before the male knew what was happening, she sent a spear of shadow magic thrusting through his neck.

She caught the body before it hit the ground, then swiftly dragged the dead weight backward, away from the wide dry gully that the enemies were using as a roadway.

As silently as her own, the five other enemy scouts vanished.

Dryads rose up out of hiding spots and made their way down the gentle slopes of the gully. A few subtle spells, a rustle of a breeze among the underbrush, and all signs that a struggle had occurred vanished.

Anna spotted Meadow and Lark among the group. Along the link, she could sense where Obsidian was keeping tabs on all his friends, but he didn't allow his concerns to divide his focus.

With the scouts taken care of, they all settled back to wait. Though it wasn't long before she heard the distant sound of booted feet on the gully's stony ground.

A short time later, the first row of combatants came in

sight. She knew from dryad and gargoyle scouts that this group was three hundred strong.

A tiny group compared to the might the Battle Goddess could summon, but this was just a raiding party. Designed to slip in, snatch their spy under cover of a raid, and then slip out again.

Rook's company of gargoyles and dryads were much smaller. Just a hundred and fifty, but enough for this task. Many more were still guarding Death's Temple and the time portal while still others were preparing to evacuate Haven.

In the lead was one of the captains to judge by the armor, but Anna didn't recognize this one, and while she hadn't interacted with each of the captains during her time in the Battle Goddess's kingdom, she did know each of the emblems. The red crossbow bolts on an ebony field wasn't heraldry she recognized.

"He's new, I think," Anna said as she touched Obsidian's mind. *"Can you get a whiff of him? Discover what he is?"*

"No, there are too many scents, but I agree, I don't think this fellow was a captain the last time we were among the demigoddess's army."

"Rook said when the Avatars attacked some of the captains had been killed. This fellow must be a replacement for someone. I wonder who?" Anna's lips compressed. *"Do you think Vaspara or Sorac might have been killed? I would have thought at least one of them would have been trusted with such an important mission as this."*

"I won't even hazard a guess, but we'll proceed with caution since we don't know this newcomer's skills or his magical strength.

It won't be a paltry thing, though. Not if the goddess deemed him worthy to lead as one of her captains."

"I agree."

During their silent exchange, the enemy soldiers had come closer. Entering the trap, unaware. Still, Anna waited. Obsidian too.

More enemy soldiers ghosted by her position. Almost two-thirds of the line had entered the trap when a questioning shout rang out. A moment of heavy silence followed while the soldiers at the head of the line waited for the scouts to respond in some way.

The scouts would never be answering.

But Rook responded for them, rising from his hiding spot almost two miles down the gully. Then he raised his horn to his lips.

At the crisp, clear sound, the one hundred and fifty dryads and gargoyles surged out from their hiding places and raced down the slopes to engage the enemy.

The trap didn't spring perfectly. A third of the enemy fighters, almost a hundred by Anna's eye, were outside the encircling dryads and gargoyles.

"Time to earn our keep," Anna called as she raced toward the closest enemy.

"Fifty for each of us," Obsidian agreed in all seriousness.

"Our friends might expect us to share."

Obsidian chuckled. *"I'll share if they're fast enough."*

Ten feet from the first enemy, Anna shifted to run on two feet, sword in one hand and shadow magic shield in the other.

Their link flared brighter, growing to encompass their minds in response to the presence of danger. There was no longer a need to speak as both Anna and Obsidian transformed into Rasoren-Kyrsu—twin souls guided by one unified will.

Blades dripping with blood, talons covered in gore, shadowy shards of magic shifting around them as they danced. The lethal brutality of a berserker's battle rage rose up within their souls, strengthening their bodies and quickening their strikes.

It did not make them mindless, though. They still had a hyper clear focus: destroy their enemies.

During their deadly, splendid dance, they accomplished much, cutting down thirty opponents in a blur of minutes. Sometimes she would distract the enemy and her Rasoren would make the kill. Other times, he would engage, and his Kyrsu would slide up like an assassin from the shadows to end their enemy's life.

And during yet other times, they fought back to back or shoulder to shoulder. The clash of their sword strikes rained down upon shields and enemy swords until it formed its own sharp-edged music.

Rasoren-Kyrsu danced, destroying all in their path.

"You both are truly breathtaking."

The familiar voice jarred Anna out of their link, and she was once again alone in her own body. An expired opponent dangled from her talons. Obsidian was panting beside her, a second warrior raised above his body, shadow magic shimmering with deadly promise.

With barely a look at the soldier, Obsidian finished him off with a spear of magic, then discarded the body as he stepped toward the familiar voice. Anna followed, circling around to stand at his shoulder.

She blinked at finding herself facing Captain Vaspara. After a sea of unknown enemies, seeing a familiar visage caused a small curl of surprise in Anna's stomach and perhaps even a little uneasy dread.

"I see the Lord of the Underworld managed what his sister could not. The cub's fully grown and lethal." She glanced at Anna. "So too is his little mother bear."

"What are you doing in gargoyle territory with such small numbers, Vaspara? I thought you were more intelligent," Anna shot back.

"I assure you, I wouldn't be here given a choice," she said in that ultra-calm tone Anna remembered. "Alas, I don't command this expedition. After the losses we've suffered, the Battle Goddess needed to replenish her pool of captains."

"You and Sorac fallen out of favor?" Anna asked as she tapped the tip of Vaspara's blade.

"Something like that. Though I'd rather face a horde of ravaging gargoyles than remain behind to be food for a blood witch's spells. Death upon a gargoyle's talons is quick and clean at least."

Anna and Obsidian snorted, both knowing Vaspara was as lethal as most gargoyles.

Obsidian tapped his sword against the succubus' next, and Anna allowed her partner to take over. She settled for killing enemy soldiers that got too close to the pair. But Anna could still track their full conversation through the link.

"You've filled out nicely." Vaspara eyed Obsidian in a way that reminded Anna of the captain's succubus nature.

"You can flirt with me later if you must," Obsidian

responded sounding bored. "Though, I must confess I'm more curious what your leader thinks he's doing here."

"The idiot leading this suicide mission is not my leader." Vaspara actually made a horrified face. "He thought if he could capture enough gargoyles, they could fuel the blood witch's spells."

Obsidian tilted his head to study Vaspara. "So this raid has nothing to do with reclaiming a certain spy-spell forged of a djinn's power and recovering what it has learned?"

Fuck it. Anna didn't know how Obsidian could make his voice sound so pleasant and innocent with blood dripping off his jaws.

"Ah, you've found it already?" Vaspara paused to look around at the dead. "If I hadn't found you, this would all have been a waste. Though how you grew so quickly and how Anna survived and recovered are intriguing mysteries. Ones I'm sure my Lady would love to discover if she ever managed to get you alone."

"Sorry to disappoint but that's not going to happen," Anna said as she rejoined the conversation.

"But what if it could?" This time Vaspara tilted her chin and looked somewhat smug. "Your return will restore my place in the Battle Goddess's army. Sorac's too, once we take you back to the goddess."

"Hmmm. From my perspective, it looks like we're winning," Obsidian countered.

"There's always more than one way to look at a problem, young one. While you have matured to a fine specimen..."

Vaspara raked him with another hungry look—and she probably was hungry after expending magic during the battle, Anna thought, but there was no way she was going to refuel using Obsidian.

"You were saying?" Anna prodded.

"There's more than one way to look at a problem to find a solution. It helps that as succubus stock, I can look into a male's mind. Especially during battle when his bloodlust is up."

"Move the story along, we don't got all day," Anna hissed.

Vaspara just nodded. "Earlier, during the battle, I crossed swords, and minds, with a gargoyle. Inside was the usual love for a woman, his family, and his friends. This time it was the friends part that was interesting. Obsidian, I assume you know Truth?"

Obsidian's wings flinched.

"Ah, he's a good friend of yours, then? Glad I kept him alive. Sorac's keeping an eye on him for me."

Vaspara was intentionally letting information drop. She was too intelligent to give away her cards. She wanted something. Something more than just a trade, Obsidian for Truth.

Beside Anna, Obsidian stiffened more, a growl rolling from between his parted lips.

"Easy, you're giving too much away. Vaspara will use whatever you give her against us." Anna hadn't seen him do that since he'd been a child. Vaspara's words had rattled him. *"You knew going into battle meant no one is safe. But by her admission, Truth is alive."*

Anna directed her next comment at Vaspara. "Just get to the part where you tell us what you want for Truth's life."

"I want a way out of this for myself and Sorac."

"He's a firedrake. Why doesn't he just fly away? Or come to think of it, why haven't I seen him try to BBQ anyone yet?"

"Come and see for yourselves. He's holding the gargoyle and two dryads a short distance to the west. Call off your attack gargoyles, and we'll see if the three of us can come to an understanding."

"If you've harmed Truth or the females…" Obsidian growled another warning.

"The females are likely Meadow and Lark. They were together earlier. Let's hope there is still something to save." Anna stepped around Obsidian and placed a restraining hand on his chest but directed her next words at Vaspara. "We'll come with you and negotiate for the release of our people."

Vaspara nodded at Anna's words and then tilted her chin to where a section of underbrush had been burned away. Clearly work of the firedrake.

By some miracle he hadn't—or maybe he couldn't—burned away enough of this surrounding tree canopy to get up into the air with his prisoners.

Once she scanned the trail with more detail, she spotted the bright red of Sorac's lava-like blood still smoldering on the ground.

Ah, he'd been hurt. One or perhaps several of the gargoyles had managed to overpower the big beast.

"You're protecting him," Anna said suddenly.

"Yes." Vaspara agreed, not even attempting to lie. "He protected me from three masters while I fought a fourth. I pay my debts."

Anna was sure whatever ran between Vaspara and Sorac

was much deeper than a debt owed. It might even be love. She filed that information away for later. Anything that could help save her friends was useful.

"Lead the way," Anna ordered the succubus.

Vaspara nodded and began to pick her way back up the northern side of the wide gully. Not once did she take her eyes off the gargoyles.

"Leave her," Obsidian ordered the others. "We will deal with this."

Rook suddenly appeared in their midst. He might even have been one of the masters who had maimed the big firedrake.

"Obsidian," he said without taking his eyes of the succubus, "have a care. Her kind can be wily and best even a gargoyle."

"Vaspara is known to me. She and Sorac still retain a semblance of honor. She will keep her word once given."

"She has not yet given her word," Rook pointed out.

Vaspara chuckled. "The master is correct. Should we make our deal here? Now?"

"No. I want to see our friends first," Anna answered before Obsidian had a chance. *You were always a shrewd tactician, Vaspara. I'm not letting you outmaneuver us during this little reunion.*

When Anna saw more of Sorac's glowing blood, she couldn't help but remember how he and Vaspara had used to work together to keep her and Shadowlight away from the worst elements dwelling in the Battle Goddess's kingdom.

Anna didn't fool herself though. They were still the enemy. She just didn't want to have to be the one to kill them. Obsidian either. And if Vaspara had hostages, then Anna was willing to trade the two captains' freedom for those hostages.

Hadn't Lord Death said that no gargoyle or dryad could be taken captive?

This might not have been precisely what he had in mind, but it was faithful to the essence of his command.

Time to cut a deal.

CHAPTER FIFTY-ONE

Vaspara led the way, Anna followed, always keeping herself between him and the succubus. Obsidian knew what Anna was about, trying to protect him but also stop him from leaping headlong into an ambush. Or doing something else foolish, like falling prey to a succubus.

He allowed Anna to lead since he'd never faced a succubus after his maturity. Now wasn't the time to discover if his special blood would make him immune to her powers.

So Vaspara led, Anna held the center, and he brought up the rear. And as the succubus had promised, they found Sorac and the three prisoners just a little west of the main fighting.

Obsidian froze.

Horror lodged like a rock in his gut.

Truth was pinned to the ground by the spikes of the firedrake's tail. One had speared through Truth's right shoulder, another at the left hip and a third in the right thigh. Others had pinned his wings to the ground. Though painful, those would do nothing more damaging than keep him out of the sky for a day or two.

The other wounds were what caused gorge to rise in Obsidian's throat. He'd hadn't felt this helpless since all those years ago when Anna was dying.

This wasn't the work of a blood witch, though. If Truth were lucky, the healers would be able to heal him enough to prevent a lengthy stone sleep.

But even sleeping in stone for years was better than death.

Still, the wounds would be monstrously painful.

Resisting the urge to growl was difficult.

Directly under Sorac's scaled belly, Obsidian spotted Lark and Meadow. They were bound in ropes of magic. The two dryad warriors struggled to free themselves, cursing when they couldn't.

Meadow gave up after a moment, her gaze upon Truth as tears rolled down her cheeks.

Anna cleared her throat, drawing his attention firmly back to her. Then she eyed Sorac and Vaspara thoughtfully. "You're both too weak to escape on your own."

The firedrake craned his long neck to stare down at her. "Correct. I am injured too greatly, my magic weakened by keeping me alive. I could not summon a portal to escape back to our lands. Vaspara would not leave me behind and had to expend a great deal of power protecting me. Now, she can no longer summon enough magic either."

"Close your jaws you great fire-breathing lizard!"

Vaspara's tone lacked anger, though. Obsidian also detected sadness and weariness. Not hopelessness. Not yet.

But she would never surrender. He knew that. She would fight to the end. The only uncertainty was whether she'd spare his friends' lives.

Anna was in his mind, reading his every emotion. And he was in hers. He knew what she was going to say before she said it. His duty was clear. For everyone's sake, Vaspara, Sorac, and every other enemy soldier needed to be captured or killed. This was war. It was his duty to see Vaspara and Sorac dead or captured, even at the expense of his friends' lives.

He should halt Anna from making a deal.

He didn't.

Anna pointed the tip of her sword at Vaspara, using the blade like a pointing finger. "This is how it's going to go down. You'll let Obsidian have Truth. I'll create a portal back to your lands. You release Lark. Sorac will go through first, and then you, Vaspara, will release Meadow before I let you enter the portal. You have my word no harm will come to you if you do as I say."

Sorac growled, his voice like rolling thunder. "What assurances do I have you'll let Vaspara go once I leave?"

"The lizard has a point," Vaspara said, calculation entering her eyes. "What if one of you crosses the portal first so there is a guarantee of sorts that both sides must behave if they wish to see their partner again?"

Anna laughed and then pinned the succubus with a look that Obsidian knew would send lesser beings fleeing. "There is no version of this event where it ends with either my Rasoren or me going with you."

Vaspara glanced away from Anna to look Obsidian in the eyes. A cunning look entered her gaze.

Obsidian just flashed his teeth at her. "Take the deal, Captain. Or there will be a bloodbath, and then there are no guarantees."

"Ah," Vaspara returned his grin. "The cub truly has grown up. Sorac and I will humbly accept Anna's deal."

Nodding agreement, he wasted no time calling on his magic and creating a portal. When he'd finished, he looked up at Vaspara and then Sorac.

"The portal will dump you out along the borderlands. If you are lucky or have skills enough, you should be able to hide until you're both full strength before having to face the blood witch or the Battle Goddess."

Sorac released Truth and then bowed his large, scale-covered neck in a show of respect. "Thank you. And for what it's worth, I was careful where I speared this one," he deposited Truth between them, forcing a grunt of pain from the gargoyle. "If you hurry, I'm sure he'll survive. You're all impressively tough bastards to kill. Anna included."

His Kyrsu laughed. "Don't go getting sentimental. I haven't forgotten who you serve. Next time we meet, it will be as enemies. Our debt to you is paid."

"It is," he agreed. He released Lark first and then shoved Meadow toward Vaspara. Then he heaved himself up onto his three legs, the other was a mangled mess, and limped toward the portal. He paused, glancing at Vaspara before he crossed the threshold.

Vaspara stood with an arm locked around Meadow's throat as she gazed out at the surrounding forest as if waiting for gargoyles to attack. When none did, she backed toward the portal.

"You'll release Meadow before you touch the portal," Anna warned.

Vaspara shoved the dryad at Anna and then continued back until her boot heels were touching the outside barrier. Then she surprised Obsidian by bowing deeply. "May your honor be rewarded one day."

"And yours," he called softly.

As she stepped into the threshold, she paused, looking back over her shoulder. "Fate will force each of us onto the battlefield, I just hope the battlefield is large enough we never face each other. Farewell Corporal Anna Mackenzie and Shadowlight, two of the bravest young beings I ever met."

Then Vaspara was gone. Obsidian rushed to his friend's side.

"Truth! Are you alright?"

The other gargoyle made a wheezing sound, and it took Obsidian a moment to recognize the sound as a laugh.

"To borrow a phrase from Anna, fuck no." Truth groaned. "Why does everyone always ask that?"

"I'm sorry. I didn't..."

But then Anna stepped up beside him, making sounds of sympathy and dragging Obsidian out of the way so the healers could see to Truth.

"Meadow and Lark are safe, Truth. We'll all be here once you wake," Anna said, her tone soothing.

"Thank you for saving them." He closed his eyes. "I tried but failed."

"You didn't fail them," Obsidian added his voice to

Anna's. "You fought bravely, my friend. Now let the healers patch up your stubborn ass before Meadow drowns us all in her tears."

As he'd hoped, that caused the other male to look toward the dryad. Something besides pain entered Truth's expression as he laid eyes on the woman he loved.

Leaving them staring at each other, Obsidian guided Anna away.

"We need to help with the sweep for any stray enemies who might be making an escape."

Anna nodded and soon they were dropping to run on all fours, hunting the few remaining enemy soldiers who hadn't already been captured or killed.

CHAPTER FIFTY-TWO

As it turned out, the last of the invaders were swiftly dealt with. Those willing to surrender were taken captive. The rest were destroyed.

Even the warriors who surrendered would still face death eventually, Anna learned.

Lord Draydrak would judge each captive's soul and determine if the person could be rehabilitated or if they needed to be sent back to the Divine Ones for healing.

The ways of the Magic Realm were efficient at least.

But it remained to be seen what the demigod would do with his Rasoren and Kyrsu when he learned they'd allowed two of the Battle Goddess's top captains to escape. Anna planned on taking the blame.

"There's no point worrying about what can't be changed. But as far as I'm concerned, that was the correct choice." Obsidian shrugged. "Perhaps next time we meet Vaspara and Sorac, maybe we'll have gained their trust enough that they'll surrender to us. Depriving the Battle

Goddess of two of her most competent captains would be a great blow."

"We can hope." Anna knew she'd failed to keep the doubt out of her tone when Obsidian sighed.

"You're correct, of course. Next time we see them will likely be across a battlefield." He paused. "The thought doesn't please me."

"Me neither." Anna agreed. "It's because they were the closest we had to allies in that place. It doesn't mean they are. We're going to need to remember that for the next time. If Lord Death is planning on letting us have a next time."

"We'll find out shortly." He jerked his chin toward the temple where it sat glowing in the sunset. They'd flown to the island after receiving a summons from Lord Dray. The other members of the war party were still doing a final sweep for survivors back on the mainland.

"We should have made a run for it," Anna said only half in jest. "We could have made it back to the Mortal Realm before anyone realized we're gone."

Obsidian only huffed but knew she didn't really mean it. Neither of them would be running away from the demigod.

Together they continued their walk up the stairs cut into the bedrock of the island. On either side spread the beautiful terraced gardens. It struck him as strange that this island, structurally the same as Haven, differed so much.

"It's odd, isn't it," Anna said, sounding deep in thought, "that the God of Death surrounds himself with green growing things, tropical birds, lizards, and insects. And likely any number of other creatures that make their way to this island. When I think of death, visions of tombs and desiccated dead things pop into my head. But, hell, tropical paradise. Whatever floats your boat."

"It must be lonely," Obsidian said softly.

"What?" Anna glanced sidelong at him. "Oh, you mean having the power he commands."

"Oh, it is," Lord Dray's entrancing voice was suddenly sharing headspace with them. *"My duty demands unquestioning dedication. Loneliness is a result of that. But I wouldn't change what I am. There is nothing more beautiful than sending souls made wise by a long life back to the Spirit Realm to reunite with all the other loved ones who've already made the journey. The joy they feel echoes back to me, and that is rewarding enough."*

They turned a corner and found themselves within feet of the massive demigod in the flesh.

"My Lord—" Obsidian began, but Anna cut him off.

"It was my plan. My action that allowed two of the enemy to escape. The blame is mine to swallow."

Obsidian squared his shoulders. "But it was my choice to allow it."

His belligerent tone said he wasn't budging. Well, Anna didn't plan to give ground either.

"Captains Vaspara and Sorac are known to us. Vaspara wished to bargain. Obsidian wouldn't have agreed, except they had Truth, Lark, and Meadow."

Dray said nothing, merely folding his powerful horse-like legs under him and kneeling on one of the manicured patches of lawn. His expression was attentive and... something else.

Was that curiosity?

Amusement?

Balls!

Had that part with Truth, Meadow, and Lark been a test? Death had once alluded to knowing every soul's destiny. It was part of his gift. It allowed him to know when each soul's life had run its course. He might have seen this in one of his many futures.

If it was a test, Anna assumed they'd failed. Lord Dray had ordered that none of the enemies be allowed to escape.

But that didn't change anything. Anna would still have acted to save her friends.

Lord Draydrak continued to study them in silence.

What the hell did he want? Usually, he'd just read their minds or say what was on his.

When in doubt...

"I'm sorry and humbly beg forgiveness."

"For what?" Dray asked.

Was that a hint of humor?

Anna glanced sidelong at Obsidian. *"You can step in at any point."*

Obsidian's tail flicked ever so slightly, but otherwise, he made no response to her statement.

How helpful.

At last, Dray took pity on her. "I saw what you did. Now you would apologize for saving three lives? And protecting your Rasoren from the grief of losing three friends?"

Wait one minute.

Come to think of it, what was the chance that Vaspara and Sorac would just happen to find three of Obsidian's friends in the middle of a battle?

"Yes, Kyrsu. You've caught me. I didn't just see the outcome; I orchestrated the event to no little degree."

Obsidian snorted in surprise, his expression much less humorous than the demigod's. "You intentionally put my friends in danger to test us?"

His betrayed tone made Anna want to reach out and comfort her Rasoren.

"The futures showed the possibility of good coming from that strange meeting. I just nudged your friends with a word that this would aid you in the future. I hope that seed of potential will grow to save many more."

"Truth knew what would happen to him?"

"No. But I did warn him some futures showed his return to the Spirit Realm. He chose to serve in spite of the danger."

"Forgive me." Obsidian bowed his head, humility returning to his every line.

Dray sighed as he looked down upon the gargoyle. "There is certainly no need unless it is to apologize for never grasping the two directives I exist to serve: Save as many lives as possible and never harvest a soul before it's time."

Anna blinked at him. What the hell was he talking about? "But you're the Lord of the Underworld. You deal in death. You are death."

"And don't you think death is necessary for all life to flourish? An old tree falls and creates room for younger ones to thrive. The diseased animal is hunted down by predators, thus saving others of their herd from getting ill as well as providing food for the next generation of predators. Can life flourish without death? No. There would be no life. Even plants compete for food, water, and light. Death is the promise of renewal."

He made it sound so sensible, but she still couldn't see the good in a tidal wave sweeping across the land and snuffing out three hundred thousand lives. Could that be because she was small and mortal?

Perhaps if she were as ancient as he, she would see the universe differently.

Though, she didn't think she'd ever change enough for that many lives to mean so little. At least she hoped not.

"It's not callousness like you envision." Lord Dray said. "It's compassion. What would happen to all those souls trapped in broken bodies beyond healing or repair? The agony of disease and rot eating away at them. Should I allow them to exist in pain for eternity?"

Dammit. That did sound like compassion when there was no modern medicine or magical healing to be had.

"By why not heal instead of kill in those instances?"

"Sometimes the Divine Ones simply wish for a soul to return home and sing of the world where they lived for a short time."

And I got no comeback to that.

She touched along the link, seeking Obsidian. *"Take over. Anytime now."*

Obsidian sat down on his haunches and looked up at Lord Draydrak. "You're truly not angry we risked the entire island to save three lives?"

"Every life is worth saving. Each soul deserves the chance to learn as much as possible. You followed the Light's directive by saving those three souls." Dray looked thoughtful. "You may have saved more than those three souls this day."

Did he mean...? "Vaspara? Sorac?"

"Yes. There are many future paths their souls might take. In one, I see the barest hint that those two might be redeemed. I am proud of your actions. Remember that compassion almost always leads toward the Light. But a theological debate about death and good and evil is not why I summoned you here."

Dray looked out across the ocean for a moment before continuing. "It is time my new gargoyle Legion meets the old. But first I must endow my Rasoren with the magic to wake them."

Wake them?

"Yes, Anna. You've only met a fraction of my Legion. The last two generations and their teachers. The previous generations sleep, awaiting the time when they are needed. That time is now."

Well, shit.

Now that she thought about it, how had she over-looked that there were thousands of ancient hamadryads? One of her lessons had made mention of the fact that the tree began to die upon the death of her dryad. If there were thousands of the healthy, living hamadryads on the island, then somewhere there must be thousands of dryads.

"How many?" Obsidian asked.

"Enough to end the war between my sister and me once and for all."

Ah. He wasn't just planning to win a few battles and send his twin's army running back to hide and lick their wounds.

"No, Anna. I plan to end my sister once and for all."

"But I thought the problem was that you can't die and as long as she's linked to you, nothing can kill her? Or am I misunderstanding?"

"It is as you say. I cannot die. And as long as I exist, so does my twin. But if I give up a vast portion of my power, that which roots me to this realm, I can return to the Spirit Realm, and if I can force her to expend much of her own power first, I'll be able to drag my unwilling sister along with me. Once home, the Divine Ones can at last mend what is broken inside her."

Anna could get on board with that plan.

"But what of you?"

Dray laughed, flashing his very white teeth at her. "I must remain in the Spirit Realm for the duration of my twin's healing—centuries or millennia as you judge time."

Anna held her silence, but he'd probably picked up on her thoughts, for he grinned broadly at her. "Yes, it will be a...vacation."

He said the word like it was unfamiliar to him. Hell, it likely was.

"But what will happen while you're gone?"

His expression turned serious. "I have safeguards in place. My swords will absorb all my power and continue to keep the cycle of life and death in balance throughout the universe. Enough talk. Come to my temple. I will grant Obsidian the power he needs to wake my Legion."

CHAPTER FIFTY-THREE

Once deep inside Death's temple—a gigantic structure that easily dwarfed the great pyramids—Dray led them to an altar room where he said he'd need some time to prepare.

As far as Anna could tell, he merely stood in the center of the room where his four swords had been driven partially into the stone. He stood in the center of the circle, his back to them, his monstrous wings folded against his equine body.

Anna kept her eyes firmly glued to the stone beneath her feet, or sometimes on Obsidian, where he stood silent and watchful at her side.

Anywhere that wasn't Dray's naked horse-like rump.

"Relax, there is nothing to see," Obsidian's voice encroached upon her thoughts, followed by a hearty dose of humor. *"Lord Dray relates as male, but since the Divine Ones have yet to bless our Lord with a mate, he chooses to remain genderless."*

Anna was about to sneak a peek when Lord Draydrak's statue-like body moved at last.

He raised his head from its bowed position and reached out to draw his swords from the stone they'd melted into. Then almost too swiftly to follow, he crossed the four blades. At the contact, they began to hum.

It rose from a deep tone to something higher and purer. A great flash of light followed, and the blades vanished. The demigod now glowed with fierce light.

Anna took an involuntary step back.

Flames in tones of blues and purples licked along his body, growing increasingly paler and brighter by the second. She shielded her eyes from the blinding illumination bleeding through his skin.

Then his form shimmered like a mirage in the heat. The next moment it disintegrated into a million bolts of light, swirling in a shimmering vortex.

Anna's breath froze in her lungs, her fingers curled around her sword's hilt.

Then, the bright, pure soul that was the essence of the Lord of the Underworld reached out with a tendril of power and touched Obsidian on the chest.

Her Rasoren grunted in discomfort. Though he held his ground. Instinctively Anna reached out to share his pain. Some force prevented her from reaching Obsidian's mind. Or any part of him, she realized belatedly.

A shield of energy now surrounded him.

Panic rose within. Her magic flared brighter in response. The part of her mind that wasn't all fear and instinct knew Lord Draydrak wasn't killing her Rasoren.

But it was still a mighty battle to keep herself rooted in place.

"Easy, Anna, my intent is not to harm your beloved partner, though it is indeed painful for him. However, this will make him stronger. Strong enough to challenge the male half of the Avatars and wrestle control of the Gargoyle Legion from him."

What the fuck? No one had mentioned Obsidian would have to fight Gregory.

Anna's heart hammered in her chest and blood rushed in her ears, but she held onto control by the tips of her talons.

"When I am finished, Obsidian will be stronger than ever, and so will you."

Anna nodded sharply and then sat on her haunches to wait, telling herself it would be over soon, and then she could comfort and pamper Obsidian after this newest ordeal.

After close to an hour, the pure, bright power with its strange mix of heat and cold pulled back from Obsidian, revealing him curled on his side.

The magic hadn't entirely faded from his skin, and she was already at his side, curling her gargoyle body around him protectively.

His skin was shifting to gray, hardening to stone as she watched.

"He will need to rest while his body adjusts to the gift I have just given him. When he wakes, the time portal will carry you both back to Haven one last time. There Obsidian will wake the rest of my Legion. Once that is done, you both will return to the Mortal Realm and face the Avatars."

Anna blew out the breath she'd been holding. "Our

training was cut short. I doubt we can fight the Avatars and win."

"It is unfortunate we don't have more time together. All I can say in comfort is that some battles require more than physical and magical strength. While Obsidian's task will be to challenge Gregory for control of the Legion, your task will be to convince the Sorceress to return to me for a long overdue talk."

"Just to talk?" Anna asked as she settled a wing over Obsidian. After what he'd just endured, she wanted him to know she was near even in sleep.

"Yes." The glowing nebulous energy contracted back upon itself, taking on shape and form once more. When she could see clearly, he'd returned to his previous fearsome form.

"I will do my best to convince her."

"Good. Our talk about Gryton is long overdue."

"Gryton? He's trouble."

"More than you know. Yet we may need him if we hope to win the war with as few casualties as possible."

Again, Anna found it strange that a being who oversaw trillions of deaths across the universe daily still worried about casualties.

Thank God he did. Otherwise, he might decide to start fixing problems with the sweep of a scythe.

"I have a question." He lowered himself to the ground, his long legs folding under him in that graceful way he managed. "What is it with the comparison with death and an agricultural implement? I am no farmer. And a scythe would make a poor tool."

"You don't talk to newly returned souls?"

"No. Almost never. They are always too excited to return home after a long journey."

Bemused by the picture he painted and that a demigod would ask her a question, she explained the origin of the symbolism.

"A reaper? But I harvest nothing for myself. I merely set a soul free." He sounded somewhat affronted.

"Well, you did say you experienced their joy, right? So some would argue you are harvesting something."

His ears cocked forward, giving him a somewhat surprised look. Anna felt her lips twitch.

"Hmph. I suppose." His expression turned more serious after a time. "While I do not like sending a soul back to the Spirit Realm before they've had a chance to learn something of value, my sister will make sure that many lives are cut short in the coming war."

Anna grunted. "Well. If the Divine Ones should ever get around to giving you a mate, she better be a healer to lighten your workload."

Death laughed with her then, and Anna realized her life couldn't get much stranger. When Dray mastered his humor, he slowly climbed to his feet.

"Rest Kyrsu. The council and I will see that Haven is ready to evacuate. When your Rasoren wakes, he will have the strength and knowledge to wake the rest of my army."

He turned and started away but paused at the base of a large set of stairs. "It was nice to talk with you, Anna Mackenzie. I look forward to the next opportunity."

Yeah, because having Death end a conversation with an 'I hope to see you soon' was always comforting.

Still bemused by her exchange with Dray, she just

shook her head and then pressed her muzzle gently against Obsidian's stone cheek, giving him a loving little lick before tucking her head against her shoulder.

She'd nap while the opportunity presented itself. There was no telling when the next chance would appear. Not with battle preparations to make and their impending return to Earth and all they'd left behind.

Now the thought of a court-martial was the least of her worries.

CHAPTER FIFTY-FOUR

Master Thayn led the way, leaping over rocky terrain and the occasional fallen tree or low hanging branch. Knowing his extreme age, it was easy to forget he could kick all their asses. And, oh, how he liked to remind them of that fact.

Obsidian ran full out to keep up with the elder, while Anna took up the rear. Though he was aware her slighter build allowed her to run faster, and she could outpace him if she chose.

Especially now, since his body was still adjusting to the gift of added strength and magical power Lord Draydrak had entrusted to him.

They'd used the time portal to return to Haven, and then made their flight to the mainland. Thayn led them farther north than Obsidian had ever traveled. They continued until the shimmering veil between the realms could be seen where it separated this small contained land from the rest of the realms.

They'd come nearly to the edge of this spell world.

Obsidian put on a burst of speed to lead them up the last short run to the summit. From this elevation, they could see much of the mainland below them and the curtain wall of the veil where it curved out toward the ocean.

He looked south and east. If the day had been clear, he would have seen the island of Haven, a dark mass on the horizon. But it was too misty this morning.

Yet when they crested the summit and peered down into the broad valley below, the mist from the ocean had not yet rolled this far inland and he had a clear view of the valley floor.

Hundreds of thousands of gargoyle statues lined the river.

"Holy shit," Anna whispered as she came to stand at his right shoulder.

"Their dryad counterparts are also spelled to dormancy inside their hamadryads. If you looked to the surrounding slopes, you'd come to recognize the trees with sleeping dryads inside."

Thousands of the trees were leafless. But his magic confirmed they weren't dead like they looked.

"Hamadryads go dormant in regions where the winter snows lay deep," Thayn explained for Anna's benefit. "During that time, a dryad can choose to sleep away the cold months within her tree. Lord Dray simply extended that ability to last for a few hundred years. When they wake, neither dryad nor hamadryad will have suffered from the extra-long sleep."

Anna whistled long and loud, surprising Obsidian since he hadn't known gargoyles could whistle.

"That's a damned lot of gargoyles. Is there enough food in the universe to feed that many?" Anna's comment was in jest, but she raised a valid concern.

"They will be hungry when they wake," Thayn agreed. "But this far inland, there will be plenty of prey in the woods. However, we have also been adding to the stores for hundreds of years and have enough in reserve to feed the army for five years. Though I doubt the war will drag on that long."

While Thayn and Anna commented about the army's strengths and weaknesses, Obsidian turned his attention inward, seeking the new wellspring of power Lord Draydrak had given him. It rose at his slight touch, eager to do his bidding, or perhaps to fulfill one of its purposes.

Whatever the cause, the magic filled him, flooding his body with the intense power until his skin frosted over. Anna stepped nearer, offering her own strength if he needed it.

"It won't be needed this time, my Kyrsu." He infused his words with an appreciation for her offer.

Anna nodded and silently stepped back, giving him space to work.

Power and instinct merged into one strong purpose, and without a hint of hesitation, he released the magic building inside him.

"Wake," he ordered as the thrumming magic raced away from him.

When he was sure the wild and turbulent power would obey his command, he fed it more of his strength.

Expanding out, away from his body, the warm wave grew in height and strength as it rolled down the mountainside. When it reached the first dormant hamadryad a quarter of the way down the slope, a blue iridescence surrounded the tree, outlining every branch.

As the wave descended, more and more hamadryads lit up with shimmering energy, the dryads inside stirring awake for the first time in centuries.

The glimmering wave of power continued to the bottom. When it touched the first line of gargoyle statues, they awoke, shifting their wings as they stretched.

Already they were turning to look up the slope, their gazes finding him unequivocally. Next, they sensed his female Kyrsu and their thoughts were awash with surprise. There would likely be much discussion about Anna once again, but he didn't doubt they would see her fierce, pure soul and come to trust her in time.

They had to.

The wave he'd released continued across the valley floor and then began to climb up the opposite side. It took a little direction from him to send it outward to continue its search for more sleepers, but the power obeyed his will.

When at last he sensed no other sleepers, he ordered the power to halt and merge harmlessly with the surroundings, where both gargoyles and dryads could tap into the bounty to weave clothing, weapons, and armor from shadow magic.

"It is done." He sounded tired even to his own ears.

"You did well, youngling," Thayn said with a big grin. "Exactly what I'd expect from one of Rook's prize pupils."

Anna thumped Obsidian along his shoulders. "Eh? Guess basic training is over."

"It is," he agreed and bumped his muzzle against hers in return. "I'm glad I finally grew into the partner you needed."

Anna laughed and swatted his flank with her tail. "You were always what I needed. I just didn't realize that your love wouldn't be a threat until far too late."

He was glad she'd discovered that much. He now hoped their love was given a chance to bloom into something as profound as the Avatars shared.

Anna snorted. "Gear down, big trucker. Let's focus on surviving the war, first."

He caressed her cheek and suddenly switched to their link. *"Even if we never become more than brother and sister in arms, what we share now is enough for me."*

Anna grinned at him, her tail flicking in an invitation to come play. *"It damn well should be. We already share one mind, one heart, and one soul. That's a far deeper connection than most anyone else will ever experience, or have you managed to forget that?"*

"Forget?" He grinned. *"With you yammering away in my thoughts all day long?"*

He dropped to all fours and batted at her tail playfully.

"Yammer?" She raced a quick circle around him before pouncing, though her talons were turned into her palms to avoid scratching his skin.

"Anna, Obsidian! Aren't you going to greet your Legion?"

Obsidian glanced over his shoulder even as his magic responded to his command.

"Come hunt with me, my brothers and sisters of the Legion."

The eldest of the gargoyles threw back his head and howled with laughter.

"I think Thayn is rubbing off on you," Anna remarked.

"Maybe a little," he admitted. *"But there is something addictive about tossing tradition to the wind and just being one's self."*

"Suppose I can see the draw." She looked out over the valley. *"Are we going to hunt for all of them?"*

"No, but enough that we'll instill a sense of family in them. They are, after all, our new family."

"Going to make for damn big family reunions," Anna muttered as she started down into the valley, her ears tilted forward on the hunt for prey.

Obsidian gave chase, happy to follow.

In fact, he'd be happy to follow his second in command anywhere.

Even toward war and an unknown future.

THE END

Thank you for reading *Legacy of the Sorceress*.

Lisa Blackwood is the author of the bestselling Gargoyle and Sorceress urban fantasy series. Her work has also landed on the Wall Street Journal and the USA Today Bestseller lists as part of the Dominion Rising Anthology. When she's not reading and writing, she also enjoys gardening and spending time with her horse and her dogs.

At present, she grudgingly lives in a small town in Southern Ontario, though she would much rather live deep in a dark forest, surrounded by majestic old-growth trees. Since she cannot live her fantasy, she decided to write fantasy instead.

BOOKS BY LISA BLACKWOOD

Gargoyle & Sorceress

Dawn of the Sorceress

Sorceress Awakening

Sorceress Rising

Sorceress Hunting

Sorceress at War

Sorceress Enraged

Legacy of the Sorceress

Sorcery & Firedrakes

Scion of the Sorceress

Sorceress Eternal

In Deception's Shadow Series (Epic Fantasy Romance)

Betrayal's Price

Herd Mistress

Maiden's Wolf

Death's Queen

The Prince's Gryphon (forthcoming)

Ishtar's Legacy Series (Epic Fantasy Romance)

Ishtar's Blade

The Blade's Beginning (short story)

Blade's Honor

Blade's Destiny

The Blade's Shadow

First Queen of the Gryphons

The King of the Anunnaki (forthcoming)

The Anunnaki's Blade (forthcoming)

Huntress vs Huntsman (Epic Fantasy Romance)

Master of the Hunt

Night Huntress

Dragon Archer

Soul Mage (forthcoming)

www.ingramcontent.com/pod-product-compliance
Lightning Source LLC
Chambersburg PA
CBHW051312190726
48290CB00001B/113